DIV

Seamus Fitzgerald

Acknowledgements

I would like to thank Dave Marsh from Liverpool for talking me in to writing this book. I would also like to thank Author Eleanor O Reilly for the support, Author Michael Mc Carty (RTE) for the guidance, Author Chris Rush for directions, Lisa Doyle for help with the characters, my children who tolerated my very early mornings, and most of all my Wife Heather who painstaking edited the work. This could not have been completed without all of your help.

ISBN- 9798443034270

For Dave Marsh (Mushy)
Thanks for the inspiration.

Table of Contents

Christmas Day 1919

Christmas morning 1919 dawned dark and gloomy. As she opened the front door of her parent's Victorian townhouse, 19-year-old Mary Bradford wondered if it would rain. She was greeted with an icy blast, the cold, bitter wind forcing her to struggle with the heavy door. She finally won the battle. She had been up since 6 o'clock, helping her family prepare for the day ahead, the normal daily chores of lighting fires, filling oil lamps and turning down beds, were followed by seasonal preparations for the Christmas dinner – cleaning and polishing the best china and silverware, setting the dining table and making a special breakfast of eggs and bacon.

When all was done, Mary sat down in the hot parlour, with her parents, George and Angela and her 16-year-old sister, Anna. Breakfast was laid out on the ancient, wooden table. It bowed slightly in the middle, its pine colour almost white from years of scrubbing. She was exhausted and hungry from all the running around and ate heartily.

"Slow down Mary! Don't eat like a navvy," her father, George said, smiling.

He was a small, corpulent man of 50 years, who always wore a black suit with waistcoat and tie and an immaculately starched white shirt and collar.

"Yes, Mary! Please do try and behave like a young lady," her mother said, imitating the Mother Superior from the local convent and making them all laugh.

When breakfast was over and the parlour tidied, they crossed the dark, chilly hallway to the front rooms. The 'Priests' Room', on the right, was only used for very special guests, whilst the room on the left, the living room, was for all occasions. George opened the door. The room was warm and cosy, the glow from the candles

1

and fire and the sweet scent of the fir tree, creating a wonderful Christmas feeling.

"Oh, what a beautiful scent I love this idea of a tree," Mrs Bradford said, clasping her hands together.

"It's really popular – even the Nuns have a small one at the Convent," Anna said excitedly, dropping to her knees and landing on a soft shaggy rug in front of the tree. She reached underneath and retrieved four presents, placed there the night before. Anna read the name tags and handed the presents to their respective owners, the family taking turns to open them.

George Bradford was first. He removed wrapping paper from what turned out to be a beautiful, silver-topped cane.

"Thank you, everyone – Just what I need to get me home on these cold nights," he said, deliberately leaning into a pose. "Do I look like a Gentleman?"

"You look like Lloyd George," Anna said laughing loudly.

"God forbid! I was aiming for Michael Collins!" George replied in mock horror.

"Not a hope," Angela teased, "he's good-looking!"

"What? And I'm not?" George said pretended to be mortified.

"We love you as you are, George," Angela pinched his cheek playfully.

"Stop you two, and open your present, Mam," Anna interrupted their moment.

Angela Bradford posed a striking figure, tall and slim with beautiful long brown hair, she wore a full-length, sky-blue, silk dress, which made her look much younger than her 40 years. She carefully removed the wrapping paper from the small package, so it could be used again, and revealed a clasped box with the words 'Powers' Jewellery Shop, Arklow', embossed on its lid.

"Open it!" Anna exclaimed excitedly, jumping up and down in front of her mother. Angela opened the box slowly. Inside was a beautiful silver pendant of Celtic design with a large, blue sapphire at its centre, supported on a fine silver chain. The pendant was accompanied by matching sapphire earrings.

"Beautiful!" Anna gasped, "And they match your dress perfectly! Let me help you put them on."

"Not just now, Anna," Angela replied, throwing her arms around her husband.

"They're gorgeous, George. Thank you so much. You shouldn't have, really!"

"There, there!" George said flustered. "You're next, Anna. I can see you can't contain your excitement" George said, embarrassed that his children had witnessed the affection he and his wife shared.

Anna ripped off the blue Christmas paper covering her present, ignoring the rule to save it. Inside was a cardboard box with 'Hamilton's, Arklow', printed on the lid. Anna opened the box, exposing a stunning, cream-coloured, velvet dress with pearl buttons. She pulled it out and held it against her body, admiring herself in the large mirror over the fireplace.

"How do I look?" She asked, whirling around, the dress pressed against her.

"Like a Princess, my dear," Angela replied indulgently.

"Steady on, Anna. You'll make yourself ill, "George said concerned.

Anna stopped and turned her attention to Mary.

"It's your turn Mary! Hurry up!"

"You'd better open it before Anna explodes," George smiled at her.

Mary carefully removed the Christmas paper and ribbons, neatly folding them and putting them to one side, mischievously smiling at her sister.

"Hurry up!" Anna prompted. "You're taking forever."

When Mary lifted the lid of the box, her smile lit up the room. Placing the box on a nearby table, she hugged both of her parents at once.

"Thank you both, so much," she said, kissing them on their cheeks.

She was delighted with her present, a two-piece outfit with an emerald green jacket and matching skirt, not quite full length - the latest European fashion, according to the salesmen at Hamilton's Shop, where she worked. She hugged her younger sister.

"We'll wear our new outfits to Mass on Sunday, and be the talk of the town."

"Oh, I can't wait," Anna said, dancing in circles again with her new dress.

"Talking of Mass, you'd better hurry up, Mary," George prompted.

Earlier, at the breakfast table, they had agreed that Mary would go to an early Mass, then watch the Christmas dinner whilst the rest of the family went to their usual Mass at 11 o'clock. Lunch would then be ready on time.

Mary carefully placed her present beneath the tree and kissed her family.

"Stay here. I'll see myself out."

She closed the living room door behind her and stepped into the chilly, dimly lit hallway. She put on her long black coat and hat, kept on an old, hallstand that had come with the house. She fought with the front door and stepped outside.

She was going to 8 o'clock Mass, normally a short walk across the bridge and up Main Street. Today, weather severely restricted her progress as the cold wind blew her long, black hair across her face. With one hand, she held her hat securely in place, using the other to lift the front of her long dress, to accelerate her pace. The journey took a full fifteen minutes. Thankfully, just as she climbed the granite steps to the Church, the heavens opened.

"Typical Irish weather! I hope it stops before Mass ends," she thought to herself.

She entered the Church porch, glad of the shelter. Feeling dishevelled, she dipped her frozen hand into an even colder font of water, and blessed herself, shivering as she did so. She brushed herself down and used both hands to open the heavy doors leading to the central aisle of the Church.

As she entered, several heads turned to see the latecomer. Embarrassed, Mary sat in the first vacant seat, at the aisle-end of a long wooden pew on the women's side of the Church. She knelt briefly, before taking her seat.

Making herself comfortable, she glanced around. The poverty gap was clearly noticeable in the way people dressed. She was sitting amongst the poorer townsfolk, mostly fishermen and labourers, accompanied by their wives and children. The men sat to the left, their wives and children, to the right, as was the tradition. The poorer townsfolk dressed alike, the men wearing the distinct Arklow Gansey, whilst the woman covered themselves with black, woollen shawls.

None of the latest Dublin fashions for these people. Some of the children had no shoes, and Mary felt guilty as she thought of the presents and Christmas dinner awaiting her, knowing that many of these people were going home to absolutely nothing. She tried to console herself with the knowledge that her Father had given his employees a 5-shilling Christmas bonus, but it did little to alleviate the guilt.

"This is 1919," she thought angrily, knowing that Hamilton's was filled with boxes of children's shoes.

The wealthier townsfolk sat nearer the Alter - the Bank Manager, Solicitors, Shop-owners, and Business people. They wore their 'Sunday Best', emphasising their elevated social standing. This is where the Bradford's were expected to sit, as her father owned a coach-making and boat repair business.

Today, she was avoiding the company of these people. Having just turned 19 the week before, she was now considered a suitable match for their elder sons, many of whom had made their intentions clear. At first she enjoyed the attention, but was infuriated when one, John Boland, angered by Mary's rejection, had made an obnoxious comment.

"Mary Bradford's pretty enough, but she's damaged goods! I should know!"

His comment drew unwanted attention, and was why she had volunteered for early Mass today. She knew the front seats would be empty, the wealthier families opting for the 11 o'clock Christmas Day Mass, for the social opportunity afterwards. It was on the steps, outside the Church, where John Boland made his insulting comment, and, aware that on Christmas Day, this gathering would be larger than usual, Mary wanted no part in it. She would steel herself to deal with it the coming Sunday.

Mary was at ease amongst these poorer townsfolk, having worked alongside many of them at a local Munitions' Factory, befriending the younger girls and attending dances with them. Sadly, none were amongst this congregation. That did not bother her. The locals kept to themselves. She would not be bothered by unwanted suitors today.

Her thoughts were disturbed by an icy blast as the Church doors opened. She risked a glance and was pleasantly surprised to see a handsome, British Army Officer, in full uniform, try to step into a pew on the men's side. The fisherman on the end refused to move, standing rigid, and arms folded, preventing the Officer from taking a seat. He tried the next pew and received the same hostile reception; this time accompanied by scolding looks and muffled comments from the shawl covered women opposite. He moved on to a sparsely occupied pew directly opposite Mary, and took his place on its end. As he sat down, he caught Mary looking at him and acknowledged her with a pleasant smile. Her heart fluttered with embarrassment! She looked away. He had to be new in town as an unwritten rule dictated that Officers and men of the Army

Barracks, located across from the Church, did not sit at the back amongst the poor of the town. They were expected to sit near the front, regardless of rank, especially when in uniform.

Mary could barely hear the priest. He had his back to the congregation and was speaking Latin. She had learnt some Latin from attending the local Convent School, and, working in the Munitions Factory – her Manager had taught her the Latin names for the chemicals used to make explosives.

Mary was comfortably distracted by the handsome Officer, sat just a few feet away. Every now and then, she would risk a glance. He caught her during the Sermon, and returned a smile. She averted her gaze, focusing on the Sermon, which sparked her interest. The Priest spoke of the Anglo-Irish War between British Forces and the Irish Rebels, angrily thumping the top of the pulpit with his fist.

"The Catholic Church does not condone this War! We're disgusted with those involved in these murders, and if caught, they will be excommunicated," he warned.

At Communion, the congregation stood together and silently queued to step into the aisle. The Officer stepped out, leaving his hat on the seat with a pair of folded brown gloves and a small prayer book. As Mary stepped out, a young man deliberately knocked the items to the floor. She did not hesitate to pick them up. As she did, she read the manufacturers name, protected by a cellophane cover. 'Kings of Bond Street, London', the same company that supplied the more expensive men's hats at Hamilton's Shop. Another man witnessed her actions and paused so Mary could place the hat and contents back on the pew. He gave a sympathetic nod.

The dull thump of the men's hobnailed boots on the black and white mosaic tiles filled the Church, as the congregation slowly lumbered its way up the aisle to receive Holy Communion. Mary could not prevent herself from stealing a glance at the Officer every time she took a pace forward. She was now standing almost parallel to him. It was as if he knew, as he suddenly turned, stared directly at her, and smiled.

"My word, he's so handsome," she privately thought.

He had a perfectly manicured, thin moustache with beautiful short, black hair, and a deep sadness clearly visible in his piercing blue eyes. She could not help herself and returned the smile with a small nod, triggering muffled comments from the people nearby. Mary ignored it. She was soon kneeling at the Altar receiving Communion from Father Mackenzie, the assistant Priest.

"Corpus Christi,"

"Amen," Mary replied, as an Altar boy slipped a brass platter below her chin. For a second, Mary thought Father Mackenzie was staring at her chest, with a clenched smile on his face, making her feel very uncomfortable as she stood to leave the alter.

As Mary returned to her pew she found herself staring at the young Officer who was kneeling, with his hands covering his mouth. He relaxed his arms and gave her a pleasant smile. She looked away shyly and quickly took her seat.

As Mass ended, Mary rose, stepped into the aisle and joined the slow shuffle to the exit. It was still raining and small groups loitered in the porch. Some stepped aside as they prepared to face the elements, fastening coats and tightening belts, but the fishermen and their wives just passed through, walking directly out into the hostile weather. Mary felt sorry for their barefooted children.

An old woman broke away from the crowd. She stood directly in front of Mary, who realised that she was about to be scolded.

"Girl, you shouldn't entertain the enemy   No good will come of it."

The old woman's words were met with nods of agreement from others in the porch, some of whom seemed obliged to add their own comments.

"Irishmen can't come home for Christmas for fear of being arrested or murdered in their beds by the likes of him," one grizzled old man commented.

They left as a group. Mary, unable to contain herself, shouted after them.

"A very Merry Christmas to you all!"

They ignored her.

"Am I getting you into trouble with your neighbours?" A male voice echoed in the empty porch. It came from behind, with a distinct English accent. Mary turned to see the Officer putting on his hat and gloves. He was young, about 25, and very tall.

"No, you're not, Sir. These townspeople can be very stubborn, you know."

"Oh, believe me, I do know, Ma'am," he replied, walking over to her.

"Kings of London," Mary said, without thinking. "Your hat," she continued.

"Oh, I see," the Officer was puzzled as to how Mary could have known where his hat came from, as it was now firmly on his head.

"My parents bought it, when I returned from France."

"I work in a shop where other Officers often place orders for 'Kings of London' hats," Mary said. "Hamilton's? It's on the Main Street."

"Ah yes, I passed it during the week," the Officer replied, his curiosity satisfied. He was now standing beside her in the doorway, and saw those that had just left, shuffling home in the heavy, grey rain. They reminded him of troops, reluctant, yet determined, shuffling towards the front lines in France.

"A huddled mass of misery," he thought, pinching the bridge of his nose.

"Are you aright, Sir?" Mary asked, concerned.

"Forgive me; they reminded me of my troops in France. How rude of me," he continued, snapping back to the present. He

9

removed a glove from his right hand and offered it to Mary. "Captain Myles Fox, Royal Norfolk Regiment".

"Mary Bradford," she replied, taking his hand with a small curtsey.

"I believe it's easing off. Where do you live, Miss Bradford?" he asked.

"Over on Ferrybank."

"Ah, that's across the bridge, isn't it? I'm still learning my way about!"

"Yes, Captain Fox. My home's just on the other side," Mary said, shyly.

"Please call me Myles." He smiled. "May I escort you home on this dull Christmas Day, Miss Bradford? The pleasure of your company will most certainly brighten it up for me."

"That would be lovely; Myles," she replied, "but you must call me Mary."

"I'm so glad I came to 8 o'clock Mass now!" Myles said, putting on his glove.

"I normally go at 11 o'clock with my family," Mary said, "but I volunteered to look after our Christmas dinner. Is this your regular Mass, Captain?"

"It's actually my first Mass in Ireland. I was only posted here last week. I'm also here for a similar purpose - the Officers assist with serving Christmas dinner, a tradition that goes back years."

Myles stepped outside and stared up at the sky.

"Shall we?" he said, offering her his elbow.

"Yes," Mary took his arm.

"I think your Father might have something to say about that, Mary Bradford!" a booming voice interrupted, in a broad, Scottish accent.

Myles and Mary turned in unison, to see Father Mackenzie standing in the porch with the Mayor, Norman Boland. Both men were of a similar height, around five foot ten, but Norman Boland

10

was much older and rather corpulent in comparison to the 30-year old Father Mackenzie, a keen sportsman and swimmer, his large and powerful frame clearly on display. Mary always thought his dark hair and rugged good looks were at odds with his angry and hostile personality. Mr Boland was dressed in a black suit and tie whilst Father Mackenzie was wearing his curates' gown and biretta. They both made an authoritative pair.

"Merry Christmas, Father. Mr Boland. How long have you been standing there?"

"Long enough, Miss Bradford," Father Mackenzie replied, firmly.

"I have my car outside, Mary. I'll give you a lift home," Mr Boland blustered.

"Both of us?" Mary asked cheekily, refusing to be intimidated.

"Well,.. I…I…," Mr Boland stuttered.

"That's very kind, Mr Boland. I'll be sure to let my Father know," Mary said.

Myles introduced himself and offered his hand. Mr Boland took it, nervously.

"Norman…Norman Boland. The Town Mayor."

"Pleased to meet you, Mr Boland," Myles replied politely, and turned towards Father Mackenzie with an outstretched hand. Father Mackenzie turned away. He unhooked the doors and retreated into the bowels of the Church, disgusted that Mary had put the Mayor is such an awkward position.

"Merry Christmas, Father Mackenzie," Mary shouted after him, as the doors closed. She did not get a reply.

They left the Church together, heading towards Mr Boland's Ford Model-T car, parked in the Parade Ground of the army Barracks.

"Please allow Captain Fox to sit in the front, Mary," Mr Boland said, moving some boxes on the back seat to make room for her. He helped Mary into the car. She read the words 'Kynoch

11

Explosives' on both boxes. Since Kynoch's had first opened in Arklow, 25 years earlier, every household had acquired ammunition boxes stamped with the Kynoch logo. Most were used for general storage - her Mother kept vegetables in one. Some poorer households had more functional uses for them, such as tables and chairs. One had been used as a crib, in her friend Susan's house serving all six siblings. The imposing Kynoch symbol, a Lion's head, was on both sides of the crib, as if protecting the sleeping child.

"Are you staying in the Bridge Hotel, Captain?" Mr Boland asked nervously.

"Yes, I am," Myles replied.

"Good. I'll drop you off first."

The journey was far too quick for Myles. He had hoped to get better acquainted with Mary, but was all too quickly standing outside the Bridge Hotel, waving them off. As Mr Boland parked outside her house, Mary's Father appeared. Mary thanked him for the lift, wished him a 'Merry Christmas', and went inside.

The men spoke briefly about National Bonds offered for sale to local business people by the Rebel leader, Michael Collins, but the inclement weather forced them to part. Mr Boland agreed to collect the Bradford's in his car, later that morning and take them to 11 o'clock Mass, in order to continue their conversation.

By lunchtime, everyone was home and eating their Christmas dinner. An excited Mary told her parents about Myles and the incident with Father Mackenzie.

"He sounds lovely, Mary," Anna said. "I hope we get to meet him?"

"He sounds very handsome," Mary's Mother said, with a twinkle.

"Oh Mam. He's tall, handsome and quite the Gentleman," Mary said, excitedly.

"There is a problem… " George injected some realism into the conversation.

"And what's that?" His wife asked.

He's English and a British solider," George replied.

"Does that matter, Dad?" Anna asked. "You were in the British Navy once, and so are many of the men of the town, so what's the problem?"

"It' these dark times we live in which will get a lot worse," predicted George. "We should keep our heads down and avoid unnecessary attention from either side," he tucked into his Christmas dinner.

"Are you telling me not to see him, Dad," Mary banged her cutlery on her plate.

"Now, now," Mrs Bradford said, placing a placating hand on her eldest daughter's arm. "Let's not argue on Christmas Day and ruin our dinner. You've put a lot of work into it, and it would be such a shame to waste it over a silly argument."

"It's not silly, Mam," Mary said angrily.

Her Father apologised. "You know that's not what I meant. Of course you should see this young man again. He sounds very pleasant. All I'm saying is it may prompt unwanted attention from the local Volunteer's. But, for now, I can alleviate the problem by buying National Bonds from Mr Boland."

Mary stood up and hugged her Father's neck.

"Thank you, Daddy!" She apologised, and sat down.

"That's better. Who's for pudding? "Angela asked.

"I am," Anna shouted loudly. They all laughed.

Mary's parents supported her independence. They were ardent supporters of the Suffragette movement, and believed the Great War and the 1916 Rising were fought for the rights of woman, as well as men. They would repeat the words in the Proclamation, *"IRISHMEN AND IRISHWOMEN,"* when questioned as why they allowed Mary to work elsewhere, rather than in the family business.

Mary was always independent. She, and her friend Susan, left school at 14, and successfully applied for jobs at the Kynoch's explosives factory, which opened in Arklow in 1895. It, was here, Mary first witnessed female discrimination as women earned half the wages of a man doing the same job, and the 'Marriage Bar' forbid women to work, once married. Mary admired the girls she worked with. They were strong, self-reliant and financially independent which infuriated male authority and the Church, whom deliberately made it very difficult for them to conduct any official business without the assistance of a male parent or sibling.

Arthur Griffith, an Irish Politician and ardent fighter for workers' rights, made a speech while visiting the factory. In his speech he declared that if the Sinn Fein Party was successfully elected, the Workers Union would review the Marriage Bar, and favour equal pay for all workers, regardless of gender. This speech greatly influenced Mary's passionate support for women's rights and suffrage.

Sunday Masses and Sunday Dresses

Sunday could not come quick enough for Mary and Anna. When it finally arrived, both girls were up early helping each other to get ready for 11 o'clock Mass. It was not Mass that appealed, but the opportunity to show off their new dresses.

They descended the large, wooden staircase together. Their parents, waiting patiently at the bottom of the stairs, were overwhelmed by the beauty of the girls.

"What happened to my two little girls?" George beamed with pride.

"They've grown into beautiful young women," Angela said, wiping her eyes.

Mary looked stunning in her emerald green skirt and jacket. It was shorter than had previously been the norm, clearly exposing her black ankle boots and woollen tights. She wore a white, low-cut blouse beneath the jacket, with black hooks, fastened tightly below her chest, enhancing her slim waist and hips. Her long, black hair shined brightly beneath a matching, large-brimmed, hat, sitting sideways on her head.

Anna was equally stunning. Her cream dress also finished just above her ankles, the top fastened with buttons rather than hooks. She wore a high-collared blouse and a cream velvet band tied in her well-groomed, shoulder length blonde hair.

As they entered the Church, everyone turned to stare at the beautiful girls. Father Mackenzie was fussing at the Altar. He paused and stared. Norman Boland stood up and allowed George to sit in beside him, whilst Mrs Bradford and the girls sat opposite with Mrs Boland. Once settled, Mary glanced around but failed to catch sight of Captain Fox.

"Perhaps he went to 8 o'clock Mass," she thought, with disappointment.

Throughout Mass, she continued to glance around hoping to see him, but got unsolicited stares from John Boland and his friends, instead. At Communion, she finally saw the Captain shuffling back from the Altar. Her heart fluttered, and she blushed as they made eye contact, acknowledging each other with a smile.

After Mass, the wealthier people congregated in small groups at the top of the outside steps. It was a dry, bright, cloudless day, but still chilly. Mary tried to stay close to Anna as she waited excitedly for the Captain to appear.

Despite her efforts, Mary was separated from her sister and overwhelmed by unwanted attention from male suitors. John Boland the son of the Town Mayor, was very persistent. He was tall and attractive, with brown hair. He was also 19-years-old, just two months older than Mary, and she had known him all her life. Mary and John had been close when they both worked together in the Munitions' Factory from the age of 14. John Boland had a dangerous job in the Cordite Mixing House, located at the far end of the mile-long factory. Mary worked in the Packing Houses, at the opposite end, nearer the town. They would meet daily for lunch in the sand dunes on the beach, exactly half way between their work stations. Here they shared their lunches and enjoyed each other's company. When John's shifts permitted, he would walk Mary home. Sometimes they would stand and talk together for hours outside her house, until hunger and darkness forced them to part. Once, during a Summer Ball, held in the Factory's Dining Hall, they fell to the floor whilst dancing enthusiastically to the sound of a military band. They paused a moment in an awkward embrace, then kissed. Their friends applauded.

"About time you two!" Someone shouted.

A bandsmen played, 'Here Comes the Bride', on his trumpet, and everyone roared with laughter.

They began to meet regularly outside of work, taking long romantic walks together. One summer's day, almost a year after their first kiss, they were having a picnic in a secluded spot on the river bank. Mary had chosen this shaded place for its coolness and privacy, beneath a tall, spreading chestnut tree that overhung the shallow, slow-moving river. John removed a patchwork quilt from the heavy picnic basket and spread it out, flattening the long grass.

He placed food and drinks on the quilt and invited Mary to join him. When they finished eating, John discarded the unwanted earthenware bottles and jars in a hollow at the base of the tree to lighten the load for the journey home. As he put the packed basket to one side Mary, lay back on the quilt and stared up at the clouds that drifted past in the blue sky. She felt a warm and happy glow as she listened to the sounds of the riverbank.

"Oh, John. I do love you," she said.

John leaned across and looked deeply into her blue eyes. He was overwhelmed by her beauty, her long black hair spread out on the quilt. He stroked her hair, mesmerised by her pale complexion and the rise and fall of her breast, beneath a satin blouse. When her chest rose, he noticed she wore nothing beneath, allowing a forbidden glimpse of bare flesh, briefly exposed between strained buttons.

"Oh, Mary I feel the same," he said, leaning down to kiss her gently on her lips.

Mary placed a hand on the back of his head as they kissed with passion. These feelings were strange to the inexperienced Mary. She remembered hearing her female co-workers share their intimate experiences in the Changing Rooms at the Kynoch's Factory. They told her to never allow religion or guilt to prevent her from enjoying new experiences and emotions.

John was also struggling to control his desire. His heart thumped so fast he thought it might explode. He risked placing a nervous, shaking hand on the softness of Mary's breast. He was expecting an immediate rebuke, but none came. Around them flowed the tranquil sounds of birds singing from the branches of the chestnut

17

tree and bees buzzing from one wild flower to the next, totally oblivious of what was occurring on the quilt a few feet away.

Both parents approved of the relationship and believed a proposal would be forthcoming. The relationship continued for two happy years and they made plans to buy a ring. Then, in February 1918, the completely unexpected news of the factory closure was announced by the British Government. This had a devastating effect on every person and business in the town and surrounding counties. John was angry. He believed the British had closed the factory as a punishment for the Easter Rising of 1916. The proof, he told anyone that would listen, was that the War in France was not over and the British still needed vast amounts of explosives.

John's anger was fuelled by the influence of his fellow workers who harboured the same beliefs. They all joined the Local Irish Volunteers. At the same time, John became distant from Mary and his behaviour became erratic and unpleasant. This was particularly noticeable when he was in the company of three older Volunteer friends, not originally from Arklow. They had arrived together from County Tyrone, to work in Kynoch's as Runners, an unskilled, but necessary job, manufacturing nitro-glycerine. It involved running between Mixing Houses with vital information regarding the temperature and viscidity of the product as it passed in overhead, lead-lined ducts. It also gave them first-hand experience and understanding of the size of the factory, and the complex procedures involved in the manufacture of explosives.

Since the factory closure, these three men and a considerable number of other Runners, had hung around the town. Some successfully gained alternative employment, whilst others earned a living from odd jobs as labourers and fishermen. The name, 'Runner', stayed with them and became synonymous when describing someone not originally from the town, but had come looking for work.

One warm June evening, Mary was running late to meet John at one of her favourite places, a popular area on the riverbank, directly below the ivy-covered ruins of an old Norman Castle that once stood majestically over the town. She particularly loved this part of the riverbank for the row of mature weeping willow trees whose hanging branches gently caressed the water below. Sometimes, when they planned to meet here, Mary would arrive an hour early, just for the pleasure of sitting beneath their shaded canopies to read or be alone with her thoughts.

This particular day, she had worked late to avoid disappointing Mrs Hamilton, the owner of Hamilton's Drapery Shop, who had employed her on a trial basis a week earlier. She would not have time to go home to change or let her hair down for their rendezvous, so would have to keep it in a bun and wear her shop clothes - a light, white cotton summer blouse and long, dark blue skirt.

Mary ascended a nearby row of steps that led from Main Street to the riverbank. Halfway down she paused to enjoy the view and inhale deeply the fresh evening air. From this point she could see across the tops of the trees on the opposite bank, undulating gently in the light breeze. Below them, the meandering river sparkled in the evening sunlight on its lazy journey to the sea. The willow branches silently swayed as if waving to her. This scene and the perfumed air always helped her unwind after a busy day, leaving her feeling happy and contented.

Mary reached the bottom of the steps and walked towards their meeting point, a bench next to the path. As she approached, she was overwhelmed with disappointment, realising that John had invited his three Runner friends again. These boys were older and taller than John, each over six feet tall, and collectively, were very intimidating. They dressed smartly, in tweed jackets, corduroy trousers, and baker boy caps, but there was something about them that Mary disliked. One sat on the back of the bench with his feet on the seat. He was leaning forward, resting his arms on his knees and holding a cigarette between his fingers. The other two were standing in front of the bench. They were smoking and laughing. John was sitting on the bench and did not see her approach.

"Finally!" John announced loudly, as Mary came into view.

"I'm so sorry to be late, John. I got caught up with an order for delivery tomorrow morning," Mary said, apologetically, as she approached the bench.

"Well, at least you're clear where your loyalties lie," John replied sarcastically.

This was their first meeting since a recent visit to the harbour to purchase fish. John had arrived late with the same Runners. Mary had been standing next to a mooring bollard when they gathered around her, continuing their conversation. As she tried to join in, John Boland berated her. When she objected to his attitude he issued a triad of obnoxious remarks at her expense. Feeling belittled she made her excuses and quickly left to the sneers and jeers of the Runners.

Mary realised that this would happen again, so feeling tired and grubby after her long day, she decided to have it out with him.

"What has got into you, John Boland? You were never like this. You've become vile ever since you started hanging around with these Corner boys."

"Corner boys, is it?" the Runner sitting on the back of the bench said, loudly in his northern accent, deliberately flicking his cigarette towards Mary, scaring her.

"We're not the ones offering 'Play Time' on this riverbank or out back of Boland's Wood Mill or in the sand dunes! Is there anywhere you haven't done it, Slut?"

Mary was horrified. She tried to deal with the feelings of shock and utter gut-wrenching betrayal that were suddenly overpowering her. Mary and John had never been fully intimate, but it was quite clear that John had lied and said that they had.

"John Boland! How could you humiliate me like that?" Mary shouted at him.

He looked up at her indifferently.

"What's wrong? I was only sharing the type of person you are, with the boys".

"How dare you. John Boland, You are nothing but a liar! Those were our most private moments to be shared with No-One, especially this bunch of vulgar Curs!"

John did not answer. Instead he took a deep drag from the cigarette he had just lit, and deliberately exhaled the smoke directly into Mary's face. She straightened up, coughing badly and waving her hands to disperse the smoke. The Runner sitting on the back of the seat started laughing, and, looked at her with cold contempt in his eyes.

"Do you know what your problem is, Slut? You need a real man!"

He reached out and squeezed Mary's breasts with his hands, hurting her.

"And I'm the man for the job!" he said, grinning and not letting go.

Mary shook with anger. She lashed out and punched her assailant squarely in the face, knocking him clean off the seat, into the hollow behind. His two associates burst out laughing. John Boland remained seated but was clearly shaken. The assailant made a quick recovery and stood up. He was missing his cap and covered in leaves and dirt. He rubbed his jaw, and retaliated, in an aggressive and dangerous tone.

"Boland! You'd better keep this bitch on a leash. She needs manners put on her and I'll do it if you won't."

He suddenly, and unexpectedly, jumped across the seat, landing just inches away from Mary. He grabbed her lower jaw with his right hand and tightly clenched it; He stuck his face down on hers, so close, their foreheads touched. Mary felt ill from fear and the

21

smell of his nicotine breath as he said, viciously, through clenched teeth.

"If you ever do anything like that again, Bitch, I'll teach you a hard lesson!"

As he said this, he brutally groped her between her legs with his left hand.

"Do you understand what I mean, Slut?"

He pushed her violently. She fell to the ground, as he went in search of his cap.

Mary felt nauseated and terrified. She turned to John, sobbing through her tears.

"Are you going to let him get away with that, John?"

John was still sitting on the bench with one arm stretched out across the arm rest holding the cigarette. He flicked it away and stood up in a nonchalant manner.

"I don't see any harm done."

He looked towards the assailant who had recovered his cap and was banging it clean on his arm. John offered his outstretched hand to help him back across the seat rather than help Mary up from the ground. Mary's fear turned to seething anger. She stood up, unaided, but refrained from hitting him. Instead, she made it clear that she wanted nothing more to do with him. She grabbed the front of her dress with both hands and stormed away, intending to put a great distance between her and them. As she left, she heard them all laughing. She briefly turned, fearful they might follow her, but was greeted by John's vacant and unemotional stare. She looked away and continued her journey, adamant that their relationship was well and truly over.

Mary cried the entire way. When she got home, and finally stopped crying, she told her family what had happened and the events that had led up to today.

That was over a year ago now, and Mary was not completely over it. For a short time, following the incident, Boland and his friends would come into Hamilton's, and browse the goods nosily, exclaiming an interest in anything they could find. Mary would go out back and wait until they left, but they soon got bored and stopped.

Now, each night when Mary finished work, she would leave in the company of other staff as Boland had been seen outside on a number of occasions. After a few weeks this also stopped. Sometime later, Mary was on the quay with her Father, waiting to get some fish. It was herring season and the stocks were abundant. She was standing to one side of her Father, when Boland appeared from behind a row of stacked fish barrels. He completely startled her, grabbing her elbow from behind.

"Please Mary can we talk back here for a moment?"

"Get your hands off me, John Boland. We have nothing to talk about. You made that perfectly clear when you proved where, 'Your Loyalties' lie, that evening on the riverbank. Are those other thugs hiding back there, waiting to assault me again?"

George Bradford was nearby, chatting to some men.

"What's going on there, Mary?" He asked with concern.

"It's John Boland harassing me again, Dad," Mary said, still harbouring a terrible anger for Boland.

"Clear off, Boland, or I'll call the Police, or worse, that man over there," George said, pointing to a man in his late thirty's standing by the dockside, alone and deep in thought. It was Commandant Pat Kavanagh, the Commanding Officer for the local Volunteers, and John Boland's boss.

"Patrick, can I have a word?" George suddenly shouted, surprising Boland with his abruptness.

Commandant Kavanagh snapped out of his thoughts, acknowledged George with a wave, and walked towards him. Mary turned to see Boland's reaction, but he had already disappeared.

After that, Mary did not have any trouble from him or his associates. Even when they passed each other on the street, they kept to themselves.

Recently John Boland had been showing an interest in her again, but strangely, he was behaving in the same obscene manner that led to their breakup. Mary could not understand him and ignored his advances. Boland refused to accept Mary's repeated rejections and continued his pursuit. Following his remarks the previous week, Mary loathed the sight of him.

Some of the other local boys, not part of Boland's group, were pleasant and complimented Mary on her new dress. She was still uncomfortable knowing that Boland and his companions were only feet away, but, Mary held her head high and refused to be intimidated.

George Boland saw his daughter looking anxious. He moved to join her but was intercepted by the Mayor, wanting to follow up on their brief Christmas Day discussion on Irish State Bonds.

"George, have you considered purchasing the bonds that we discussed on Christmas Day?" The Mayor asked.

"Yes, I did Norman, but 100 pounds is a lot of money for me to take a risk on."

"There's no risk, George. These bonds are guaranteed by Collins personally, and the new Government, the Dail."

"I know that, but half of them are in prison and the other half, on the run. What if the British win this war?" George asked, lowering his voice and trying to be subtle.

"That's not going to happen. This won't go away, George. It's the start of a 'Terrible Beauty' as Yeats said. The Phoenix has truly risen, and will not stop until the British are beaten. Investment made by you now, is just a loan to the new Republic. You will be paid back, in full, with a healthy dividend. Unless, of course, you don't support our cause? You were in the British Navy after all?"

This remark angered George.

"Yes, I was Norman. Just like Dalton and Connolly were in the British Army, along with well over 300,000 other Irishmen, not to mention all the Arklow men that have been, and still are, in both the British Merchant and Royal Navy. So, if you want to question people's loyalties, Norman, because they were in some form of the British Services, perhaps you can start with yourself - were you not a sailor back in the '90s?"

"Yes, that's true, George. My Father insisted that I join the Merchant Navy for experience before taking over the family business. I apologise about the loyalty remark, but, please, George, we need more Irish businessmen, like yourself, to help us out with financial support."

"I have every intention of supporting the new Government, Norman, but I fear how purchases will be logged? If it all falls apart, what will happen to those records"?

"George, records are kept individually and collectively of, every member's time donated and lives sacrificed, every meeting held, every order given, even down to every bullet issued. This is not a rag-tailed organisation like it was in the past. Collins has it all carefully controlled and monitored. Every penny for the daily budget is accounted for, as are the donations from England and the States. These are evenly distributed throughout the country, so a large donation is not going to go unnoticed or missing and the donor will be registered and reimbursed when the state is finally founded."

"Christ, Norman, is that not dangerous? What if those records were to fall into the wrong hands? We could all end up in prison or worst, shot!"

"That's a risk we are all willing to take, George."

"Call into my office tomorrow at 10 o'clock, and I'll have a cheque waiting for you. It will be written out to yourself. You can process the funds through your own accounts, just in case things go wrong. I have the girls to think of" George relented.

"Thank you, George. I'll do that and give you a receipt. I'll drop the bonds over to your house when I receive them. I can assure you that you won't be disappointed when this is all over. Now, about your girls, George. Well, Mary, in particular. Did you know she was in the company of a British Army Officer on Christmas morning?"

"That was Captain Fox, the new CO of Arklow," George replied.

"Yes, that's who it was. It would be better for all of us if Mary was to avoid any future contact with him, George," Norman said, in a whisper, looking over his shoulder in case anyone was listening.

"Norman, please do not tell me, or my Daughters, who to talk to. You know how independent Mary is, and how she would react to such an instruction. Now if this is to do with your son, John, well, he had his chance and destroyed it."

"No, it's not about John, George. It's about preventing members of the British Forces getting close to the public and winning their trust. It has got to stop and that's the order we have received from Dublin."

"What! You're ordering me? I'm not in your Army, Norman," George shouted loudly, causing heads to turn in their direction.

"Calm down, George. I'm doing no such thing," Norman said in a whisper to avoid drawing further attention to their conversation.

"I am just telling you what I have been ordered to do. We must be seen to suppress any relationship between Irish Citizens and the British Authorities, whether it's business or personal."

"Suppress business relationships, Norman? The IRA has directly approved my repairs to Army trucks and coaches, which I have been doing unhindered. You have even supplied goods from your yard to carry out those repairs."

"That's different. It's to our advantage that we have access to their transport and know their movements. We hide things in their trucks for transportation to Dublin."

"Stop Norman! I don't need to know, nor want to know," George said.

"True, George, very true. There are some things you're better off not knowing."

When Norman finished speaking, he removed his spectacles and cleaned them with a handkerchief to avoid the stares from others.

"You're right, Norman. I'd rather remain unaware of your clandestine activities. Just drop into my Office tomorrow morning at 10 o'clock. I'll have the donation ready. Now will you please excuse me? I must find Angela and the girls."

George turned to see his wife standing at the opposite end of the Church with Father Mackenzie. They were quite secluded. Father Mackenzie had asked Angela to step to the side of the Church, away from everyone. He had indicated that he wished to have a private conversation about her daughters. Angela had accepted his unusual invitation more out of curiosity than concern.

Once alone, Father Mackenzie firmly stated his concerns about Mary's attitude and her lack of respect for him and Norman Boland on Christmas morning. He also highlighted how, in the Church's opinion, Mary dressed inappropriately and provocatively. Angela was surprised at first, but surprise quickly turned to anger.

"What does the Church find offensive regarding her attire?" she asked curiously.

"Well, she should try and compose herself, especially the top part of her body, Mrs Bradford, and not wear clothes that enhance the womanly parts found there," Father Mackenzie stuttered, cupping his own hands against his chest for emphasis.

Angela, who was just a little smaller than Father Mackenzie, could not control her feelings, and burst out laughing at his comments and the funny sight he posed shaking his cupped hands in front of his powerfully developed chest,

"Compose herself, Father," she said, seeking composure herself.. "Since when does the Church take any notice of a woman's ample assets?"

"Since they became a distraction, Mrs Bradford," Father Mackenzie said firmly, annoyed that Angela was not taking him seriously.

"A distraction, to whom, Father?" Angela asked. "Not you, I hope?"

"Take a look for yourself," Father Mackenzie said in a disgusted voice, stepping back to the front of the Church and pointing towards Mary who was surrounded by boys. Even from that distance she presented a noticeable and attractive figure.

"All I see is a group of boys showing a healthy interest in an attractive young woman, Father," Angela said, following him back to the front of the Church.

"In Germany, six years ago, the Bishops joined together and issued a pastoral letter attacking these new fashions and banning girls from partially exposing their breasts. I have to say that I fully agree with them. Unlike you, Mrs Bradford, I don't see a 'healthy attraction'. I see a very 'unhealthy attraction'. Your daughter should be sent back to the convent," he said, almost frothing at the mouth.

"Or perhaps the Laundries, Father?" Angela retorted.

"That would be no harm either. I could make the arrangements immediately?" he replied, wiping his mouth with a handkerchief.

"You will do no such a thing, Father Mackenzie! My daughter is a well-developed and desirable young woman, extremely capable of accepting any challenge life puts before her. She is independent and confident, and comes from a very respectable family. It's no crime to be beautiful and choose your own clothes, whether they enhance your natural assets or not, and all those boys know that Father, including their parents. So, if the Church has issues with

28

any of that, then perhaps, it's time the Church composed itself. Also starting at the top!"

"Like Mother, like Daughter," Father Mackenzie said, storming off to challenge Mr Bradford, who had just finished talking to Norman Boland.

Suddenly Captain Fox appeared from the central doors of the Church. Everyone stopped and stared at him. Father Mackenzie hesitated, then went in through a nearby side entrance to speak to someone he had noticed standing in the shadows.

Captain Fox was in the company of Mrs Hamilton, who was leaning on his left arm. Mary, on seeing them both, immediately broke away from the group of boys and went over to say hello. The boys dispersed. The politer ones joined the group of girls that Anna was chatting with. The others joined John Boland who was leaning against the Church wall with the Runners, smoking cigarettes.

John Boland stood where he could observe Mary. Captain Fox looked towards them, receiving hostile looks in return. He was briefly reminded of his troops in France, and of one particular morning during the second battle of the Somme, when he and his men, haggard and tired, were all lined up ready to go over the top. He remembered the disgusted looks directed at him from the long-serving soldiers, who understood that they were going to their almost certain death, and that their deaths, like so many others, would be of no advantage to the War or its outcome.

He was brought back to the present again by a woman's voice.

"These are terrible times, Captain. It was very sad about that poor policeman last month."

It was Mrs Boland speaking. A rather elegant woman of about 50 years well dressed in velvet, dark blue, dress and wearing pearls.

"I was only posted here last week, Ma'am. I have been in convalescence for over a year in Norfolk. So, I am unfamiliar with what exactly is going on in Ireland now."

"Well, it won't be long before you find out, Captain!" John Boland said loudly from the centre of the group of boys, who all laughed at his comment. Everyone else ignored him, except the Mayor, who turned his disapproving glare on his son.

"I see you know Miss Bradford, Captain? A wonderful girl. She is one of my best employees. Very efficient," Mrs Hamilton said, quickly alleviating the sudden unwanted tension created by Boland's remark.

"Yes, I had the pleasure of her company on Christmas Day. It was raining, and Mr Boland was kind enough to give us both a lift."

"Not by choice," John Boland interrupted again, causing more sniggering.

The Mayor and his wife were embarrassed by their son's behaviour. They made their excuses and left, taking their son with them. Norman Boland had in his possession, incriminating documents, and could do without the unnecessary attention. He walked briskly to his car to dispose of the items in a hidden compartment.

"What the hell do you think you're playing at Boy, antagonising that Officer?" Norman Boland asked his son sharply. John Boland leaned against the car and inhaled deeply on the cigarette he was still smoking.

"So what, Pops. He's only a Brit, and he'll get his comeuppance soon enough, Thomas Donnelly has his eye on him," John Boland said, flicking the remains of the cigarette onto the ground and crushing it with the toe of his shoe.

"I collected State documents and bonds from Thomas Donnelly, just before Mass, and was still in possession of them when you started shooting your mouth off, jeopardising the whole operation. Mr Donnelly is a wanted man and is still here, for God's sake, Boy! Now get in the car."

"I'll walk, Pops," John said casually, seeing the Runners leave the Church grounds and make their way towards him. Norman also looked at them.

"No! You bloody well won't, get in the car, so I can keep an eye on you until these documents are safely delivered. This is not a schoolyard game, John."

When ready the Boland's drove away. Some of the others witnessed the admonishment from the steps but chose to ignore it.

"Where are you from, Captain?" Mrs Hamilton asked, changing the atmosphere.

"Norfolk, Mrs Hamilton."

"Oh what a lovely part of England, I often sailed with my late husband from Arklow to Kings Lynn and would catch the train back. But that was many years ago," she mused.

Mrs Hamilton was a lovely, sincere woman, in her late 60s and dressed entirely in a lacy black full-length Victorian dress out of respect for her late husband. Her conversation with Captain Fox created an atmosphere of trust. Soon everyone was engaged in conversation about the sailing history of the town. Those that spoke with Myles found him pleasant and charming, especially the women. After some time, the crowds dispersed. Captain Fox intercepted Mary, her parents and Anna.

"Sorry Mary. I did wish to speak with you, but I seemed to be rather, well permanently engaged."

"Yes, you were very popular, Captain," Mary replied teasingly.

"Not amongst the young men, though," he replied.

"Ignore those boys," Mary's father said, introducing his wife and Anna.

"It's an absolute pleasure to meet you all, and Mr Bradford, with your permission, I would like to invite Mary to the New Year's Eve Ball to be held in the old Munitions Factory this coming Thursday?"

George laughed and pointed towards Mary.

31

"She's only there. Why don't you ask her yourself?"

"I would be delighted," Mary said, before he could ask.

"Oh, that's excellent, Mary! Thank you. I'll collect you from your house at 7 o'clock on New Year's Eve," Myles replied, excited by Mary's response.

They left the Church grounds together in the chilly but bright sunshine. Myles offered Mary his arm, which she gladly took.

Father Mackenzie was standing inside the doorway at the front of the Church. He was scrutinising the whole affair while in company of a sinister-looking stranger, wearing a trench coat with a fastened belt and a tilted fedora hat. He stared at Myles with utter contempt on his face as he inhaled deeply from a cigarette.

"What do you know of the English Captain, Father?" He asked, in a whisper.

"Very little He only arrived here last week, but that Mary Bradford that he's with, she's real trouble. She almost jeopardised a shipment of explosives stolen from the Kynoch's Factory. Norman Boland was transporting the boxes in his car on Christmas morning. Because of her, the Mayor was forced to give that Officer a lift to his quarters with the explosives still sitting on the back seat. It could have been the end for us all if the Brit had turned around and enquired about the crates."

"We'll keep an eye on them, Father," Thomas Donnelly replied, as he flicked the cigarette out through the porch door. They both turned and surreptitiously disappeared into the bowels of the Church, without removing their hats.

New Year's Eve

Mary was at fever-pitch waiting for 7 o'clock on New Year's Eve. Finally, Captain Fox knocked on the door and was greeted by Mr Bradford. He invited Myles into the dimly lit hallway. Mary had been getting ready since 5 o'clock, with Anna's help. She had borrowed Anna's Christmas clothes, and the contrast between her black hair and the cream of the dress was stunning. Myles was speechless at her beauty as she glided down the old wooden staircase, with Anna in close attendance.

"My, you look absolutely beautiful," Myles exclaimed.

"Thank you," Anna said, giggling.

"I mean your..," Captain Fox paused, realising Anna was teasing him

"You look very beautiful too, Anna," he continued.

"Thank you, Captain Fox," Anna replied.

"Are they for me?" She asked, pointing to the flowers Myles held in his hand.

"Oh, stop teasing, Anna," Mrs Bradford said, smiling.

"No, they're for your Sister," Myles replied, handing the flowers to Mary.

"Thank you. They're very beautiful," Mary said, passing them to her Mother.

"We must get going if we are to get a seat. I'll have her home just after midnight," Myles said to George.

"That's fine but as I've said before, Mary's an independent woman, so I'll not be waiting up,"

Myles helped Mary into her long, black winter coat which she removed from the hallstand. He smiled to himself when he saw a small brass label between two large iron coat hooks stating, 'Mary's coats', and next to it, another with 'Anna's coats'.

"Is that in case you forget who owns which coat?" Myles said, pointing to the labels.

"Dad put them there years ago when we were learning to read and write," Mary said, as she struggled to fold the large hood on her coat.

"Please allow me help. You won't need it in the car." Myles said assisting Mary in folding up the hood.

"First flowers now a car. My, I am being spoilt tonight," Mary said, as she quickly brushed the front of her coat down with her hands before leaving for the car.

Both parents and Anna followed to see Mary off. The car was chauffeur-driven by Myles's good friend, Captain Percy Harper, who was in full uniform and holding open the back door. He was a tall, dashing young Officer from Kent, with an athletic build, short blonde hair and a thin moustache. Myles introduced him to Mary and her family as they gathered around the car.

"What a lovely looking car," Mrs Bradford said to Percy.

"Perks of the job, Mrs Bradford," Percy replied jovially.

"What sort of car is it?" George asked.

"It's a Vauxhall D-Type Staff Car, Mr Bradford. A bit cold for this time of year, but simply dapper in the summer," Percy replied in his charming English accent, as Myles helped Mary into the back seat, before joining her. Percy shut the back door and jumped into the front. Shouting, "HAPPY NEW YEAR, EVERYONE," he put the car into gear and drove away.

"Have fun," Anna shouted after them as she and her parents went back inside.

The New Year's Eve Party was organised by the Countess of Wicklow to raise funds for the new hospital she had recently sponsored. She had permission to use the Dining Hall from the factory liquidators, who were also in attendance. The hall stood next to one of the many factory entrances, all of which were still closely guarded by armed Soldiers – the factory had closed with such short notice, that the machinery and raw material still on site could still produce explosives. There was also a lot of completed product and military equipment stored, awaiting shipment to England, and it was attracting the unwanted attention of the local Volunteers.

Over the years, the Kynoch Factory had kindly allowed its Dining Hall to be used by anyone wishing to hold an event, regardless of whether they worked there or not. Because of this generous act, it had gradually developed into a community hall for the town. Many travelling entertainers took advantage of this hospitality, as did local clubs and societies, who often held functions there to raise money.

The Dining Hall was a large, wooden, building, surrounded by a covered veranda. It had two entrances, one on the street side and one on the factory side. Inside was a large open space with a wooden floor which could be used for dancing. Sometimes it was filled with seated tables for dinner parties, or rows of chairs for other forms of entertainment.

The Kitchen was in another room, separated by a long serving counter. The floor in front of this counter was worn white by years of hungry feet shuffling along in disciplined queues, waiting to collect their dinner. There was a small stage in the right, next to the serving counter, where the bands and entertainers preformed.

The hall was warm and cosy. It was illuminated with electric light, with multi-coloured bunting hanging from the beams that crossed the open apex roof. There was a Christmas tree covered with decorations in one corner, and above the tree, a homemade banner with 'Happy New Year' painted on one side, dangled from the wooden beams. Small groups of soldiers in uniform were sitting with their wives and girlfriends at tables and chairs set around the edge of the dance floor.

Mary was engulfed by a rush of fond memories. This building had been a major feature of her daily life in Arklow. This was

35

where she had seen her first moving picture, starring Mary Pickford. As a result, every girl in the town wanted to be an actress. It was here that Mary first tasted ice cream sold by a visiting American. It was also the place where she first danced with a boy and where she had her first kiss.

When she worked in the factory, she helped to organise some of the functions put on to entertain the staff. She felt a little sad from the memories. She thought of the first time she ever visited the hall, back in 1908, when she was only seven, and Anna, just 5. Their Father brought them to see a dancing bear. According to the poster, this bear, named Boris, had come all the way from Russia. It was on a warm Friday evening in late February. They were extremely excited as they queued on the veranda next to the entrance door. It was getting dark and a little chilly as the crepuscular sky enveloped the silent factory. Suddenly, without warning, electric lights mounted high on poles, started to flicker on across the entire works, penetrating the evening twilight with bright yellow triangles. Those standing in the queue discussed this marvel of modern science. Then, without warning, two more electric lights came on directly above their heads, lighting up the entire veranda. No-one had seen electric lights this close before. They were astounded and applauded loudly. The Electrician, who had just switched on the lights, exited the hall. He was a young man, dressed in blue overalls and wearing a flat cap. He chuckled and rubbed Anna's head as he passed by.

"Better than a dancing bear," he said, in a Dublin accent, a big grin on his face.

He smiled at Mr Bradford.

"These girls will keep you busy," he said jovially.

George returned the smile saying, "they already are, believe me."

"I can imagine," the Electrician said, as he exited the veranda onto a narrow path which cut through the carefully manicured sand dunes. Their eyes followed his journey with awe, watching him disappear into the darkness between the illuminated poles. Whenever he briefly emerged beneath the yellow pools of light, the children shouted,

"There he is."

Everyone watched him walk to the end of the path, and then disappear into the vastness of the factory. Mary held her hands out in the bright yellow light.

"it's just like daylight! Do you think we could have it in our dark hall at home?"

"Don't be silly, girl," a man said, in front of her. "That would never happen. How would you get the stuff into your house?"

"And it would be dangerous," the woman next to him said. "I work in the factory, and that Dublin Electrician told me that electricity can kill you. I wouldn't have it in my house, pouring out all over the place if it broke."

"And look at all the insects it's already attracted. Every moth and fly in the world would end up in your house," another man said.

Anna was still totally mesmerised and pointed at the yellow incandescent light that shone above her head.

"Look Dad, it's the sun," she said.

This made the crowd laugh loudly.

"What would you like to drink, Mary?" She snapped back to the present.

"Yes, a mineral, please, Captain Harper," Mary said.

"Please, call me Percy, Miss Bradford."

"And you must call me Mary,"

"Agreed! Now, get a seat quickly and I shall return, post haste," Percy said, as he made his way towards the counter where a small beer keg had been placed.

Myles was a perfect gentleman, not once leaving Mary's side. He was fully aware that this was not her usual society and understood that she might feel a little uncomfortable. He was also aware that some of them would consider Mary's family and friends as Rebels and Fenian's, and would be feel a little apprehensive about her presence. He was thankful that this was not the case as he introduced her to his fellow Officers, NCO's and men.

As the evening progressed, the hall filled up with Dignitaries' from the town, who introduced themselves to Myles and Mary. Most were from rich, Protestant families, like the Kearon family, wealthy Ship owners who traded with her Father. Others ran successful shops and farms which generated employment amongst the townspeople.

Later in the evening, Lord Wicklow and his wife, the Countess, arrived in the company of Lord and Lady Carysfort. They briefly mingled amongst the crowd, personally thanking everyone for their support of the fund-raising event.

Between them, these families owned the whole town and surrounding countryside. Everyone in town, including her parents, paid them ground rent. When Mary shook their hands, she mulled over the Rebel objective that, in the new Republic, Tenants would have the opportunity to purchase their own property. She kept these thoughts to herself.

Mary felt even more uncomfortable when Percy introduced the local Reverend, Anthony Hammond, and his wife, Grace. His predecessor had created bitter animosity amongst the Catholic population a few years earlier, which resulted in violent religious riots. These wounds were still sore. She recalled getting caught in a demonstration one Sunday morning, as she and her friends were rounded up like cattle by armed Dublin Police, who had arrived by train, to prevent a full-scale riot.

A large crowd gathered outside the Catholic Church, raising objections against the Reverend, who was preaching about the downfall of Catholicism. This Reverend carefully chose the timings of these orations, travelling to the poorest areas of town on Sunday afternoons, when most families were home. Some thought him mad, including the Police, who often arrested him for inciting riots. It would have been funny had it not been so serious. So serious, in fact, that it was discussed in Westminster. Thankfully, it ended with the demise of the Reverend, allowing the town to settle back to normality.

Mary need not have worried as the new Vicar seemed unperturbed by his Predecessors' actions. His wife, Grace Hammond, proved to be a wonderful, caring woman from Hampshire. She was intelligent, independent and rather irreligious, easing Mary's fears when she made it clear that she disagreed with the religious divide and all it represented. She supported the Suffragettes and showed signs of being an atheist. Grace Hammond invited Mary around for tea in the New Year.

The evening started with a light buffet, served from the counter. When everyone had finished eating, the tables and chairs were cleared away, and a small three-piece band started to play. The entire evening was lively. Everyone danced, sang solos, and even played the instruments when the band took a break.

At midnight, Captain Fox raised his glass to his friends and their companions.

"Happy New Year. Let's hope it's good one.

"Here, Here." They replied chinking glasses.

The band played 'Auld Lang Syne' and everyone joined in. Captain Harper enthusiastically invited the guests outside to watch fireworks he had organised.

"How delightful," Grace exclaimed, clasping her hands together as an excited Percy left the hall. "Come Mary. We'll watch together," Grace said, taking Mary's hand and leading her to the exit door, Myles and her husband following.

They stood together on the road with the crowd. Across the road, Captain Harper disappeared between two large pillars that led to an abandoned brick factory.

"Is it not dangerous to light fireworks in a munitions factory?" Mary asked Myles.

"Don't be concerned, Mary. It's the old brickworks across the road. Most of the garrison are presently billeted there," he said, reassuring her with a smile.

The outside air felt chilly after the heat of the hall. Mary snuggled into Myles. Her face brushed his medals when suddenly a bright flash followed by a deafening bang startled her into letting go. Grace noticing linked her other side. Another firework exploded, lighting up the sky with a kaleidoscope of colours, casting an eerie glow on the cheering and clapping crowd below.

"It reminds me of the ghastly explosion that happened here two years ago, "Grace said.

"Yes, I remember Mary said, turning to Myles for comfort, but was horrified by what she saw, his whole body shaking all over.

"Myles, Myles," she said, "whatever's the matter?"

Another firework flashed and exploded, lighting up the surrounding area. Myles ran to the car. He curled up beside it and coved his head with his arms, while continually repeating a line from a nursery rhyme.

"All the King's horses and all the King's men, couldn't put Humpty together again."

Most of the crowd were too pre-occupied by the fireworks to notice, but Grace Saw, and knew he needed help. She propelled Mary forward.

"Quick, go to him. It's shellshock. I've witnessed it many times. The fireworks have triggered it."

Mary ran to his aid, followed by a uniformed soldier.

"Get Captain Harper," Mary instructed the soldier, as another firework exploded, followed by more cheering from the crowd.

"Right you are, Ma'am," he replied.

Percy and the soldier arrived quickly, and helped Myles into the back seat of the car. Mary followed assisted by Grace and Percy.

"Don't worry Mary. He will have recovered by morning. You've been wonderful company. Good Night and Happy New Year," Grace said.

As Mary settled into the back of the car, Percy said."

The fireworks were a dammed bad idea. I was never in France, myself, Home Front for me. My Dad likes to influence my postings,"

He stopped outside Mary's house, got out and opened the door for her.

"He's asleep," Mary said, as she took Percy's hand.

"He'll be fine by morning," Percy said, "I'm sure". "Thank you for everything, Percy. Please let him know that I had a wonderful evening. Good night and Happy New Year."

"I will, and many happy returns," Percy said, waiting until Mary's front door was closed, before leaving. Across the road Thomas Donnelly stepped out of the shadows, extinguished a cigarette and walked back towards the town.

41

Myles' Story

Myles was admitted to the Countess of Wicklow's Memorial Hospital next door to the Kynoch Factory. A Doctor insisted he stay for at least a week,

Mary planned to visit Myles the following Sunday. She arrived at 5 o'clock, and a nurse directed her to his bed in the centre of a long row, on an open ward, lit up by overhead oil lamps.

Myles was sitting up in bed wearing sky blue pyjamas. He was writing in a leather diary as Mary approached. He was clearly delighted to see her.

"Oh Mary. Thank you for coming. I do hope it hasn't put you out?" He said, placing the diary on a bedside chair.

"I wanted to come," Mary said, sitting down on the empty bed next to his. "How have you been?" She asked tentatively, removing her gloves and opening her coat.

"I'm fine, but please allow me to apologise for my behaviour on New Year's Eve. It was most unbecoming of me."

"No need, Myles. Mrs Hammond told me about shell shock."

"Shell shock," he said, smiling wryly.

Myles looked over at Mary. He seemed to be making a decision.

"Mary, I want to tell you about myself, but, in doing so, I have to accept that you may choose not to see me again. If that is the case, please know that I understand and will accept your decision."

"I can't imagine anything you might say that would have that effect," Mary said confidently.

"I want to be honest with you, Mary. I don't want any secrets between us. So please hear me out."

"Okay Myles" Mary said making herself comfortable.

"I was an only child growing up on my Father's Estate in Norfolk. It was a modest holding, with eight sub-tenant farmers, and an Estate Manager. His name was Steven Wade. He lived in a large house on our Estate with his family, two sons and one daughter, Annabelle."

Myles paused for a moment.

"Sorry Mary," he said, his thoughts returning to the present. "We as children all grew up together – we were family. It was a lovely childhood, exploring woodlands, helping with the harvest, swimming in the lake. At 18, I went up to Oxford. Annabelle and her brothers stayed home. When War broke out in 1914, the boys and I volunteered. It's strange to think now, but at the time, we really believed it would be over by Christmas. How wrong we were!"

Myles paused, and fumbled with the blanket as he reflected on this part of his life. He glanced over to Mary who was listening intently. He continued.

"Before I left for France, Annabelle and I got engaged. I don't quite know why, but a lot of people did. We have since realised that it was a rather foolhardy decision, kind of like a schoolyard dare."

Mary could not contain her disappointment. Myles glanced over to see her reaction and found her close to tears. Seeing her distress, he threw back his blankets, placed his bare feet on the wooden floorboards and took both her hands in his.

"Oh, Mary. I just want to be honest. Please let me finish before making a judgement."

Mary could not reply, and sat tearfully, as he gently held her hands.

"I truly loved Annabelle. I still do, dearly, but in the heat of war, I realised that it was more of a brotherly love. You see, our regiment was a 'Pals Regiment', that is where everyone knew each other been from the same villages around Norfolk. There were people under my command that had spent their lives working on our farm. Good people that I had known all my life. At first, I was glad to share this exciting adventure with them, but then...then... they started to die in the most horrendous ways possible."

Myles paused, lost in thought. Mary held her breath. Finally, almost imperceptibly, he shook his head once, as if to dispel these tormenting memories.

"At first the shock and horror was unbearable. I didn't sleep for weeks. Then, just as I started to think the worst was over, another dear friend would be killed. Eventually, I became almost immune to it, maybe even accepting it, and each time it happened, I was thankful that it wasn't me."

Myles looked directly into Mary's eyes.

"I know that sounds callous, Mary, but I think it was the only way to keep my sanity and continue to do my duty in that hell. Replacements arrived, and I very deliberately refused to get to know them. Irrationally, I thought that if I didn't know them, it would be easier to cope when they were lost. Of course, it didn't work," Myles sighed deeply.

"As an Officer, you become familiar with your men. They trust you. And when you're ordered to send them to their deaths, it's devastating, especially when you survive."

"It had a terrible effect on me. I refused to return home for my leave. I knew Annabelle could offer no comfort, for I had sent these friends of ours to their deaths, and could not bear to face their families back home. Instead, I spent my leave in Paris. Then, in January '1916, something happened - the most brutal death of all. It still haunts me."

Mary was mesmerized as she slowly started to understand his pain and suffering.

"We were about a mile behind the front lines. I was tasked with taking over two dozen wounded men to the safety of a field hospital further back. It was a dull, misty morning with a light drizzle. The detail consisted of five ambulances. I was due leave and was looking forward to a respite from the constant shelling. The area we were in was more dangerous than the front line, constantly shelled at random by the enemy with 'Whizz Bangs' and 'Smokers'."

Mary frowned, having never heard of these. Myles elaborated.

"They were two types of shells. One you heard a whizzing sound, just moments before it exploded, but the Smokers were worse. They exploded, without warning, travelling faster that the speed of sound. They exploded on impact in a cloud of black smoke. The enemy would deliberately concentrate fire power on all the main access roads to and from the front line, mapping them daily with their spotter planes. They would strike, with deadly accuracy, causing absolute carnage. To keep the supply roads open, the debris would have to be cleared quickly. Horses were the worst and hard to be cleared quickly. Sappers were deployed every half mile or so along these roads, armed with the equipment to fill in shell holes, remove damaged vehicles or the macabre task of removing dead horses and men."

Mary could almost picture the scenes of devastation.

"On this day, one driver never turned up. We believed he was killed by a random shell, the convoy was stalled. The Traffic Corps Officer ordered us to abandon the driverless ambulance to the horror of its occupants. Suddenly a young nurse brushed back the canvas of the Ambulance and announced that she would drive. Her sudden, unexpected appearance was completely at odds with that nightmarish scene of utter devastation."

"Can you drive?" I asked, offering to help her down.

"Off course I can, Captain. Now steep back" She replied grinning.

She hitched up the front of her dress exposing puttees and army boots and jumped, splashing in the shallow mud that covered the road.

"Puttees and boots?" I asked with surprise.

"Practical and better than shoes, Captain. When in Rome! I'm from the Voluntary Aid Detachment. One of Katherine Furse's girls," she said, walking with great confidence to the front of the ambulance.

"She appeared to be around 20, and wore a white head dress, which had wisps of blonde hair hanging loosely around her ears that supported two sapphire earrings. She added colour and beauty to that miserable world and looked completely out of place sitting in the front of the Ambulance wearing her immaculately pressed blue uniform and starched white apron with a large red cross on its front. She fired up the engine and smiled."

"Let's go Captain."

"No woman should ever have to be exposed to that world of utter carnage, yet there she was, right in the heart of it, attending the injured and witnessing, first hand, everything that this man-made mincing machine could do to destroy all that lived."

"I see why they call you Angels. You look just like one, Miss… Miss…?"

"My name is Garland. Nurse Marie Garland, and, before you ask, Captain, I am betrothed to another," she said teasingly, holding up her left hand to display an engagement ring. It had a large blue sapphire that matched her earrings.

"I fear you've misunderstood my intentions, Nurse Garland," I replied, continuing the joke. "I merely intended to thank you for your help by requesting the pleasure of your company in the Officers' Mess, this evening. My fellow Officers would certainly benefit from some civilised conversation that would provide a delightful change to the usual mundane military conversations we always seem to have."

"That would be a delightful change for me, too. Do you mind if I bring some friends, Captain?" She replied, with a wink.

"The more the merrier. I look forward to it," I said, pleased to have a little normality to look forward to that evening as I walked back to my truck.

"Come on everyone!" A Traffic Corps Sergeant bellowed. "It's your slot. Keep to the left at all times, and keep at least two truck lengths apart. Don't bunch up, under any circumstances. If your vehicle gets hit or breaks down, get it off the road as quickly as possible. Don't try to repair it. Don't try to recover the dead. The trick to staying alive on these roads is to keep moving! The Sappers will help. Now Move!"

The convoy moved out, leaving behind clouds of blue exhaust smoke that filled the damp morning air. With difficulty, the recommended distance between the five trucks was maintained.

The road was solid and well maintained, allowing the trucks to slurp their way unhindered through the shallow, brown mud that covered its surface. On either side were deep, open, dykes full of grey, muddy water. Temporary bridges had been placed across these dykes on one side only, allowing access for working parties that were stationed on the opposite banks every 1,000 yards or so.

The sight of small crews of men armed with shovels, horses, and chains, standing openly in the rain to quickly clear away artillery strikes, was quite concerning. Even their friendly salutations did nothing to reassure.

After ten minutes or so, a small convoy of brand new and immaculately clean trucks passed in the opposite direction, heading towards the front. The canvas covers were removed, exposing a clean, shiny army of men, their faces solemn, as they entered this bleak, unknown world for the first time, clutching their new and well-oiled rifles. Some stared at the large Red Cross on the sides of the ambulance trucks, probably thinking about the condition of the occupants. Others stared across the once lush landscape, now reduced to mud and tree stumps. This colourless destruction went on as far as the eye could see, disturbed now and then by the flash of shells exploding in the distance.

After 15 uneventful, but very tense, minutes, the convoy came to a busy intersection. Here, the traffic police were directing the approaching convoys onto the roads leading to the north and south of the front. We briefly waited for instructions, giving me the opportunity to run forward and check on Nurse Garland. She had removed her head dress and was smiling broadly, clearly delighted to be behind the wheel and in charge rather than bouncing uncontrollably in the rear.

"Is everything alright?" I asked.

"Fine," she replied.

"Still on for tonight then?" I teased her.

"I can't wait," she said, chuckling away.

"You should wear your helmet," I told her, concerned for her safety.

"Just a short respite," she replied, patting the steel helmet on the passenger seat. "They're rather cumbersome, you know."

"Maybe so, but they also save your life," I reminded her with a scold, just as a whistle blast instructed us to move on. I splashed back through the mud to my truck.

The convoy continued in a westerly direction. The random shelling increasing as we neared the primary road. At this point the dykes on one side were full of abandoned trucks and wooden carts. On the opposite side, the horrific sight of the corpses of animals and men fused together in the muddy landscape, greeted the eye. The convoy was still in range of enemy artillery and now in a well-known danger zone. The earlier drizzle had turned to torrential rain, reducing visibility, the single wiper proved ineffective against the deluge.

Suddenly, a massive explosion occurred in front of Nurse Garland's truck, knocking it sideways, before it came to a halt. I stopped as quickly as I could, barely avoiding driving into the rear of it. The truck behind slammed into the back of me, knocking my truck forward, with great force. I was thrown across the steering wheel, smashing my face into the window. My helmet saved me from a more serious injury. I jumped out, wiping the blood from my eyes, and ran forward, my heart pounding in my ears. I could see smoke and fire coming from the front of her truck. Already, Sappers were over the wreck like ants, attaching chains and extinguishing the fire with water retrieved from the dyke.

As I approached, I realised that her truck had received a direct hit to the engine from an artillery shell, most likely a smoker. The entire front of the truck was gone; the wheels remained and were burning, still fixed to the stumps of the chassis.

Nurse Garland had been cut clean in two. Her top half lay motionless on the road in the filthy mud. The lower half still sat in what was left of the cabin. For comfort, she had hitched her dress above her knees, clearly exposing her puttees and boots, feet still on the pedals, and above them, the angry redness of a destroyed body.

I feel to my knees next to the top part of her body that lay on the road. I vomited. I felt completely useless and guilty, for allowing her to drive. She looked peaceful staring into the sky. I closed her eyes. She seemed to be sleeping, her beauty intact, she looked like a porcelain doll, broken in two. I took her hand. It was still warm.

"I'm so sorry!" I repeated rocking back and forth, feeling utter horror at this complete destruction of someone who should never have been part of this desolate landscape. The nearby pools of muddy rain became red as the cross on her white apron.

I was interrupted by a baton tapping my shoulder. It was the Colonel in charge of the Sappers.

"Come now, Captain. I don't want to be rude, but there will be time to mourn the dead when it's all over. Some wounded have survived and we need to move them to your truck. If the enemy sees that smoke, we're for it. Now come, quickly."

I placed her hand gently on her chest and turned to assist the Sappers loading the surviving wounded onto the back of my truck. Then, they attached chains to her ambulance and hitched them to a pair of Shire horses, standing in what was once a field on the opposite side of the dyke. As two soldiers drove the horses on and the wreckage was dragged off the road, into the dyke. It rolled and slid slowly down the bank, landing upside down at the bottom, sinking slowly into the tenacious mud. The lower part of Nurse Garlands body was still inside. One of the soldiers jumped onto the upturned wreckage and detached the chains, whilst the other led the horses away, dragging the chains up the muddy embankment behind them.

"Quick everyone! Let's get this convoy moving," the Colonel shouted, using his baton to direct the other drivers back to their trucks. "Come now, Captain! We can't afford to wait or we'll all be joining the dead," he said, pointing his baton at three bodies taken from the ambulance and now lined up on the other side of the road.

I turned to take a last look at Nurse Garland and was horrified to see that her corpse was gone, cast into the dyke on the opposite side of the road by two Sappers who were now inflicting the same fate on the three bodies removed from the ambulance.

"We try to keep the dead separate from the wreckages," one of the Sappers shouted through the rain, when he saw me staring at the shattered remains of the Nurse.

He was a short, stumpy Corporal, his companion, a large, corpulent Sergeant. I could not speak. I stared at her torso, now face up amongst the bloated and disfigured corpses of long dead soldiers, their uniforms and bodies hard to identify, as they merged together in the mud of the shallow dyke. The only resemblance to their human form, were their blackened skulls, devoid of flesh, grinning at me in the most macabre way.

I tried to keep it together as I watched the wet mud pour down the bank in brown rivulets, slowly devouring her beauty. As I wiped the rain from my face, I noticed blood on one of her ears, where no blood had been earlier. Her earring was gone. I looked at her outstretched arm. It was already half consumed by the liquid mud, but not enough to disguise the fact that not only was her ring missing, but her entire finger was gone.

Anger overwhelmed me. I was about to jump into the dyke to confirm my suspicions when I noticed that the Sapper Corporal standing just a few feet away, was looking at something in the open palm of the Sergeant's hand who was holding a virgin white sandwich in the other. They were actually having lunch after completing the gruesome task of disposing of the corpses. He was laughing as he poked something blue in the open palm of his hand with a pointed finger before taking a bite from the sandwich. I saw a large wire cutter tucked into his webbing belt and realised he had Nurse Garland's earrings and ring in his palm.

"You Bastards!" I screamed, trying to grab the jewellery from the Sergeant's outstretched hand. Startled by my actions, he staggered backwards, almost falling into the dyke. He dropped both the jewellery and his sandwich into the mud.

"What's the matter, Sir?" the Corporal asked.

I shouted for the Colonel. He walked over.

"What now? Get into your truck and move out. You're holding things up."

"Those bastards robbed the Nurse's corpse. They cut off her finger for a ring!"

"Begging your pardon, Sir. We always remove personal belongings from the deceased, to send home to their families. The Captain here, tried to snatch everything from me, and the whole lot fell into the mud," the Sergeant lied.

"Well done, Sergeant. Captain, I don't have time for this now please MOVE OUT!"

I looked down and saw a half-exposed earring lying on the surface of the mud, but before I could retrieve it, the Corporal pressed it deeper into the muddy road, with his boot, arrogantly pushing his face into mine, whispering with foul-smelling breath.

"All the King's horses and all the King's men, couldn't put Nursey together again. Was she your fancy piece, Captain?"

"Colonel, this ain't no place for a woman. Unless she's a Suffragette wanting equal rights? Well, now she's got 'em," he laughed, exposing stumps of dirty black teeth.

"You thieving bastards," I seethed, drawing my pistol.

The Colonel, a sudden look of terror on his face, froze for a moment. He tried to direct me to lower my pistol with his outstretched hand, still holding his baton, and looking for the entire world like an orchestra conductor.

"There's no need for that, Captain. It's just a misunderstanding," he stuttered.

"Misunderstanding!" I shouted, still pointing my pistol at the cowardly pair, who looked more petrified than the Colonel.

Suddenly a massive explosion knocked us all to the ground, showering us with mud and stones. It was a smoker and almost hit my truck.

"Please Captain Fox!" My other drivers pleaded.

I could barely hear anything but ringing in my ears, I knew I had to move. I helped the Colonel to his feet. He seemed uninjured. Surprisingly he was still clutching his baton. As I looked around, both NCOs, had absconded across a bridge and were running in the same direction the horses were taken.

"Please, Captain. Get a move on for the sake of the injured. We can follow this affair up later," the Colonel pleaded with me.

I stared at the terrified faces of the wounded, sitting uncomfortably and soaked through in the back of my uncovered truck.

"You're right Colonel," I said. "We will follow this matter up."

I got into the truck, started the engine and joined the convoy as it slowly moved on. Fuelled by anger, I drove to the opposite side of the road to take a last look at the final resting place of Nurse Garland. Her lonely corpse still looked radiant, amongst the recent dead, and the skeletal remains of the long dead. Like a hungry snake, the viscous mud slowly absorbed her body into the underworld of this man-made Hades.

Two rats appeared from the dyke, sniffed the blue sapphire earring that was partially exposed in the bottom of a boot print. Ignoring it, they raced towards the abandoned sandwich, gnawing on its contents, in total disregard of the pouring rain."

Myles stopped speaking. The hospital room was filled with a solemn silence. He was still holding Mary's hands. She looked into his hollow eyes. Now, for the first time, she understood the pain and suffering he was experiencing. She could not speak. She sat on the bed in absolute shock, repulsed by Myles story and the horrors he had witnessed.

"My Dear Mary. I'm sorry for burdening you with this, but, for the first time, I feel that I've met someone who can help me to heal."

"I want to help you, Myles, but why didn't you tell Annabelle? Surely she would want to help also?"

"I truly wanted to, Mary, but she'd already lost both her brothers, and I didn't want her dwelling on how they might have died, or what happened to their bodies." He paused. Her brothers were like family to him, and he felt their loss acutely.

"We met the following Christmas," Myles continued.

"I was ordered to escort a prisoner back to England. He was to face trial for a murder he had allegedly committed in London, before the War. We got delayed in Liverpool so I foolishly allowed his handcuffs to be removed so he could eat. While I investigated the delay, the prisoner over powered his Guard shot him with the pistol I had supplied and disappeared on the busy Platform,

"I had to stay for a fortnight to assist with the enquiries that followed. Thankfully, I was absolved of all responsibility. His Battalion Officer had omitted to tell us just how dangerous he was I was in England and due leave, so I plucked up the courage to go home for the first time since the start of the War."

"Was she pleased to see you?" Mary asked, anxiously.

"It's hard to say," Myles replied. "Was I glad to see her? I don't know the answer to that either. We had both changed so much. We were older - no longer the giggly school friends with the world at our feet. Annabelle suffered greatly because of that confounded War. She lost her brothers, and her Father died soon after. My Father had to hire a new Estate Manager, so Annabelle and her mother had to move into the Gate Lodge on the Estate."

"That must have been so difficult for them," Mary sympathised.

"It was obvious that Annabelle had not recovered. We met in the Drawing Room. Our parents were there. It was a strangely formal meeting. We had tea and cake in front of an open fire. I was delighted to see her and kissed her cheek. She barely responded. We sat together on the settee. It was very uncomfortable, as if we were meeting for the first time. The parents talked about our future together. They thought I should return to Oxford after the War, to complete my studies. Annabelle said nothing. She just stared into the fire, a sad smile on her face. When our parents left the tension became unbearable. She barely spoke. I stood up and walked towards the fireplace, carrying my cup and saucer.

"What's wrong, Annabelle?" I asked, my cup rattling in my hand.

"How was your journey?" She replied, steering the conversation to mundane pleasantries.

I was surprised by the question. Lost for words, I distracted myself with a study of the ornaments on the mantelpiece, each in exactly the same positions they had been before I left. The talk of returning to Oxford, of picking up my life again as if nothing had happened made me realise that I was forever altered by my experience. I picked up a small Wedgwood figurine, a blue and white porcelain Angel. Its perfect simplicity reminded me of Nurse Garland. My hands shook. The continuous scraping of the spoon as Annabelle's stirred her tea pierced my brain, reminding me of the incessant rain that fell that day. The cracking flames and heat from the fire took me back to the burning truck. I tried to put the figurine back on the mantel to make it stop, but my hands wouldn't stop shaking. I dropped that perfect figurine. It fell to the ground and broke in two. I stared at the two halves, and heard the words uttered by that despicable Corporal.

"All the Kings horses, all the Kings men....,"

I knew I was still in the Drawing Room. I looked to Annabelle for reassurance, for comfort. She was staring at me, that same polite smile on her face. She asked again,

"How was your journey from London?"

It wasn't her fault. She had no idea where my thoughts had taken me. But the sound of her voice, the politeness of her tone, left me feeling scared and lost. I was angry. I threw my cup and saucer into the roaring fire.

"Two years, Annabelle! We've been apart for two years, and all you can ask is how my bloody journey was from London," I shouted at her across the room.

My sudden outburst startled her. But she quickly recovered and continued to stir her tea. I bounded over to the settee, grabbed her hand and threw her cup aside.

"Stop stirring your bloody tea," I shouted, trying to provoke a reaction.

"Better than throwing it into the fire," she replied, calmly.

I was suddenly overwhelmed with guilt. I sat down next to her, and took her hand. It was soft and warm. I begged her to forgive me.

She stroked my hair. "There, there, Myles."

I turned to kiss her, thinking, we could move forward together, but she rejected me. She put her finger on my lips. "I don't think that would help, Myles."

That was when I knew, for certain, that we would never be able to rebuild our shattered lives together. We were both just too damaged.

Annabelle and I met again at the end of the War, in December '18. I'd been injured at the second battle of the Somme, in August of that year.

"I heard a lot about that awful battle. What happened?" Mary asked concerned.

"We had gone over the top following a seven-day artillery bombardment. To our surprise, we were successful in crossing No Man's Land and capturing our target, a quarter mile section of enemy trench. My orders were to hold that section, whilst the rest of the Division pushed on deeper behind enemy lines. Their target was to cut off a major supply route further east."

Myles paused. He was surprised that he was sharing so much of his trauma with this lovely woman, a woman he had known for less than two weeks. But, looking into her eyes, and seeing genuine concern, he knew, without doubt, that she would not judge him, and that he could tell her anything. Maybe, in sharing his troubles with her, he would begin the long process of healing. Taking a deep breath, he continued.

"As we settled into the abandoned German trench, we prepared for a counterattack. On pulling back some corrugated iron leading into a dugout, we discovered that the trench was not completely abandoned. German troops started crawling out of the exposed hole. They looked like drowned rats, and put up no resistance, surrendering immediately. Some spoke broken English, identifying the entrances of other dug-outs. We helped them to recover their buried comrades. In less than an hour, we had amassed over 200 German troops, all surrendered immediately. It was the strangest thing. They had simply had enough. They had lost the will to fight," Myles said, pensively. He let out a deep sigh, before continuing.

"Once we had secured that section of trench, we sat it out with our prisoners as ordered. As we waited for support, everyone began to relax, and my men and the German troops, swapping food, cigarettes and badges. One of the German officers introduced himself, in fluent English. He had studied at Oxford for three years prior to the War. We chatted over shared experiences and discovered a mutual Latin Lecturer. After that, our conversation dwindled, as we recognising the futility of war."

"When support finally arrived, we escorted the German prisoners back to our lines, handing them over to the military police. We then set out for the kitchens, feeling exhausted but relieved. Suddenly, an artillery shell exploded next to me killing three of my companions. I remember little after that. I awoke days later, in a hospital just outside Paris. As I regained my senses, I felt terrified to inspect my body. I hesitated twice before slowly lifting the white sheets. A Nurse, who had seen me waken, said, "Nothing to worry about, Captain. You're intact, and have scored a Blighty."

"What's a Blighty?" Mary asked, inquisitively.

"A wound that's bad enough to get you sent back to dear old Blighty, meaning England."

"How scared you must have felt, Myles. Did you get back to "dear old Blighty' she asked?

"Yes I did," he laughed at hearing the English phrase spoken in an Irish accent.

"I was shipped back to England, given a Military Cross, and, whilst convalescing, the War ended. When I finally got to go home Annabelle and I agreed that we would give it one last try. Our families wanted it to work; I explained to Annabelle that the horrors of War had not left me and that I was no longer the person she had once known. I was honest. I told her that I might be difficult to live with, and was willing to accept that she may want to terminate our engagement. Her reaction was unexpected. She had also changed. She had lost both of her brothers on the same day in September 1916, at the Battle of Fleurs-Courcelette. Her father had never recovered, and had died a few weeks later. The War stole so much from both of us. It was clear that we both had our demons. I think, at the time, we both thought we could help each other. I kissed her forehead gently, and agreed that we would work together to try and rebuild our relationship, helping each other overcome the grief and scars the War had inflicted on us. We kissed gently just as our parents re-entered the room. They foolishly thought all was mended, but sadly it wasn't."

Myles paused. He looked at Mary with fear in his eyes, but, instead of resentment, he saw understanding and sympathy. He continued.

"We cared for each other and tried to fill the void and carry on as if nothing had happened. But I began to feel an enormous guilt for having survived when so many others had died, especially when I met their families in the village. Annabelle did nothing to make it worse, but her grief at the loss of the men in her family was overwhelming. As the months passed, we drifted further apart. I felt restless, so instead of returning to Oxford as expected, I re-joined my unit. My parents were angry and we had the most awful row, and it was quite some time before I returned home for a visit. When I did return, Annabelle and I agreed that if either of us met someone else, each would release the other from the engagement. If I'm honest, Mary, and I do want to be honest with you, we were relieved. Somehow, that simple conversation made the remaining time we had together so much lighter. We were friends again. We had the most wonderful time together before my departure to Ireland. We happily explored the fields and woodlands together feeling the same love we had as children, but we both knew this was a love of a brother for a sister, not that of a future husband and wife."

"Do Annabelle and your parents know you're in Arklow?" Mary asked, tentatively, secretly relieved at what Myles had just told her.

"Oh yes, of course, I informed them as soon as I arrived. I don't believe they are aware of just how hostile this country has become, though, and I would prefer to keep it that way. No need to put them through any unnecessary worry."

Mary could see Myles was getting tired, so she helped him back into bed. When she was sure he was comfortable, she touched the Medals on his uniform.

"Is this the medal you got for capturing all those Germans?" She asked.

"Yes, it's a Military Cross. I see it as a reward for saving lives, not taking them."

Mary picked up his hat and studied the cap badge.

"This badge on your hat, it looks like the front of a penny, Myles."

"It's Britannia. The regiment adopted it years ago. It is similar to the back of a penny, The King's on the front," he explained.

"I'm sure the King won't mind my mistake," Mary said, trying on the hat. It was a little too big and covered her eyes. Myles laughed as he reached out to straighten it.

"I do love it when you laugh, Myles. It hides your sadness," Mary said. "Do you think Kings of London would make a cap that fits me?"

"I'm sure they would, but they mustn't know it's for a woman. They're rather old school, I'm afraid,"

"Well, if they're like that in this day and age, I'd rather get my hat elsewhere," Mary said in an exaggerated and petulant tone as she placed the hat back on the chair.

Myles laughed again, attracting the Matrons attention.

"Come, Miss Bradford. It's almost 6 o'clock and the Captain need's his rest."

Mary kissed him gently on the forehead.

"I'll come again tomorrow," she said.

Mary kept her promise. It was a short walk from her house to the hospital and the following day was unnaturally warm for January. On entering the ward, she was surprised to see the beds were empty. A nurse directed her to a door leading onto a veranda.

The veranda overlooked a large lake, which was used by the Kynoch's factory to pump water all over the mile-long site in the event of a fire. The water was dark, almost black in colour, and surrounded by golden reeds that quivered in the bright sunshine. There was an abundance of different coloured water fowl that silently explored its sparkling surface. In the distance, she could hear the lonely cry of gulls drifting over the tops of the sand dunes, sometimes coming in to view as they glided high above the shore line on the cool sea breeze.

It was the first time Mary had stood on this veranda. Suddenly her thoughts were interrupted.

"Over here, Mary".

She turned to see three soldiers sitting in bath chairs. They were each covered with blankets and had been placed in a row overlooking the lake. They were seated out of the breeze, allowing them to enjoy the warmth from the January sunshine. She recognised Myles immediately. He was on the end, an empty wooden chair next to him.

"Over here, Mary," he called again, patting the empty chair. She acknowledged the other two soldiers as she passed. Both had bandages on their arms and heads, and did not reply to her greeting.

Mary leaned over and gently kissed Myles on the forehead.

"You look much better today, Captain."

"I feel better, Mary. Thank you for visiting again."

"What's the matter with those two?" She asked, in a whisper, as she sat down.

"They're licking their wounds. They got into an altercation with some locals in the Brooke House. They insisted the customers sing, 'God save the King', and then started a fight when everyone refused. They came off worst."

"They're lucky to be alive," Mary said, trying to look discretely towards them.

"They wouldn't, had it not been for the RIC who happened to be passing. They rescued the pair of fools as they were being dragged down a back lane. Unfortunately, a local man was shot in the fracas."

"Oh my God! Is he alright?" Mary exclaimed.

"Yes, for the time being. He was arrested immediately after being discharged from hospital. He is now being held in Kilmainham, awaiting trial."

"He deserves to be hung, the bastard," one of the injured men muttered.

Mary was furious. She stood up and faced him.

"Does he now? Does he really? A man, sitting in a pub, minding his own business, when he's approached by two eejits who demand he sing ridiculous songs against his will and, because he refuses, he gets shot. And now he's threatened with hanging. Well done, boys! You should be really proud of the uniform you wear. I'm sure your King will be delighted. He might even give you a medal."

"Shut up, you Fenian bitch. Captain, why are you with this Fenian whore?" The solider asked.

"How dare you Private. Apologise, this instant or I'll have you up a charge," Captain Fox shouted, as he tried to stand up.

The Matron appeared through the open doorway.

"Meyer! Will you ever give it a rest? You can't be left alone for a minute. You'd raise murder in HELL. So you would."

She wheeled him back to the ward, ignoring his pleas to stay.

61

She reappeared a moment later, and asked Myles if the other man was also making a nuisance of himself. They looked over, and realised that he was fast asleep.

"Let him rest Matron." Myles replied.

"Just call me if you need anything, Captain," she said.

"My, you're a fiery one, Miss Bradford," Myles said smiling.

"I'm sorry if I embarrassed you, Myles, but when I worked in Kynoch's there were hundreds of English soldiers stationed there just like him. They had us women demented, cornering us, blatantly groping and molesting us. We never dared complain for fear of losing our jobs. That soldier reminded me of those times. He could be one of them, for all I know."

"That's disgraceful! I'm so sorry that you were made to endure such reprehensible behaviour. Let's not allow it to spoil our afternoon."

"I agree! Here, I brought you a present."

Mary produced three oranges from the large silk purse she was carrying. Myles looked at the oranges and the colour drained from his face. He started to shake. His eyes glassed over. Mary realised something was wrong.

"Myles, Myles, are you alright?" She asked, shaking him with one hand.

He seemed to snap out of it, turning to her as he pinched the bridge of his nose.

"I'm so sorry, Mary. The tiniest of things can trigger a reaction, and those oranges reminded me of something, well someone, actually."

"Was it the girl on the battlefield that you mentioned yesterday?" asked Mary

"No, no, it was way before that." Myles said, "But I'm sure you don't want to hear all my horror stories, Mary,"

"I do, if it helps. You've been through so much, so it's the least I can do to listen, and maybe help a little.

Myles saw the sincerity in her eyes. He felt relief from sharing his experiences with her yesterday, so decided to continue, sensing the openness between them.

"It was my Batman actually," he continued. "He was such a lovely man. He returned from leave in Paris and brought with him a bag of oranges. We were delighted when he announced that he could make orangeade using some sugar, and carbonated water that he had also acquired."

"His name was John Nancarrow. He was older than us, about 30, and regularly entertained us with stories about his home in Cornwall. He made it sound idyllic. It was a Saturday evening, around 7 o'clock. He went to collect the carbonated water from his kit bag. He brushed back a blanket we had hanging over the doorway to keep out the draught, and stepped outside. Suddenly, he fell backwards. We thought he'd tripped. There was no sound, no mark, and no reason. He just stepped out through the doorway, and then fell backwards.

"Get up, you fool," someone said, but I knew it was a Sniper. It was as if his whole body had just switched off, like an electric light. Some soldiers arrived and took his body away. Like so many others, one minute he was there, the next, he was gone."

"Oh my God, Myles. That's terrible," Mary said, reaching for his hand.

Myles placed his other hand on Mary's. He felt content and more relaxed than he had in years. He had slept soundly the night before. Finding someone he could be open with in the way he could with Mary was so unexpected. He saw a future with this passionate and fiery, Irish girl. He did not want to make the same mistake that he had with Annabelle, carefully hiding behind polite conversation. He wanted Mary to know him, the real him, with all the visible, and invisible battle scars that he carried. He leaned sideways, still holding her hands, and looked into her eyes.

"What I'm about to say, I've not admitted to anyone, including myself. I'm sharing it with you as I want to get better. Please, just listen. If you think me mad when I'm finish, you can walk away. I will understand. I've seen men, good men, driven mad by their experiences in the muddy fields of France. I have seen them share their darkest fears with doctors, and be incarcerated in an asylum. I am haunted by demons, Mary. But you are different. I should not fear the worst from sharing how I feel with you."

Mary was full of compassion for this man who sat next to her. She could tell he was a genuine, gentle and caring person who seemed to carry a great burden of guilt and pain, inflicted on him by a foolish war he had found himself caught up in.

"I promise that whatever you tell me, Myles, I will not think you mad, and I have no intentions of abandoning you."

Myles smiled at her and continued.

"Before the War, I believed in God. My belief was nothing special. Just a part of who my family were - Catholics in England, difficult at times, but not unsurmountable. Now, Mary, I question those beliefs, and I wonder about His existence at all."

"But you go to Mass, Myles. That's how we met," Mary whispered, surprised that anyone could even think to question the existence of God, let alone announce it.

"I know, Mary. I still attend Mass because I want to eradicate doubt. I want to feel the way I felt before. What I saw during the War caused me to question God's existence. So many unnecessary deaths so much slaughter. Thousands of bodies broken, their insides scattered to the four winds for vermin to feast on. Good men, twisted together like a Chinese puzzle. Manicured moustaches and clean shaven faces, blue, brown, and green eyes. Severed hands and arms that once held, caressed, and tucked their children into bed at night, bloodied lips, on shattered faces that once kissed, and were kissed. These were God-fearing men, their families praying daily for their safe return and God answered those prayers by destroying them, in the most horrific ways."

"It's unimaginable," said Mary, "yet for you, it's real. Horribly real," she squeezed his hand, urging him to continue.

"It was after the battle of Marne when I started to question my religious beliefs, and my sanity. During that Battle, I witnessed the existence of Evil, real Evil, Mary... pure Evil in the form of the Devil and his assistant, Death. I see Death as an entity that's always around us, waiting to strike at any moment. It was the presence of Death, not God, which I was witnessing daily, and God and Man seemed powerless to stop him."

Myles twisted his fingers together and stared blankly at some white coloured water fowl that squawked loudly as they swam together.

"Even though I was in the presence of Death daily, it was the killing of my Batman that changed everything for me. It felt like Death had personally introduced himself to me that day – not a proper handshake, more a quick salutation in passing. I started to have a particular hallucination. I started to believe that I was Death's choice that evening, and my Batman accidently prevented it. So, as a punishment, Death decided to be devious with me for his own entertainment, regularly appearing to me during random killings."

Myles paused, considering how best to explain.

"Before the war, I had always perceived Death to be the black-cloaked, skeletal Grim Reaper looming menacingly, holding his scythe. But in my hallucination, he was nothing of the sort. He appeared in a human form. He was extraordinarily tall, almost seven feet in height, thin and gangly, and stood with a slouch. He was sloppily dressed in old and distressed evening attire, with immaculately polished shoes. He had long arms with huge hands, like paddles, hanging limply by his sides. His fingers were long and bony. His forefinger supported a long nail, almost the length of a table knife."

"It's funny how the mind works. Sitting here now, I know that this is nothing more than a manifestation of a Gentleman we saw when visiting a Yarmouth beach for my 8th Birthday. It was a summer afternoon and a tall Gentleman dressed in immaculate evening attire, with the shiniest shoes ever seen, walked through the crowds, talking loudly to himself. He started to wade out into the sea. Some men standing nearby, rescued him, but the memory of him and his attire stayed with me for years."

"What a strange connection," Mary said.

"It really is. At the time, I was unaware of the connection, but now, sharing the detail with you, I'm able to see it differently, more rationally."

"I'm glad, Myles. I'm glad I can help please go on."

"The first time I saw this manifestation, was in a front line trench. He was standing behind an NCO who was addressing a row of soldiers. I had no idea what I was seeing. I stopped in my tracks, wondering how he wasn't getting shot he was head and shoulders above the parapet, and dressed to be noticed! He turned and stared at me, with a half-smile. His face was clean shaven, his parted lips, thin and blood red, exposing sharp, yellow, pointy teeth. But it was his eyes that were the most striking. They were black as ink, hollow and empty. He turned back, looked at the soldiers, raised his arm, and then, ever so gently, tipped the rim of one soldiers' helmet with his long finger nail. The soldier collapsed to the ground. The entity then turned and clumped away, his limbs moving in large, exaggerated movements.

I fell to my knees, shouting at the scattering troops, "Did anyone see that?"

"Yes! It's a sniper," a panicked NCO said racing past.

"Best get out of here, Sir, until the area is cleared."

"The next time Death appeared to me was the aftermath of a failed attack on the enemy's front line. It was twilight. I was in our trench watching for returning survivors when he appeared clumping his way across No Man's Land, touching those that survived with his long translucent finger nail, as they tried, in vain, to get back to the safety of the trench."

"I fired several shots at him, to no avail. I thought I was going mad. I asked some soldiers if they could see him. Their bewildered stares served to warn me of my deteriorating mental condition. Death does not discriminate. He treats everyone the same, from Kings to beggars, Death knew he was the Master of this World and could take all of us, anytime, anyplace, without fear of answering for his actions, without fear of retribution, without fear of God."

As the low winter sun slowly migrated into the western sky, dark shadows replaced its brightness on the veranda and a cold breeze replaced its warmth. Myles stopped speaking and was staring across the pond, reflecting on what he had said.

Mary was stunned and found it difficult to comprehend what Myles had told her. She studied his face, thinking of the horrors he had seen and kept inside. She could not get out of her head the image of him kneeling over the dead nurse. It was no wonder he had behaved the way he did on New Year's Eve. The other soldier started shouting for the Matron.

"How long have you been awake?" Mary asked.

"I was never asleep. I just didn't want to be wheeled in like that other fool."

Mary was horrified to think that he may have heard their entire conversation.

Matron appeared in the doorway.

"Get me away from this pair of lunatics before I end up cutting my wrists."

"I see that you're as charming as your friend," Matron said, wheeling him inside.

Myles was still staring into space when Matron reappeared.

"Come now, it's time for the Captain's supper. You can visit again tomorrow Miss Bradford."

Myles came round and thanked Mary for the oranges and passed them to the Matron.

"How lovely! I'll squeeze them and make juice."

Mary looked at Myles, thinking of his Batman.

"Don't worry, Mary, I don't think anyone is going to shoot Matron."

"What did you say?" Matron exclaimed, startled.

"I said that's a lovely idea, Matron. We can share it at supper." Myles said, smiling at Mary.

Mary kissed him and made her way home in the chilly evening twilight. She was so engrossed in thoughts of Myles and his stories that she did not notice a man on the other side of the road, leaning against a wall. He folded his newspaper and followed her into town.

The Raids

The following Monday, Myles returned to work, feeling refreshed, both mentally and physically, following his respite. He twirled a pencil, procrastinating before reading the orders of the week, just delivered by a despatch rider. He thought about his conversation with Mary, and felt at peace for the first time in years. He suspected that his feelings of contentment stemmed from more than just his relief from sharing his troubles, but also from the growing feelings he had for Mary Bradford. He could not get her out of his mind. He had never felt like this with Annabelle even after they were engaged. As he thought of Annabelle, he felt a sense of betrayal prompted by his affection for Mary. Even the thought of their amiable agreement should either find someone else, brought little relief.

He was confused as to how to progress the situation. Tell Annabelle - Maybe? Avoid Mary - Never! Transfer back to England? These thoughts swirled around his head in a chaotic mess.

"Damn what's a man to do," he said out loud, snapping his pencil in frustration just as Percy walked in to the room.

"Excuse me, Myles, but what are the orders from Dublin?" Percy asked, embarrassed at having to interrupt a private moment.

"Sorry Percy. I've not read them yet," Myles said and opened the leather case from Dublin Castle. It contained documents marked 'Secret', which he examined carefully, putting aside all other thoughts as he focused on the job in hand.

"We have a Mrs Byrne and her two sons downstairs, enquiring after her husband?"

"We have no one detained. Who is her husband?

"John Byrne, arrested over Christmas for the attempted murder of Myers and Bagshott."

"Oh no!" Myles sighed, picking up a page from the pile on his desk.

He stood, handing the document to Percy. It was from Dublin Castle, with orders to inform the family that on Friday 9th of January 1920, John Byrne from Ovoca, and formally of Arklow, was killed as he tried to escape from military custody in Dublin. He had been held for questioning for the attempted murder of two British soldiers. Arrangements would be made for the repatriation of the body, later that week.

"Shall I inform them, Myles?" Percy asked, noticing the distress on Myles' face.

"Jesus Percy! Can I not have just one day without death rearing its ugly head!" Myles said vehemently. On seeing the startled look on Percy's face, Myles calmed himself.

"I apologise, Percy. I will inform them myself, but thank you for offering."

Myles entered a room, next to the main door. It was an old Guard room, now used as a waiting room. It was small with a well-worn wooden floor, the walls were painted turquoise and peeling in places, it had one window that had not been opened in years, iron bars and faded whitewash on the glass, darkening the room still further. There were two seats on either side of a trestle bench. A large, lit oil lamp had been placed in the centre of the table.

"Good morning." Myles said to the family, closing the door behind him.

He was taken aback as the woman grabbed both his hands, pleading with him.

"Oh Captain! Please release John, he's done nothing wrong. We're a simple family, three girls and two boys. These are our boys." She said with pride, pointing to the two young men.

"They work in the Copper Mines with their Father. They're good lads, Captain, and never did a day's harm to anyone, just like their Father. My husband walks the five miles into town once a month to visit his brother. It's usually on a Saturday and he stays over, but because it was Christmas he dropped in on a Monday and ended up getting shot. Dear God! If only he'd gone Saturday. We've heard nothing since. We don't know if he's dead or alive, and nobody will tell us anything?"

At that, she burst into a wailing cry.

"Please sit down, Mrs Byrne," Myles said, steering her towards the chair.

"Begging you're pardon, Captain, but we've a letter from the Director of the Ovoca Copper Mines in London, vouching for the honesty and loyalty of our Father," the older boy stated proudly.

"Even when Kynoch's offered almost twice the wages, our Father stayed loyal to the Mines. That's why the Director sent this letter, so we could pass it on to you, Sir." The boy finished, offering the letter for Myles to inspect.

Myles face filled with empathy as he looked at the two boys, aged around 15 and 17. It reminded him of other families brandishing letters from dignitary's to army councils, pleading an amnesty for their conscripted sons, only to have it fall on deaf ears.

"Mrs Byrne. Boys," Myles said, building up the courage to inform them of his death.

"I'm afraid I've just received some unfortunate news from a dispatch rider who left less than 10 minutes ago. You may have seen him on your arrival?" He added, hoping to soften the pain of what came next.

The boys looked at each other and nodded as they recalled seeing and talking about the motor cycle as it left the Barracks.

"What did it say?" The older boy asked, his voice quavering.

"There's no easy way to say this, but we've been informed, by Dublin Castle, that your Father was killed last Friday, whilst trying to escape. Arrangements will be made to repatriate his body."

An uncanny silence fell across the room, broken only by the flickering wick of the oil lamp. As understanding dawned, Mrs

Byrne slumped to the floor without a whimper. Myles rushed to her aid but was pushed aside by her sons.

"Get your filthy, murdering hands off her, you fucking English Bastard!" The older boy shouted as both boys attended their unconscious Mother.

"Is there anything I can do?" Myles asked a tremor in his voice.

The boys did not reply, crossing to the door, carrying their mother.

"I can arrange a lift back to Ovoca?" He said, opening the door for them.

"Give us our Father back, Captain. That's something you can do. Preferably alive!" The older boy said, as he exited the room.

"Captain," he continued, as Myles followed them into the hallway. "The only thing you can do now is to keep your head down! My Father came from a large family – an honest family at that. None of us have ever supported the IRA. But now, their ranks will swell, I can promise you that."

"Are you threating me?" Myles asked wearily.

"Yes I am!" He replied, through gritted teeth.

Myles decided not to pursue the threat, dismissing it as an understandable and emotional response. As he watched them disappear into the bright sunlight, two staff cars roared into view, followed by three truckloads of troops. A driver jumped out from one of the staff cars and opened the back door. Myles watched inquisitively as a Brigadier General exited the rear of the car.

"Can this cursed day get any worse?" Myles muttered to himself. He quickly rearranged his office as a reception for these unexpected visitors. He was with Captain Harper and a second lieutenant, when the Commander in Chief of Ireland, Brigadier General, Sir Henry Wilson, entered the room, with a civilian man and three other high-ranking Officers.

The Arklow group stood to attention. Myles saluted.

"As you were," the General said, without returning the salute, refusing to sit in the chairs provided for him and his entourage.

"Can we get you anything, Sir?" Percy offered as Myles returned to his desk.

"We're not here for refreshments, Captain. We're here to discuss the total disrespect these locals have for their superiors."

Myles took an immediate dislike to him. He had met this type of pompous Officer many times in France, the offspring of English Aristocrats, honed and trained in public schools to run the affairs of the British Empire. They cared nothing for native traditions, suppressing them instead, with an iron fist. In France, these high-ranking Officers were famous for briefly appearing on the front line before a large scale offensive, disappearing before it started, taking no responsibility for the thousands of men who would die or be maimed as a result of their ridiculous ideas. They would sit on Court Martials, their sole intent to ensure the defendant did not get a fair trial, and an example was set for the other ranks.

Myles stared at his medal ribbons - MBE, DSO, South Africa Campaign, India Star, Egypt Star and many others. He noticed two ribbon bars that represented the Eastern front, and his contempt for this man increased. "How many of your own men did you kill at your Kangaroo courts or send to their deaths on ill-conceived attacks to earn those," he thought to himself.

"Glad to see you back, Captain," the General barked. "I find a gin and tonic an excellent cure for return bouts of campaign sickness".

"Thank you for the advice, General, but it was not malaria that I suffered from".

"Well, whatever… This gentleman is Detective Freeny, from Dublin Castle," the General said, introducing the civilian. He was tall, powerfully built and in his early 30's. He looked dangerous, almost too big for his wool suit.

"Captain Fox, Mr Freeny has gathered invaluable information on the membership of the local IRA in Arklow. Your orders are to assist with their immediate arrest, so Mr Freeny can question them."

"We shall get to it immediately, General," Myles replied, sarcastically.

Freeny marched over to Myles desk.

"Listen to me, Captain," he said, slamming a sheet of paper down on the desk containing the names of local IRA suspects. He leaned across the desk, closing the gap between himself and Myles, hoping to intimidate him with his large frame, but quickly realised that Myles was immune, twirling a pencil with both hands, just below his chin.

Freeny, feeling a little intimidated himself, took a step back and straightened his jacket. He spoke through gritted teeth.

"Surprise is the ultimate weapon here, Captain. Make these arrests now, this morning, and these animals won't have a chance to conceal damming evidence."

Freeny turned towards the General, making his expectations known.

"General, I expect full cooperation from your Area Commander and his men."

"What! What! Of course, Mr Freeny, of course," the General spluttered. "You heard the man, Captain Fox. I expect you to give him your full support."

Despite his immediate dislike of Freeny and his anger that high ranking officers would allow a civilian to tell them what to do, Myles took the list and calmly stood up.

"Sirs, I cannot organise the arrests of...," he paused, counting the names on the page," Of 11 men, first thing on a Monday morning, Firstly, I would need more time and men, and, secondly, if the people named on this list are guilty of membership, I can assure you they are well on their way to a safe house, as we speak."

"That type of response caused the War in France to drag on for years, Captain. You're the Army, God dam it! You can use the men that I have brought with me. Now, Get on with it, and no excuses!" the General bellowed.

Myles composed himself before responding.

"General, a 'Trevelyan' approach will result in far more serious consequences for us all," Myles said.

"Trevelyan Approach! What the hell is that, Captain?" The General shouted.

"Sir Charles Edward Trevelyan was an English Civil Servant, famous for the quote, 'Those dammed Irish', when he was drafted in to resolve the Famine crisis back in the '40s. His approach failed miserably, may I add," Percy informed the General.

"Sir Charles Edward Trevelyan didn't fail, Captain. He successfully averted a crisis, and was awarded a well-deserved Knighthood," one of the Aides interrupted.

"What? And now these dammed Irish use his name to describe failures, like Captain Boycott? What ingratitude! They deserve what they get!" The General spouted.

"We did not come here for a bloody history lesson on the begrudging Irish. We came to resolve a major threat to Crown forces. Do you recognise any of the names Captain?" Freeny asked, angrily.

Myles slowly realised that they had no intention of leaving until he made an attempt to carry out Freeny's plans.

"Yes, two," he replied, deciding that, in order to get rid of them he would have to cooperate with their ridiculously unprepared plans.

"Who are they, Captain?" The General asked.

"The Town Mayor, and a local Priest. General with all due respect, Sir, I cannot arrest a Priest. The whole town would be up in arms."

"You will arrest him, Captain, even if you have to drag that dammed papist from his altar whilst practicing his voodoo. And if the natives rise up, well, they'll just have to face our old friend, 'Maxim'! We bought two with us, just in case."

"Sir! Are you really suggesting we fire machine guns into a crowded Church?" Percy asked horrified.

"Yes, Harper! Those 'damned natives' of Amritsar can attest to its success!" The General said.

"The Jallianwala Bagh Massacre, Sir," Captain Harper replied in astonishment. "I beg to differ. That assault on the native population was a total disaster,"

"I did not come here to listen to your cowardly and sanctimonious opinions, Captain Harper. Now, get your men ready! We'll arrest the Priest first as he's only across the road. I will personally conduct the operation from this office."

"I'm sure you will," Myles thought to himself.

"What an excellent idea, General," Myles said, surprising everyone. "This window commands a superb view of the driveway to the Priest's house."

The General walked over to the window, brushed aside the lace curtain and looked out. The tree-lined driveway on the other side of the street was clearly visible.

"Excellent idea, Captain."

"Just be sure to be careful of hidden riflemen, Sir," Myles replied.

"What! Yes, of course," the General blubbered, stepping back.

"Now, Captain Fox, go with Detective Freeny and carry out as many arrests on that list as possible. Get moving!" He shouted, hoping no one noticed his fear at the mention of a hidden sniper.

As Myles predicted, the arrests were a disaster. Word of the raids and the arrival of a high-ranking General with three trucks full of Police and troops had spread to all Area Commanders, alerting the whole county, not just the town. As Myles had predicted, the people on the list went into hiding, and all weapons and papers were safely hidden.

The visiting soldiers, many of whom were Irishmen from the Dublin Fusiliers, reluctantly crossed the road to the Church, secretly delighted to discover that the only person present was a housekeeper. She informed Captain Harper that all the Priests were out conducting parish duties, and would not be back until later that evening.

"Back to the Barracks, men," Percy ordered, grateful the raid was unsuccessful.

The troops crunched their way across the gravel drive, heading back to the Barracks. The General expressed his disappointment at Percy's report.

"Damn! Let's hope the others have more success. We shall have to await their return as they have the list, and I do not have a copy. That will be all, Captain."

"Very good, Sir."

Percy made a hasty exit, before the General changed his mind, but the General's fear of snipers meant he had no intention of conducting any more raids, preferring to remain in the relative safety of the Barracks.

Myles and Freeny did not have much luck either. They forced their way into two houses only to find them empty. The rest were fishermen cottages, full of screaming children, cared for by older siblings, due to the sudden absence of both parents.

They were invited into Norman Boland's house by his wife, who reluctantly allowed them to carry out a disciplined search, personally supervised by Myles. Nothing was discovered.

Freeny was fuming when he got back to the Barracks, almost two hours later. They gathered again in Myles' office, to discuss outcomes and further actions. This time, the General and his party sat on the chairs provided. Percy and the Lieutenant stood to one side, and Myles sat at his desk.

"I think they were tipped off, General," Freeny said, refusing to sit. "Not one person on the list was at home."

"I don't know how anyone could have known, Detective? These plans were made under strict security and only released last Friday," the General said, nonplussed.

"Perhaps it was the sudden arrival of two staff cars and three lorries' full of armed troops that aroused suspicion, Sir?" Myles suggested.

"We're not dealing with uneducated peasants. All we've achieved here today is to warn them that we know who they are, and as a result, they are likely to remain in hiding."

"Maybe so, Captain, but, knowing we're on to them will keep them on their toes. I want you to continue your pursuit and bring these criminals in for questioning, delivering the chief suspects directly to Dublin. I shall dispatch a group of Police Special Reserves later this month to assist you and the local police with these arrests."

"May I ask what 'Police Special Reserves' are, General? Myles asked, curiously.

"Indeed, Captain," the General said, excitedly. "As we speak, we are recruiting men in England to assist the RIC, who are woefully under-staffed with all this commotion in country. We expect our first batch of recruits next month."

"Take this list and get me results," Freeny said, slapping the list on Myles' desk.

Myles stood, staring coldly at Freeny, showing the utter contempt he felt.

"General," he said, ignoring Freeny, "May I suggest that you try to avoid going through the village of Inch if your journey is taking you South, Sir."

"Why is that?" One of the Aides's enquired.

"Well, Sirs, following this morning's debacle, we have announced our intention of making further arrests and that

78

particular area is renowned for ambushes, going back to 1798. Just last year a policeman was murdered there. So I advise you avoid it."

This rattled the General.

"Come, Detective Freeny. We'll change our planned route and go back to Dublin. Perhaps we can surprise some small towns on the way. We don't want to make it easy for these damned upstarts," the General said, preparing to leave.

Freeny reluctantly agreed.

"They wouldn't dare attack a convoy of troops, General," the Aide injected.

"Indeed not, but its good practice to change one's plans! There's no more we can do here. We leave everything in your capable hands, Captain Fox," the General said, delighted to make a hasty exit.

"Good bye, Captain Fox, Captain Harper. Keep up the good work." Both men came to attention and Myles saluted.

"Come, Detective Freeny. We have work of our own to do," the General said, tipping his baton off the peak of his hat as a returned salute.

"Get me results, Captain," Freeny barked, as he tapped the list on Myles' desk. He left through the door ahead of the Colonel.

"Good day, gentlemen," the Colonel said, following Freeny through the door.

"That went well," Percy said sarcastically, loosening his tie and closing the door.

"I'm trying my best to win the trust of the locals, and was doing it with some success, I might add, until this debacle. It's like a game of snakes and ladders. I was just a few moves away, and that fool caused me to slide down a snake to number 1 again. What other disaster can possibly happen today? I should have stayed in the Hospital," Myles shouted angrily.

"Shall we get some lunch,"

Percy said, trying to ease the tension.

"A good idea, Percy. The Railway Hotel I think. On me, assuming we don't get shot on the way," Myles said, sarcastically, as he placed Freeny's list and the dispatch papers into the safe. He picked up his hat, seeing the 'Kings of London' label he thought of Mary and his personal dilemma.

"Bloody Snakes and Ladders, Percy," he said, as they left for lunch.

As a direct result of the British raids, the local IRA was forced to organise a secret meeting for all senior leaders. It was to be held a week later, at 7 o'clock, upstairs at the Brooke House. People arrived early, in ones and twos, collected a drink at the bar, and inconspicuously made their way upstairs.

The room, originally part of the living quarters, had been converted into a function room years earlier. It was directly above the bar, allowing staff and customers alike to warn attendees of a potential raid by banging the ceiling with the handle of a brush kept nearby, for just such a purpose.

A huge, oval, wooden table, almost black in colour, dominated the room, surrounded by ten matching chairs, four on either side, and one at each end. The table sat on a threadbare rug that did not completely cover the wooden floor, a scattering of single chairs were placed against the walls, which were covered with thick, hessian wallpaper. A fire burned brightly in an enormous black, marble fire place, above which, an ancient black mirror hung, its glass speckled with age .On its mantel two oil lamps sat either side of a black marble clock, displaying the correct time, the glow from these lamps mixed with the light from the flames created a soft yellow light that barely penetrated the smoky atmosphere. The curtains on the three windows had been closed tightly, preventing any light from entering, and any sign of life from exiting.

The room was full of local IRA Commanders and their Lieutenants. The Commanders sat at the table, discussing recent events, whilst their seconds stood or sat on chairs directly behind them, chatting amongst themselves.

The clock chimed 7 o'clock, silencing the room. Thomas Donnelly, the senior IRA Area Commander, entered on the final stroke. As he closed the door, cigarette smoke swirled around him making him look like a wolf on a misty, moonlit night.

"Good evening, Gentlemen. Thank you for attending in these dangerous times," he said, assertively taking the seat at the head of the table between Norman Boland and Pat Kavanagh.

"First things, first. Pat. Have lookouts been placed?"

"They have, Thomas," Pat Kavanagh assured him.

"Is the emergency escape route opened?"

"Yes," one of Pat Kavanagh's men said, as he lifted back a section of the hessian wallpaper, revealing a hole, two-foot square, cut into the thick stone wall, large enough for a man to crawl through to access the printing works, next door.

The guard outside, knocked on the door and opened it, allowing the Runner to enter. He was carrying a tray with jugs of water, glasses and two small oil lamps. He evenly placed the items on the table, stood back, and leaned against the wall.

"Can we continue?" Donnelly asked Norman Boland, in a condescending tone.

"Yes, Mr Donnelly," Norman replied, glaring at the Runner.

"Good. Now, let's begin," Donnelly said, placing documents on the table in front of him. "I presume you're aware of the surprise raids carried out by the Brits last week? Unfortunately, they made a number of arrests on their way back to Dublin, due to unexpected changes. Thankfully most of the arrests were on suspicion rather than proof, so most suspects have already been released, they also executed Mr Byrne of Ovoca, some weeks ago, saying he was shot trying to escape. I can confirm that neither he, nor any of his family, were Volunteer's, but his death will be avenged."

The atmosphere in the room was electric, filled with the buzzing sound of assent.

"Quiet, please!" Norman Boland, the Chairman of the meeting, said loudly, banging a pen against an empty glass. "Mr Donnelly is not finished."

"Thank you, Norman," Donnelly said. "Our biggest concern over these raids is not that the Brits knew who to arrest, but the houses they chose to raid." Donnelly paused, allowing the impact of his statement to sink in. "I will make this very clear to you all, two of those houses were very safe indeed, only known to a handful of people, indicating that we have a Spy amongst us, in Wicklow."

There was a tumultuous uproar amongst the patrons with a barrage of accusations competing with oaths of allegiance, and much fist-banging.

"Jesus, if we are fighting among ourselves like this now, what the hell will it be like when it's all over?" Pat said to Boland and Donnelly.

"Calm down, gentlemen, Please calm down!" Norman shouted, above the din. Silence and order replaced the turbulence created by the accusation.

"Gentlemen, I am not suggesting, for one minute, that we have a Traitor in this room. I am merely saying there may be one close to our ranks. If the British had been successful in making arrests at all of the addresses they raided on Monday, our organisation would never recover. Make no mistake, I mean 'NEVER'!" Donnelly paused, looking at each of the Commanders seated at the table.

"Even though we knew raids would take place, allowing us time to move weapons and men, we were shocked by the extent of their knowledge. Dublin Central Command is convinced the Castle has somehow infiltrated us. Our new orders are to focus our efforts in finding out exactly who he is. So therefore…"

"What if it's a, 'her'?" A random voice interrupted from the side.

"Who said that?" Donnelly asked, incensed at being interrupted mid-speech.

"It was me, 'Ciaran Payton' from the Arklow branch," the Runner said, stepping forward and holding up his hand as if in school.

"What do you mean boy?" Norman Boland asked contempt in his voice.

"My Commandant ordered me to follow a local girl, Mary Bradford," he said, pointing at Pat Kavanagh, "and I've noticed she spends a lot of time with the new Brit CO. She could be our Informer."

His comment generated a lot of mumbling and head nodding amongst the other Commanders and their men, eager to pin the blame elsewhere and move on.

"I think we should cut off her hair and banish her from town for being an Informer and having an affair with a Brit Officer," Payton continued.

"Shut up boy!" Norman Boland demanded. "I have never heard such tripe in all my life. This has nothing to do with who the informer is. That girl could not possibly know who we are or where we stay, and, mores to the point, would not inform, even if she did. I can vouch for Mary and her Family, Mr Donnelly. They help the organisation in other ways. This 'Blow in' from Tyrone has a personal vendetta against the girl, because she spurned his advances."

Donnelly remained silent. He was mulling over the fact that the name 'Mary Bradford' had been mentioned to him twice, in the last few weeks.

"I asked you to follow the new CO, Payton, not the girl," Pat admonished.

"But I couldn't help it, Commandant – She's always with him," Payton said, apprehensively, trying to defend his comment.

"Keep your eye on her, Patrick," Donnelly said to the Commandant. "This girl's relationship could be an advantage to us in the future. However, replace Mr Payton, as I agree with Norman, there is no room for personal vendettas. Leave this girl in peace, Mr Payton. That's a direct order. Do you understand?"

"Yes, Mr Donnelly," Payton stuttered.

Pat looked at Payton, directing him to leave. Payton left the room without objection. He went downstairs for a drink, angrier at not being able to punish Mary than for being asked to leave the meeting.

When Payton first met Mary through John Boland, almost two years earlier, he was infatuated with her, his infatuation being one of pure lust, rather than any pretence of love. Payton convinced Boland to share personal details of his relationship with Mary, but after her outburst on the riverbank, he realised that Boland had lied to keep face. This only served to inflame Payton's desire, but, knowing that Mary would never be with him willingly, he decided it would happen by force, if necessary.

He had deliberately interrupted the meeting with the water and lamps, in order to stay and raise the issue of Mary's relationship with the new CO. He had hoped that, as the bringer of information, he would be given the task of cutting off her hair, a regular punishment for Irish women in relationships with British soldiers. He intended to use the opportunity to violate her, assisted by his two Runner friends.

"There will be another opportunity, Miss Bradford," he said to himself, as he sipped his drink at the bar.

Upstairs, the intense meeting was drawing to a close. Norman Boland read the minutes, confirming the agreed activity for the next few weeks. Arms and funds were limited, so Commanders had to make do with the little they had, improvising where necessary.

The Arklow branch was to commit a clear act of retaliation to demonstrate that they were still very active, and to emphasise the ineffectiveness of the British raids. The RIC Sergeant in Ovoca had made himself a legitimate target, failing to object or intervene in the arrest of Mr Byrne. He was to be given 24-hours' notice to leave the country. If he failed to act, appropriate action would be taken.

No-one was to return to the raided houses for the time being. They were all to take extreme caution. The exception was Norman Boland. His high-profile positon as Mayor meant he could not stay hidden, so he agreed to present himself at the Barracks the following day, to be cleared of all suspicion.

Finally, a discrete investigation was to be carried out by all Commanders, each supplying a piece of false information, designed to entrap the Informer.

As everyone dispersed, the proprietor's wife entered and started tidying up for the next meeting, a Town Council meeting, due and the   following   night.

The Hanging Stone

The following Sunday afternoon, Myles collected Mary from her house. Patiently tolerating a long discussion between Mary and her sister over which coat and hat were most suitable for the weather, he finally got her away. Mary planned to take Myles to 'the Hanging Stone', a large, free-standing monolith, about 30 feet high, that hung precariously over the edge of a cliff. It was located on the seaward side of Arklow Rock. This monolith was a favourite place for local children to play, most of them having painted their names on it, at one time or another.

The weather was dry, but a strong, chilly breeze blew directly off the sea. Mary decided to use a short cut across low-lying farmland next to the shore, in an area called 'the Fishery', hoping to benefit from the shelter it offered.

A path, known locally as the 'Mass Path', snaked its way across this low-lying farmland. The path started at the top of a small hill, and from there, Myles could see the whole plateau of farmland and a sprinkling of small, thatched dwellings. Most had white smoke rising from their chimneys, bending at right angles as the wind caught it. Myles was reminded of the dugouts at the front, although these cottages looked a lot cosier. Mary gave a brief history of the path, as they followed it to their destination.

"It was during the Penal Laws. The English would not allow the Catholics to practice their religion, so a Priest would secretly hold a Mass out at the Rock, and this was the path they used."

"Are you sure you're not a Rebel, Mary? Myles asked, with a smile.

"Well, it's very difficult to give any history lesson about this town and its surroundings without mentioning some atrocity committed by the English," Mary retorted, defending herself.

"I was only teasing, Mary," Myles laughed, as they approached the Rock Hill. Here the road ran straight over the top, with smaller tracks leading off in different directions.

"Which way now, Mary?" Myles asked.

"This one," she said, pointing to a track leading to the seaward side.

They both followed the steep, dirt track to the top, passing a few houses on the way. As they approached the top, the path levelled out, becoming a grassy, stone-walled laneway, with thick gorse bushes on either side.

"It's not far now," Mary said. "Just down this laneway and across a field."

Here it was breezy and a little chilly, so Mary snuggled into Myles as they walked down the grassy laneway. He did not object, feeling pleasantly comforted by it.

Halfway down the laneway, they came across a small whitewashed cottage, with a red door and two windows buried deep within its mud walls. Protruding through a red corrugated iron roof was a stone chimney, puffing out clouds of white smoke, quickly dispersed by the wind. To the side of the cottage, an old man was struggling to retrieve a bucket of water from a well, flush with the ground. He was dressed in brown trousers and an old black coat, tied up with string, and had well-worn hobnailed boots with black leather gaiters, reminding Myles of German jack boots.

Myles did not hesitate to offer to help the old man.

"Please allow me," he said, stepping onto the granite flagstones surrounding the well.

The old man stood up and moved back from the well.

"I won't object. These old bones aren't what they use to be," he said.

Myles lifted the heavy pail and followed the old man into his cottage. A large cloud of wood smoke tried to escape through the open door.

"Quick, shut the door," the old man instructed Mary, as she stepped through.

The inside of the cottage smelled of wood fires. It consisted of a large, open-plan room, with a huge stone fireplace in its centre; a small fire was burning beneath a cast iron pot of water, which was suspended on an iron chain, hanging from one of three metal bars that were fixed across the chimney opening.

"Put it here, please," the old man said, pointing to a chair, beside a dining table.

Myles placed the pale of water on the chair, removed his hat and looked around. It was exactly as he imagined – small and dark, but very cosy. Sitting on a grey slate in the centre of the table was half a loaf of homemade bread, beside it, a blue and white stripped jug with a muslin cloth covering its butter milk contents. A dresser was standing by a wall in front of the table, displaying a set of Delph plates. Several family portraits hung on the other walls, which were once whitewashed but now had a dull brown appearance, caused by years of smoke. The most dominant picture was a large religious print of an Angel standing over a child collecting water from a stream. The caption read "My Guardian Angel". A well-worn wooden ladder, its sides shining from use, led up to an open platform, unmistakably a sleeping area. Above this platform and clearly exposed along the entire length of the roof, were ancient, twisted, wooden branches gone grey with age. These were the original roof trusses used to support the thatched roof that had been covered over by the red corrugated iron. Over the fire place, mounted directly in the centre of the chimney breast, hung a black, hardwood crucifix, with an ivory figure of Jesus, its once magnificent whiteness now a dull yellow.

Next to the fireplace, a buttermilk churn stood surrounded by a shovel, spade, scythe, and several other random tools, required daily on a working farm. Two shafts of light entered through the small windows, brightening up the cottage and illuminating the floating dust particles, as they sliced their way through the smoky atmosphere.

"Would you like a cup of tea? I was just about to make one for myself," the old man asked, picking up a poker and stoking the fire.

"Is that a halberd, Sir," Myles asked, indicating the poker. "May I have a closer look?"

The old man laughed as he passed over the poker.

"You English have funny names for everything. That's a pike head from 1798, from the Battle of Arklow. I've found loads over the years."

"Yes, I recognise it now. There are some on the railings surrounding the Priest's monument in the parade ground," Myles said, handing the object back to the man.

"Ah, that's Father Murphy. He was a leader in '98," the old man said, placing the pike head by the fireplace. "Now do you want a cup of tea and some bread?"

"No, thank you, but I would like a drink of water, please?" Myles replied.

The old man passed Myles a ladle, which he took, drinking thirstily from the bucket of fresh, well water. It was cool and refreshing.

"Do you live alone?" Myles asked, as he took another ladle full of water.

"Yes, I do now, since my wife Esther died a few years back. She was never right after our only boy died in the War."

"I am very sorry to hear that," Myles said, as he placed the ladle on the table.

"It was the Battle of Mons in 'late October 14. He was one of the first to die, before they even started to dig trenches. Our only boy, John, and his friends, answered Redmond's call after that speech out at Woodenbridge. They believed the promise of Home Rule in return for signing up, but, it never happened," the old man said, bitterly. "Most were killed in the first few weeks. Then, when it was over, the English Government deferred its promise. Giving us one of these in return for his sacrifice."

The old man opened a drawer in the dresser and removed a large copper disk and three medals, which he placed on the table next to Myles.

Myles picked up the disk and looked at it.

"It's the first time I have actually seen one of these 'Death Pennies'," Myles said, examining the disk with great care and respect.

The name, John Tracy, was etched in a small square above a lion's head, with the words, 'He died for freedom and honour', around the edge. A figure, presumably Britannia, was holding a wreath in an outstretched arm, over the name.

"I'm so sorry, Mr Tracy. Many honest and good men died in that terrible war."

"They died for nothing! Especially the Irish," the old man retorted, overwhelmed by sadness and anger. He had met so many uniformed Officers, all full of apologies, so many officials, so many friends. He was sick of hearing how sorry everyone was.

"Read what it says 'round the edge," the old man asked Myles, through gritted teeth.

"He died for freedom and honour," Myles replied.

"Freedom! What Freedom?" The old man shouted, angrily. "Wasn't that War fought for the freedom of small nations? Well you can't get any smaller that Ireland, and we're still waiting. But it's not going to happen, is it Captain. It was all lies. Your King, your Government, your Army, and your glorious Empire, all lied. They promised Home Rule and went back on their word, and now kill or arrest anyone who objects or tries to do something about it themselves." The old man paused.

"Listen carefully, Captain," he continued, lowering his voice to a whisper, "I can see you're a good man and probably don't deserve the fate that awaits you if you stay here, so take my advice and get out. Leave your Army and go home, because the War that has started here now, is not like '98 or '16. This is it. The big one and it won't end until you Brits are forcefully removed from this Country, once and for all. From the birds in the trees, to the dogs in the street, the Irish people have truly had enough of you, your lies, your laws, and your downright deceit." The old man banged his fist on the table. "Your Government is too stupid and too arrogant to accept that times have changed. Just like the War in France, they will fight to the last man and the last bullet, sacrificing hundreds of young lives for their own glory. Then, when all is lost, just like in France, they'll sit around a table and sign an agreement with their enemies. Even then, I don't doubt they'll attempt to justify hanging onto some part of this country, whether through laws or taxes or occupying some remote hill or army Barracks, they will desperately try and hang onto it as long as they can." The old man pointed his finger at Myles. "Mark my words, regardless of all their arrogant justification, their desperate hope to cling onto some authority here, will come back to bite them, and bite them it will!"

This outburst on the waste of War, and the hopeless prediction of the future was the last thing Myles expected to hear from a clearly educated old man, living on the side of a hill. He felt claustrophobic as panic began to set in, several items in the cottage seemed to transform into those used in trench warfare. The ladder, and the tools bought back bitter memories of working parties crossing No Man's Land at night, many never returning, felled by the constant bark of a distant machine gun.

He loosened his tie and placed his finger around his collar. An open fire was a common trigger that could accelerate these panic attacks. Other triggers competed – the small wooden cross over the fireplace, the picture of the Angel looked like the fabled 'Angels of Mons', assisting British Forces with their bows and arrows.

He looked at the picture again and thought of the old man's son. He could imagine his body, discarded and broken somewhere near Mons. His face must have betrayed his thoughts, a sudden outburst from Mary, banishing the awful memories.

"Sir," she said, directing her gaze to the old man. "This man saved hundreds of lives in the trenches. I know that if he could, he would give us all a full Republic tomorrow morning. He is a good and honest man, you are right. He is truly sorry for the loss of your son, but he does not deserve your admonishment."

Mary defended Myles, acutely aware of his distress and the unfairness of the situation.

"You're from here! An Arklow Girl, with an English Officer now there's trouble brewing, take my advice, both of you and leave this country as quick as you can. No good will come from staying here. Believe me, there will be no happy ending for you both, in these turbulent times. The only thing you can be guaranteed to get from this is one of these, Miss," the old man said, pointing at the disk.

Myles glanced at the named copper plaque still lying on the table. He saw the scythe leaning against the wall beside the churn. The gangly man came to mind. Did he tip John Tracey on his head before he died, he wondered to himself? The gangly man had not come to mind since Myles had spoken to Mary about him in the hospital, fearing a relapse; Myles knew to go, now. Struggling to take control, but gaining a great deal of strength from Mary's presence, he politely took his leave.

"Thank you for the water Mr Tracy. I am, truly sorry for the death of your son. If there is anything that I can do for you in the future, that will ease your terrible burden, please do let me know and I will do everything in my power to assist."

"Get me my son back, Captain," the old man sighed.

Myles was about to open the door but hesitated.

"If only I could."

He lifted the metal latch with a loud click, and left, Mary following behind. Outside the cottage, the breeze refreshed him.

92

Myles inhaled deeply, clearing his mind and dispersing the claustrophobic feeling that had threatened to overwhelm him.

The old man stood in the doorway, smoke billowing out above his head.

"I'm sorry, Captain. I miss my son so much, and you reminded me of him. His death was such a waste." He went back inside, closing the door behind him.

"My God, Mary. These people really do dislike us."

"Well, not all of them." Mary said.

"Believe me, it's all of them. Your family is the only exception."

He placed his hat on his head, and cheerfully said.

"Come and show me the Hanging Stone – I'm so looking forward to seeing it."

They walked to the end of the laneway and crossed a large grassy meadow towards the sea. The breeze seemed stronger in the open, causing long, erratic waves to race across the top of the bright green grass. At the end of the meadow was a steep cliff. Here, just below, on a large ledge, standing proudly was the Hanging Stone. There was a steep, dirt path leading down to the ledge and continued around a corner, heading back towards the town. A small group of children were on this path, running around the Stone, whilst others were climbing on top of it.

Mary's dress was unsuitable for the couple to climb down to the ledge, so they sat on a small outcrop of rocks, by the meadow. Mary plucked some primroses from the rocks and handed them to Myles.

"Why thank you my fair maid. I shall keep them forever," he said with a cheeky smile.

Where they sat, commanded a beautiful view of the large, graffiti-covered Hanging Stone and the surrounding ocean, a vast green plateau that sparkled in the sunlight. It was covered with small, white-crested waves, which looked like playful, wild horses, chasing each other to the shore, eventually giving up and dissolving back into the vastness of the dark green sea. Above, seagulls soared, looking like floating letter M,s as they used the air currents to propel themselves high above the cliff face, their melodious call penetrating the cold sea breeze.

Mary gave Myles the history of the Hanging Stone.

"Every Easter morning, the stone drops into the sea to wash off all the paint and moss, and then climbs back up for another year. They say it appeared during the 1798 Rebellion. Some English Red Coats on horseback were chasing a Priest. Just as they were about to catch him, the stone jumped out from the side of this Cliff, landed on them, horses and all, and the Priest successfully escaped."

"My God, Mary! If those stories are true, even the stones here hate us."

"Of course, they're all true. Everyone knows that," Mary exclaimed, folding her arms and turning sideways to frown at Myles. He was sitting with his forearms resting on his knees and twirling the primroses between his fingers.

"Don't you believe me, Captain Fox?" She said laughingly, the sea breeze causing long streaks of black hair to flicker across her face.

"Of course,!" he said, "I'm sure they're all true."

Mary looked into his eyes and could see that the sadness and pain had returned.

"You're thinking of what Mr Tracey said, aren't you?" Mary said with empathy.

"Yes, I am, and I must say, I rather agree with him. To receive a large copper disc for the life of your son, rather than fulfilling a promise, how could one disagree?" Myles said, sadly. Taking her hand and looking into her eyes, he continued.

"I must confess I almost had a turn in that house. You being there prevented it, and for that I'm extremely grateful."

94

He tried tucked Mary's hair behind her bonnet, but the strong breeze undid his work.

She smiled, this time, taking his hand and kissing the back of it. Myles had been feeling uneasy since leaving the cottage, but the touch of Mary's lips soothed him. He stroked away the rivulets of dark hair dancing across Mary's face, this time, leaning over to gently kiss her on the lips.

Mary placed her arms around his neck, accidently knocking off his hat, as they fell backwards into the thick, wavy grass. The seagulls hovered and darted on the breeze high above, their sonorous sound filling the air.

John Boland was hiding nearby behind a clump of bramble bushes. He had followed the couple on their entire journey. Overcome with grief and loss, he watched them embrace each other.

"Damn you to hell Payton!" Boland said knowing with certainty that he had lost the only woman he would ever truly love. John knew that he had allowed Payton, and his own stupidity, to ruin his life.

"You absolute Bastard, Payton," he cursed to himself, punching the grass with his fist. He stood up and left, in his grief, completely unconcerned that he might be seen.

Mary and Myles were interrupted by the children, laughing as they caught them in their embrace, shouting and pointing with outstretched arms. Myles sat up and replaced his hat. When the children saw that he was a solider, they changed. Instead of pointing fingers, they pointed imaginary rifles.

"Bang! Bang! Bang!" they shouted, pointing at Myles.

Myles pointed back, using his fingers as a pistol.

"Ker pow!" he said loudly and mimicked the kick from a gun.

Two of the boys fell together. The others continued shooting. Then the fallen stood up, and they all ran off together, laughing.

"Even the children want to shoot us, Mary. We really have no hope.

Myles helped Mary to her feet and they headed back towards the town. As the sun set, it cast their shadows as one, across the undulating   grass   in   the   windy   meadow.

A Fortnight of Attacks

The following Monday morning was bright and dry. Kathleen Dunne, the wife of the Ovoca RIC Sergeant, opened the front door of her house and flooded the dark hall with bright sunlight. She stepped out into the morning sunshine and was greeted by the sight of two large dray horses attached to a long, flat-bedded trailer, loaded with kegs of beer. A small group of men had placed two planks against the back of the trailer and were cautiously unloading the wooden kegs, one by one, rolling them into the side yard of Fitz's Pub, directly across the road. Kathleen was a pious woman. Her immediate thoughts were for the women who struggled to feed their children whilst their husbands spent their hard-earned money on that Devil's liquid.

Ignoring them, she pulled out a cloth from her apron pocket and started to dust down the front door. She was preparing to polish the brass knocker when a telegram boy came skidding to a halt next to her, on his oversized bicycle.

"You'll destroy your good shoes, young Tom." she said, turning towards him.

"I can't stop any other way, Mrs Dunne", the boy replied, handing a telegram across the handlebars.

She took it and shouted down the hall,

"Joe, it's a telegram have you a coin for young Tom?"

Joe Dunne appeared in the brightly lit hallway, shaving soap still on his face. He was not wearing his tunic and had one hand buried in the pocket of his uniform trousers.

"Oh, I think I might find a bob or two for young Master Tom," he said, and winked at Tom as he shuffled up the hall towards the front door.

Suddenly, a man with a handkerchief across his face broke away from the cart. He ran across the road, pointing a revolver. He fired twice, hitting the RIC Officer in the chest. Joe Dunne collapsed to his knees, a shocked and bewildered expression on his face. He looked up at his screaming wife and a terrified Tom. The gunman fired again. Joe fell forward onto the hard terracotta floor with a great thump, his hand still fumbling in his pocket for coins. A large pool of dark blood appeared beneath him. His white shirt soaked it up, thirstily. The gunman pushed Tom of the bicycle, mounted it, and disappeared across a nearby bridge.

A few nights later, a small group of armed men attacked one of the guarded entrances to the Kynoch Factory, killing a solider and seriously injuring another. They took the soldiers' rifles and ammunition, disappearing into the night.

The following Saturday afternoon, a Prison guard from Wicklow Jail, was shot dead whilst fishing on the beach. That Sunday night, the RIC Barracks in Arklow were attacked with a homemade bomb. The bomb detonated, blowing up the gate, and damaging the plinth of the Father Murphy statue, which stood directly across the road.

The following Tuesday, the Aughrim RIC Station was burned to the ground, with no fatalities. A week later, after a series of non-fatal attacks on off-duty Soldiers and Police, across the County, the RIC Barracks in Rathdrum were, unsuccessfully attacked, resulting in the fatal killing of two IRA Volunteers and one Police Officer.

At 3 o'clock that Friday afternoon, Myles stood outside the bank, waiting for Percy. He dismissed the two soldiers posted to guard the bank, leaving him feeling vulnerable, acutely aware that he was a potential target. He thought the public felt the same as they gave him a wide berth. Myles mused on his surroundings, considering the town well-planned. He looked across at the County Court House, an old building nestled behind huge poplar trees that swayed in the breeze. In its grounds, protected by iron railings and granite pillars, stood the remains of the old Norman Castle, mostly destroyed by Oliver Cromwell, 400 years earlier.

The remaining tower and some defensive walls had been incorporated into the structure of the Barracks, built 50 years later, on top of the ruins. Across the road, towering above the Barracks stood the Catholic Church, dominating the square. Outside, the stone statue of Father Murphy, the famous leader from the 1798 Rebellion, stood tall on a stone plinth, pointing an accusatory finger towards the Barracks in which he had been fatally injured whilst attacking it in June 1798.

A horse-drawn cart pulled up outside the Barracks, the workmen repairing the damaged gate, unloaded wooden planks. The name, 'Bradford's Coach Repairs' was painted on the side of the cart. Myles thought of Mary. He had not seen her properly since their tryst at the Hanging Stone, almost three weeks earlier. They had spoken briefly to each other in passing, and had made hasty arrangements for a stroll together, but, because of the intermittent attacks he had to cancel. He decided to pay her a visit before she finished work and arrange a proper engagement over the weekend, come hell or high water! The very thought of seeing her lifted his sprits from the dreadful few weeks he had just experienced.

Percy came out of the bank and stopped on the high steps, laughing at Myles.

"What's so funny, Captain? "Myles asked.

"Look," Percy said, pointing towards Myles feet.

Myles looked down. A small white dog had cocked its leg and was urinating on his brown boots.

"Get away," Myles said, pushing the dog away with his boot. "Christ Percy. Even the dogs in the street hate us."

"Come on; let's get lunch in the Railway. It's on me," Percy said as they crossed the road for the hotel.

They made their way to the lounge, surprisingly busy for a Friday afternoon.

"What can I get you, gentlemen?" The barmaid asked, as they sat at the counter.

"Two lunches, please," Percy said, removing his hat and gloves.

"And two pints of Porter, please," Myles said.

"With everything that's been going on for the last two weeks, how do you manage to be so happy, Percy?" He asked, as he settled down on the stool.

"Well, to be honest, my Father is organising a transfer for me, away from this death trap."

"Really! When were you going to tell me?" Myles asked, feeling betrayed.

"When it was confirmed and approved. I've not heard anything back yet."

"But you could have mentioned it to me, Percy?"

"I apologise. There was no deceit intended, I'd only asked him last Wednesday"

"To be honest, I feel you're running away from your responsibilities, Percy."

"You've said it yourself Myles. This War is already lost. What difference would my death, or yours, make to the 'Powers that be'?"

"That's defeatist and somewhat treasonous."

"So be it, Myles, but it's true. Working with you has shown me that life is not about being stuck in a trench in France, or watching your back as you cross a road. Tell me honestly; is this ridiculous war like the one you fought in France? Percy asked, feeling angry that Myles had challenged his loyalty to him.

Myles was shocked. He knew that Percy's viewpoint had been altered after 3 months under his command, listening to his experiences from the War in France.

"I'm sorry, Percy. I agree, your death will make not the slightest difference to the course of this war. I will make no objection regarding your request."

"Thank you, old friend," Percy said, feeling relived.

"Gentlemen! Forgive the interruption. Derek Rouse is the name, and insurance is the game," a man in an orange checked suit stated. He placed his card on the counter. Myles picked it up. It read, Derek Rouse, Good Life Insurance Company, London.

"We live in terrible times, Sirs. That's why I'm offering you a simple insurance policy, just in case the worst happens, so that you can rest easy, knowing your loved ones will be looked after."

He removed his bowler hat and placed it over his heart. Myles looked at the funny-looking, round man, dressed in a comical suit, and burst out laughing.

"Nothing to laugh at, Sir," the man said, feigning sincerity, and placing a small case on top of the counter. He opened it. Inside, were a selection of small .22 derringer-type pistols, and a host of insurance policies. Percy picked up one of the guns.

"What the hell is this – a Novelty from a Tom Smith Christmas Cracker?"

"That, my good man is a Belgium .22, six-shot pistol, with folding trigger. It can be concealed anywhere on the person, and can save your life in unpredictable circumstances. It's free when you sign up to the deluxe insurance package".

"I think I would rather take my chances with one of these," Percy said, tipping the butt of his pistol.

"I could have you for gun running," Myles said, curiously examining the pistols.

"They are all perfectly legal and above-board, I can assure you, Captain".

"Sirs, your lunch is ready," the Barmaid said, interrupting the salesman. "They're on your usual table in the dining area."

"Thank you, Betty," Percy said, as he stood up.

"Take my card," the salesman said. "If you change your mind, I'll be here."

Out of politeness, Myles took the card and placed it in his pocket.

As they were about to enter the dining area, Pat Kavanagh came through the doors, followed by the Runner, Payton and another man.

"Allow me, Sirs," Payton said, holding the door open with a flourish. "Don't sit too close to the windows now lads, will ya's," he continued.

"Shut Up, Payton!" I apologise, Gentlemen. Sit wherever you like, and enjoy your meal," Pat Kavanagh said, and continued across the smoky room to the exit.

Myles watched him leave.

"Excuse me, Percy," he said, following Kavanagh out through the exit.

"Mr Kavanagh, may I have a word with you?" Myles called after him.

They turned together, an expression of total surprise on their faces.

"Alone, Mr Kavanagh, if you don't mind."

"Go on ahead, there lads. I'll soon catch up with ye.

His companions objected, but Commandant Kavanagh insisted. They left, waiting directly outside the main door. Pat Kavanagh walked towards Myles, curious to hear what he had to say.

That Sunday afternoon was overcast. Myles stopped the staff car directly outside Mary's house. He got out, and as he walked around to the passenger door, he looked up at the grey sky and wondered if it might rain later. Mary appeared at the top of the steps, with her entire family. They all descended, crossing the front garden to greet Myles.

"Good afternoon, stranger," Mary said, as Myles removed a glove to shake hands with her parents.

"Good afternoon," he replied, kissing her lightly on her cheek.

"Hello Myles," Mr Bradford said, offering his hand. "These are terrible dangerous times" he commented.

"Yes indeed," Myles said, shaking his hand firmly. He turned to Mrs Bradford. She looked beautiful dressed in a long ivory dress and wearing her blue sapphire pendant and earrings. Myles stared at the sapphires and thought of Nurse Garland and the Sappers – surprisingly the memory faded with no ill-effect. Feeling happy, Myles ignored all other thoughts, kissing the back of her hand, in greeting.

"I must apologise for my absence. I've been rather busy for the last few weeks."

"We have missed you at Sunday morning Mass, Captain," Mrs Bradford said.

"For that, I must also apologise. I now attend 8 o'clock Mass, where I receive a much more honest resentment from the congregation."

"I know what you mean, Captain. Nothing like an honest man to tell you the truth," she replied, with a chuckle.

"We don't resent you," Anna, interjected, inspecting the interior of the car.

"Oh, I know, Anna," Myles said, "and I thank you for that."

"Please let me go with you in the car? I won't be a nuisance," Anna asked.

"No. They have not seen each other for a few weeks, Anna. Please allow them some privacy," Mrs Bradford interjected.

"We're only going for a short drive, Anna, and shan't be long. I'll drive you around town when we get back, I promise," Myles said, closing the side door.

"Thank you! I'll look forward to it," Anna said, bubbling over with excitement.

Following farewells Myles drove off, turning onto Sea View Avenue, towards the old Kynoch's Factory.

"Where are we going?" Mary asked inquisitively.

"Hostilities against the Army have increased and I must accept that I'm a target. I refuse to place you in danger, so, rather than confine ourselves to quarters, I thought it would be nice to go for a walk in the relative safety of the old factory works. That way, I can guarantee your safety."

"How exciting! I can show you where I worked," Mary said, feeling nostalgic.

Myles drove alongside the lake. The unexpected noise of the car engine disturbed the water fowl that were peacefully resting on the black surface of the pond. Some squawked loudly in protest as they raced across the rippling surface towards the protection of tall, golden reeds that shimmered in the watery light of the afternoon sun.

Myles stopped the car next to a sentry post and helped Mary out. Looking up at sky, he noticed the sun trying to penetrate the foreboding black clouds on the horizon. A soldier came out of his hut to meet them.

"Good Afternoon, Captain Fox. All's well. Nothing to report," he said.

"Good afternoon, Private Fuller. Thank you for the report. This is Mary. She and I will be going for a stroll across the factory this afternoon. Please ensure we are not disturbed. We should take two hours. If we're not back by then, please alert the other guards," Myles said, adopting standard procedure with his staff.

"You're being very cautious, Captain Fox," Mary said, smiling at the soldier.

"You can never be too careful, Ma'am," the soldier said, as he held open a small side gate, allowing them to enter the site.

The huge Factory stretched across the dunes of the north beach for over a mile. There were a multitude of buildings. Some were large, abstract concrete constructions, like the large Water Tower and Chemical Mixing Houses. Others were made of brick and stone, like the huge Warehouses, Generator Stations, and Drying

Rooms. Most were small wooden huts, with paper-like walls, surrounded by high sand banks, designed to direct accidental explosions upwards. A network of roads and railway lines latticed the entire site, connecting every building and open area together. All roads were lined with electric street lighting. The factory looked like an unoccupied town.

An overwhelming sadness engulfed Mary as she walked through the factory. She thought of how busy and noisy these now silent and empty buildings once were, and how crowded these roads and paths were when the huge workforce of 4000 men, women and children occupied the site. She stopped outside the Generator House, opened the door and entered, explaining that this was the heart of the factory. She remembered, with fondness, the Dublin electrician, who she often sat with during lunch, and his brief explanations of how electricity worked. His chair sat next to a wooden bench covered with abandoned newspapers, as if waiting for him to return.

Mary, overwhelmed with sentimental memoires, walked towards the end of the factory to an area known as Spion Kop. On the way, she explained to Myles the roles of the other buildings in the production of Cordite. She pointed out the Water Tower, used as a meeting point, and the Laboratory, where the English Chemist taught her the Latin names for the chemicals. Then the Drying Houses, where the Gun Cotton was dried under careful supervision. They crossed a small bridge, leading to a secluded area.

"This was the most dangerous area of the factory, and completely out of bounds. These were Mixing Houses. The raw ingredients came in here on the overhead troughs," she said, pointing up at a lattice of lead-lined, wooden troughs that filled the sky. "They ran into those buildings, where they were mixed to make nitro-glycerine."

Myles was fascinated. "Was it not dangerous?"

"A large explosion did happen here one night. 27 people were killed, including my Mother's brother. We all thought it was an attack by a German U-boat, but no one knows what really happened.

"I am sorry to hear about your Uncle, Mary." he said

He gently took her hand as they followed the road that led to their destination.

Myles was astonished at Mary's knowledge of how the factory operated. She knew the workings of each building, and many of the unusual items and their uses, like steel presses, brass extruders and the filters in the Acid Houses. He was intrigued at just how large the site was, and the very complex, and dangerous, procedures involved in the manufacture of Gun Cotton and Cordite. But what fascinated him most was the amount of equipment still in the buildings. It was as if all the people had just left for the day, and were going to return in the morning. There was evidence of a hasty exit everywhere. Experiments were still set up in the lab, boxes of finished and unfinished products lay everywhere. Some of the machines had raw ingredients still attached, and there were boots, hats, and hand tools everywhere. He had even seen a half-painted door, the paint pot and brush still beside it. Everything and everywhere looked as if it was just waiting for the owners to return.

The Dublin Company that had purchased the site from the War Office had been forced to cease dismantling activity by the IRA. The IRA intended to keep the factory in good working order, hoping that when an Independent Irish Government was established, it would reinvest in the factory, and start production again. The IRA heard a rumour that the dismantler was ordered, by the British Government, to leave the factory in such a state that it could never produce explosives again, but right now, it looked as if the work force could return, and start production within a week. The IRA were aware of this, and, not only threatened the Dublin

106

dismantlers, but extended the threat to all locals who may have been tempted by the large wages on offer from the dismantlers.

They finally reached their destination - the top of a hill known as Spion Kop, named after a famous battle in South Africa, for which Kynoch's had supplied most of the munitions. The hill commanded a beautiful view of the sea and a nearby crescent-shaped beach. From behind it, Myles and Mary were able to overlook the entire site and the town in the distance. They sat together, silent in their own personal thoughts. Mary was thinking of the time when she worked there, and Myles, about the complex procedure of making explosives, and that he would, most likely, have used product produced here.

"Tell me," he said, breaking the silence, "how do you know so much about the factory?"

"I loved working here. I was always exploring the unrestricted areas during my breaks. I would often visit people and ask them what they did. Most were delighted and proud to explain their jobs. There were so many different roles, and I would always volunteer when help was needed in other areas, from cleaning the danger areas to packing in the warehouses.

"My, you were busy. It must have been fascinating."

"Oh, it was," Mary said, excited at the memories.

"And to think, I may have used ordnance in France that was made by you. Myles looked over Mary's shoulder towards the sea. He saw random squalls disturbing its surface, and its horizon was dominated by dark foreboding clouds.

"I think it is going to rain, Mary. We should get back before it comes down on us," he said, standing up and offering her his hand.

As they walked back across the factory site, the light began to fade. It became dark and overcast. Suddenly, the clouds opened and it started to rain.

"Quick! Through here," Mary said, laughing. She grabbed the front of her long dress and started to run along a sandy path between two very tall, sand dunes.

On the other side, a long concrete building stood with doors on either end. Myles raced ahead of her. He tried to push open the door, but found it locked.

"You have to pull, Myles. It fools everyone," Mary said, catching up with him.

"That's unusual," Myles said, pulling open the door and stepping inside.

"It's a precaution against fire and explosion. Most of the doors here are like that," Mary said, as she removed her bonnet, shaking the rain from it.

"What was this building for?" he asked, curiously, as he spied rows of wooden lockers on the walls. In the centre of the room were large, blue, wooden trestles, bolted to a diamond patterned brick floor,

"This was the ladies changing area. We came here to remove our clothes and hang them in the lockers. We then went through this door," Mary said, opening a door in the centre of a wall that divided the long building. It led to a similar room also with lockers and trestles. Myles followed her. This room had a slight echo as she spoke.

"Here we put on the factory-issued clothes, to avoid contamination, and accidently taking dangerous residue home, which could explode in our houses."

Mary opened what was once her locker. Her old factory uniform was still hanging inside, her hat, a blue one-piece dress, a white apron and a pair of wooden clogs. She wistfully picked up the hat and apron. She went over and sat down on a trestle in the centre of the room. She fondled the hat for a moment, and then laughed loudly.

"Is something funny?" Myles asked.

"I was just thinking about how much I enjoyed working here."

"I can imagine it was fun." Myles said.

"Yes, it really was and I miss it, especially the company of the other girls. I was just thinking of this one time when I was changing my clothes, in this very building, and Father Mackenzie accidently walked in. I was wearing very little," she said, looking up at Myles who was standing by a window.

"He got such a fright! He kept saying he was looking for the lavatory, and tried to pull open that door from inside. He didn't know where to look," she said, chuckling. "I got up and pushed open the door, covered only with this apron." Mary placed the apron across her body and continued.

"He thanked me and ran off through the dunes."

"That was very naughty," Myles said, walking over to join her on the trestle.

"It was, I suppose, but I was only sixteen at the time. He never said a word to me about it afterwards," she said, gently stroking the back of Myles hand.

She turned and stared into his eyes, while leaning her head in towards his. Myles' heart was thumping. He wrapped both arms around her, and kissed her lips, passionately. Mary did not resist and slowly lay back on the trestle, bringing Myles with her, continuing to kiss. Myles pulled the apron from between them and discarded it on the floor; Mary removed his hat and placed it on top of the apron. On seeing the label 'Kings of Bond Street, London', she smiled as they both succumb to their desires, while listened to the rhythmic sound of the rain on the tin roof.

Over at the sentry post, the Yorkshire soldier told John Boland to move on. Boland, not wanting to attract attention, pulled down his cap, turned up his collar and prepared for the wet, arduous journey back to town angry that he had lost track of his quarry.

109

The Black and Tans

Monday morning, 29th of March 1920, was damp and dull. The edge of yesterday's storm lingered over the town, but the worst had passed during the night, with a brightening of the sky on the eastern horizon. Myles walked across the wet Barrack's courtyard, a spring in his step. He was thinking of Mary and their shared passion, other thoughts secondary to his memory of their tryst in the factory.

As he walked past the parked trucks, the stale smell of the damp canvass reminded him of transporting troops and equipment in France. This time, the memories did not linger and his thoughts quickly returned to Mary.

Myles walked to the back of one of the trucks. Lifting the canvass, he noticed that a sizeable amount of domestic and military equipment had been carefully packed into the back of the truck.

"I wonder what's going on." He thought to himself.

Continuing to the office he noticed the wet cobbles were covered with dead leaves and twigs. He located the source, a tall evergreen in the Court House, next door, swaying and rustling in the wind.

"What a mess," he thought

Suddenly a voice called to him.

"Captain, a word if you please."

It was Sergeant McCuskey, the RIC Chief. He appeared in the doorway of his office, a small, separate building to one side of the main block, and directly below the tall trees. The roof was also covered in twigs and leaves. Sergeant McCuskey, an irascible, but honest man from Donegal, with 40 years' service with the Police Force all over Ireland. The last 15 years had been spent in Arklow, where he intended to retire. He had gained the respect of the locals and the IRA, known to have a firm but fair attitude, avoiding

Crown interference, when possible. Now, with a sharp increase in Crown activity from Dublin Castle and the Army, Sergeant McCuskey believed the trust he had spent years establishing, had been eroded. In the last few months, he was refused a seat amongst the locals at Sunday Mass, where before he was inundated with smiling offers.

Myles walked back towards the Sergeant.

"Good Morning, Sergeant. What can I do for you?" Myles said cheerfully, reflecting his current mood.

"Well, don't you look like the cat that got the cream, Captain Fox," the Sergeant said, responding to Myles' happy demeanour.

"You Irish have analogies for every situation, Sergeant," Myles replied laughing.

"There are two Gentlemen in my office wishing to speak with you, and they won't be long in taking back the cream," he said,

Myles entered the office, followed by Sergeant McCuskey. He immediately recognised Freeny, who was sitting with a strangely dressed man in front of McCuskey's desk.

"Gentlemen, this is Captain Fox, the CO of Arklow and surrounding districts," Sergeant McCuskey said, as he sat down in the chair behind his desk.

Freeny remained seated, whilst the other man stood up and offered his hand to Myles. He was a little taller and a few years older but of the same build.

"Hello Captain Fox. I'm Captain Jeremy Richards of the 'Kings Own Scottish Boarders', he said, shaking Myles hand firmly.

"That's not a regular Army uniform," Myles said, as he looked Richards over.

"No, I'm no longer in the Army, Captain. This is the uniform of the newly formed Royal Irish Constabulary Special Reserve. R.I.C.S.R, for short. The uniform is a mixture of a Police and Army uniform due to shortages," Richards said, holding open his long white trench coat to clearly display the mixed uniform to Myles.

He looked threatening, dressed in tall brown boots, kaki cavalry trousers, a deep green police tunic, a Sam Brown belt with holster, and a Tam O'Shanter hat, supporting a large RIC cap badge.

"Gentlemen, we are not here to discuss the latest military fashions. We're here to deal with the increase in subversive activity in County Wicklow," Freeny bellowed angrily, slapping a red folder down on the desk.

"Royal, Irish, Constabulary, Special, Reserve. That sounds like a French Brandy, Captain," Myles said, as they both sat back down, ignoring Freeny's outburst.

"It does rather, but I prefer the name, 'Black and Tans', which the Irish have affectionately given us."

"There's no affection in that name, Captain. It's after a pack of Kerry beagle hunting hounds," Sergeant McCuskey interjected.

"Yes, I read that in a paper recently. We were formed a few months ago by Churchill to assist the RIC with their duties, 'to face a rough and dangerous task', according to the recruitment drive," Richards said, taking a pipe from his pocket and banging the bowl in his cupped hand.

"But what would this Country have that could be more dangerous than Gallipoli, or the trenches of France, Captain Fox?"

"It would be foolish to underestimate the IRA, Captain," McCuskey said.

"I don't, not for one minute," Richards replied, turning to look at McCuskey.

"At least in France and the Dardanelles we knew who and where the enemy was, and could keep a safe distance," Myles said, adjusting his leather Sam Brown belt into a more comfortable position, and stretching his legs out across the floor.

"Except for the dammed Snipers," Richards said. filling his pipe with the tobacco he had removed from a leather pouch.

Myles stiffened at the mention of the word, 'Sniper'. He leaned forward and pinched the bridge of his nose, hoping to avoid being overwhelmed by memories. Since returning from France, that one word, 'Sniper', had the power to completely disarm him and make him question his own sanity. If ever there was a word he hated, that was it.

He had learned to avoid using it, when describing his war experiences, referring to them as 'Camouflaged Riflemen' but, when it came up, out of the blue as it just had, it could easily lead to a relapse. He had no desire for that to happen in present company, so he planned to make an excuse and leave. But as he pinched his nose, he was surprised. The memories were there, but the reaction was not. He remained calm and completely in control of his emotions and actions. Thoughts of Mary came flooding back, rekindling his happiness and supressing all other negative thoughts.

"Yes, those dammed Snipers, Captain Richards. You'll find the countryside and towns of Ireland are littered with them."

He felt an inner satisfaction after using the word without difficulty.

"Snipers, Snipers, Snipers," he said to himself, noting there was no memory recall, no gangly man, no nervous anxiety. It was now just another word.

"Mary, I believe our tryst yesterday has cured me," he thought, smiling to himself, as he settled back in the chair, stretching his legs out once again.

"Gentlemen, can we please refrain from comparing past conflicts and get down to the business at hand," Freeny interrupted, opening his red folder.

"Now, first of all, following the murder of Sergeant Dunne in Ovoca, the district, has been without a police presence for almost a month. That cannot continue. It is Dublin Castle's intention to station Captain Richards and six Special Reserve Constables there to establish a strong Police presence and let the community know

113

that we are in control. We must eradicate any idea the IRA might have, that they are responsible for law and order in this area. Once settled, Captain Richards will round up the suspects in Sergeant Dunne's murder, bringing them here to Arklow for interrogation, and trial for his murder."

"Why don't we kill them straight away, saving the bother," Myles said angrily.

"And not get a chance to interrogate the bastards. Where would be the fun in that? Freeny replied.

Captain Richards exhaled a long plume of smoke, filling the room.

"Captain Fox, the Castle has acquired a list of safe houses where we might apprehend these peasants. We also have the element of surprise, so it should be an easy task, to be completed either later this week or early next."

"The last time the Castle tried to apply those tactics, it proved a total disaster," Myles said, as he sat up in his chair.

"Captain Fox, if you had done what we required of you during my last visit, we might have apprehended some of those thugs, and prevented these recent murders." Freeny stated.

"You were with me during those searches? Please remind me of what I failed to do, that might have prevented the increase in IRA activity," Myles snapped back at Freeny.

"You failed to follow up on arrests."

"Mr Freeny, as you know, I'm not authorised to make arrests. That's the job of Sergeant McCuskey here," Myles said, pointing at a weary looking Sergeant. "I can only offer him the support of the Army when he's carrying out such matters. Had you and the Brigadier, not been so hasty with your actions last month, most of the suspects would've been successfully arrested over the following days. But NO! Both of you failed to agree with my suggestion of postponing the action and went ahead with a botched attempt of searching houses, resulting in all the suspects going to ground and an increase of subversive activity over the following weeks."

"Well, we can now get across that little anomaly. Captain Richards has the same authority as the Army and Police. We will conduct these raids with or without you."

"Mr Freeny, I have no objection to assisting the Police, but I do object to the unnecessary use of force when conducting raids, as it only serves to increase hostility in the general population. Some train drivers have refused to carry uniformed soldiers and shops and bars are adopting the same policy. Every time we take action against using force, we increase our isolation within the local population."

"So, WHAT are you suggesting, Myles? Should we wait for an invitation? Or maybe send one ourselves? Richards said, interrupting Myles.

"We cannot mollycoddle these criminals," he continued, pausing to relight his pipe.

"A strong, swift iron hand is what they need," he said pointing the stem of his pipe towards Myles. "This will confirm, once and for all, who is actually in charge of this God-forsaken Island, and my men and I are the ones that are sure as hell going to do it. As for train drivers, shop keepers, and anyone else who insists on continuing this boycott, they will receive the same harsh treatment, and that is a direct order from Churchill, himself. It's time to sort out this rabble, once and for all, Captain Fox".

"Churchill is not here dealing with the outcome of such actions, Captain Richards. We are! There will be more violence, which I can guarantee, especially if you apply the methods of your old Regiment, used in Dublin five years ago".

"I presume you're referring to the Bachelor's Walk Massacre? Unfortunately, I was stationed in India at the time, so missed all the fun, but I can assure you it did not blight the Regiment's history."

Richards eyed Myles over the top of his pipe.

"Captain Fox," Freeny said irritably, "we're not here to discuss recent history, but re-establish Crown authority in the Ovoca district. We also need to plan raids on rebel houses, and, you'll be pleased to hear, we'll adopt your idea of settling in first, conducting raids after a week or two of careful observation. Now, you were invited here to be introduced to Captain Richards, and we also need you to supply a truck and 10 men to escort the Captain and his constables to Ovoca, and spend the day helping him re-establish authority in the old RIC Barracks. So, if you don't mind, Captain, please see to the transport immediately. I have other urgent matters to discuss which don't concern you. You will leave in 30 minutes. Thank you, and good day.

Myles realised he was not wanted and stood up, disgusted at how Freeny had spoken to him. He was about to lash out, but a sympathetic glance from Sergeant McCuskey caught his eye.

"Any of that cream left, Captain?" Sergeant McCuskey asked.

Myles, puzzled for a second, recalled their earlier conversation. Thoughts of yesterday's tryst came rushing back.

"I do believe I have, Sergeant," Myles replied, with a wry smile.

"I suggest you take a good, long drink before you say something we'll all regret," Sergeant McCuskey advised him.

"Thank you, Sergeant, excellent advice. Gentlemen, I shall have the trucks and men ready in 30 minutes. Please don't keep me waiting," Myles said.

The journey to Ovoca was uneventful. Myles sat in the front of the supply truck with Captain Richards and the driver, whilst the six Tans and his men sat in the back of a second truck. They pulled up at the Police Barracks, and noisily dismounted shattering the silence of the sleepy village. Richards opened the front door and they entered.

The building was musty and completely devoid of furniture. Daylight flooded the hallway, highlighting a dark stain on the red tiles. Myles paused, before following Richards, who was opening every door and glancing into each room. He opened the door at the end and stepped into a large kitchen. After a brief inspection, he tried to open the back door.

"What happened to Mrs Hughes," Richards asked grunting as he struggled with the swollen back door.

"She went back to Kerry, where she came from."

"I suppose you wouldn't want to stay knowing your husband's murderer could be standing next to you in the Post Office," Richards said,

"Ah, got it," he gasped, as he dragged the door across the kitchen floor.

Both men steeped out into a large, enclosed cobbled courtyard. The morning air was cool and refreshing. To the left, was a 12 foot wall, with a water pump and trough in its centre. Directly in front were rows of outbuildings, and to the right, a large wooden double gate, chained shut. After inspecting the outbuildings, Richards commented.

"They'll make good holding cells, with a little work. What's on the other side?"

"The River Ovoca," Myles replied.

"What? There's a river on the other side. Let's have a look," Richards said excitedly, as he unlocked the gate. The Officers walked to the centre of a high bridge, overlooking the back wall of the courtyard.

"This is ideal," Richards said, as he studied the wall that swept all the way down to the edge of the river, and was over 30 foot in height.

"We'll convert those buildings into cells, immediately. No one will be able to escape unless they what to go for a swim. What's the river named again?"

"The Ovoca." Myles said.

"How original," Richards replied laughing as he returned to the barracks. "Reverse the supply truck into the yard," he bellowed, signalling the driver.

Soon the truck was unloaded. Metal beds, oil lamps, and general kitchen equipment, together with crates of rifles, grenades and ammunition littered the yard.

"Do you really need that much weaponry?" Myles asked, studying the boxes of rifles and grenades.

"We mean business, Myles."

"But there are only six of you. There's enough equipment here for twenty men."

"Six of us for now, Myles, but our intention is to make Ovoca the hub of RICSR activity throughout the entire county."

"The RIC have been reluctant to hold weaponry in isolated barracks as the IRA has been very successful in acquiring it."

"We're not the RIC, Myles. We're the 'TANS'! Those IRA bastards are welcome to try anytime!"

"Be careful what you wish for, Captain," Myles replied, as he acknowledged his Sergeant, who had just finished separating the soldiers and RICSR into two columns.

"Troops ready for inspection, Sirs," the Sergeant said, falling in on the end.

"May I take this, Myles?" Richards asked.

"Be my guest," Myles said, offering up the parade with a sweeping gesture. He was getting annoyed with Richards' refusal to use his rank when addressing him, especially in front of the men.

"Gentlemen, we are dividing into two patrols, of five Soldiers and two RICSR Officers. Captain Fox and I will lead a patrol each. The Sergeant and two Police Officers will remain in the Barracks,"

"Very good, Sir," the Sergeant said.

"The task of each patrol is to search houses and farms, derelict and occupied, and anybody you see fit to search along the way.

118

The first patrol will take a truck, towards Woodenbridge. The second will cross the village on foot, heading towards the old Woollen Mills, located at the end of the village. It will search shops and people along the way. Any questions?"

"No questions Sir," the troop bellowed, coming to attention with a loud stamp of feet.

"Myles," Richards said, looking towards him.

Remembering the words of Sergeant McCuskey, Myles managed to control his anger, calmly issuing a rebuke to Richards.

"It's Captain Fox, when addressing me in the presence of the troops," he said purposefully, loud enough for all to hear.

Richards stepped back, a cocky grin on his face, unperturbed by the comment.

"Men. You wear the uniform of the Crown, and with that comes respect. So, treat the general public with the same respect you would expect to receive."

"What about, shoot first, ask questions later," a voice shouted from the ranks, causing an uproar of laughter from the entire column.

"Shut up!" The Sergeant bellowed, stepping out from the ranks.

"Thank you, Sergeant," Myles said. "You are from the West Yorkshires, which has an unblemished record. Please keep it that way. Carry on Sergeant."

"Very good, Sir. Fall out! The Sergeant roared.

The two sections dispersed, one heading for the truck, whilst the other marched out through the gate under the watchful eyes of a small, yet bemused crowd that had gathered on the side of the road. Myles jumped into the front of the truck as it took off. Richards, holding a pistol in his hand while his unbuttoned trench coat flapped dramatically in the wind, led the other section through the village.

Myles' patrol found nothing useful. They searched the grounds of a nearby ruined Church and graveyard, finding only scratches

119

and cuts from the brambles. They called into a few farms, hoping the element of surprise might unearth something, but, unsurprisingly, they were met with nothing but hostility. They investigated two abandoned farmhouses and a parked truck, which also proved fruitless. Their final destination was the Woodenbridge Hotel, where they received a surprisingly warm welcome from the Manager. No objections were raised to the questioning of staff and guests and the Manager volunteered the Visitors, Book for inspection.

"Who are those two strangely dressed men, Captain?" The manager asked.

Myles looked up from the book. The Manager was pointing at the two RICSR Officers, both sitting on a long settee in the reception, brazenly flirting with two female guests, who seemed very uncomfortable with the attention.

"They're the new Royal Irish Constabulary Special Reserve, Sir". Myles said.

"Sounds like a Cognac, Captain".

"That's what I thought. A newspaper's branded them 'the Black and Tans'."

"An appropriate name, Captain," the Manager replied, eyeing the odd uniforms.

Suddenly one of the ladies jumped up and yelped as if stung by a bee.

"How dare you," she shouted, slapping one of the Tans across the face. The Tan also jumped up, grabbed the girl's wrist, and twisted, utter contempt in his eyes.

"Sir, you're hurting me," she whimpered, bending over to alleviate the pain.

Myles slammed the guest book closed and shouted.

"Unhand the lady immediately, Constable!"

The Tan threw the girl aside. As she made a hasty retreat he turned his attention to Myles.

"You're not in charge of me, Captain."

"Yeh, you can't tell us what to do," the other one challenged getting up from the settee.

"Try me, Gentlemen!" Myles said coldly, as his own men approached.

"Let's leave this dump. We can come back later, Roger," the assailant said.

"Yes, preferably at night," Roger replied, laughing as they walked towards the exit.

A well-dressed, elderly Gentleman, standing nearby, witnessed the commotion.

"Sirs, you're a disgrace to your uniforms. I shall report this to your superiors," he said in disgust.

The assailant snarled at the gentleman, whilst the other lunged towards the man, arms outstretched, as if to grab him. Startled, the Gentleman fell backwards losing his balance. As he fell, he pulled a pot plant, off a marble plinth, spilling it contents over himself and the floor. The Tans laughed as they walked out, happy with the carnage they had created.

The staff and guests gasped in unison. Myles was horrified. He ordered his men to assist the Gentleman, and walked over to the two women, still standing at the bottom of the stairs.

"I apologise for that appalling display, Ladies. I can assure you that their behaviour will not go unpunished. Are you alright, Ma'am?"

"No, I am not, Captain. He assaulted me and almost broke my arm," the injured girl sobbed, holding her bruised arm.

"I do not accept your apology. You will be hearing from my Father's solicitors," They both angrily ascended the stairs without waiting for a reply.

Myles sighed and faced the Manager, who also admonished him. Myles apologised profusely, and wearily left. Outside, was warm and sunny. Everyone was back in the truck and the engine running.

He jumped in and ordered the driver back to Ovoca. When they pulled into the yard, he discovered the other patrol had returned and were fitting out the station with beds and other domestic equipment. Myles went in search of Richards with his Sergeant and the two Tans. They found him in a room he was setting up as an office.

"Ah, there you are, Captain," Richards said, as they entered. "This village is a lot smaller than expected. Our patrol was over in less than half an hour. How was yours?"

"Rather uneventful, except for the unacceptable behaviour of these Officers."

"What did the rascals do?" Richards asked, smiling.

"Rascals! They behaved like common criminals, assaulting two female guests and injuring another, also damaging hotel property in the process."

"Ah, just letting off steam. No-one was seriously injured, I presume," Richards replied distractedly.

"Steam, Captain? These men violently assaulted a young woman who intends to press charges, as does the Manager for damages, and another male guest."

"Listen carefully, Fox," Richards said, through gritted teeth. "As I said earlier, the time has come to stop mollycoddling these natives, regardless of their social status. Now, I believe what really happened was that my two Officers questioned a suspected female subversive, who refused to cooperate, and became hostile, which required my men to use necessary force to protect themselves. I must praise my men for neutralising the situation before it became uncontrollable for you and your men, Captain. Isn't that what happened, Constables?" He finished, looking at the two sniggering Tans.

"Yes Sir." They replied together whilst grinning.

"Good. You may both leave," Richards ordered, smiling directly at Myles.

"Captain Richards, I must object." Myles said

Richards angrily slammed his fist on the desk.

"Captain Fox, I have been extremely patient with you, but my patience is wearing thin. I have my orders, and your interference is not going to stop me carrying them out. Do you understand?"

"Yes, I do understand, Jeremy," Myles said calmly. " If you think behaving like common criminals is a good way to win trust and respect, then good luck to you. I think we're done here."

"I do believe we are," Richards replied.

"Sergeant, gather up the men,. Good day, Captain Richards," Myles said, leaving a bemused Richards standing at the desk.

The truck bitterly objected to climbing the steep hill out of Ovoca, It belched out thick, black smoke as the Sergeant struggled with the gears.

"God help that village, Captain." He said.

"God help Ireland, Sergeant," Myles sadly replied.

"Why's that, Captain?"

"We've only seen a small nest of these vipers. Imagine how the rest will behave?"

"God help us all," the Sergeant said, as the truck ceased its objections, finally reaching the top of the hill, where the road levelled out. Myles relaxed now that the truck was no longer under pressure.

"We haven't seen the last Richards and his thugs," He said pensively.

"I'm sure of that," the Sergeant replied, as the lorry chugged back to Arklow.

The following Sunday morning, Myles and Pat Kavanagh met, in the centre of a catwalk that ran the length of the south pier. They had arranged the meeting weeks earlier in the Railway hotel. Once reassured they were not followed, they stood next to each other, and stared across the calm sea that glistening and sparkled like liquid silver in the brightness of the morning sunlight.

After receiving details of future raids Pat Kavanagh inquisitively asked a content looking Myles.

"Have you ever personally faced death Captain?"

"Thank you for meeting me this morning." Myles replied ignoring the question.

"I did think you might decline the invitation. However I must stress that you can never reveal the source of your information regarding the upcoming planned raids. To anyone."

"Your secret's safe with me, Captain Fox. That afternoon at the Hotel, you seemed very sad, but now that sadness is strangely masked by a twinkle. What has happened to you, Captain Fox?"

Myles smiled but refused to answer.

"It's Miss Bradford! I've seen that look before!" "Very clever! That leads me to another reason I requested this meeting. I intend to propose to Miss Bradford, and take her to my Father's estate in Norfolk. Until then, I want your assurance of her and her families' safety. Call off your hounds - Boland and his friends are following us, night and day."

"Ah now, without incriminating myself, I don't quite know what you mean?"

"Please don't take me for a fool, Commandant. I'm asking you, man to man, to leave Miss Bradford alone. I know the IRA policy regarding locals fraternising with the enemy, especially young women, but I can assure you that she is not a spy. She is not intending to betray anyone, on either side, so can I have your word that you will leave her alone until such time as I can get her out of here?"

Kavanagh looked at Myles.

"Seeming as you are such an honest man, Captain, then yes, I will get my men to back off until you both leave for England. But, I must warn you that another has an unusual interest in you, and I have no control over him. He is the equivalent of an IRA, G-man.

124

"Do you mean Collins and his Squad? Why would they be interested in me?"

"Not Collins, but one of his men has been enquiring about you and your history."

"I've only been in the country for a few months. What on earth could I have done to warrant this personal interest?" Myles asked concern in his voice.

"Is it the murder of Mr Doyle from Ovoca?"

"No, it goes back further than that. I genuinely don't know, Captain, but, Officer to Officer, I will try to find out and keep you informed."

"Thank you, Commandant. I appreciate it. If there's anything I can do in return, please let me know. "

"Get out of my country," He suggested wryly.

They both laughed, staring over the wall once again. A silhouette of a young man and dog walking on the shimmering shoreline caught their attention. The shore looked as smooth as a billiard table. The dog disturbing a flock of Lapwings that flew up into the morning light, squawking loudly in protest.

Kavanagh turned towards Myles.

"Thank you for the information on the upcoming raids, but what puzzles me most is your lack of fear at being branded a traitor? Why are you taking such a risk, have you 'gone native'?"

Myles laughed at the thought of it.

"No Commandant, I've not gone native. I'm proud of whom I am and the uniform I wear. I have already sacrificed six years of my life for it. I know the inevitable outcome of this so-called, 'Anglo-Irish War'. It will end in a year or two. A treaty will be signed as it was in the Great War. But many will die before those signatures are collected. If I can save lives, on both sides, during this arduous journey to the table, then I will. If my actions are uncovered and I'm considered a traitor, then so be it. But, if we could ask the families of those that would have certainly died, had I not acted, whether they think I'm a traitor, I wonder what their reply would be?"

The two men turned away and stared out across the sea, lost again in their own thoughts. The sound of the waves lapping the nearby shore and the distance cries of the lapwings soothed them. After a few moments, Myles broke the silence.

"Does the same fate not await you, Commandant?"

"Mine will be death or success, Captain. But if I do survive I will go back to being a Mechanic, occasionally meeting up with comrades for a drink."

"Do you really think you can go back to a normal life after killing people?"

"Doesn't every Soldier?"

"You consider yourself, a Soldier?" Myles asked, turning back to Pat. "I've known real soldiers. Not those that only joined up for money and pageantry, but 'Real Soldiers', who unselfishly sacrificed everything they had to save the lives of others."

"What makes me so different from you, Captain? Kavanagh replied, "You spent five years of your life in France killing Germans?"

"In the end our intention was survival, not killing Germans, especially when faced with ridiculous orders. It would have been easier to jump overboard on the journey over, rather than take part in some of those infamous futile battles. That would have saved so much time and money Can you imagine? Instead of corpses rotting in No Man's Land and the ditches of the supply lines, we could have sailed back to England, picked up another few hundred thousand and got them to jump over the side on the way back to France. The money and trouble that would have saved when considering the tactical advantage we gained in the first few years of slaughter in that War!"

Myles was aware of the anger bubbling up inside. He turned to the view of the shoreline once again, in the hope that its therapeutic effect would calm him.

Pat Kavanagh was stunned into silence. He felt great sympathy for Myles as he watched his eyes glaze over, with that glassy hollow look of sadness and emptiness that he had noticed in the hotel.

"Captain Fox," he said. "I can't, and don't want to imagine what you've witnessed in France, but you have to realise that this War is not going to stop until the English have left Ireland for good. After the executions in 16, the Irish people have had enough. They want the English out for good. The seeds of discontent firmly planted in 1798 have grown strong and are ready for harvest. It is not England that will reap the benefit of this harvest, but Ireland."

"Is it so bad that we may save the lives of our comrades with a little cooperation during that harvest? You said you don't wish to image what I've witnessed, well Commandant, you can judge my actions for yourself." Myles took a deep breath.

"You asked me earlier if I had ever faced death. The answer is yes. In fact, you may think me mad, but I actually saw death manifest itself on many occasions. I haven't just seen hundreds of dead, or even thousands, but tens of thousands, men, women, and children, killed in the most horrendous ways imaginable. The next time you're in a busy church look around at the size of the congregation and then double it. Treble it, actually, and that might give you an idea of how many men I've seen die on a single day in France. I was surrounded by death. Not one hour went by without me witnessing death at work."

Myles briefly paused, breathed deeply and continued.

"At night, if I succumbed to a restless sleep, Death would remind me in my dreams of his handiwork. During the day he would take many a good man that I greatly respected. Because of this I hated Death, but he didn't care, knowing that, in the end, he would win. He always wins. So, if I cheat that bastard from taking more souls, regardless of what Flag they fight under, then I will have won that round. I have no fear of being judged for that, by God or Crown."

Pat Kavanagh looked at Myles. He blessed himself, his voice shaky in response.

"Good God, Captain, what have you witnessed? " He, too, was denied the therapeutic effect of the sea.

"Captain Fox, you must take Mary to England immediately. Don't wait. When this War is over, when we have gained out liberty, come back. It will be safe for you to raise a family without having to constantly look over your shoulder."

"If it were only that easy, Commandant, unfortunately I have some pressing business to complete before I can even consider such actions."

"Is your loyalty to that uniform more powerful than your love for this woman? If I were you, Captain, I'd be getting myself and Miss Bradford away from here as soon as possible. You've sacrificed enough. Man was not born to suffer as you have. Give it up, this loyalty of yours, or it will just keep taking until you've nothing left to give and then what? A brief ceremony followed by a few lines in a newspaper to mark your passing? Then you'll be completely forgotten, remembered only by those that loved you."

Kavanagh turned towards the low wall and thumped it with both his fists.

"God, you English can be so bloody stubborn."

He noticed a couple approaching the base of the pier.

"We cannot be seen together," he said, offering his hand, which Myles accepted.

"Take my advice and leave," he turned and walking back towards town.

Myles sighed deeply as he watched him leave. He pondered the advice knowing it was exactly what he should do, but first he needed to be officially released from his promise to Annabelle.

He had shared his innermost thoughts and feelings about the War with a complete stranger and felt no anxiety. Mary's influence clearly gave him peace.

"Let's do this, Mary," he said aloud.

The following Tuesday morning, at 10 o'clock, Myles received a surprise visit from Captain Richards, who knocked and entered his office.

"Ah, there you are, Myles. I'm glad I caught you. Slight bit of bother that you might be able to help with," he said, as they both shook hands.

"What can I do for you?" Myles asked.

"Well, Myles, that bloody No. 3 Leland truck has given up the ghost, right here, on the Main Street of Arklow. It's been playing up for a week, So, I need to borrow one of your trucks, if you'd be so kind."

"I'd love to oblige, but our only truck is currently on patrol, and not expected to return for at least another three hours," Myles said, glancing at his watch.

"Damn and blast!" Richards exclaimed.

"We're due to assist the RIC with surprise round-ups in Wexford Town at noon."

"We can phone ahead and let them know," Myles said, pointing to the phone on his desk.

"Do you know any mechanics, Myles?" Richards asked, ignoring the suggestion.

"Actually, I do," Myles replied, thinking of Commandant Kavanagh.

"Great. Can you contact him? I'm sure he'd oblige," Richards asked as he walked towards the door.

"I'm sure he would," Myles said sarcastically, following Richards.

Word was sent to Kavanagh through his niece's shop, as Myles and Richards walked down town to the delayed convoy, consisting of two Leland trucks and a staff car. The side panels of one truck were open and two uniformed men peered inside.

Some of the armed Tans were keeping a controlled cordon around the vehicles, clearly irritating the passing public. A small group of bemused locals had gathered on the footpath, just in front of the convoy, to watch the spectacle.

"Any luck?" Richards asked the two men.

"No, Sir. We might as well be looking into a field of barley," one replied, in an Irish accent.

"Captain Fox has sent for a local mechanic. It shouldn't be long, Sergeant."

Myles noticed two armed Tans harassing some local girls as they passed.

"Sergeant! Control the men!" Richards ordered on seeing Myles' distain.

"Ah, sure the men are getting restless," the Sergeant replied, pointing to the back of the truck where more Tans were jumping out onto the street.

"That's not the point. Control them." Richards said, clearly for Myles' benefit.

Myles was surreptitiously beckoned from the crowd.

"Excuse me, Captain Richards, I shan't be a moment," he said, on seeing Pat Kavanagh enter a nearby Butcher's shop. Myles followed.

"I got your message! Now get those Tans off the street, Captain," Kavanagh said, rocking on his heels.

"Good morning to you too, Mr Kavanagh, but I believe you're best placed to do that, been a mechanic after all?"

"Do you think I can just casually walk out into that nest of hornets, fix their car, shake their hands and then leave?"

"I see what you mean," Myles said, as he noticed the Tans were continuing to harass the public. "I want them on their way as much

130

as you, Mr Kavanagh, so if you know of anyone else that can fix their confounded truck, let me know?" Myles replied.

"Mr Fitzgerald, the Electrician, would be able to fix it. He can fix anything!" the Butcher said, from behind the counter.

"Good idea, Mr O'Connell," Pat said. "Get your boy to fetch him, please."

"Let me know when he arrives," Myles said, as he re-joined Richards.

Soon, a very irritable man and his dog were stood at the back door of the shop.

"I'd be grateful if you'd give Fido something to eat, while I get these Curs off the street," he said, marching out of the shop to the truck. The Tans refused to let him pass, but a quick nod from the Butcher prompted Myles to intervene.

"I think this might be our mechanic."

"Do you want your truck repaired or not, because I've better things to be doing with my time," the Electrician shouted angrily.

"Let him pass," Richards instructed.

The Electrician made a few adjustments, and then shouted to the driver to try the ignition. The truck roared into life, raising a cheer from the crowd.

"Thank you. Now, what do I owe you?" Richards asked, opening his wallet.

"I don't want anything, Captain," the Electrician said, as he walked away.

"Thank you, Myles. I knew I could rely on you," Richards said, as he jumped into the staff car.

Soon the Tans were on their way and the crowd drifted away. Myles was outside the Butcher's shop, when Percy appeared, with Mary on his arm.

"Look who I found, Myles," Percy said. "I heard you had a bit of bother, so I came to assist, and found this young lady sheltering in a doorway."

Before Myles could reply, the Electrician exited the Butcher's shop, closely followed by his dog carrying a large bone in its mouth.

"Good day, Gentlemen, Miss Bradford," he said, tipping his cap.

Myles was about to thank him when Boland and the Runners ran from the shop next door, deliberately knocking into him. A startled Myles was going to say something when Boland made an ugly comment.

"Oh look! The Bradford whore is sharing the Brits!"

"How dare you!" Percy said feeling incensed.

"How dare you!" One of the runners said mimicking Percy's voice perfectly, the others burst into exaggerated and mocking laughter.

"Now look here, Boland," Myles said, firmly, interrupting the laughter.

Boland, without another thought, recklessly tried to smash his fist into Myles' face. Myles, although taken by surprise, was able to avoid the punch, and side-stepped. Boland lost his balance, and fell. This prompted the mimicking Runner to try and punch Percy, completely missing. Mary screamed in fright, attracting the attention of passers-by. Boland recovered, and was squaring up to Myles when, a loud voice interrupted.

"I'd think twice about that, if I was you!"

It was Sergeant McCuskey, with three armed RIC Officers. They were standing across the road when Mary's scream attracted their attention. The three assailants stood down. The mimicking one banged his cap on his forearm.

"Just a bit of fun, Sergeant, which got a little out of hand that's all. No damage done."

"Really? Gentlemen," he said to Myles and Percy, "would you like to press charges?"

"No Sergeant, there's no need for that."

"Be on your way, the lot of you," McCuskey said.

The three assailants skulked off, without speaking.

"Will that be all, Captains, or would you like one of my men to escort you back to Barracks

"That won't be necessary, Sergeant. Thank you,"

"Damn it Myles! Why not have all of them locked up for one night, at the very least? They insulted Mary and physically attacked both of us. If that doesn't warrant being locked up, I don't know what does," Percy complained.

"I have my reasons, Percy, are you alright, Mary?"

"I'm just a little shaken. Earlier, I was harassed by the Tans. They insisted I empty my purse. Thankfully, Percy came along and rescued me, only to then be verbally abused by those corner boys."

"Come, Mary, we shall escort you to work," Percy said, offering his elbow. Mary took it, and they walked up the street.

Across the road, a dark shadowy figure observed the altercation from the doorway of the Royal Hotel. He beckoned the assailants to follow him, as he slipped deeper into the hallway of the hotel. Boland and the Runners followed. In a dark and secluded corner, Thomas Donnelly turned on them, aggressively.

"That's not what I asked you to do. Whose big idea was it to start a fight and nearly get everyone arrested? Get in here NOW! You bloody fools."

Donnelly opened the door of a side room. They followed him, like sheep.

Mary felt a growing distance between herself and the townsfolk now that she was stepping out with a British soldier. This distance was becoming a rift and the altercation on the street had not helped. At first, it was the odd comment and scalding look, but, occasionally, people would deliberately knock into her, sending her shopping flying. Mrs Hamilton had been forced to ask Mary to work in the store room, as some customers refused to have her serve them. She was also finding it difficult to get a seat in Mass, especially if attending alone.

She now attended 11 o'clock Mass with her family for support, but on the steps, after Mass, even her family were treated to caustic remarks.

"Lovely, long black hair. Shame to see it all cut off."

A week after the altercation on Main Street, Mary and Myles were sitting on a bench in the gardens of the Railway Hotel, overlooking the river. They were enjoying the beauty of the evening sunset. Mary laid her head on Myles shoulder.

"The town is starting to break me, Myles. Please take me to Norfolk with you."

"I know it's difficult, Mary," Myles said, as he admired her face in the enchanting glow from the setting sun. "I'm due leave, and have arranged to go to England for two weeks. It's my intention to speak with Annabelle, and request a release from my vow. I've already mentioned you in my letters, so I'm sure it's just a formality. I'll return in a fortnight, retire from the Army, and take you to Norfolk where we will marry and happily live out our lives."

"Oh, Myles, that's wonderful. I don't know what to say.... Is that a proposal?"

"Of course, Mary. I'm completely and utterly in love with you. Please say you'll marry me?" Myles asked, taking her hands, as he knelt before her, looking into her surprised face, glowing in the golden yellow of the setting sun.

"Mary Bradford, will you do me the great honour of becoming my wife."

"Yes. Yes. Yes, I will, Myles," Mary said, jumping up with excitement.

Myles stood up and sealed the pact with a kiss.

"Mary, we can't go public with this until I return from England."

"Oh, I understand, Myles, but retire from the Army? What's brought that on?"

"I recently received some advice from...well a friend who reminded me of many comrades killed in service. All they received for their ultimate sacrifice was a few hastily scribbled lines in a local paper. I don't particularly want to be remembered in a similar fashion."

"Oh... Myles! I'm so happy! This is the happiest day of my life. I really do love you, and I can't wait to meet your family."

The Runner

Ciaran Payton was in the bedroom of his digs. He opened his shirt and hung his braces around his waist. He used the floral pitcher and basin of warm water placed on a small marble-topped dresser by his landlady. It was 10 minutes to six, and he was looking forward to his supper. The aroma of cooking wafted up from the kitchen, filling the house, increasing his hunger. Suddenly, the landlady called up to him. He looked at his watch, drying his hands and face.

"You're early, Mrs Wolohan," he thought to himself.

She called out again, so he descended the staircase in his open shirt. There was a problem. The front door was open and a uniformed telegram boy, dwarfed by an oversized Post Office bicycle, stood outside.

"It's for you Mr Payton. Food's almost ready," she said, heading to the kitchen.

"Are you Mr Ciaran Payton?" The boy asked.

"Give it here!" Payton said impatiently. As the boy waited for his tip, Payton opened the telegram. On reading it, his colour drained and he staggered.

"Is everything alright, Sir?" The telegram boy asked.

"Clear off, you stupid brat," Payton shouted, slipping his braces back on.

The telegram boy shuddered in fear, silently noting that Payton's Irish brogue had changed to perfect English. He mounted his bicycle and sped away.

"Damn!" Payton said, under his breath, realising his mistake and he watched the boy disappear. He read and decoded the message again.

Your dad's not well. ---- *The raid was a set-up.*

He's not expected to live. ---- *They're on to you.*

Come home. ----*Get out now.*

He raced back to his room, removed a small brown case from the top of the wardrobe, threw it onto his bed, and started packing hastily. He struggled as he removed a loose floor board from beneath the bedside chair. Below, a small wooden box, and a short revolver were hidden. He tucked the gun into his belt, and removed a bundle of money and an identity card from the box. He donned his coat and hat, grabbed the case and raced downstairs, only to be met by his landlady.

"Ah, there you are Mr Payton. I thought you didn't hear me calling," she said, holding a white dish cloth in her hand. She noticed the case.

"Was it bad news? She asked, panic in her voice.

"Yes I have to leave immediately, please take this," he said, handing her five pounds. "Good-bye, Mrs Wolohan. I'll not be back. Thanks for everything."

He raced out of the door, leaving it open behind him, and a bewildered-looking Mrs Wolohan standing in the hallway, clutching a white five-pound note.

It was half past 6 and getting dark. Myles and Percy had finished for the evening, and were leaving the Barracks when Payton appeared, causing a commotion with the RIC Officer on the main gate.

"What's going on, Constable?" Percy asked loudly.

"This man is demanding to see the Sergeant. I've told him to come back tomorrow, but he insists."

"I must speak with Sergeant McCuskey. I have valuable information for him. I also need to phone Dublin Castle, immediately," Payton demanded in a very English accent. Not recognising him at first, Myles instructed the Officer to admit him.

"Thank you, Officer," Payton said, stepping onto the cobbles. Percy suddenly recognised him as the assailant involved in the scuffle on the main street.

"Payton! What the Hell?" Percy demanded, as the Constable closed the door.

"All in good time. I really need Sergeant McCuskey and to phone the Castle."

"NO!" Myles said, looking at the suitcase. "You will explain right now, or I will have the Constable arrest you for subversive activity."

"This should explain everything," Payton said, holding out his identity card.

Myles took the card, opened it and read its contents. Percy and the Constable could not help but notice the surprised look on Myles face.

"You had us fooled, Detective Steadman," Myles said, passing the card to Percy, who was equally surprised to read the details below a stamped black and white photo.

Detective Steadman, John,
Dublin Castle, G Division,
DOB 13/07/1895.

'On Active Service' was stamped in bold red ink across the entire document.

"You're a G-man, Mr Steadman? Myles is right, you did have us ALL fooled."

"A bloody G-Man, here in Arklow?" the Constable asked, surprised as anyone

"You're lucky to have made it to this gate, Sir, if your friends are on to you."

"Those bastards are not my friends! Now, can I see the Sergeant and phone Dublin, please."

"This way, you can use the phone in my office. Constable, please send word to Sergeant McCuskey to meet us immediately, thank you? "Myles said.

They made their way to Myles' office, whilst the RIC officer left to inform the Sergeant. When Sergeant McCuskey entered the room, Steadman, who was sitting behind Myles' desk, was just finishing his call to Dublin Castle.

"I will see you at 11 o'clock, tomorrow morning. Thank you again, Sir, and good night." He finished the call and replaced the receiver.

"Ah, there you are, Sergeant. I have information for you, and need you to do two things for me," Steadman demanded of the Sergeant, taking full charge of the situation.

The Sergeant was completely perplexed by his accent, tone and attitude.

"How about you tell me who you are, and what you want before you start issuing orders, Mr Payton."

"My name is Detective John Steadman, alias 'Ciaran Payton'. I am an undercover agent working for the G Branch of Dublin Castle. I was sent here two years ago to infiltrate the local Sinn Fein branch and locate Liam Mellows who was operating in the area at the time. I was sworn in with the local Column, but tonight, my identity has been uncovered, so, I need to get out immediately."

"A bloody Spy and Castle G Man! Do they know you're here? "The Sergeant asked.

"Yes, I just told them. They're sending a car for me tomorrow morning."

"Not the bloody Castle, I mean the local volunteers, for God's sake. Because they'd stop at nothing to get at you, let me tell ya."

"No I don't think so. I'm sure I wasn't followed, but this Barracks is full of Police and Soldiers they wouldn't dare attack it."

"You're the one who's lived with them for last two years, so I'm sure you know what they're capable of? With so many attacks on Police Stations and Barracks across the country, we only station three men here at night. We store no arms or ammunition, only the trucks that you see outside."

"So, am I safe here?" A panicked Steadman asked.

"Well, it's probably the safest place right now, until the morning, at least."

"I'll detail a section of men to stay overnight," Percy interjected. "We'll collect them from the old brick factory in one of our trucks. It shouldn't take long."

"Very good, Sirs. Thank you, "Mr Payton, we will conduct our affairs in my office downstairs," the Sergeant said, directing Payton to the door. About an hour later, ten soldiers were installed in the billets. Myles and Percy were leaving again, when the RIC Sergeant and Steadman entered his office.

"Mr Payton, I mean Steadman, you played your part well, especially that fight on the street." Percy stated.

"That was that fool, Boland, pissed off that he'd lost his whore to the Captain," Payton pontificated, confident in his safety having shared considerable amount evidence with Sergeant McCuskey.

"How dare you, Steadman," Myles protested loudly. "You've put us at risk by coming here. You expect us to help you, and then insult us. I should leave the Barracks gate open, or better still, inform your old CO of your exact whereabouts."

"It's well-known that you and Mr Kavanagh have been cosying up together during early morning assignations, on the pier!"

"What are you insinuating, Steadman?" Myles demanded, horrified that this G-man had been spying on him. "Have you been spying on us as well?"

"Comes with the job, Captain."

"How dare you question my loyalty, you callous bastard," Myles yelled angrily.

He threw his gloves and hat onto his desk, crossed the floor, grabbing Steadman by his open shirt and forcefully slapping his whole body against the wall.

"Are you going to give me a dammed good thrashing, old boy," he said, mimicking Myles voice. He sweated as Myles looked coldly into his eyes.

"Did you learn that in spy school?" Myles said, barely restraining himself.

The phone rang. It was Dublin Castle for Steadman.

"It's for you, you Scoundrel," Percy said, placing the receiver on the desk

"You pompous bastard," he said, reaching for the telephone. "You haven't heard the end of this, Fox," he continued, straightening his hair with his fingers.

Myles was about to grab him when Sergeant McCuskey intervened.

"Don't lower yourself to his level, Sir. I know you're better than that."

"You're not worth it, Steadman. I need air. The stench is over-powering."

At that, both Army Officers left Steadman and the Sergeant alone in the office.

Steadman sat at the desk to take the call. When finished, he addressed McCuskey.

"Sergeant, we have a problem. Two agents were going to try and contact me this week, as a matter of urgency; I need to get a message to them tonight to cancel all future contact. The Castle has just given me their addresses. Could you see to it that these messages are delivered this evening?"

The Sergeant sighed. "Are they local?"

"Yes, well within a ten mile radius."

"I'll send a Constable's up to collect them," the Sergeant said as he left.

Steadman took a pen from a wooden stationary set and wrote out two coded messages on headed paper. He placed each note in a separate envelope and wrote out the addresses. Nosily glancing over Myles' desk, he noticed some personal stationary, with Myles' details as CO of Arklow. He lifted a blank page and stroked the

141

paper with his fingers, slowly conceiving a perfidious plot to extract revenge on Myles.

A Constable entered and Steadman gave him three letters to deliver.

"Post the nearest one first, Constable, it will make your journey easier."

"Ah, the Bradford residence. I know exactly where that is," the Constable said, reading the addresses on each of the sealed envelopes before leaving the room.

Steadman, alone in the office, stretched out his legs, and tried to relax, but an inner nervousness prompted by his deceitful plan would not allow him to settle. He quickly jumped up from the chair, grabbed his case, coat and cap and left the office, heading for the billet next door.

Most of the soldiers had left kit scattered around the room. They were playing cards in another room, as Steadman entered their sleeping room. Steadman placed his belongings on an empty bed, but, instead of settling down, he surreptitiously removed a tunic and hat from one of the other beds, went downstairs and out into the courtyard. The night air was refreshing having been cooped up in the offices all evening. He noticed it was the West Yorkshire regiment he was sharing the billet with, as he put on the tunic and cap.

"Open up," he said, in a Yorkshire accent, as he approached the main gate. "I drew the short straw and have to go on a cigarette run. Do you need any?" He asked the bewildered looking RIC Constable manning the gate.

"I'm fine, thanks. The password is 'Flag'," the Officer said, closing the gate.

"Bloody Paddies! They're everywhere in this God damned shithole," Steadman said, under his breath as he stopped to investigate what he could feel in the pocket of the stolen uniform. He pulled out a Zippo lighter and a pack of cigarettes.

"Nice one," he said to himself, as he removed a cigarette and lit it. He inhaled deeply, paused for a moment to admire the lighter before flicking it closed, and putting it back in the pocket. He made his way to the Kynoch Factory entrance.

Mary Bradford was in the parlour of her house with her sister and mother. They were sitting around the large kitchen table, repairing clothes beneath an oil lamp. The only sound was the constant ticking of a large, wall clock, mounted above the door. The contents of an old wicker sewing box were scatted across the table, spools of thread, paper cards with a selection of needles and an old sweet tin full of mixed buttons all added to the chaos of repair. They were so immersed in their tasks; they failed to hear the knock on the door.

Mary's Father called from the Hallway.

"Mary, it's the police and they're looking for you."

"What did your Father say?" Mrs Bradford said shocked. She promptly stood up, placed her work on the table and left the room, followed by the Girls.

Mr Bradford and a local Police Constable were standing in the hall. His dark uniform and large helmet gave an impression of authority.

"There you are, Miss Bradford. I was asked to deliver this message," he said.

"Who's it from, Constable?" Mary asked, on seeing her name and address on the front.

The Constable paused, suddenly realising that he did not know exactly who Steadman was and had never questioned why he was sitting at Captain Fox's desk.

"Captain Fox, I presume. Well, his office at least," he replied. "I was just asked to make sure you got it. I have two more to deliver, one to Woodenbridge and the other to Ovoca, and at this hour of the night. Let's hope the wolves aren't out tonight hunting for Constables on bicycles."

"Good night, Constable. Safe journey," Mr Bradford said, as he closed the door.

"What does it say?" Anna asked excitedly.

Mary had already opened the envelope and read the contents.

"It doesn't make sense, Dad," she said, and passed him the letter.

Good Evening, Dearest Mary,

Firstly, please accept my apologies for contacting you in this manner. I beg you to meet me outside the Kynoch entrance on Seaview Avenue, at 9 o'clock this evening. Please come alone. I promise to explain everything when we meet.

Yours, most affectionately,

Captain Myles Fox

Commanding Officer, Arklow.

"Well, it's very unusual," Mr Bradford said," but it does look legitimate to me."

"It sounds all very romantic, to me," Anna said.

"Perhaps he has a big surprise for you, Mary," Mrs Bradford said.

"Grab your coat, Mary. I'll go with you," Mr Bradford said.

" No He said to come alone," Mary said, blushing slightly as she thought about their recent romantic tryst in the changing rooms.

"Are you sure, Mary? It's late and a little unusual."

"Don't worry. I won't be long," she said, as her Father helped her into her coat.

It was a short walk to Seaview Avenue. It was a still, cool evening. The air carried the perfumed scent of a damp landscape, settling down for the night. The only noise disturbing the silence was her steps, crunching on the gravel path. She could see the sentry hut and the yellow street lights of the factory in the near distance, as she made her way along the dark path that ran parallel to the large lake. As she approached the hut, a voice shouted out from behind a bright hand-held carbide lamp.

"Halt! Who goes there?"

It was the same young sentry, now wearing a helmet and pointing a rifle at her.

Mary stopped in her tracks.

"It's me, Mary Bradford. I'm meeting Captain Fox."

Recognising Mary, the sentry relaxed, and slung his rifle back over his shoulder.

"Oh, it's you, Miss Bradford. I haven't been told about a visit from our C.O. Come and wait, whilst I will make a call and try and locate him for you."

"Thank you. I was afraid you might shoot me," Mary said relieved.

"Don't worry, Ma'am. After the fatal raids, we don't carry live ammunition, some agreement with the locals and our C.O, but don't tell anyone," he said, jokingly.

As they approached the sentry hut, the silhouette of a uniformed figure stepped from the shadows, a few feet behind them, and called out.

"Mary! Over here!"

"Ah, there he is. You can't mistake that posh accent, now can you, Miss Bradford? I wonder what his game is, at this hour of the evening."

"I have an idea," Mary said, feeling embarrassed.

"Well, I'll be over here if you need me," he said as he headed back to his post.

Mary walked towards the figure which had stepped back in onto a narrow sandy path that led towards the edge of the lake.

"Where are you, Myles?" She whispered, picking her way along the sandy path.

Suddenly, Steadman appeared from within the tall bushes, startling Mary.

"Well hello, Bitch!" He said, callously. "I owe you this," and punched her hard, on the jaw. She collapsed into the undergrowth, drifting into unconsciousness.

Back at the Barracks, the Company Sergeant, a giant of a man, six feet six inches tall, and filling every inch of his uniform, shouted with excitement, slapping his cards down on the table.

"Two pairs, Kings and Queens! Now pay up, O Reilly, ya, little bastard,"

"Jesus Sarge, I haven't got 10 shillings on me. You'll have to wait till payday."

"Well, you can give me that fine Zippo lighter of yours as collateral," the Sergeant said, leaning back smugly, on his chair.

Reilly fumbled in his pockets.

"It's in my tunic. I'll get it," he said, heading across the hall to the other billet.

Suddenly, Reilly reappeared in a panic.

"Sarge, my tunic, hat and web belt are missing. I think that Castle agent has taken them, because he's not in the billet. Or else, the IRA have snuck in and dressed him up to smuggle him out of here."

The Sergeant jumped to attention and barking orders.

"You! Get McCuskey here, now. You! Check with the gate sentry. You two! Carry out a complete search of the building. You! call Captain Fox."

Myles' office was full of panicked soldiers and police, when he entered.

"We can rule out kidnapping, Sir, as the Sentry confirmed he let someone out fitting Stedman's description an hour ago," the Sergeant said to Myles.

"I don't understand this," McCuskey said, walking towards Myles with two un-crumpled headed pages. "I left the agent at your desk writing coded messages for two other agents. I had my man deliver those messages tonight. But read the pages I found on your desk. They're clearly not coded," he handed the crumpled pages to Myles.

146

The pages were two failed attempts at a letter, addressed to Mary, requesting an assignation at the Kynoch's Factory. Myles expression changed to absolute anger.

"That bloody bastard. Quick, Sergeant. Load up the truck and follow me. Percy! You're with me," he ordered, racing out of the room.

Mary slowly regained consciousness and found Steadman kneeling across her waist. He was wrestling with the buttons on her blouse, having successfully removed her coat. She felt groggy, and looked up at him through a blurred haze. As her senses slowly recovered, she realised who he was, and what he was trying to do.

"Please Stop! Stop!" she screamed

"I'm fulfilling my promise to you, bitch!" Steadman replied menacingly.

He paused for a moment, and removed his stolen tunic and cap.

"I need that clean, so I can get back into the Barracks once I'm finished with you, Bitch," he said laughing in his excitement.

"Help! Help! Someone, please help!" Mary shrieked, as loudly as she could.

"Shut up, bitch. No-one can hear you," Steadman smacked her face.

"Please don't," she whispered, as she slowly succumbed to his punch.

"What's going on in there?" A voice shouted from the road side.

Steadman turned, only to be blinded by a beam of light from a hand-held carbide lamp. He held up his hand to shield his eyes. Mary called out again,

"Please help me!"

The solider pointed his rifle at Stedman.

"You're not Captain Fox! Stand up! Now!" he said, stepping onto the path.

Steadman surreptitiously removed the short revolver from his waistband, turned, and shot the soldier at close range. The solider fell back, landing hard. His lamp fell into the bushes, sending a beam of white light upwards, into the night sky.

"Look what you've made me do, you've ruined everything," Steadman growled,

His intention was to kill Mary after violating her, then include her name as an informant, suggesting the IRA were responsible for her death. But now he had a dead Tommy on his hands.

"Think man, think," he said, banging his forehead with the heel of his hand.

"I could blame his death on you, Mary Bradford! Maybe you enticed him with your naked body, so you're IRA Pals could shoot him, but you got killed in the crossfire. I'll just throw your naked corpse on top of his, after having my fun, of course. Then I'll head back to the Barracks, not forgetting the cigarettes, return the uniform, and no-one will ever know! Perfect! Now let's get on with the fun!"

He grabbed Mary's blouse and was about to tear it apart when he suddenly reared up, like a show horse about to jump a fence, before falling on Mary, his head lolled forward, and his oily black hair fell around his face. Mary was petrified. She could see a shining piece of steel, dripping with red watery slime, sticking out of his chest. Steadman slowly raised both arms, gently touched the tip of the steel with his fingers, muttered something incomprehensible, and then fell sideways, with a thump.

Mary shrieked loudly and kicked her way out from beneath him. Once free, she sat up and saw the young soldier, still lying on the ground, but holding his rifle. He had attached a bayonet to it, and plunged it deep into Steadman's back, with every last ounce of energy he could muster.

"Are....you.....alright....Ma'am"," he asked, struggling to hold the friendly smile on his face. His head slowly dropped into the sand, and he passed out. His carbide lamp continued to send a shaft of bright, white light upwards, into the sky.

Mary could hear the sound of approaching vehicles penetrate the silence of the night. She burst into tears as she saw a familiar silhouette, followed by several more, running towards her.

On Leave

Following the attack on Mary, Myles postponed his trip to England. Two days later, still livid, he bumped into Kavanagh, in the foyer of the Railway Hotel.

"Can I have a private word please? Mr Kavanagh,"

"What can I do for you, Captain?" Kavanagh replied.

"In private!" Myles repeated, angrily looking at Kavanagh's companions.

"Go on ahead, lads. I won't be long," Kavanagh assured them.

Once alone, Kavanagh went on the defensive, anticipating Myles' fury.

"Now, before you start making accusations Captain, neither I nor the local brigade, had anything to do with what happened to Miss Bradford. It was one of your own, as you well know. I've told you what you should do, and if you'd listened to me, this wouldn't have happened."

"What about the attack on the street? For God's sake, I was helping you."

"I didn't authorise that attack either. I was just as shocked when I saw it happen. I was still in the Butchers! But, as I told you, someone else has an interested in you. I wasn't made aware beforehand, but he was in town that morning, Captain."

"Are you in charge of these thugs, or not, Commandant?"

"I understand your anger, but, like you, I also have superiors that I must report to."

"Has this person got a name, Commandant?"

"Now, now Captain. Don't be asking me things that I can't be telling ya. Just like you couldn't tell me that Payton was a spy, I can't be passing on information about my CO, now can I?"

"I knew nothing about Steadman… I mean Payton," Myles said, frustrated.

"Would you have told me about 'Steadman' if you did?" Kavanagh asked, picking up on Myles' mistake.

"Of course, I wouldn't, out of duty and loyalty."

"Now there's that word again! 'Loyalty'. That will be your downfall. Loyalty or love - I was really hoping you'd made your choice by now."

"Listen here, Mr Kavanagh," Myles said, through clenched teeth, "I have made a choice and I have no compunction in telling you what that is. Yes, I intend to take Miss Bradford away as soon as I can. I'm going to England next week to make preparations. So, I want your word that both Mary and my men will be safe from your thugs, during my absence."

"Well now, that's a bit of a problem, as I'm away too. My second will be looking after things, but I cannot tell the Area Commander about our private arrangement because if HQ found out, I just might end up in a ditch meself!"

Suddenly the main doors swung open and the Insurance salesman entered with a confident swagger.

"Christ, here comes 'Burlington Bertie'," Myles said, rolling his eyes. Kavanagh grinned and doffed his hat.

"Captain, it's been a pleasure." He said leaving. "Good afternoon, Captain Fox. Have you had any time to think about our deluxe insurance package, yet?" The salesman asked.

"No!" Myles said abruptly, He momentary paused, and reconsidering said. "Well, actually yes, I have. Does it still come with those Derringer pistols? "They're Belgium pistols, and yes, they do. Please step into my office, Sir," the salesman said, pointing to a table in a dark alcove beneath the main stairs.

The following Monday, Myles was leaning on the handrail that surrounded the open stern deck of the Mail boat. He was enjoying the warmth of the bright, morning sunshine, as he watched the sprawl of Kingstown slowly disappear behind the horizon.

151

"Ireland - What a beautiful but hauntingly sad country you turned out to be."

His fellow passengers started to disperse as the warmth of the sun had been replaced by a chilly sea breeze. A familiar voice interrupted his thoughts.

"Ah, there you are now, Captain."

He turned and was surprised to see Pat Kavanagh leaning across the same rail.

"Christ, you're like a bad penny, Kavanagh."

Pat smiled and turned to Myles.

"Well, Captain, I'd rather be a bad penny than a bleddy honest Englishman."

"I don't understand, "Myles said, feeling confused. "Ah, ya have me heart broke, Captain. You see, I actually like ya for an Englishman that is, and I know I can trust ya as well, and that bleddy well kills me..."

He removed two cigarettes from an open Players box and offered one to Myles. Covering a lighter with both his hands he lit his own first and as Myles leaned in, Kavanagh whispered a name.

"Thomas Donnelly. I hope I won't regret that, "he said, stepping back. "Last night, he admitted having a personal vendetta against ya. Now that's the sort of thing that makes me nervous, and him very unpredictable, and a danger to the both of us. Do ya get me meaning, Captain?"

He silently walked away, leaving an astonished Myles standing alone on the open deck. Myles composed himself while stared at the hovering gulls.

"Thomas Donnelly? Why does that name ring a bell with me?" He mused, as he extinguished the cigarette and went inside to find the restaurant.

Ten minutes later, Myles was sipping a cup of tea, reading his journal at a table in the busy dining area. An entry caught his attention.

"My God!" he exclaimed loudly. He quickly closed the journal and left, finally understanding why Mr Thomas Donnelly wanted him dead.

Two days later, Myles was sitting with Annabelle in the Drawing Room of his parent's house. He was out of uniform for once. She wore a beautiful, knee length white dress. He had told her everything about Mary, and, seeing his obvious happiness, she had willingly consented to end their engagement. He even received a cheeky smile from Annabelle as he described his feelings for Mary.

"Oh, Annabelle, I have so dreaded this," he said.

"Myles, for me this is a great relief. I knew we were lost to each other when you returned from that confounded war. I could see that you were only a shell, hollow and empty and there was nothing I could do to help you, as much as I tried. I'm happy to see you full of happiness and ideas for the future. Go and bring Mary back. I will welcome her into our lives with all the love she deserves, for the happiness she has given you."

"You're such a dear friend and I love you for your understanding. I know I've not been easy to be around since returning from France."

"Shhhh, my dear," Annabelle said, placing a finger on Myles mouth. "Now go and invite your parents in, before they explode. I can hear them pacing outside."

"You can come in, now," he announced happily.

They both stood up as the parents entered the room.

"Mr and Mrs Fox. May I present to you, your son, Myles, who has finally come home after six years," Annabelle said, smiling as she swept an outstretched arm towards Myles. Mrs Fox, suspecting what had happened, rushed to Myles and embraced him.

"Welcome home, my dear son."

His Dad, just as excited, offered his hand.

"Welcome home, my boy!" Myles happily shook it.

They sat down to tea and cakes, and listened intently as Myles described his plans for the future. He would marry Mary, leave the army and study intensive farming, so he and Mary could run the estate.

Mrs Fox glanced at Annabelle, who returned a smile of relief. All was well.

The Monday after Myles had left for London, Steven Kelly a local fisherman, recently engaged to Mary's friend, Susan, entered Hamilton's asking for Mary.

"I want to discuss our wedding plans," he said to a suspicious Mrs Hamilton.

"Mary is busy preparing orders. You'll have to go out back to speak to her."

"Thank you I won't be long," he said, opening the door to the back corridor. He found Mary sitting at a small desk. She was delighted to see him, but as she stood up, she knew something was wrong.

"Whatever is the matter, Steven?" She asked.

"Mary," he said, fear in his voice," I have to make this quick. Commandant Kavanagh told me I should tell you about any attacks on the army that might be planned whilst he's away. It's about Captain Harper. He's supposed to be at a meeting with the Council tonight, in the Brook House. Please do what you can to stop him going."

Without another word, he made a hasty exit.

Mrs Hamilton, assessing the situation, took charge.

"Mary, we need to get that message to Captain Harper immediately, without raising suspicion. Come out into the shop in five minutes, and announce that Captain Harper's shirts are ready. I'll get the parcel boy to deliver them with the bill and a note," Mrs Hamilton wrote a brief note, explaining everything.

"Let's hope he can read Latin," she said.

Shortly afterwards, the parcel boy was standing in front of a surprised Percy, waiting for payment.

"I don't remember ordering two shirts," he said, jovially, to the boy as he opened the envelope containing the bill. His joviality was replaced with horror, as he read the ominous warning in Latin. He paid the delivery boy and left to cancel his attendance at the meeting, without raising any suspicion.

Two days later, Father Mackenzie had a late-night visit from Thomas Donnelly.

"Come in," Father Mackenzie said, delighted to see him. "Go on into the lounge and I'll get you a drink." Once sitting comfortably, with a drink in hand, Donnelly produced the note, written in Latin.

"I want you to have a look at this, Father, and translate it," Donnelly said.

Father Mackenzie reached over and took the note.

Evitar reunion esta noche. Asesinato planificada.

"It's Latin. It says, 'Avoid meeting tonight. Assassination planned.'"

"Just as I suspected! We have an informer in our ranks. He must have passed it over to that playboy, Harper, sometime on Tuesday. Who speaks Latin in the Parish, apart from yourself? "Donnelly asked, in an accusatory tone.

"I don't know." Father Mackenzie replied nervously.

"Well I want you to find out;"

"How did you come by it," Father Mackenzie asked, passing the note back.

"The bin men collecting the rubbish from the Barracks, we thought it was secret code. Do you recognise the writing?"

"No, but do you think that harlot Bradford had anything to do with it?" Mackenzie asked.

"No, how could she? " Donnelly looked perplexed at the suggestion.

"And why would you suspect her?"

"She's the mistress of a British Officer, "Mackenzie said, refilling both glasses.

"I get the feeling you don't like this girl, Calum."

"She's a traitor and not to be trusted," Mackenzie snarled, as he took a drink.

"To put your mind at ease, Miss Bradford's been watched and has spoken to no one. We'll find our informer Calum, have no fear," Donnelly drank up. "I must leave. We'll be in contact."

"I'll see you out," Mackenzie said

A week later, the 9 o'clock train pulled into the station, and hissed to a steamy stop. The doors were flung open, and a multitude of people descended, mingling with the crowd waiting on the platform. Mary was amongst them. When she saw Myles, she could not restrain herself, hugging and kissing him as soon as he stepped off the train.

Percy took Myles' bag.

"The car is outside."

When settled in the car Myles could not postpone his excitement any longer and presented a letter.

"Here, read this. It's from Annabelle. She gives us her blessing, and hopes to meet you soon."

Mary read the letter, delighted with its contents.

"Myles, this is wonderful!" She snuggled into him as she handed back   the   letter.

The Engagement

Later that week, an excited Myles arranged to meet Mary's parents for lunch in the Railway Hotel. He asked their permission for her hand in marriage, explaining his future plans now that his official resignation from the Army had been accepted. Mary's mother cried openly when he mentioned taking Mary to Norfolk at the end of June, but she accepted it was for the best. George was delighted, and suggested that Myles come for Sunday lunch, where he could officially propose to Mary. Myles agreed and later that afternoon went into a local jewellery shop to purchase the blue sapphire engagement ring that Mary had admired.

Myles arrived punctually at 1 o'clock that Sunday. He found Mary waiting eagerly in the doorway. She was wearing a white apron, which covered her green Sunday dress, conjuring up pleasant memories as he recalled the last time he had seen her wearing such an apron. He greeted her with a gentle kiss before stepping into the hall. As he stopped to hang up his coat, Mrs Bradford called out from the front room.

"Just a minute Mam, it's been hectic here all morning," Mary said, anxiously.

"I can imagine! Go Mary, I won't be long, "Myles said, taking advantage of her absence to remove the ring from his coat and place it in his tunic pocket. In doing so, he accidently removed Annabelle's letter. He held it up, kissed it and smiled to himself.

"Thank you so much, Annabelle. Today it will be official."

"What's keeping you, Myles?" Mary called out. "We're all waiting."

He hastily placed the letter into his hat with his gloves, and, as he hung it on the coat rack, Mary's coat with the large hood, fell to the ground.

"I am on my way," Myles replied, as he picked up the coat and placed it back on the rack, covering his hat.

Lunch was delicious. Afterwards, when everyone was relaxed, Myles asked Mary to stand up. Mrs Bradford reached across the table to take her husband's hand. He replied with a gentle squeeze and offered her his hanky. Anna looked as if she was going to explode with excitement, but somehow managed to contain it, and for once, remained silent.

Myles went down on one knee and took her hand.

"Mary Bradford, would you do me the great honour of becoming my wife?" Mary almost collapsed with excitement.

"Yes, Yes, I will," she replied enthusiastically, looking at her ecstatic family.

"The ring, the ring. "Anna cried, unable to control her excitement any longer.

"Ah, yes, the ring," Myles said, realising it was still in his pocket.

As he fumbled for it, there was a sudden screech of brakes outside, followed by a loud bang and a woman's shriek. Myles rushed to the window to investigate.

"Oh my God, a woman's been knocked down," he said. Without hesitating, he ran from the room to offer assistance. Mary and her family followed.

A shocked driver was standing over a woman's body lying on the road.

"She just ran out. I couldn't stop," the driver kept repeating.

"I'll see how badly hurt she is," Myles said, stooping down. He carefully placed a hand on the woman shoulder. To his horror, the woman rolled over and pointed a Webley revolver directly at him. He fell back into a sitting position, as he recognised his assailant as John Boland, disguised as a woman.

Terrified and shocked, Myles tried to scramble away. Abruptly he stopped.

"You!" He shouted, at seeing the person standing directly behind Boland. He crossed himself, stretched out his hand in an attempt to defend himself, and shut his eyes. "Mary I love you," he whispered.

A loud bang filled the air. The bullet passed straight through Myles' hand and hit him directly in the chest with a hollow thump, sending him flying backwards.

A dog in a nearby garden started to bark incessantly. As the smoke cleared, Myles' body could be clearly seen splayed out on the dusty road. Boland jumped up and threw the dress to one side.

"Quick," Boland's accomplice said. "Search his pockets and take his pistol."

Struggling to open the stiff leather strap, Boland found the holster empty. He searched Myles pockets, removing the small, brown package containing the ring. Unsure of what it was, he stuffed it into his own pocket before he and his accomplice, made good their escape up a nearby avenue that crossed open marshland.

The supposed car accident had already attracted a small crowd. They stood silently, in shock at the callousness of the attack. No one dared to follow the assassins as they disappeared into the marshland.

When Mary saw Myles fall, she screamed. Mrs Bradford gasped, as she comforted Anna, who buried her face in her mother's chest. Mr Bradford, no thought for his own safety, ran over to Myles. Mary's mouth suddenly became dry and parched. A hollow, painful vacuum replaced her lungs, restricting her breathing into large gulps. When she tried to follow her father out onto the street, she realised she could not walk. Her arms and legs felt like molten lead. The back of her knees failed to control this sudden shift in weight, and she fell in a heap. She stared at Myles' body lying on the dry, dusty road. Unable to comprehend the situation she started to crawl towards him on her hands and knees, all the time, fighting her own body that vehemently opposed every movement, as if deliberately preventing her from ever getting to him.

She finally reached him, and gently lifted his heavy head onto her lap, crying uncontrollably. She looked around at the vacant faces staring silently down at her.

"Please help!" She pleaded, as she cradled his head and stroked his face.

The women in the crowd turned away, unable to witness such grief.

Mary looked at Myles' chest. There was no blood, only a smoking hole. Myles groaned. Mary realised he was still alive.

"Oh Myles," she said, laughing with relief as she stroked his face. "Don't try to talk. Help is coming."

Myles lifted his hand towards her; she willing took it.

"Your father's gone to fetch the Doctor," a voice shouted from the crowd.

"Do you hear that, Myles? The Doctor's coming. Everything is going to be alright. We will be in Norfolk before you know it."

"Oh Mary…" Myles struggled to speak. "Do you know what I am thinking of?"

"Don't speak, my love," Mary replied, while tightly squeezing his hand.

"Primroses….Mary….at the Hanging Stone." Myles started to cough, painfully.

"Shush, shush, my love. Please don't try to speak,"

"My Irish primrose…I do love…." Myles tried to speak again.

"Shush, shush," Mary comforted him. His face relaxed. His hand went limp, and let go. He was gone. Mary continued to stroke his face, sobbing, willing him to live.

"Myles please…please don't leave me. We have our whole lives to live together in Norfolk, in a garden full of primroses." She broke down completely.

Someone helped Mary to stand up as her father and the Doctor arrived.

The Doctor looked over the body and turned to Mr Bradford. With a small shake of his head, he confirmed the worst. Mr Bradford retrieved Myles's greatcoat from the hall stand, and placed it over the body. This was too much for Mary. She passed out in the arms of the helping stranger.

That evening, the RICSR arrived at the Bradford's door.

"Come in," Mary's mother said, exhausted by recent events. "Mary is upstairs. The doctor has given her something to help her sleep."

The three RICSR officers barged through the door, knocking a horrified Mrs Bradford to the ground. "We're here to arrest Mary Bradford for assisting in the murder of one of his Majesty's Officers."

The three policemen raced up the stairs to locate Mary. Mr Bradford and Anna appeared from the front room to investigate the sudden commotion. When George saw his wife on the floor, he rushed to assist her, but was restrained, at bayonet point, by two soldiers who had followed the Policemen into the house.

"What the hell is the meaning of this outrage?" He shouted. "This is my House!"

"Stay down, you Fenian Bitch," one of the soldiers shouted at Mrs Bradford, who was trying to get up.

The other Soldier cupped Anna's chin with his hand.

"Well, well, what have we here then? Another Fenian temptress!"

"Get your filthy hands of her," George shouted, furiously knocking the soldier's hand away from a now crying Anna, who quickly retreated behind him for safety.

The solider replied by cracking his rifle butt in George's face, splitting open his forehead. He collapsed in the living room doorway. Anna shrieked as she tried to help her unconscious father.

Mrs Bradford shouted out his name, trying to go to her husband, but was restrained by a sharp jab in her side from a bayonet. The pain took her breath away and she collapsed to the floor again with a loud groan. She tried to stop the blood that suddenly appeared on her white blouse with the heel of her hand, but the pain became unbearable, so she stopped.

"I told you to get back, bitch," the assailant shrieked, in guttural English.

The other solider grabbed Anna's wrist and pulled her away from her father's unconscious body, savagely twisting it.

"Now where were we, 'Temptress'?" He was interrupted by the sudden appearance of the three policemen, violently dragging Mary down the stairs.

"Mama, Mama," was all Mary could say, as she tried to comprehend the scene below. She was dragged outside to a waiting truck.

"Come on, you two," the last Police officer said to the soldiers, totally ignoring the carnage they had created. The first soldier released his grip on Anna's wrist with a shove. She fell, landing in a sitting position.

"I'll be back, temptress, so wait for me!" He said, with a malevolent smile that exposed filthy brown teeth. They all left. Anna bravely took control, running across the street to fetch the doctor.

"Oh my God! What happened?" the Doctor asked, on seeing the chaos in the hallway.

"I'll make some tea," Anna said confidently, having been reassured that her parents' were going to be fine.

Mary was brought to the foreboding, 18th century military Barracks that had dominated the Main Street of Arklow for over 200 years. She was dragged from the truck, across the cobbled courtyard and down a narrow staircase that led to the small, cramped, underground cells. Here, the two soldiers unceremonious threw her to the floor of the nearest one. A loud eerie vibrating sound echoed through the air, slowly fading into silence, as its ancient wooden door was slammed shut.

The cell was in the bowels of the Barracks. Over the centuries it had hosted many a suffering prisoner. Some had left their marks on its stone walls, which could be read in a shaft of moonlight that shone through a tapered window, high on its back wall.

Confused and terrified, Mary picked herself up, and sat on a folding, wooden bench that doubled as a bed. Her mind raced. She relived every punishing minute, over and over again. She sat there, silently sobbing as she realised that she was still wearing her Sunday dress, the one that Myles had always admired.

At the thought of Myles' senseless death, her agony became unbearable and she lay on the bench, and wept, uncontrollably.

Without warning the cell door opened. The two soldiers entered carrying a storm lamp which they attached to a hook hanging from the ceiling. They were followed by a tall man, with broad, stocky shoulders – his frame filled the doorway. He was clean shaven and had short brown hair and wore civilian clothes. A pernicious air of authority emanated from him. He was the Dublin Castle G-Man. His name was Alan Freeny.

"Search her," he ordered, as he placed his jacket on the floor and started to roll up his shirt sleeves, exposing strong, muscular arms.

"With pleasure," one of the soldiers replied, rubbing his hands. He was small and fat, but looked powerful. He walked over to Mary, who was now cowering in a corner.

"I believe your sister is waiting for me. I'm looking forward to breaking her in," he said, salaciously stroking Mary's long hair.

Before Mary could comprehend the statement, he viciously grabbed the front of her dress and tore it open; sending buttons and hooks flying across the floor. He grabbed the top of her white blouse and ripped it off, exposing her breasts. Mary screamed out in

163

protest and pain, desperately trying to cover herself with the remains of the ripped garments. The soldier paused for a moment.

"Ah, so that's how you tempted the young Captain. You Fenian Bitch!"

He spun her around, and in one quick, fluid movement, pulled off her top garments, causing pain as the cuffs stuck on her wrists. To overcome this, he slammed her face down onto the cold, stone floor, placed his foot on her back, and violently pulled. The cuffs eventually gave way, and, with a repugnant laugh, he cast the clothes across the cell. They landed next to Freeny who callously kicked them to one side. Mary curled up in a ball, looked towards Freeny, and begged for help. He ignored her pleas.

The other soldier was tall and thin. He assisted the first with lifting the screaming and kicking Mary from the floor. They stretched her out, face upwards, across the wooden bench. He viciously held her outstretched arms whilst the other violently removed the rest of her garments.

"Get her ready," Freeny said, approaching a naked Mary, pushing his braces to one side and unbuttoning his trousers.

Suddenly, Percy, his Sergeant and three armed Privates burst into the cell. The big Sergeant knocked Freeny to the ground with a single punch. Percy pulled the smaller soldier from Mary so hard, that he landed in the narrow corridor, completely winded. The tall solider let go of Mary's arms, and stepped back, holding his hands up.

"We're just following orders, Sir."

"Thank God, Percy. I don't know what's happening?" Mary said, curling up on the bench, trying to hide her nakedness.

"Everything will be alright, Mary," Percy said, as he covered her with his tunic.

"I'm a detective from Dublin Castle and this is a Ministry matter," Freeny said, as he stood up from the floor and rubbed his jaw. "You have no business here!"

"This is my Barracks, Sir, and since when did defiling a woman become a Ministry matter?" Percy commanded, leading Mary from the cell.

"She's a criminal wanted for the murder of one of his Majesty's Officers. You have no right." He said trying to pass the Sergeant.

"Sergeant, please escort Mr Freeny, out of the Barracks, before I lose my temper with him, and ensure that both of these soldiers are charged with assault." Percy said trying to restrain his anger.

"Yes Sir," the Sergeant said as he twisted Freeny's arm and frogmarched him from the cells.

The Trial

Due to the seriousness of the accusations against her, Percy could not release Mary from military custody. He placed her in the direct care of Sergeant McCuskey, who, in turn, transferred her to the old guard room, below Myles and Percy's office.

From here, they monitored official visitors, and discreetly allowed private visits from her parents, who brought her a change of clothes. Dublin Castle hastily set a trial date for the following Friday, allowing very little time for Mary to build a defence.

The day before the trial, Percy's Commanding Officer made an unannounced visit from Dublin. He summoned Percy into Myles' old office.

"I will cut to the chase, Captain Harper. The Regiment has received several demands from the Ministry requesting your transfer. I investigated the origin of these requests and discovered your father is the driving force behind them. I never like it when interfering Parents use their positions to protect their cowardly sons. However, given recent circumstances, I shall put aside my grievances, and cooperate with this instruction. You will accompany Captain Fox's body back to Norfolk, tomorrow morning, and from there, you will join the Regiment in Egypt."

"Sir, I must protest," Percy said, horrified at the prospect of leaving Mary.

"Protest be dammed, Man. These are my orders," the CO barked.

"I can't miss the trial. I have evidence to support Miss Bradford. She's innocent of these ridiculous charges, and saved my life, Sir, "Percy pleaded.

"There's no evidence of a threat to you. It was a Council meeting, for God's sake, man. She hoodwinked you, Captain, just as she did the late Captain Fox.

166

"Sir, I must protest…"

"Do not question my judgement, Captain. You leave for Kingstown this evening and that's the end of it. Good Day!"

"Sir with all due respect…"

"Good day, Captain," the Colonel bellowed as he stood up.

Percy knew there was no point in arguing. He saluted and left.

That evening, Myles' coffin was placed on the back of a truck to be taken to Kingstown Harbour for the early morning ferry. Before leaving, Percy spent his last few hours with Mary. He was comforting her when Sergeant McCuskey entered.

"The truck's ready, Captain," he said, solemnly. "I'll look after Miss Bradford from here."

Percy stood up and forced a smile.

"Thank you, Sergeant. Mary, you could not be in better hands."

Mary started to cry as they embraced for the last time. Percy stepped back, straightened his tunic and swallowed hard.

"Everything will be alright, Mary, I promise." He turned and left quickly, attempting to curb his emotions. At the truck, he passed a letter to Sergeant McCuskey.

"Tom, if things don't go right for Mary, please can you see that she gets this."

"You're a good man, Captain Harper, and it has been a pleasure knowing you," McCuskey said, taking the letter and offering his hand.

"Likewise, Tom," Percy said, shaking it.

The driver started the truck. Percy jumped in, completely overwhelmed by grief.

The trial was set for 9 o'clock, Friday morning. Six armed soldiers escorted a handcuffed Mary on the short journey to the Court House, next to the Barracks. She felt dirty and scruffy and her long black hair was unkempt. Outside the Court House, a small group of women were protesting her innocence with homemade banners and posters. They were clearly members of the Cumana Na

167

mBan. She glanced at their faces, only recognising Marie Curran. She entered the Court Room. It was dark and gloomy compared to the bright sunshine outside. The wood-panelled interior combined with a large painted Royal Coat of Arms emanated totalitarian authority.

Mary was un-cuffed and seated in the defendant's box. She glanced around the room and tried to comprehend her surroundings. Directly opposite her was the witness stand, and beside it, a separate wooden enclosure for a jury. To her right, below the Coat of Arms, were three large, throne-like chairs. All overlooked a large, red linoleum-covered area that looked like a giant table, with two small staircases leading to its surface, at opposite ends. Pairs of black gowned figures with white wigs sat around this table, fussing through papers. In front of this was the busy, tiered viewing gallery.

Mary searched through its sea of murmuring faces and found her parents sitting next to Grace Hammond. They acknowledged her with smiles of reassurance.

"All rise!" said the Court Clerk, as three gowned Judges entered.

Mary was nervous and confused. She had not spoken with her council, and only noticed that he was sitting at the linoleum table, directly below her, when she stood up. He ignored her loud whispers and sat back down, when instructed by the Court Clerk.

The Bradford's family Solicitor had been unavailable, forcing them to accept state-provided Council, and Mr Bradford was concerned they might be biased.

Following a brief description of the case, the first witnesses were called. These were the two soldiers that had eavesdropped on her and Myles from the hospital veranda. Both swore, under oath, that Mary wore the dress used by the murderer when visiting Myles in hospital. They agreed that Mary was hostile with them, condemning the actions of the British Army in Ireland, and telling them they deserved what they got.

The Prosecution slowly climbed the stairs, positioning himself between the witness box and Mary. Suddenly, in a theatrical manner, he pointed towards her, and bellowed.

"Is this true, Miss Bradford? "

"Answer the question," the Judge demanded, when Mary hesitated.

"It was not like that, your Honour."

"Yes or No?" The Prosecution roared.

"Well yes... but...but," Mary spluttered, not fully understanding the question.

"No more questions, your Honour," the Prosecutor smugly stepped down.

The next witness was the Life Insurance Salesman. He confirmed that Captain Fox initiated an insurance policy a month earlier, and named Miss Bradford as the only beneficiary.

"We now have 'Motive', your Honour," the Prosecution declared. Stepping back, he produced a small pistol as evidence.

"Do you recognise this gun, Mr Rouse?"

"Yes. It was a complementary gift to Captain Fox for purchasing the policy."

"You're Honour. This gun was found in Miss Bradford's possession on the night of her arrest," the Prosecutor declared.

Had Mary been standing, she would have fainted at the sight of the gun. Myles had insisted she have it, following the attack by Payton. He had given her shooting lessons in the old factory, and she kept it in her room, where the Police found it on the night of her arrest.

"You're Honour. Captain Fox never replaced his side arm after losing it during the War. I believe he purchased this one for personal protection, and you, Miss Bradford, stole it from him," the Prosecutor declared, dramatically spinning around and pointing an

169

accusing finger at Mary. "You deliberately took this gun from the good Captain, so he would have nothing to defend himself with on the day of his murder?"

"No, no, that's not true," Mary cried, pleading with her Barrister, who deliberately looked away, fussing with his papers. "Myles gave it to me after I was attacked," she sobbed, realising he was not going to intervene.

"Ah, the alleged attack. I call my next witness, Sergeant Owen McCuskey."

The Sergeant, unaware that he was to be called, was totally unprepared as he sat in the witness box.

"Sergeant, a simple yes or no will suffice. We have evidence, from several sources, that Mary Bradford flirted with Mr Payton, or Stedman, if you prefer, enticing him with her provocative behaviour."

"Lies!" Mary screamed across the court room.

"Silence! Silence in my Court," the judge thundered, banging his gravel. "Any more outbursts like that, Miss Bradford, and you'll spend the rest of the hearing in a cell. Mr Smith, please control your client. You may continue, Mr Frost."

Smith gave Mary a scolding look, whilst Prosecutor Frost thanked the Judge and continued.

"Sergeant McCuskey. Is it possible that Mr Payton/Stedman, totally infatuated with Miss Bradford, had arranged a final assignation with her? And that, during this final, lustful tryst, she cried, 'rape', knowing the Guard on duty would come to her aid? Unfortunately, the Guard's best intentions resulted in a fatal injury to Mr Payton/Stedman, but not before he was forced to defend himself, discharging his pistol at the Guard, who sadly succumbed to his injuries, later that night."

"I never heard such codswallop in all my life," McCuskey exclaimed. "Payton stroke Stedman as you describe him, was an utter thug, liar and a reprobate who…."

"We are not interested in a character assassination; a simple Yes or No will suffice."

"Please answer the question, Sergeant, "the Judge interrupted.

"It's possible, your Honour, but that's not…"

"No more questions, your Honour," Frost interrupted, stepping down.

"But that's not true," McCuskey persisted.

"Enough! You may step down, Sergeant," the Judge said. Mary accepted a sympathetic nod from McCuskey, as he walked away.

"Aren't you going to cross examine him," Mary pleaded with her Barrister, Smith. He stood up, holding some papers aloft, climbing the platform, and hissing at Mary as he passed.

"Don't tell me how to do my job, Miss….Miss….?"

"Bradford!" Mary declared, in a loud whisper. "You don't even know my name, for God's sake."

"Of course, I know your name. The Defence calls, Miss Grace Hammond," Smith suddenly announced.

Mary felt a warm relief, as she listened to Grace describe the wonderful happy relationship she had witnessed between Captain Fox and Mary, elaborating on Captain Fox's intentions, following his engagement to Mary.

"Thank you, Miss Hammond," Smith said. Mary's relief was soon replaced with dread, as she watched the Prosecution ascend. He slowly approached Mrs Hammond,

"Miss Hammond, you stated that Captain Fox had proposed to Mary Bradford that afternoon, and that they were both very much in love."

"Yes, that's true," Grace replied.

"Lies!" The defence suddenly roared, startling Grace and the entire court room.

"Captain Fox was already engaged, as stated on his service records. Are you questioning his honour, Mrs Hammond?"

"He obtained a letter from his fiancée, releasing him from his promise. He showed it to Captain Harper, Mary's parents and I," Grace said.

"The parents of the accused cannot give evidence and Captain Harper is out of the country, so, without the letter, there is no proof of any of this," Frost said.

"Ask Annabelle Wade, in England," Grace interjected.

Unexpectedly, the Judge interrupted with a very clear and distinct instruction.

"I will not be told how to run my court, Mrs Hammond, but, for the record Miss Wade was contacted. However, without proof of the letter being written prior to the incident, her statement cannot be submitted as evidence. That is the end of the matter."

Mary watched Grace step down. She reflected on how Percy had, unsuccessfully, searched Myles' body and his personal effect, for the letter. They had no idea where it could be. Her thoughts were interrupted as, to her surprise, the Prosecution called Father Mackenzie to the stand.

At first, she took comfort from his large, authoritative frame, dressed in his biretta and cassock, but that was short-lived when he announced that he had condemning evidence he wished to submit.

"Father Mackenzie, what evidence have you brought to the court," Frost asked.

"I have a membership list for the Local Cumann Na Bann group. Mary Bradford's name and signature are on line 42, stating she joined the organisation in 1916," he said confidently.

Mary was completely confused, having never been a member of Cumann Na Bann.

"On examination, Detective Freeny from Dublin Castle has confirmed the document's authenticity. It is accepted as evidence," the Judge announced

"It's lies! That is not my signature. Ask Father Mackenzie where the document came from," Mary screamed.

172

"Why are you doing this to me, Father?"

"Quiet," the Judge roared, banging his gravel. "This is your last warning. One more outburst and you'll be locked up for the rest of the proceedings, Miss Bradford. Do you understand?"

Mary was too shocked to answer.

"I asked you a question, Miss Bradford. Do you understand?"

"Yes, your honour, but that's not my signature," Mary cried openly.

"You may leave the stand, Father Mackenzie."

"Thank you, your Honour," Father Mackenzie said, looking directly at Thomas Donnelly, who was sitting in the Gallery. Donnelly acknowledged him with a barely imperceptible nod. Father Mackenzie looked at Mary briefly, and then left the Court Room.

Smith looked away, ignoring her pleas and muffled whispers. He had no intention of questioning the authenticity of the document. Anger overwhelmed Mary.

"You're useless, Smith. You'll pay for this!" she hissed through clenched teeth.

Smith, horrified by the threat, turned and looked at Mary. He was about to reply when the Judge banged his Gravel and announced a short recess.

"I will not be threatened, Miss Bradford. I have done everything possible for you. Now, let us hope that the Judge will be lenient." He left without another word.

After a short recess everyone re-entered to hear the final judgement.

"I have carefully considered all aspects of this case. I have taken into account, the possibility of Captain Fox's alleged marriage proposal, which, without clear evidence, I am forced to dismiss, considering it a feeble attempt to divert the course of justice. Also, knowing that Miss Bradford has been seen, on many occasions, in the company of the deceased, verifies that she was deliberately

173

misleading the good Captain. I have also ruminated over the fact that the accused has financially gained from the demise of Captain Fox with the recent insurance policy. After carefully considering all this evidence, I have reached my judgement. For the charge against Mary Bradford of deliberate conspiracy and entrapment, which led to the murder of Captain Myles Fox, I find the accused, Guilty as charged!"

A loud swoon emanated from the gallery followed by the buzz of objection.

"Silence! Silence In court," the clerk demanded.

The Judge continued.

"I have dismissed the death sentence due to the age and sex of the accused, leaving me with only one option, and that is to sentence Mary Bradford, to 25 years hard labour, to be served at His Majesty's pleasure in Holloway Prison, London."

He banged his gavel. "Take her down, Constable."

There was a loud uproar from the gallery, Mary's parents cried, desperately trying to console one another. On seeing them both, Mary collapsed. She had to be carried from the Court Room by two Police Officers to a truck, which was taking her straight to England, with no farewells from family or friends. Before the truck left, Sergeant McCuskey passed her Percy's note.

"Be strong child," he said, holding back tears as he watched the truck depart.

In the Judge's chambers, Freeny raised a glass to the Judge.

"Well done, you're Honour. Another Fenian bitch out of the way."

Across the road, Thomas Donnelly raised a glass to Father Mackenzie.

"Well done, Calum, another traitorous whore out of the way."

Father Mackenzie was disgusted by the toast, feeling no relief from his actions. As he had left the Court House earlier, he finally realised that his feelings for Mary were of love, not hatred. He conjured up a distant memory of her face, her smile – the smile that would never again be bestowed upon him. He remembered their walks along the river, her conversation and witty humour. The way she laughed. Now, that was destroyed. He had been complicit in eradicating the only person he would ever truly love. He had betrayed her. He glanced up at cross on the steeple of the Church, silhouetted against the clear blue sky and thought of St Peter, for whom the Church was named. Peter had denied Christ just as he had denied Mary. She would no longer be a young woman when she was finally released from prison, and Father Mackenzie knew he was to blame. By the time he reached his front door, his tears were falling.

Father Mackenzie realised that removing the source of his torment did nothing to relieve his inner turmoil. His immoral thoughts of Mary were now replaced by feelings of treachery and deceit. The image that most haunted him was the look of betrayal on Mary's face as he presented his evidence. It felt like the kiss of Judas. This image haunted him, day and night. He felt like a traitor, especially on learning that the list was actually genuine, and that his evidence had led to the deaths of the Carlisle Sisters, two Wexford women, whom he had known and liked.

A week after the trial, Thomas Donnelly paid a late night visit. His presence brought no relief to Father Mackenzie as they sat down and opened a bottle.

"How have you been, Calum?" Donnelly asked, taking a sip from his glass.

"Not good, not good at all, Thomas. I'm having serious doubts about what we did." He was about to take a sip but hesitated, placing the glass back on the table. "Did you know the list was real, Thomas?"

"Yes, I did."

"What? You knew? How could you? Do you know it led to the death of the Carlisle sisters," Calum said, with anguish.

"They were just another pair of untrustworthy whores, Calum."

"How were they untrustworthy, when the Brits killed them?"

"They just were. Just casualties of war, Calum," Thomas replied dismissively. Taking another sip, he leaned forward.

"Look here, Calum. Ireland can afford the loss of the odd bitch or two. These Suffragettes demand equal status, so they can't complain when they get it, can they?"

"No, I don't know what this country can afford. But I do know that you said the list was fabricated and that the other names were fictitious," Callum retorted angrily.

"That Castle G-man would have discovered that in minutes, and your traitorous whore would have been released," Thomas said, unapologetically.

"My traitorous whore, so, were the Carlisle's' yours? Is that how you got that cut on your face? Calum asked, referring to a vicious-looking cut that had appeared on Donnelly's cheek, a few day' earlier. "I have been accused of stealing that document from their office. The entire Wexford branch of the IRA is threatening to kill me, unless I go back to Scotland. I am an outcast in my own Parish!"

"Stop worrying about it. I'll deal with them. We got rid of the Officer and his whore. That's what you wanted, isn't it?"

"Stop calling her that!" Calum was almost purple with rage.

"Now I get it. How stupid of me. You obviously still have feelings for her. I grant you that she was a good looking, buxom young woman, but she's probably the entertainment of some British prison warden now, thanks to you," Thomas taunted.

"Get out! Get out now!" Calum screamed, pulling a startled Thomas from his chair and dragging him into the hallway. He punched him as he threw him out the door. Thomas fell hard on the gravel. The Housekeeper rushed to the door to investigate the commotion. She stood beside the Priest as Donnelly, still kneeling and rubbing his jaw, looked up at him with a cold expression.

"You'll regret that Mackenzie." With that, Donnelly disappeared into the night.

"What's going on, Calum? His petrified Housekeeper asked.

"Never mind Bridie just go to bed, please," he replied, kissing her forehead.

Calum went back into the room, and stood silently. The bottle of whisky was still on the table. The glass Thomas was drinking from was now lying on the floor. He walked over and picked the bottle up. He briefly looked at it. He let out a loud sigh and violently threw it into the unlit fireplace.

He walked to his desk and sat down. He spent the remainder of the night writing his confession, requesting Mary's release, in return for his full co-operation in the prosecution of Thomas Donnelly. Early the next morning, before Mass, he surreptitiously posted the letter. About a week later, he incautiously answered a knock on the door and was horrified to see an armed Thomas Donnelly and two others standing there, in broad daylight,

"You look surprised, Calum. Were you expecting someone else? Donnelly asked, sarcastically.

Calum nervously stepped back.

"What do you want? You're not welcome here anymore."

"Oh, you made that perfectly clear in this letter," Donnelly said, removing it from his pocket with his other hand.

Father Calum Mackenzie felt his whole world collapse, like the trapdoor beneath a condemned man's feet.

Freedom

The Anglo-Irish War raged on throughout 1920. The British introduced another Military militia group, the Auxiliaries, in November of that year. These proved to be even more ruthless and lawless that the Black and Tans. Their actions alone ensured an escalation of IRA retaliation.

It was not until 1921 that all parties finally came to the table, and a Treaty was signed, in London, on December the 6th.

Failure to achieve a fully independent Republic split the Sinn Fein Party and the entire country. The main consternation was the partition of six counties in the North of the country that would remain under British governance, along with some strategic Ports in the South that would remain under British control. The abolition of the Irish Republic declared in 1916 and again in 1919, was a major thorn in the sides of many Republicans, who had sworn to preserve it.

The newly-introduced administrative rules also caused great distress amongst those opposed to the Treaty, particularly as any new Government would have to swear loyalty to the crown. Michael Collins, when questioned as to why he would support such an order, was clear that he would swear any oath to get his hand on the helm, and that this was only a stepping stone to a full Republic, but his rhetoric fell on deaf ears.

Eamon De Valera who was elected as the first President of Ireland in 1919 by the first Dail, gained great support for his opposition to the Treaty. Many established IRA leaders, throughout the country, rallied to his cause. He was a great orator and his skill in the debates that followed between the Pro and Anti-Treaty Parties, served to widen the divide between them. This animosity between one-time loyal comrades seeped out across the entire country. The Military Barracks that had been taken over from the British by the IRA were now under the control of, either the Pro or Anti-Treaty supporters.

It finally came to a head on the 14th of April 1922. Two prominent IRA figures, Rory O'Connor and Sean Lemass, with over 200 IRA members, occupied the Four Courts building in Dublin. A fierce standoff ensued between them and the Free State Army.

Michael Collins and the other signatories to the Treaty were put under intense pressure by the British to dislodge these Rebels. Collins made a number of failed pleas to O'Connor and Lemass. On the 22nd of June 1922, Sir Henry Wilson, the notorious Commander of the British Army in Ireland throughout the Tan War, was assassinated on a street in London by two IRA men. Following this, Lloyd George issued an ultimatum – he would tear up the Treaty and occupy the entire country, once again, if the Free State did not do something about O'Connor, who, he deemed to have sent out murderers from his openly rebellious headquarters, in the heart of Dublin. This threat forced the Minister of Defence, Richard Mulcahy, with the support of the Taoiseach, Arthur Griffith, to reluctantly make the decision to forcibly remove the rebels. On the 27th of June 1922, the Free State Army shelled the Four Courts with 25 pounder guns borrowed from the British. The Battle for Dublin was ignited, throwing the entire Country into a brutal and vicious Civil War with devastating results.

The Civil War lasted almost a year, ending abruptly on the 10th of April 1923, with the death of Liam Lynch, the leader of the IRA forces, who was mortally wounded in the Knockmealdown Mountains. His successor, Frank Aiken, reluctant to continue the Civil War, issued an order to dump arms, not long after he took command.

The Country found it hard to settle back to normality. With the deaths of so many leading figures such as Collins, and Griffith, and a bitterness created by atrocities committed by both sides during the conflict.

The worst of these were the high-profile executions of IRA leaders and men, carried out by the Free State, on the instructions of Kevin O'Higgins, the Minister of Justice, and supported by Richard Mulcahy, the Minister of Defence.

Rory O'Connor and Liam Mellows and two others were executed on the 8th of December 1922, and throughout the entire Civil War, over 70 others faced the firing squad. Sean Lemass survived, hiding out in safe houses in Wicklow and Wexford. The people of Ireland were reminded of these atrocities daily - buying groceries from a one-time sworn enemy. Hearing mass from a Priest, who had previously condemned them from the pulpit, or forced to seek help from a reluctant councillor bearing a grudge. Necessity sometimes forced this animosity to be put aside, but it was always far from forgotten.

Mary was released in the autumn of 1923, under an agreed amnesty for all Republican prisoners. She and Percy had kept in contact, his letters giving her the strength to survive her incarceration and assaults.

Following his enforced Egyptian assignment, Percy's very influential father had him transferred to the Directorate of Military Intelligence (DMI), a branch of the War Office, based in London. Percy was able to collect Mary on the day of her release.

She stepped through a small hatch door in the main gates, immediately blinded by the autumnal sunshine. She shut her eyes and was savouring its unrestricted heat on her face, when a familiar voice rang out.

"You're a sight for sore eyes."

Even though Mary was wearing the dress she had been arrested in, and was sporting a prison hair-cut, she looked stunning in the bright autumnal sunshine.

"Oh, Percy," she said, embracing him tightly, fearing he would vanish.

"Easy on," Percy's companion said with a laugh.

Percy released Mary and introduced his friend.

"Mary, I would like you to meet Andrew," Percy said.

"Why, if I wasn't in love with Percy here, I'd whisk you away myself," he said, scrutinising Mary's appearance, while pinching his chin with his thumb and forefinger.

"Hello Andrew," she said, offering her hand with a smile. "It's a pleasure to finally meet you. Percy's told me so much about you."

"All bad, I hope," Andrew replied, accepting her hand with a dramatic flourish.

"Come now, Mary. We have lots to show you before you go back to Ireland," Percy said, excitedly.

"Our first stop is Selfridges. My friend is going to dress you like a Goddess," Andrew said, scrutinising Mary further. "It's all been arranged, so no objections," he continued, opening the car door. Mary was treated like a queen. She was given a room to herself in Andrews's large apartment, and his older sister, Liza, accompanied them on their excursions. Mary felt relaxed and was having fun, for a change, helping her to supress the pain of the past few years.

On one excursion, they passed a shop in Bond Street. Mary stopped, the array of items in the window catching her eye. She looked up, saw the name over the door and tears started to fall.

"Whatever's the matter," Liza asked, comforting her.

Mary silently pointed up at the name of the shop, which read: *Kings of Bond Street. Gentlemen's Hat Makers. Est. 1766*

"This is where Myles bought his army cap which sparked our first conversation."

"Oh you poor dear." Liza said giving her a consoling hug. Mary composed herself, and they walked to the nearest tube station. That evening, they decided to eat in. When finished, they sat in the lounge, comfortable in each other's company.

181

"Mary, I'm so sorry about earlier," Percy said.

"If we'd known we would have avoided that street."

"It's alright, Percy. I'm very grateful for such wonderful friends. Thank you for your kindness."

Mary told them how she had first met Myles on Christmas Day, and how she fell in love with the handsome, young soldier immediately. She wept when she talked about the proposal and his assassination. She felt relived and tired having not spoken to anyone about it before.

"Bedtime!" Andrew said, noticing how exhausted Mary looked.

Liza offered to share her bed and Mary accepted. Percy knocked the door, and entered. Liza was sitting in front of a dresser, with Mary brushing her hair.

"I just came to say goodnight, and apologise, once again," Percy said, and kissed both girls' good night. Before he left the room, he paused, and said to Mary.

"By the way, we never found Myles' hat. I donated mine for the funeral."

"It must've been left on the road, Percy. I was too distraught to notice," Mary mused.

"Very strange. Perhaps one of the Rebels took it. Good night!" he said, and left.

The next morning they set out on a prearranged trip to Norfolk. It had been arranged, at the request of Myles' family, who were eager to meet her. Mary was hesitant at first, but the thought that she could place flowers on Myles' grave, sustained her and helped overcome her fear of meeting his family.

The drive to Norfolk was pleasant. Mary loved the autumnal countryside, reminding her of Ireland. They finally arrived at Drake Manor House.

Mary's tummy was full of butterflies, as they drove up the winding drive to the large sandstone house. Mary could picture a young Myles running up the driveway and playing on the lawns. It was a large country house, with ten bedrooms. Andrew parked the car outside the main door, which opened immediately. A middle-aged, well-dressed couple came out. The woman ran over to Mary and, without introduction, gave her a huge hug.

"I'm Myles' Mother, she said, squeezing the life from Mary. It was such a relief to be welcomed so warmly. "Oh, Mary, you're even more beautiful than he described. Come in, come in. There's someone inside who wants to meet you."

"Who could that be?" Mary asked,

"You'll see, my dear," she said, taking Mary's arm.

They were led into a large drawing room, where a beautiful young woman was sitting alone on a settee. The woman stood up. She looked a little nervous. Mary realised who she was, and rushed over to her. The embraced, emotionally.

"Oh, Annabelle," Mary said, emotions threatening to overwhelm her. "I'm so sorry that I couldn't protect Myles. He loved you so much."

"There's no blame, Mary," Annabelle said, as they tried to compose themselves.

A maid brought in tea and they were all soon engrossed in their memories of Myles. Mr Fox produced some photo albums which had a photo of Myles in his uniform, before he left for war. Mary asked if she could have a copy of it.

"Of course, my dear," Mrs Fox said. "There's something else we want you to have, too."

Mr Fox retrieved from a nearby dresser. a brown, leather-backed journal, and a small, black velvet box. It was Myles' medals and his war journal.

"I can't take them," Mary said surprised. "They belong to your family."

"Please," Mrs Fox said. "We've discussed it. You are family, and it's what Myles would have wanted."

Mary opened the journal at random and exposed a charcoal sketch of a couple sitting in front of the Hanging Stone in Arklow. Below the sketch, fixed to the page, were three pressed Primrose's with the words, 'From my very own Beautiful Irish Primrose'.

Annabelle gave Mary's hand a reassuring squeeze as she glanced at the open page. They shared a warm smile, tears in their eyes as Mary continued to turn the pages.

Annabelle stayed beside Mary all afternoon, giving comfort and receiving it, in return. A visit to the churchyard where Myles was interred was arranged for the following morning, so everyone retired early.

The next morning was bright and dry, with an autumnal chill. They drove the short distance to the 12th century stone Church, circled by a low stone wall with a Lych-gate entrance. The surrounding grounds were covered with ancient gravestones, most of which were bent and angled across a small network of gravel paths.

There was a mature old Oak tree at its centre. It dominated the other trees and bushes which bordered the gravel paths. Most were losing their leaves, covering the Church grounds in an array of mixed, autumnal colours.

Mrs Fox sombrely lead the way across a narrow, leaf-covered path that wound between the ancient gravestones. Mary was escorted by Annabelle and Liza, one on each arm, and the men brought up the rear. Mary fell to her knees on seeing the small, white, military gravestone that stood alone on a stretch of manicured lawn. It was embossed with the Norfolk regimental badge, and, underneath, simply read, 10457 Captain Myles Fox, M.C. Died in Ireland, 20th of June 1920, aged 26.

She suddenly relived every terrifying second of that day especially the painful journey across the road to his body. She reached out and placed one hand on the top of the headstone and with the other she traced his name, weeping uncontrollably. The group stood back to allow her privacy to grieve alone. Mary slowly composed herself sat back on her knees and placed the pressed primroses from the journal onto the grave. She whispered.

"From your Irish Primrose, my Love,"

She turned and looked at the small group and through tears thanked them. As Annabelle and Liza helped her back to her feet, the Vicar approached and introduced himself. A conversation about the tragedy of war followed while everyone sheltered beneath the canopy of the large oak tree. Mary found the Vicar very comforting and understanding. He made her feel welcome.

Soon it was time to leave for London, as Mary had to catch the Saturday train from Euston to Holyhead. Following many hugs, tears and promises to keep in touch, the visiting group set out on their journey. Mary silently sat in the back of the car with the journal and medals on her lap. Liza snuggled in beside her. Mary was deep in thought about the anticipated journey back to Ireland.

Saturday morning was sunny, but still chilly. Andrew drove to Euston Station. After parking the car, they gathered on the concourse amongst the rushing crowds. Mary thanked Percy for his kindness. After many tears and kisses and a heart-breaking platform departure, Mary found herself sharing a first class compartment with a couple who smiled, and chatted with her all the way to Dublin.

She finally arrived at Arklow railway station at 9 o'clock that night. George and Anna were waiting, and both rushed forward to greet her as she stepped down from the train. Mary burst into tears on seeing her family for the first time in years.

"My, you have grown!" She said hugging her sister,

"Come on, I have lots to tell you," Anna said excitedly, as they walked to the car. Mary's Mother was waiting in the open doorway of the house, and ran to the car as it pulled up. She dragged Mary out and gave her a long hug. After a brief cup of tea, an exhausted Mary was soon in a deep sleep, in her own bed, for the first time in years.

She woke at 8 o'clock the next morning, and joined her family for breakfast.

"Please don't ask me about what happened. I'm not ready yet," Mary said

Her family understood and agreed to wait.

"Will you be coming to 11 o'clock Mass with us, Mary?" Her father asked.

She gave him a bemused look.

"After what Mackenzie did to me, I don't think so, Dad. He's a Priest and he blatantly lied. How could he do that to me, and why?
"

Her parents looked at each other with grave concern. Before they could answer diplomatically, Anna bust out loudly.

"He's dead, Mary!"

"What? "A clearly horrified Mary asked.

"Father Mackenzie is dead! They say the IRA murdered him because of the document he gave to the court. All the women on it were arrested and two were killed trying to escape."

"Oh my God! Is this true?" Mary asked her parents.

"Yes, my dear." Mr Bradford said.

Mary felt robbed. During her time in prison, she had carefully planned to bring justice down on those that were involved in her incarceration, and Mackenzie was on the top of her list. Now he was gone.

Mary excused herself from the table.

"Maybe I'll go to Mass next week, but now, I'm going for a walk, alone. I need to make sense of the last three years, and digest what you've just told me."

"That's perfectly understandable," her Mother said, squeezing her hand.

Mary walked down Seaview Avenue, Mary and entered the old munitions factory through the now abandoned sentry hut, totally unchallenged. As she ambled through the site, she was horrified by

186

the destruction. Every building was in a state of ruin. Most were missing their rooves, doors, and windows. Entire walls had been demolished, to assist with the removal of large machinery. Only the foundations of the Dining Hall remained, and all of the tall chimneys were gone. She was walking towards the Water Tower when she met a man walking a dog.

"What happened to the factory?" she asked.

"It's been slowly sold off, piece by piece, by a Dublin company," he replied

"Did it ever open up again?"

"No, rumour has it that before the Treaty, Lloyd George and Churchill intended that the factory would never produce explosives again, and a deal was struck with the Scrap Company to make sure of it."

She thanked him and continued her journey, ambling along the factory paths and railway lines, which still snaked through the natural sand dunes and man-made sand hills. They were all covered in long marram grass and overgrown. She remembered how clean these paths and hills were kept when the factory was operating.

She came to a stop outside the Women's Changing Room. She slowly entered. The roof, windows, and doors were removed, exposing the blue sky above.

Inside, a large section of the stone-tiled floor was covered with sand that had blown in through the missing door. The changing bench was partly buried, its baby blue paint peeled in flaky patches, and the exposed wood, bleached white by the weather.

Scattered around it, and half buried in the sand, were bits of the blue factory uniforms. Hats, aprons, clogs, and the odd rubber boot. Mary sat down on the bench, and stroked the wood with her gloved fingers, reflecting on her many romantic trysts with Myles on this very bench. She realised she was not yet ready for the happy memories of her time with Myles. The years had taken their toll. To distract her thoughts, she pulled one of the partially buried cloth hats from the sand to study it. Suddenly, she remembered, now with distain, the time that Father Mackenzie had walked in on her as she was changing. She remembered his apologies as he tried, desperately, to avoid glancing over towards her. She had never seen anyone so embarrassed. When she realised he was the new curate, she felt mischievous, and so with the intention of increasing his embarrassment, she walked across the room, partially-clothed. She was glad that she had embarrassed him, but this was small consolation for what he had done to her. Little did she know, at the time, that this tiny mischievous action was the seed that would lead to their destruction.

The next morning, Mary was surprised to receive a telegram from Commandant John Mills of the Irish Free State Army, requesting a meeting later in the week, at Mary's home in Arklow.

Out of curiosity, she accepted, so, the following Wednesday afternoon, Mary and her Mother found themselves having tea with Commandant Mills and his secretary in the priest's room of their house.

John Mills was a 26-year-old Cork man and his secretary, a Miss Sylvia Horan, also from Cork, and the same age as Mary. They represented the Military Service Pensions Collection (MSPC), a department founded in June 1923, to acknowledge and reward injured members of all branches of the IRA, and the widows and children of its deceased members.

Since its establishment, this new department had been inundated with applications, not only from the families of the injured and deceased, but living members and those that took great risk by assisting the Flying Columns, during the Anglo Irish War. The huge number of applications led the Free State Government to set up a new department to deal with them separately, which was to officially open in 1924.

Because Mary was still an officially recognised member of Cumann Na mBan, the MSPC were offering her a job to separate and investigate the validity of these claims in the Leinster area. She was also to request copies of personal diaries and detailed accounts of actions against the British to assist with the claim, which would also give the new Free State an opportunity to preserve the history of its foundations for future generations. If she were to accept the post, she would have to surrender her membership of Cumann Na mBan, as that organisation still supported the Republican cause.

Mary was flabbergasted. She wanted to tell them the truth, that she had never been a member of Cumann Na mBan, but her instincts and prison experience, convinced her to remain silent. She saw this as an ideal opportunity to collect information on some of the more sinister characters involved in Myles' murder, and her arrest. She listened, with great interest, as they told her how she could work from home or the Dublin office, and that all of her expenses would be paid, including any travel required to validate claims.

She told them she would accept the offer, but wanted the rest of the week off, as she had only just got home, and needed time to settle in. The Commandant and Silvia were delighted and left the details of their office in Dublin, before departing.

The following Sunday, Mary felt ready to go to Mass with her family. It was a cold, wet, miserable morning, autumn quickly changing to winter. The family gathered in the hallway to witness Mary remove her old winter coat from the hall stand. It had hung in the same position since the night of her arrest, and, under Mrs Bradford's strict instructions, no-one was to touch it, except Mary. The hall was dark and gloomy. Mrs Bradford lit an oil lamp, creating an eerie, yellow glow.

"I wish electricity would come to town," Mary said. "We had it in Kynoch's."

Her Mother raised the lantern above the rack.

"There it is, on the end," her sister said." I hope it still fits. It's been there since you were taken. Mama wouldn't let anyone touch it until you came home"

"I wanted you to be the first to remove it, Mary."

"Thank you, Mam," Mary said, lifting the coat.

Suddenly Her parents and sister gasped in unison.

"What is it?" Mary said, "You look like you've seen a ghost." She turned towards the rack to see what had caused the commotion. Myles' hat was still hanging on the peg where it had remained completely hidden from sight since that terrible day.

"Oh, Mary," her Mother said, gently touching her arm. Mary could not speak. She stood there, holding her coat, staring at the hat. Finally the spell broke.

"It's alright....I'm alright. Myles is obviously trying to tell me something."

She reached up and removed the hat. Myles's gloves and the letter fell out. This was too much for Mary, and she sank to the floor, tears falling.

They decided not to go to Mass. They comforted Mary, who finally felt ready to share some of what she had suffered over the past years.

Monday morning was cold and frosty. Mary felt a little anxious, sitting in the back of her Father's car, on the short Journey to the Station. She was clutching a small case, and enjoying the sight of the frost-covered trees, as they twinkled in the luminous orange glow of the low rising sun. She felt content for the first time since her return.

After an uneventful journey, Mary was welcomed into the Dublin office by Commandant Mills. He took her small case and escorted her upstairs to an office, and showed her a desk, completely covered with, and surrounded by, boxes of files.

"Are these all pension requests? "She asked, astonished by the sheer number.

"Yes, and that's only for Leinster. If we had half these people during the War, it would have been won it in weeks, not years," the Commandant said wryly.

Sylvia entered from a small kitchen. She welcomed Mary, and briefly explained the task at hand. Mary thanked her, and sat at the desk, taking a few minutes before she opened the first File. It was a Farmer from Hacketstown stating he had hidden guns and ammunition on his Farm and given shelter to Flying Columns. The request included times, dates, names and details of the equipment stored. It was an interesting read, and Mary put it to one side for follow up. She started to sift through the piles of applications, dividing them into the towns and rural areas of Leinster. She was soon busy, spreading the files out on the floor around her desk. The Commandant, in passing, stopped and gave her a smile of approval. She looked up, returned the smile, and carried on. Suddenly one name caught her attention - Norman Boland, Arklow. She sat back in her chair and opened the file, with great anticipation, reading it, over and over.

Mary returned to Arklow that Friday evening, and joined her family for supper. Throughout the meal, she talked excitedly about Dublin and her new job. George squeezed his wife's hand, both silently acknowledging that Mary was really home.

That Sunday, Mary accompanied her family to Mass.

Afterwards, she joined Anna, outside who was now on the receiving end of all the attention. On seeing Mary, the potential suitors edged away.

Mary stood on the Church steps, studying the ruined Army Barracks. It had been burnt down by Anti-Treaty forces during the Civil War. She realised that little had changed in the routine of the town, as a smiling Mrs Hamilton approached her for a chat, and a group of boys risked approaching Anna.

Mr Boland and his wife appeared. When they saw Mary, they paled with shock, trying to make a hasty retreat. Mary walked directly over to them.

"Where's your murdering son, hiding?" She asked Norman Boland, shocking everyone to silence.

"Now, Now Mary. A lot of terrible things happened during the War and a lot of good people died. We're very sorry for what happened to Myles, but I assure you, we had nothing to do with it,

""Nothing to do with it, Mr Boland!" She declared loudly, blocking their path.

"So, your request for a state pension is false? That statement you made about planning raids with Thomas Donnelly and stealing explosives from Kynoch's are all lies, are they, Mr Boland?" Mary asked. "Oh, and how you used your car to transport weapons and ammunition across the country, with the help of Father Mackenzie Is that all lies as well?"

Mr Bradford tried to interrupt Mary, taking her arm and quietly asking her to stop, as she was making everyone feel uncomfortable.

She pulled away from his grasp.

"No Dad! I'm not finished. Well, what have you got to say, Mr Boland?"

He was speechless, pouting like a fish out of water. Finally, he found his voice.

"How on earth do you know any of that, Mary?"

"Because of my apparent membership of the Cumann Na mBan I am employed by the Military Service Pensions Department. My job is to root out the liars making false claims for state pensions and compensation. So, tell me again that you had nothing to do with my fiancée's death?" Mary asked coldly, in control for the first time in years.

Mrs Boland erupted in hysterical tears.

"We're sorry Mary....so, so sorry.... we also lost John...We had to send him to my brother in Canada because he was a wanted man. They would have hung him if he'd been caught. He's not been home since," she said through gasps of breath.

"At least he's still alive, Mrs Boland, unlike my fiancée," Mary retorted.

"Yes, we are grateful for that," she wept.

"He stole my engagement ring when he rifled my fiancée's body after shooting him and I want it back."

The Boland's looked at each other in horror, not just at the thought of their son committing murder, but because both remembered a package he had asked them to hide before absconding to Canada. This package was still hidden in their Grandfather clock.

"Mary," Norman Boland said, composing himself. "We truly are sorry for the wicked thing our son was involved in. I know it would be impossible for you to forgive him, or us, for that matter, but if it brings you any solace, I think I know where your engagement ring is. If you and your family would care to call to our house on your way home, I will give you a package that may contain your ring."

Now Mary was speechless. Her father confirmed the arrangements, and they left.

The Boland's front room was spacious and full of ornaments and pictures. The Bradford's sat around an immaculately polished mahogany table. They had refused an offer of refreshments from Mrs Boland. Norman entered, breaking the uncomfortable silence. He was carrying a large, item, covered in oil cloth.

"John gave this to me the night he left," he said, placing the item on the table. He removed the cloth, exposing a Webley revolver, six bullets, and a small box, with 'Powers Jewellery Shop' printed on its lid. Mary could not take her eyes off the gun. She reached out and touched the barrel.

"This is it isn't it, the gun that killed him?" she said.

"Norman, why did you bring that dreadful thing in here?" His wife asked, distraught.

"I don't want it in our house anymore. I don't want to see it again," Norman said.

"There are six live bullets here? There should be a shell case from the one that killed Myles. Where is it?" Mary asked.

"I don't know. This is what John gave me that day. For safety, I took the bullets out of the chambers. I never came across a spent shell case."

"Never mind the gun Mary. I think this is what you're looking for," Norman said passing the jewellery box to Mary.

She slowly cracked the lid. Embedded in the black cushion of the box was a beautiful blue sapphire stone surrounded by diamonds, mounted on a silver band. The sight of the ring rendered her speechless. She recovered momentarily and closed the lid.

"Thank you. Thank you both. Father, please take the gun," Mary said, standing up.

"I apologise for my behaviour earlier. Although no excuse, I have been through a lot."

"Oh, my dear we have prayed so hard for your safe return," Mrs Boland said, approaching Mary and taking both her hands. "And our prayers have been answered. We are so sorry for what our son was involved in. You have no idea how terrible it's been on us, too."

"I think I might have more of an idea than most," Mary said, gently returning a reassuring squeeze before leaving with her family.

She tried not to show any sign of weakness, but, once in the back of the car, she finally succumbed, and wept uncontrollably.

Father Mackenzie

Mary soon settled in and enjoyed the routine her job demanded, especially when it was necessary to work from home. Before the Christmas holidays, she had brought home several cases to work on in January.

One particular case intrigued her. It was a request from a Bridie Mackenzie, living near Woodenbridge. After reading through the request, she discovered Bridie Mackenzie was Father Calum Mackenzie's Housekeeper and sister. Mary chose to start with this one, so on the 2nd of January 1924, after an enjoyable Christmas break, she drove through the Vale of Ovoca, in her father's borrowed pony and trap,

A deep snow had fallen the night before, burying the tangled hedgerow beneath a brilliant white smoothness that twinkled in the early morning sunlight. Out in the open Mary felt exhilarated as she trotted through the coolness of the snow-covered valley. The muffled clip clop of the hooves barely resonated amongst the tall, wintery fir trees that lined the steep sides of the valley.

Mary arrived at a small, thatched cottage, just off the main road. Its single chimney had a tube of thick, white smoke rising vertically into the air. As she pulled into the yard, a woman in her mid-40s, dressed all in black, stepped out to greet her.

"Good morning Miss Mackenzie," Mary said smiling, as she stepped down. "I'm Mary Bradford from the Ministry of Pensions."

"I...I recognise you," the woman stammered, in a Scottish accent. "Are you not George Bradford's daughter, the one they took away?"

"That's correct. May I come in? I want to discuss your claim for compensation from the State," Mary asked, removing her bonnet and gloves.

"What happened to your lovely, long black hair? Did the Tans get to you?" The woman asked, startled at the sight of Mary's cropped hair.

"Ah, that's another story," Mary replied.

"Oh my! What would Calum think? Come in, dear, we have lots to talk about."

Mary felt a pang at the mention of his name but followed the woman into the warm and cosy cottage. To her left, through an open door, she could see the foot of a bed resting on the bare wooden floor. In front of her was a large, stone fireplace, complete with a welcoming fire, chairs placed on either side.

"Take a chair my child, whilst I make a cup of tea,"

She prepared a pot of tea on a nearby table, and joined Mary by the fire.

"As you can see, Mary, I haven't got very much, since leaving Arklow."

Mary looked around. Apart from the table and chairs and a shelf over the fireplace supporting some cooking pots, there was nothing in the cottage, not even a picture.

"Did you not bring anything with you from the Parish house, Miss Mackenzie?"

"The Church owned everything and I was only given three days' notice to quit. No-one would help because of the evidence Calum gave at your trial. Apparently, it led to the deaths of two other girls? I'd have been homeless, if not for the kindness of Mrs Hammond, who arranged this cottage for me through Lord Proby."

"Ah, Grace. She's a kind woman," Mary said, taking a sip of bitter tea.

"That she is, lass. It was also her suggestion, that I contact the Pension Office."

"Well, I'm sure we can help," Mary said, trying to swallow the rancid tea

196

"Did you know that Calum had fallen for you?" Bridie asked unexpectedly, causing Mary to splutter the tea back into the cup.

"Pardon! "Mary said, in complete shock.

"Yes, he was deeply in love with you"

This statement left Mary astounded. She placed the cup on the hearth stone.

"I wasn't aware. Please, explain." Mary stuttered.

Bridie Mackenzie brushed down her dress and said..

"Well, where to start, wee lass? I suppose at the beginning. We were born in Scotland, to Irish Nationalist parents. We grew up listening to the history of Ireland and the injustices inflicted by the English. Our Grandparents were evicted during the Famine, and forced to immigrate to Scotland. They brought their Fenian beliefs with them, and passed them on to Calum. Between that and his strong religious beliefs, he left for Salamanca, in Spain, to train as a Priest. When he finished, in 1916, he was offered a temporary post in Arklow. He accepted and invited me over as his Housekeeper. We were happy for three years, until the Tan War started. Calum joined the IRB, and hosted secret meetings in his house. Thomas Donnelly was a regular visitor, using the house to store weapons and people." She paused, as if considering what to say next.

"It was around this time that the drinking started." She paused again, weighing up the bigger betrayal – to admit that her brother was not perfect, or to never explain his actions to the one person who deserved to hear the truth.

"You see, before that, Calum didn't really drink. Then Donnelly started staying in town, our house being the perfect hideaway. They would sit up until the wee hours, polishing off a bottle, discussing Irish politics. Soon, Calum started to drink alone. When I placed a blanket on him before retiring, he would be muttering loudly. It was always your name on his lips. I would catch him looking at you, from the windows. One evening, he

197

confided that he was infatuated by you. He knew it had become unhealthy."

"I am totally speechless Miss Mackenzie. I never knew," Mary said, picking up her cup to try the contents again, only to discover it tasted worse.

"Why should you, dear? When he saw that you were walking out with a British Officer, he changed. He was consumed with jealousy, and the drinking got worse. He confided his feelings about you and the Englishman to Thomas Donnelly."

"His name was Myles', Miss Mackenzie," Mary interrupted.

"Yes of course. Donnelly promised Calum that he would sort out the both of you. Sadly, he did just that a few weeks later."

"Where did Father Mackenzie, get the document? "Mary asked, mesmerised.

"A few days after you were arrested, Donnelly gave my brother that list of names and convinced him to offer it as evidence against you. He told Calum that it was not real, and that the names were made up of people already in Jail. Donnelly told Calum that the document would 'sort out his traitorous whore'. " Bridie crossed herself, reflecting on the incident.

"The night before your trial, Calum told me how he felt about you. I have to confess that after hearing what he said I reluctantly agreed that you were a temptress, and, for his peace of mind, it would be necessary to have you sent a way."

"A 'temptress?" Mary asked, horrified.

It was plain to see that Mary had no idea of the feelings Father Mackenzie had for her. The Housekeeper felt duty-bound to describe the frustration he harboured.

"He told me that his obsession with you started, back in 1916, when he first arrived in Arklow. Town dignitaries invited him on a tour of the Kynoch Munitions Factory. The tour ended with lunch in the Dining Hall. He asked for directions to a washroom, and, misunderstanding his instructions, he accidentally walked into the

Ladies Changing Room. You were alone and half naked. You screamed, and tried to cover yourself. I don't know if it was mischief or what, but he believed that, when you realised he was a Priest, you deliberately crossed the floor, in a state of undress, and opened the door for him. He panicked, apologised and left, but the sight of your near-naked body possessed him for years. It was like an injury that wouldn't heal. You really became his obsession."

Mary was too shocked to speak.

"When you started walking out with John Boland, he desires became even stronger. Eventually, he confided in the Bishop, who suggested a particular woman friend could help him, for a small fee. The details were thrown into the fire. Calum believed that if you were sent away his torment would end, so he and Donnelly hatched a plan for this to happen."

Bridie sighed and picked up her cup. She took a sip, before replacing the cup back by the fire. She looked directly at Mary.

"Mary, I'm sorry for supporting Calum's plan, but he was my brother, and you never saw him at night. That is what really made me believe it would be better if you were sent away.

Mary could not reply. She receded in shock. She thought about the accidental meetings on the river bank or on the beach, and realised that there was nothing accidental about them, at all.

"I had no idea, Miss Mackenzie. I don't know what to say or think. All because of the changing room incident? I just can't believe it, I really can't," Mary said, staring into the dancing flames of the fire.

"What happened to him?" Mary asked, desperate to make sense of it.

"A few weeks after your trial, late one night, Thomas Donnelly arrived, unannounced, as he often did. But on this particular evening, Calum and he had an unmerciful row. Calum discovered that the list was genuine. He was furious that two women had been killed, as a result. The row moved into the hallway."

199

"Get out! Get out, now!" Calum shouted "

I rushed in to the hall to investigate, and saw Calum punch Donnelly, before throwing him out the door onto the outside gravel. I have never seen such an evil look on any man's face, ever before. Still on his knees, he wiped the blood from his lip, he looked up at Calum, with cold eyes."

"You'll regret that, Mackenzie," he said, then disappeared into the night."

Bridie Mackenzie took a deep breath.

"A week later, I returned home with the shopping. I went into our store room, and found my brother hanging from a bed sheet" she paused, fighting back the tears. "The Coroner's report said, 'Suicide', but I think Thomas Donnelly came back."

"O my God," Mary exclaimed. "I feel responsible. I should have never…never…. In the factory that day…. I…. I was only playing … Oh, can you ever forgive me," she said, also starting to weep.

"Och now, hush dear. It's not you that needs forgiveness," Miss Mackenzie said, stroking Mary's hand.

"You were never to know. You did nothing wrong, only fall in love with a man that made another man jealous. Calum was only human after all, but he was also a priest, and, although it pains me to say, he should've been a better man."

"Thank you, Miss Mackenzie, thank you for understanding," Mary said, composing herself, but feeling little relief from Bridie's words of comfort. "Well, if you can prove his membership of the IRB, and if you have any records of his activities, I don't see a problem with your composition application. Bridie got up and went into the bedroom. She returned carrying Calum's journal. It contained a record of meetings, stored equipment, people that had been sheltered and most of all, his membership of the IRB. Mary had a quick look.

"This is exactly the type of records the State has requested to back up claims. There will be no issue with your request, I'm sure."

Mary placed the journal and letters in her bag, and stood up to leave.

"I will be in contact. I promise," she said, leaving.

Miss Mackenzie saw her out, and before Mary got into the trap, she thanked her again, with a hug. Mary drove away, her mind in complete turmoil.

Bridie Mackenzie waited outside her cottage, until Mary disappeared from sight.

"My God, Calum Mackenzie, 'tis no wonder you fell for her. She really is a beautiful young woman," she said to herself, as she kicked light snow from her boots before going back inside.

Judge Lavin

In April 1924, Mary became overwhelmed reading a request at her desk. Tears streamed down her face.

"Whatever's the matter, Mary? "Sylvia asked,

A few minutes later, Mary was sitting in the small kitchen. Looking up at Sylvia and Commandant Mills, she saw the concern etched into their faces. Taking a drink of water, she tried to compose herself.

"This is what Myles must have felt when he suffered from shell shock."

"What do you mean?" Silvia asked.

"Sometimes triggers caused him to relive terrible experiences from the War. The triggers could be as simple as an orange or a group of people sheltering from the rain. I didn't understand at first. It seemed odd when I would find him staring off into space, a melancholic look on his face. He ended up in the hospital, and during this convalescence, he explained to me what was actually happening in his head. It was only then I realised how serious this condition was."

"A lot of people came home from France with it, Mary," John said, reassuringly.

"But it seems it's not just confined to soldiers, John. I've just read a name on that report, and it took me back to Kingstown Prison and the unwanted attention of a Black and Tan Officer."

"Here, take, another drink," John said, offering Mary the glass. He had suffered at the hands of the Black and Tans, and his own horrible experiences gave him some insight into how Mary was feeling.

Mary drank thirstily.

"Thank you, John," she said, handing back the glass.

"I feel I should try to explain it," Mary said, apprehensive, yet needing to share her experience with her friends. Sylvia's presence gave her strength.

"The night that I arrived in Kingstown…. I mean Dun Laoghaire," Mary said, correcting herself, to using the new name for the port.

"I with several other women, were kept in a local Police Barracks until the following Monday when we would be escorted to England. I was thrown into a windowless cell with a wooden bench, chained to the wall. I sat on it, and cried. Later, two Black and Tans entered, carrying an old storm lamp. I thought they were bringing me food and water, but I was wrong. Following them was Captain Jeremy Richards, the Tan Officer from Ovoca. From the violent look on his face, I feared for my safety, I curled into a ball to protect myself, mentally preparing for the worst. But I need not have worried about being violated. His intention was clear from the onset."

"Stand up you Fucking Fenian whore," he shouted and punched me in the face. The power of the blow knocked me senseless.

"I said, STAND UP!" He roared again. Terrified and still trying to recover from the blow, I struggled to my feet. He struck me again, this time in the stomach. It winded me and I fell onto the bench.

"He was my Friend, you fucking bitch, and you had him killed." His statement surprised me, but the pain in my body made me reply, without thinking.

"No, he wasn't! He never liked you!"

"This made him really angry. He grabbed my hair, and slammed my head down onto the bench. He hitched up my skirt, kicked my legs apart, and trusted his groin, hard against me." Mary shuddered at the memory, but, bravely continued.

"I felt the weight of his body pressing down on me and I could smell the stench of his tobacco breath.

"I could have you here and now, you fucking murdering bitch, but I wouldn't lower myself to be infected by a murdering Fenian whore."

"He jumped up, grabbed my hair and slammed my face into the bench, almost knocking me unconscious. He pulled me off the bench by my hair, and flung me across the cell. The other two Officers kicked me, only stopping when Richards demanded they didn't kill me but, leave some for the Prison Wardens in Holloway'." Mary replayed the scene in her mind.

"They left, taking the lamp with them. I crawled to the bench. I was delirious; I thought maybe it wasn't real. It was a dream, a nightmare and I would wake soon. But it did continue…. for three long years. But, I could never regret my love for Myles. Instead, I started to think about the people involved in my incarceration. I swore I would survive to get justice for both of us."

"Oh my God, Mary, How on earth did you survive? " A shocked Silvia asked.

"The thought of justice on those responsible sustained me, but I never knew how I could fulfil that promised to myself. Today, I read a name in a file, and the memories, never far away, overwhelmed me, but I just don't know what to do about it."

"Was it Richards?" John Mills asked.

"No, Judge Andrew Michael Lavin," Mary replied, pronouncing each syllable.

"Really!" John exclaimed. "Excuse me a moment," he said, rushing to his desk.

"What has Lavin got to do with it?" Silvia asked.

"If Lavin had contacted Myles' family, as he said, he would have known that they would have travelled to Ireland to defend me. Annabelle told me that neither she, nor Myles' parents were ever contacted. He lied Silvia! He lied in Court, and his lies cost me three years of my life," Mary replied, choking up.

"I thought so," John said, as he returned to the kitchen. "I had a request from a Solicitor in Mallow, a few months back. It had to do with land rights, which is not our department, but his client is a close friend, so, as a favour, I contacted the Land Department. They sent me the original title deeds, confirming my friend's family had been granted the land by the 12th Earl of Cork, 'For loyal service'. These deeds were presented to the County Judge, in person. The Judge decided to keep hold of them to check out their authenticity, and then later, denied that he ever received them. The Land Department did not keep a copy. My friend is distraught. The Court Case is in two weeks. Guess who the Judge is? None other than, Judge Andrew Michael Lavin."

"My God! He must have stayed here after the Treaty," Mary exclaimed.

"Yes, and I have another friend investigating the whereabouts of the deeds."

"But, why would he want the deeds?" Silvia asked, as they returned to the office.

"That is what my good friend is trying to find out," John said, with a wry smile.

Judge Andrew, Michael Lavin came from a well-established West British family that could trace it origins back four generations. Born in Dublin to a wealthy merchant, and armed with his Law Degree from Trinity College, he became a Lawyer. He was now in his mid-50s, was now a Judge, and still sitting on the bench. He hated the Irish. He believed the entire Irish nation, regardless of position, should be subservient to him and all West Brits, a name the Irish used when referring to these wealthy families.

He was a small, weasel of a man, intoxicated with his own self-importance. He got pleasure from keeping people waiting, and applied the full force of the law on even the simplest of cases. The

205

lack of judges in the country forced the new Free State to keep him in his role, despite previous loyalties. This new power increased his ruthlessness towards Irish defendants. His reputation for being corrupt, stretched back across his entire career, but he skilfully used his position and knowledge of the law to cover his actions, which bordered on criminal. The new Free State chose to ignore his reputation, especially during the Civil War, when he was despised by the people, but loved by the authorities, for his efficiency in incarcerating over 100 IRA members, issuing the death sentence on more than 20.

On a warm Tuesday morning, in the second week of May 1924, John, Silvia and Mary set out for the Mallow District Court, spending the night in a nearby hotel. The case that interested them was due to start at 10 o'clock. When they entered the Court Room at half past nine, they were surprised by the number of people already present. After much shuffling, they finally got to sit together at the back of the public gallery. A very attractive and well-dressed woman, in her early 30s, sitting in the front row, turned and waved as they sat down. John subtlety returned the acknowledgment with a brief nod of his head.

"That's Susan Geraghty," Mary said excitedly. "How do you know her, John?"

"I should be asking you the same question, Mary, "John replied, surprised.

A voice interrupted their conversation.

"ALL STAND!" Judge Lavin entered the chamber.

A uniformed DMP policeman, standing next to the main door, also discretely nodded towards John, as everyone obeyed the instruction to stand. Mary had mixed emotions on seeing Judge Lavin again. He had not changed at all. He was still dressed in the same faded red gown and dull ancient wig of the old British justice system. Everyone sat down. The Clerk read out the details of the case.

"The Plaintiff, Sir Anthony Worthington MBE, who purchased 200 acres of land from the State, is taking action against the defendant, Mr Noel Morris, for illegally squatting on 20 acres of this land. Sir Anthony seeks permission from this court to have him lawfully removed. He also seeks to recuperate 2 years of rent arrears from Mr Morris."

"How does your client plead?" Lavin asked, unethically banging his gavel, giving everyone the impression, he wanted to finish the case as quickly. "My Client, Noel Morris, does not make a plea, your Honour," the defendant's solicitor replied, loudly. "Mr Morris believes he will not get a fair trial here today, given that you, Andrew Michael Lavin, are the presiding Judge.

"What! What! How dare you!" Lavin screamed.

"Officer, remove this man from my Court, now!" He bellowed at the DMP officer, briefly wondering why there were DMP officers present, rather than anyone from the newly formed, Garda Siochana.

"That is not going to happen, your Honour," a senior Detective from Dublin Castle said, as he stood up in the front row. "Let the defence finish."

"Who are you?" Lavin demanded, pointing his gavel at the Detective.

The defendant's solicitor interrupted, before the detective could reply.

"My client, in the presence of his wife, handed to you, in your office, a legal document which proved that he is the rightful owner of the 20 acres of land, four weeks ago. Is this not correct, you're Honour?"

"I am not on trial here. This is my Court, and I will not answer to anyone," Lavin spurted, angrily. "I demand you all leave, before I charge everyone present with Contempt of Court. I find the defendant guilty and rule in favour of the Plaintiff. Now move on to the next case."

He banged his gavel, in a feeble attempt to administer his authority, hoping, in vain, that everyone would accept it and move on.

"Overruled," a voice said loudly, as another gowned Judge lavishly entered the Court Room, surrounded by four more DMP officers.

"What's going on here? Who are you? Lavin demanded.

"My name is James Geoghegan I represent the Department of Justice and Reform, and I hereby take full control of this Court and its proceedings. You are relieved of your duty and position, Mr Lavin. Please continue," he instructed the Defendant's Solicitor, as he and the police surrounded the speechless, Lavin.

"The document, to which I refer, proves that the 12th Earl of Cork presented the disputed land to my client, Mr Noel Morris, as a reward for saving his 8-year-old son from drowning, during a fishing accident in 1902. You officially stated, last week, that you were never presented with such a document. However, not only has the document been recovered, but, correspondence, signed by Sir Anthony Worthington, M...B...E..," the Barrister deliberately highlighted each letter, holding the letter aloft. "This letter promises you, Mr Lavin, the sum of 1,000 pounds, if the case is ruled in his favour." "Those documents were in my office! How did you get them?" Lavin bellowed, still believing himself immune to the authority of the land. He glanced around the room and caught sight of Susan Geraghty. He shouted, pointing at her with his gavel.

"You! You did this, you, Bitch!"

Judge Geoghegan, placed his hand on the gavel, and took it from Lavin.

"It's over, Lavin."

He turned towards the DMP Sergeant.

"Sergeant, arrest this man on the charge of Perverting the Course of Justice, and arrest Mr Worthington, for attempting to bribe a State Judge. Take them both away."

Worthington had the sense to remain silent throughout, but Lavin refused to go quietly. He had to be dragged from Court, shouting and screaming, to tremendous applause from the gallery.

"I am a Judge. I was a Judge before you bastards took over this God-forsaken Country. I know people and I will have you all locked up for this. Imbeciles! Idiots! Fools! You think you know the law, you know nothing. Do you hear me? You know nothing! I will watch as you are all thrown into jail for this, you ignorant halfwits."

He could still be heard screaming obscenities in the courtyard, outside.

"By the power invested in me by the Irish Free State Government, I hereby rule that the case against Mr Morris is dismissed, on the grounds that he is the lawful owner of the land. All costs are to be paid by the Plaintiff. This courtroom is suspended until next week.," Judge Geoghegan pronounced.

On the journey down, John had said that he had a surprise for Mary regarding Lavin, but this was totally unexpected. Mary recovered her power of speech.

"I have got to speak with Lavin before they take him away," she stammered.

"No problem," John beckoning the Detective.

The Garda Detective led the trio into an enclosed courtyard. Here, a wagon was parked, the rear door open. Inside, a rather subdued Lavin, sat handcuffed between two huge DMP Officers.

As they entered the yard, Mary noticed the Crown Coat of Arms, removed from the Court Room some years earlier. It was leaning against a wall in a dilapidated state, its once-colourful paint peeling and its wood splitting from long exposure to the elements. It reminded her of old figureheads on the abandoned schooners in the Arklow River. She also noticed Lavin's wig lying on the ground, amidst struggle marks on the surface gravel. She picked it up and approached the back doors of the wagon. She fondled the wig while staring at Lavin. He was still wearing his red gown but looked so different without the wig, a bald, sly, angry-looking man who, unexpectedly, asked her a question.

"What business do you have here, child?"

Mary overcome by fear diverted her stare to the inside of the faded wig. She could not believe what was sewn onto the silver, embossed label,

'Kings of Bond Street, London'.

Mary took this as a sign, fear replaced by anger.

"Do you remember me?

"Should I?" he replied."

"Yes. You found me guilty for assisting with the murder of my fiancée. You lied, when you told the Court that his family, were contacted in England."

He looked at her with a puzzled frown, and then suddenly recounted the incident.

"Ah yes. The Freeny girl from Arklow. I sentenced you to 25 years hard labour. How are you out?" "Freeny? I was not his girl, Mr Lavin," Mary said, "He was the man whom you helped to frame me, ensuring my incarceration, regardless of the evidence that was available to prove my innocence."

"Innocent! Everyone's innocent until proven otherwise. I found you guilty, because you were, and that's that," Lavin said, avoiding eye contact.

"I was guilty was I? Like Mr Morris was guilty in today's debacle, I suppose?"

Lavin looked at her with an inquisitive frown.

"Have you anything to do with this affair?"

"No. You, have done that all by yourself."

"Are you with that confounded woman, Geraghty?"

"Perhaps," she replied, with confidence. "Take him away, Detective," she said

"You little Bitch!" He screamed.

"Fenian bitch, please," she replied, slamming the doors of the wagon.

Susan Geraghty appeared.

"Well, hello Stranger," she said to Mary, a broad smile on her face.

"Oh, Susan. It really is you? I've missed you so much," Mary said, as they embraced. When they finally separated, Commandant, Mills thanked Susan.

"Susan, I don't want to know how you got those papers, but thank you."

"All men have their weaknesses, John," Susan said smiling.

"By the way, how do you know Mary? " He asked, as he stood back.

"We shared a cell in Holloway Prison," Susan replied.

"Yes, we did, and Susan kept me safe there," Mary said, quietly staring at the abandoned Royal Coat of Arms and reminiscing on her own Court Case.

"Come now, let's all go back to the hotel restaurant and catch up over lunch," Silvia suggested, noticing that Mary was becoming melancholic.

"That's a wonderful idea," Mary said, placing Lavin's wig on top of the unicorn, before turning to leave with the others.

As the small group left the courtyard, the wig fell to the ground, landing upside down and exposing the Kings of Bond Street label to the elements, where it unceremoniously lay, awaiting the same fate as the Royal Coat of Arms.

Three months later, Commandant Mills approached Mary's desk.

"Mary, I have every friend in every department looking for Alan Freeny and they have uncovered absolutely nothing. It looks like he may have gone back to England in 1921. He has simply disappeared."

"Thank you for trying, John. I really appreciate it. We'll just have to wait. If he's still in Ireland, his name may yet turn up."

"Let's hope so," John said, walking away. Suddenly he stopped and turned back.

"Your friend in the Home Office in England? Could he dig up something?"

"What an excellent idea," Mary said. "I'll copy all the information we have and post it to him, and hopefully he'll come up with some answers."

"Great. I'll ask Silvia to help," John said.

The following Saturday morning, Mary was standing at the post box, outside the old Kynoch Stores. The shop, on Ferrybank, was still open, and privately run by a Mr Sweeney. She recalled standing at this very spot once with Myles, as he explained what the crest meant, sandwiched between the letters G.R on the red-letter box, before he posted some letters home.

"So, Captain Fox, If G.R. stands for George Rex what does V.R. mean? Mary had asked, cheekily.

"That's Victoria Regina, Mary, the Kings Grandmother. My word, thinking about it, we are in this country a long time."

"Well, not for much longer, Captain," Mary had replied, laughing.

"Why, you little Rebel rascal," Myles had said, as he tried to pinch her hips, chasing her up the steps to the shop.

"Your messages are ready, Mary," Mr Sweeny said from the shop doorway. Mary was snapped back to the present by the interruption. She smiled and acknowledged Mr Sweeney with a wave.

She turned to the post box and quietly whispered, whilst running her hand across the G.R. crest, now painted over with bright green paint.

"Myles, I miss you so much. You seem to be everywhere."

She posted the letter to Percy containing all the information she had on Freeny.

"Just coming, Mr Sweeney," she said, and ran up the steps, pretending Myles was behind her, trying to pinch her hips.

One warm, bright, Friday morning in June, Mary planned to leave for home, early. She was quietly working when the door opened and Susan Geraghty burst in, large as life, brandishing three newspapers, and shouting excitedly.

"Mary, Mary, you have got to see this!" She threw the newspapers onto her desk, knocking some documents onto the floor.

"Oh Susan. Now look what you've done," Mary scolded her friend as she got up to recover the fallen papers.

"Never mind that. Read these headlines."

Curiosity got the better of them all. John and Silvia joined them, taking a newspaper each. The headlines said that Judge Andrew Michael Lavin had been found guilty on five counts of Fraud, three counts of Perverting the Course of Justice, and six of Criminal Behaviour, all during his short stint as a Judge in the new Irish Free State. Further investigations into other cases that he had presided over during British rule, meant that he had now received a sentence of 10 years, to be served immediately.

"Well Mary. That is one of your Ghosts put to rest," Silvia said smiling.

"Yes, that's true, but I don't feel any sense of pleasure. It's more akin to remorse, as it shouldn't have happened in the first place."

"True," John said." But think what further damage he could have done if he had been left in power."

"Oh shut up, both of you! This is a great day for Ireland and its future. It will warn any other skulking rats that they're not safe, even if their job is held in high esteem, and that goes for you too, John Mills. So never get above you station!" Susan said laughing.

"You're quite something, Susan Geraghty. How on earth did you put up with her in prison, Mary?"

"I never did tell you about how Susan and I met, did I. When I first arrived in Holloway, I was put with a group of four women. Two were 17-year olds from London and lifelong friends. The other was Susan Geraghty, who, apparently, had been in Holloway twice before."

Mary smiled at Susan and received a wicked grin in return.

"We got on well from the start, and stuck together. Poverty had forced the London girls into prostitution, and they had stolen extra money from a client, whilst he was sleeping. It turned out that he was a well-connected Statesman, and it was not long before both girls were apprehended, receiving 2 years each. We were forced to strip naked and shower in front of two male guards. We were given prison uniforms and put in separate cells. The next morning, the two friends were crying, uncontrollably. I took it that it was because of the situation, and they never said anything throughout the day. That night we were put back into our cells. I soon found out why those girls were crying, as this time, it was our turn. The two guards came to our cell. One insisted I accompany him to the Watch Room whilst the other was going to stay with Susan. As I was forcefully being led away, Susan shouted at the guards".

"Gentlemen! That young lady, as you well know, is a member of Cumann Na mBan, as am I, and I can guarantee you, that whatever you do to her tonight or in the future, will be repeated on the female occupants of No 1 Argyle Road, London, and 124 Covent Garden, London. Do I make myself clear?"

"The guard holding me, released his grip, stormed back into the cell, and violently grabbed Susan by the throat, pinning her to the wall. He ripped open her prison uniform with his free hand."

" I can do anything I want, to you, Bitch, even kill you."

"Susan replied confidently, albeit with restricted breath," As I said... whatever you do to me.... Or Miss Bradford, will be

214

repeated....On Louise.....whom, I believe is......named after your mother..... And your youngest Eliza.... will not be safe either."

"He released his hold and threw Susan to the floor."

"Let's leave these lesbian bitches alone," he said to his accomplice. Susan stood up, fastened her top, and said, "Fenian bitches! Get it right, David."

"He completely ignored her and left, leaving the cell door open. We never had any more trouble from either of them again, and they were soon moved on, but I will never, ever forget that first week."

"God! How must you both have felt?" Silvia asked.

"I'm so sorry, but at least you had each other for support," John said.

"Sadly, Susan wasn't there all the time, but she gave me the strength to survive after her release."

"We women have to stick together," Susan said," and, look on the bright side, I make a wonderful friend."

"Yes, and on that note, what are your plans for the weekend?" Mary asked, changing the subject. "I'm going home to Arklow and would love your company."

"That sounds wonderful. I would love to spend time by the sea. I'll be back in an hour," Susan said, delighted as she left the office to pack her bag. An hour later, both women were sitting on the train, excitedly making plans for the weekend ahead.

Detective Freeny

A few months later, due to the quantity and quality of the information they had accumulated on the activities of the IRA during the Anglo-Irish War, Mary's department was asked to assist with authenticating claims for compensation made by Companies and small Businesses that had been forced to cease trading with the British Government, by the IRA. Some businesses had not survived as alternative sources of income could not be found.

One unusual claim caught Mary's attention. It came from Hammond Lane, the company that was dismantling the Kynoch explosive factory. They were claiming for losses because they were forced to cease dismantling the factory from 1920 to 1922, by the IRA. The IRA were acting on the suggestion of Arthur Griffith, the then Minister of Home Affairs in the newly elected 1919 Dial. He believed the factory could be re-opened when the Anglo-Irish War ended. Unfortunately, Griffith died during the Civil War, and his suggestion was never followed up.

As she assisted on this case, Freeny's name came up twice, suggesting to Mary that he might still be in the country. On both occasions, the evidence was in the form of letters, sent by Freeny to the company, insisting they comply with the original instructions to render the factory incapable of producing explosives again. Freeny had signed both letters as a representative of his Majesty's Government. This confused her as these letters were posted in July 1923, well after the Anglo-Irish War, and used over-printed Irish Free State stamps.

One-week later, Mary was casually comparing the new and colourful Irish stamps on her daily post, against the over-printed English stamps, the Irish Free State had first used. The words "Rialta Sealadac na Heireann 1922" (Free State Ireland 1922) were printed in black across the King's head. Suddenly she noticed that one of the English stamps was not over-printed – it was a letter from Percy. She opened it immediately, excited to find an abundance of information and photographs about Mr Alan Freeny,

On receiving Mary's request, Percy was delighted to assist, having never forgotten the large, evil man that had challenged him on the night of Mary's arrest, always suspecting he had something to do with his rapid transfer to Egypt.

Mary spread the documents and photos across her desk. The information went back before 1900, but, unusually, all records on Freeny stopped in 1922. It was like he had vanished. She called John and Silvia over to share her excitement. John saw the photographs and was shocked into silence. The colour drained from his face as he picked one up.

"What the hell does this evil bastard, Alan Dillon, have to do with Alan Freeny?"

"That is Alan Freeny, John. Who's Alan Dillon?" Mary asked with surprise.

"This isn't Freeny. It's Alan Dillon, from the CID. I should know. John said feeling frustruated.

"Tis no wonder we could not find him if he is using an alias" Silvia said, while studying a photograph.

"He's one of the original members of the Criminal Investigation Department, set up by Collins. No one knows where he came from. He just arrived with the department, back in '22, at the start of the Civil War. He was a ruthless bastard. I reckon he is personally responsible for up to 10 republican deaths. He hated your lot and still does."

"What do you mean by 'my lot', John? And, more to the point, you said 'still does'?" Mary asked, turning to face John.

"Women... and especially the Cumann Na mBan."

"Where is he now?" Silvia asked.

"He's a member of the new Garda Special Branch."

"You seem to know a lot about him? Mary said."

217

"This one Mary…." John said, shaking with anger, "This one, I will get great pleasure in taking down, regardless of Collin's order against reprisals for atrocities committed during the War. This excuse for a human being is both a murderer and a misogynist."

"It sounds very personal, John," Silvia said.

"It is, Silvia. It's very personal."

"How's you know so much about him?" Silvia asked.

"Because when you meet the Devil, you never forget," John said as he slumped down beside Mary. "Mary, you have your demons, as did your Fiancée, but this bastard…. This bastard is one of mine."

"What happened, John? "Mary asked gently, recognising the all too familiar vacant stare signifying past trauma.

John composed himself in the chair and stated.

"Back in 1922, my Brigade amalgamated with other Dublin Brigades, to form the Dublin Guard. Our duties were mostly ceremonial, officially taking over the Dublin Army Barracks and Government buildings from the British. To look the part, we were issued with dark green uniforms, with brown leather webbing. When the National Army expanded, the new troops wore dyed British uniforms, but we kept our green uniforms, which made us stand out."

"The takeover was going to plan across the country, but, the dubious conditions of the Treaty created a divide that soon escalated. There was much unrest, and that divide soon became an unbridgeable rift, with the creation of two formidable forces - the Pro- and Anti- Treaty Forces."

"Civil War was looming. Anti-Treaty forces took over the Four Courts, here in Dublin, and when the British Government forced the Irish National Army to fire on them, the powder keg was ignited, throwing the whole country into a brutal and unwanted Civil War. Months later, when Dublin was finally secured, the Dublin Guard focused its attention on the rest of the country, assisting with taking back the British Barracks and Coastguard Stations that were occupied by Anti-treaty supporters. It was a disaster as many Rebels set fire to those buildings, before disappearing."

"That happened in Arklow," Mary interrupted.

"And in Cork," Silvia said, as she sat down.

"They did it everywhere. Once the major towns were secure, the conflict moved into the countryside. It became a War of Attrition, with horrible atrocities committed by both sides. The worst were committed by the National Army, or Free State Army, as we were called, although I preferred this name to the nickname, 'Green and Tans' that we were giving."

"Flushing out the rebels from the countryside was not an easy task, and, ironically, gave us a taste of what the British had to put up with!" John gave a humourless laugh.

"During one of these exercises in County Kerry, I first met Alan Dillon or Alan Freeny as you know him. It was a beautiful, autumn morning - one of those mornings where the sky is a radiant blue. It was chilly, but not too cold. We had separated into two columns to apply a pincer movement on a strategic bridgehead, leading into Tralee. We had been informed that the IRA planned to blow it up."

"My men and I approached the ancient, stone bridge from one side while a Captain O'Connor approached from the other. My men formed two sections, walking on both sides of the road. As we neared our goal, we could see that the other column, led by Captain O'Connor, had already surprised and captured five rebels, without discharging a single shot. The rebels had been caught in the act of planting a large land mine, on our side of the bridge. Under the orders of Captain O'Connor, these five men had been stripped of their arms and tied to the land mine. Their weapons lay in a heap by the side of the road. Sentries had been posted."

"We cautiously approached the scene. The prisoners looked dirty and hungry. Captain O'Connor was fussing with a plunger detonator, still attached to the mine. I walked over to discuss our course of action."

"I'll be with you in a minute, Captain," he said, as he, and a civilian, inspected the detonator. As I waited, I looked at the pile of captured weapons. A British army cap badge, embossed on the butt of a rifle caught my attention. It was common practise for members of the Cork Flying Columns to personalise captured rifles with insignia, taken from the previous owner. I had just picked up this rifle to study the badge, when a loud shout, in an English accent, interrupted me. It was directed at two of my men, who had recognised an old comrade, tied to the land mine, and were trying to untie him."

"Get your men back, Captain," the voice roared again, this time, directed at me.

"What the hell's going on?" I asked, walking towards the Englishman and O'Connor.

"Your men are attempting to free the prisoners, control them, or I will!" The English civilian shouted.

"Get away from the Prisoners, lads," I ordered as I passed the pit containing the mine and the anti-treaty rebels. "Who the hell are you?" I asked, feeling angry at this large, dangerous-looking Englishman.

"This is Alan Dillon, CID," O'Connor replied, struggling with the detonator.

"It was then that I noticed that the detonator cords were still attached to the plunger, and I was suddenly suspicious of their intentions.

"I hope you're not intending to blow these men up, O'Connor. They're former comrades, for God's sake. I won't allow it. I'll stop you by force if I have to."

"Shut up, Captain. These are not men; they're murdering criminals that deserve to die in the same manner they had planned for us. Only last week, this bunch murdered five local soldiers with a similar bomb, and attacked a supply truck, murdering the two occupants' as they attempted to surrender. Don't tell us they deserve to live, Captain." Dillon stated.

"I drew my pistol and pointed it directly at Dillon."

"I will not allow the National Army to lower themselves to the same level as your bloody Tans. Now step back, Mr Dillon."

"What are you going to do, Captain? Start a Civil War within a Civil War?" Dillon replied, grinning.

"Lower that pistol, and get your men out of here," Dillon ordered, as he indicated O'Connor and his men, pointing their rifles and pistols at me.

"Look here, John." O Connor said, lowering his pistol. "We're not going to blow them up. It's just scare tactics. I'll untie one to defuse the mine," he jumped into the pit and untied one of the prisoners, who stood up and rubbed his wrists.

"Now, get your men well back, in case there's an accident," he said, walking quickly back towards the bridge, closely followed by Dillon.

Suddenly, one of my NCO's shouted.

"Move back, Move back! As he directed our truck and men back down the road.

I decided to assist and had caught up with him when suddenly there was an unmercifully loud explosion. The ground behind us belched up a large wave of soil and stones, followed by a vicious-looking plume of dark, orange flame and thick black smoke that mixed together as it mushroomed high into the morning sky. The directing soldier was knocked face down onto the road, whilst the rest dived for cover in the nearby ditches. This deafening explosion and accompanying wave of heat, was followed by a roaring silence that raped our ringing ears.

221

The damp, iridescent leaves that were stripped from nearby trees now filled the silent blue sky, twinkling in the bright morning sunlight, as they slowly floated back down to earth like autumnal confetti. It was beautiful, in a macabre way.

Suddenly, without warning, soldiers from the groups that had dived for cover, jumped up and, leaving their rifles and equipment, ran, hard and fast past me, and down the country road. They stopped, about 200 yards away from the blast site. As they caught their breath, they turned and looked towards me.

I felt a sprinkle of rain on my face. That's funny, I thought, looking up at the clear blue sky. Then I felt it again, and heard a splat on the bonnet of the nearby truck. Instantly, the other men got up and ran. Most were covered in sprinkles of red, which looked like blood. I wiped the rain from my face. It was also red. I suddenly realised what had happened. When a human hand landed near my foot, I too ran, and joined the first wave of fleeing soldiers, all of whom, it turned out, were experienced veterans from France.

It felt like hours before we regrouped and dared to venture close to the destructive scene. A massive hole replaced the site where the men had been tied. Dillon appeared, also splattered with red specks.

"Well Captain, that's how to deal with criminals," he said, pointing to two red and black, smouldering human torsos, lying on the edge of the crater. The remains had been stripped of anything that once resembled a human being. I felt sick. I wanted to shoot him, on the spot, and would have done, had I my pistol to hand.

The eerie silence was slowly replaced by the sound of arriving carrion, bickering with each other as they picked at the human remains strewn across the naked trees. O'Connor approached, pleased with himself, and ready to justify his actions.

"I know you're angry John, but this is the only way to deal with these bastards. Earlier I received direct orders from Kevin O' Higgins, the Minister of Justice, to deal with these insurgents in this manner."

"Justice! You call that justice. That was cold-blooded murder," I screamed at him. "Those men were our Comrades, our fellow countrymen, for God's sake. You lied to me O'Connor and you will regret what you've done here. That I promise you"

"Are you threating me, Mills?" O'Connor asked angrily.

Dillon interrupted. "Oh, I don't think the good Captain here would threaten you Captain O'Connor. How could he, when all you are doing is administering the law and following direct orders. The only one to suffer regret will be you and your men, Captain Mills, for failing to follow orders." His lips narrowed, and he leaned into my face, his cold eyes upon me. "Now, I advise you to take yourself and your men and go back to Tralee. Get yourselves a drink and spend the night congratulating yourselves on a job well done."

At that, he smugly turned and walked away.

"Take your truck back to the Barracks. You'll find some coffins stored there. I'll get my men to collect up the remains," O'Connor said.

It was too late and pointless to argue. I turned and walked away. As I left, I noticed the rifle with the embossed cap badge lying half buried in the side of the crater. Ironically, the badge was a skull and crossed bones, with the motto "Or Glory" on it. This isn't glory, I thought to myself, as we left that awful scene of destruction.

That evening, it seemed the entire population of Kerry had gathered outside the Barracks, demanding justice. It was worse than anything the British had done during the entire conflict. Those people never got the justice they sought that night. Neither of the two men responsible was ever punished. No matter how much I tried, I was blocked by the Minister of Justice, Kevin O'Higgins. He, Dillon, and people like them, are responsible for the deaths of 77 Republican prisoners during the entire Civil War."

John finished. Staring into space, he fumbled with the photo. Silvia collected a glass of water from the kitchen and passed it to him. He drank thirstily.

"Mary, we can't rush into this. We've got to get it right, no matter how long it takes. This... this .... Bastard, will have powerful allies. Remember, 'those that wait are well-rewarded'," he said, as he threw the photo back onto Mary's desk.

It was in June 1926, almost two years later, when Mary and John were satisfied they had gathered enough damning information to confront Alan Freeny/Dillon, and secure an arrest. Mary was horrified at what this terrible man had done. He was personally responsible for the deaths of 50 men and women in both England and Ireland.

He was born in the East End of London in 1890, as Anthony Littlejohn, to a prostitute mother and unknown father. He grew up in a world of violence, witnessing brutal robberies and murder on the streets of London, as well as savage beatings inflicted on his mother by vicious clients, all of which conspired to create the sadistic psychopath that he truly was.

At just 16 years old, he found himself alone in a room with his only friend, Tracy Hicks, an attractive 16 year old, with well-groomed, blonde hair, and the daughter of another prostitute. They had grown up together, always sharing the little they had. They were sitting together on the bed their mothers' used to entertain customers. Tracy's ambition in life was to become a journalist and get out of 'this vicious circle of hell', as she described it, for she feared that she too would end up following her mother's example.

Tracy was practicing her writing. She had an open copy book on her lap, and often spoke of her ambition to eventually work for a newspaper.

Littlejohn stared at her, lustfully imagining what she would look like naked. Unable to contain his desires any longer, he silently removed a small, leather cosh from its hiding place beneath the bed, used by his mother for defence against abusive clients. He slowly raised the cosh behind Tracy, and smacked her hard across the head, knocking her out cold. She slumped to the floor, her pencils and books falling around her. He quickly checked her eyes before lifting her unconscious body onto the bed. He raped her, a number of times, before she regained consciousness.

When their mothers' returned, they found him sitting on the bed beside the now fully-conscious, and clearly upset, Tracy, behaving as if nothing had happened. Tracy ran to her mother's side, explaining what he had done. A fight ensured. The women stripped Littlejohn and threw him out onto the street, an act reserved for the most abusive clients.

Later that night, Littlejohn crept back into the tenement and callously murdered both women, whilst they slept. He raped Tracy again, stabbing her multiple times, and leaving her for dead. Somehow she survived. He was apprehended a week later by the London Police, and interviewed by a civilian about the callous murders. The civilian was both shocked and impressed by his complete lack of empathy, but what astonished him more, was that Littlejohn displayed no feelings of remorse given that his victims were family, and all women

This man worked for the London Criminal Investigation Division (CID). He felt that an emotionless man like Littlejohn could be of great value to him. His attitude to women would be particularly useful in investigating militant organisations like the subversive National Union of Women's Suffrage Society (NUWSS), formed three years earlier and causing untold damage, with demonstrations and fires across the city. Following a discussion with his Superiors, this man persuaded CID to take temporary custody of Littlejohn, recruiting him, under strict conditions, to investigate certain members of this new movement.

They made him an offer to either work for CID or be hung for murder. The simplicity of the offer gave Littlejohn no choice but to opt for the CID.

Littlejohn used his experience of living on the streets to carry out this task, his actions soon leading to a number of high-profile convictions. CID were impressed and kept their word in not pursuing his conviction, dismissing the women as a couple of unwanted prostitutes that no-one would miss. They lied to Tracy, telling her that Littlejohn had perished, attempting to swim across the Thames. A body was identified, and the case was abruptly closed.

CID now employed Littlejohn on a full time basis, giving him a new name and identity. He became Detective Alan Freeny, and, within four years, at the age of just 20, he acquired an office at New Scotland Yard and two assistants. He quickly rose to the rank of Detective Chief Superintendent. His reputation for ruthlessness was legendary, especially in extracting information from women, with some dying in his custody.

In 1914, his department came under extreme pressure to explain the death of a wealthy woman, the wife of a French aristocrat. Freeny was implemented and forced to take the offer of a temporary transfer to Dublin, assisting Dublin Castle in eradicating the newly founded organisations, Cumann Na mBan and the Irish Volunteers. He soon settled in and one again, conducted this task with ruthless efficiency.

When the Anglo Irish War ended, and the Civil War started, the Irish Ministry for Home Affairs created their own Criminal Investigation Department (CID), with Head Quarters at Oriel House, Dublin. Their task was to identify men and woman of the irregular forces, who continued to act in a subversive way, engaging in hostilities against the new Government.

Still unable to return to London, Freeny offered his services to the new Irish CID. His past loyalties were conveniently ignored by his old enemies. He soon proved, once again, his efficiency in intelligence work and unique ability in eradicating, these irregulars.

Following many successful arrests of high-ranking members of the Anti-Treaty forces, the Minister for Home Affairs issued Freeny a permanent position, and a new identity – he became Detective Alan Dillon.

It was not long before Dillon's reputation preceded him. He was infamous for his brutal interrogation techniques and merciless assassinations in the field, both male and female suspected Republicans. His actions became more ruthless as the Civil War progressed. As it ended in May 1923, Oriel House was disbanded in the October with most of its high profile members transferring to the Dublin Metropolitan Police (DMP). That organisation, in turn, became the Garda Special Branch when the DMP amalgamated with the new Garda Síochána in April 1925.

Mary, with Percy's help, had collected a considerable amount of damming evidence against Freeny when he worked for the British, both in London and Ireland. There was one British, and four Irish atrocities, committed by Freeny, that could be classed as cold-blooded murder, not extra judicial killings.

The British case was that of Lady Constance Bowman, the English wife of a famous French Aristocrat, murdered on a visit to London. She had left her Chelsea hotel to meet with friends, but never arrived. Her half naked and battered body was found in a side street the next day, near Chelsea Bridge. Freeny and his two cohorts were major suspects - on that same day, they had arrested a number of Suffragettes that had held a demonstration against the King as he opened a new tram line across the bridge. A number of people witnessed Freeny chase a small group of woman down side streets, issuing merciless beatings with a cosh. Although Lady Bowman was not involved in the Suffragette movement, her body was found nearby. On her body were similar marks to those on the girls that had survived Freeny's beatings. Rumours were rife that he

227

was responsible for her death, deliberately staging it to look like a robbery. Under severe pressure from Parliament, CID transferred Freeny to Ireland, with immediate effect.

Whilst Percy was collecting evidence and eye witness accounts against Freeny in England, Mary had located witnesses associated with the four Irish cases. They were willing to come forward and testify. In reading over the evidence, she came to realise how lucky she was to have survived her encounter with this man – if he was involved in an interrogation, the women did not survive. Their battered and naked bodies found nearby, a few days later.

Of the four Irish cases, one bothered Mary more than the others. This was the murder of two sisters, both genuine members of Cumann Na Ban who were arrested a few days after her trail. They were both in their late twenties, and, supposedly, died whilst trying to escape from the back of a moving truck, as they were escorted to Dublin, by British soldiers. One of those soldiers later married an Irish woman, and had remained in Ireland. He had given a statement and was willing to testify.

Mary read the soldier's statement again, as she had, many times.

We arrested six women during a raid on a Wexford office that printed and issued propaganda leaflets and newspapers. Freeny instructed that these women be transported immediately to Dublin in pairs between three trucks. I was in the centre truck with Freeny and five other soldiers. We were sitting opposite each other in groups of three, next to the tailboard when the convoy set out. We were on full alert for ambushes as we were on the back roads. The two girls were in their late twenties and were quite obviously sisters. Both were pretty and wore short dresses and white blouse, as we did not allow them to return to the office to collect coats. They sat in the centre of the seat, opposite me, holding each other's hands and staring ahead. Freeny was sitting sideways, forward of them, sifting through photographs and papers taken during the raid.

He suddenly jumped up and thrust one of the photos in the girls' faces, shouting, "IS THIS MICHAEL COLLINS?"

They did not reply and continued to stare ahead. This made him angry. He removed a small leather cosh from his pocket and struck them both across their faces.

"Look at the picture. You pair of Fenian BITCHES!"

One soldier objected, saying, "they're only girls, leave 'em alone."

Freeny turned to reprimand the soldier, but lost his balance and fell over. One girl made a noise that Freeny took to be laughter, though neither girl actually laughed.

This infuriated him and he stood up, pulled the girl up by her arm, saying, "You think this is funny, well laugh at this." With that, he flung her out over the tail board. It happened so fast that we could do nothing. The other soldiers jumped up and rushed to the back of the truck and saw the woman bounce along the road .The driver of the truck behind swerved to avoid hitting her, but failed, causing him to crash into a ditch. Two soldiers' threw up, as the rest of us turned to confront Freeny, who was now holding the other woman, like a rag doll, in front of his large frame. He had both her arms pinned behind her back. "Now lads, don't be rash," he said grinning, quickly manoeuvring himself to one side of us, and then, just as suddenly, he pushed her out too. Someone shouted "NOOO", as she tumbled head first over the tail board. She managed to catch it, and was hanging on for dear life. Before anyone could comprehend what had just happened, Freeny lashed out with his foot, smashing it into her face. She fell backwards, to her death.

"No witnesses, boys," Freeny said.

One of the other soldiers, who could no longer contain his anger, smashed the butt of his rifle into Freeny's face, rendering him unconscious. We recovered the women's bodies and brought them to Portobello Barracks in Dublin. We all made complaints *and statements about what had happened, but, a few weeks later, we were told there would be no further investigation and that we would be court-martialled if we ever mentioned it again. It has haunted me ever since."*

On Tuesday morning, the 6th of April 1926, Mary removed a large red file from the cabinet. It was labelled, 'The Man with Three Names'. She placed it on her desk. Looking around the office, she nodded towards Commandant Mills as a sign that she was ready to proceed.

"Are we all ready? John asked, placing his hand on his desk phone. "When I make this call to Dillon/Freeny... there will be no going back."

Everyone nodded in agreement and took up their positions. John nodded to Mary as he lifted the receiver and phoned the Garda Special Branch, asking to speak with Alan Dillon. He felt a nervous energy flow through his veins, as he was put through.

"Garda Special Branch. Detective Dillon speaking," came the disembodied English accent from the other end of the phone line.

John explained who he was and why he was calling. He explained that their department were investigating a fraudulent pension claim which had resulted in the arrest of woman called Susan Geraghty, who, it turned out, was a known member of the subversive organisation, Cumann Na mBan. It was also a name flagged by Detective Dillon as a contact, in the event of her arrest.

"That woman is of no interest to me anymore," Dillon replied coldly.

"Fine. We're only following procedure. But, before I go, when I mentioned your name to her, she told us that you're not who you say you are. She claims you're actually Alan Freeny, an English CID Officer, still on the British payroll."

There was a short pause before Dillon answered.

"Hold her there. I'll be right over." He hung up.

John put down the receiver.

"He's taken the bait. It's now or never! Everyone ready?"

They took up their positions, anxiously awaiting Freeny's arrival.

Freeny arrived at the Office of Justice and Equality, his large frame intimidating. He was wearing a fedora hat and an open gabardine overcoat.

Mary recognised him immediately. She felt a dreadful fear course through her body as he entered the office. He had not changed, still emitting an authoritative and dangerous persona.

"Where's Geraghty? He demanded, with no preamble or introduction.

"I am here, Mr Freeny," Susan said, deliberately using his old name, waving mockingly from across the room. She was sitting on a chair in the corner, flanked by three Policemen.

"Take her and follow me," Dillon ordered, livid that she had used his old name.

"It doesn't work like that, Mr Dillon," Commandant Mills said, as he walked into the room from the Kitchen, and stood behind Mary, seated at her desk. Another man, standing beside Silvia's desk, spoke up.

"My name is John Moran, Superintendent of the Dublin Garda, Store Street Branch. I am here because we are investigating civil crimes against the people of Ireland, before, during, and after the Anglo-Irish War. I am arresting you for the murder of Anne and Niamh Carlisle. Also, for the cold-blooded murder of three men in Limerick, during the battle of Kilmallock, and the outrageous murder of two IRP members and their detainees in the village of Dunmanway, County Cork, on Thursday the 11th of November 1920. Have you anything to say?"

Freeny was stunned into silence by, what he regarded as absurd accusations. He hesitated for a moment, before exploding into heinous laughter, startling everyone.

"The IRP! Don't make me laugh, Moran. Were you a member of that bunch of idiots, parading around with armbands, pretending to be the RIC?"

Moran pressed on, determined that this evil man pay for his crimes.

"Yes I was a member. The Irish Republican Police were a legal organisation, founded by Arthur Griffith, the democratically elected Minister for Justice. That November morning, we arrested Mary Murphy, aged 16, and her brother John, aged 19, for stealing a cow from the Earl of Cork. As we were escorting the prisoners to the local Court House for trial, over 20 Tans' and Auxiliaries appeared, from nowhere, and blocked all exits to the square, detaining us and all locals present. You instructed us, pistol in hand, to knell down and face the two accused, already kneeling. I remember the fear on their young faces as they held each other and wept openly, trying to explain to you that the cow was theirs and that the Earl's men had taken it, by accident, from the wrong field. You paced up and down behind them, patiently listening, whilst inspecting your pistol, deliberately lulling them in to a false sense of security. When they finished, you callously shot each one in the back of the head, right in front of us all.

"Justice!" You shouted, "You came here to witness Justice? This is Justice, and you'll find yourselves on the receiving end if you continue to support these subversives"

You paused, and then went on to say, "Disgusting bitch," because you had walked in the blood, running from the girl's head wound. But the vilest thing that I have ever witnessed is what you did next. You kicked the girl over onto her back, flicked her shawl to one side with the barrel of your pistol, and deliberately wiped your bloody foot on her chest. You continued as if getting some perverse pleasure from it, only stopping when a local man, called you an "English Pervert".

You were about to pistol whip him, when I interrupted, telling you who we were and what we were doing. You smugly turned to the crowd and shouted out.

"IRA, IRB, now the IRP! Am I to suffer the entire Alphabet from these fools?"

You then shot me and my two comrades through the front of our heads. Afterwards, the Tans and Auxiliaries ran riot through the town, seriously injuring a number of civilians and destroying property. Thankfully, I survived," Moran said, brushing back his fringe to display an angry scar on the side of his head.

"Thank you for that trip down memory lane, now, Fuck Off, Moran, before I finish what I started in Cork. Did you ever hear such crap in all your life! The 'democratically elected Minister for Justice', the 'IRP' - if I wanted to hear a comedian, I would have gone to a show. I've enough to do without having to listen to these ridiculous statements. Hand over Geraghty so I can leave this fucking circus."

Moran calmly picked up the phone, and requested a car and more Officers.

"Bring as many as you want. Bring the whole fucking Irish Police Force. I'm not leaving without that shit-stirring bitch over there. Do you understand, Mr Moran?"

"Did you kill Lady Constance Bowman?" Mary asked, still fearful of Freeny.

"What did you say?" He asked, turning to Mary, his face purple with rage.

"Answer the question," John ordered angrily, noticing Mary becoming agitated.

"What the hell is going on here? Is this some sort of conspiracy?" Freeny asked, looking at all the faces around the room, before settling on John.

"I recognise you Mills. You' tried to save those rebels in Cork. The crows filled their bellies that day. Are you also going to arrest me for that, too?"

He stepped back to address the entire room.

"Listen, all of you, and listen carefully. Men like me are a necessary part of the system. We allow 'Civilised Society and Democracy' to function. We are the gears and cogs that run the parts of society that no-one wants to see, like the sewers beneath the streets or the slugs and cockroaches that deal with your rubbish. Have you ever admired an immaculately groomed horse, standing proudly on a lawn? Well, go to the back of the stables and see the piles of shit that the stable boys have to deal with. I do the same so that you can all live in your ideal civilised society."

He glared at them all, before continuing.

"Don't embarrass yourselves by trying to take the moral high ground. You cannot seek justice for what these cockroaches and stable boys have had to do to achieve your great Free State nation. The only noticeable change in this country will be the design on its stamps and coins. Behind the scenes, the same sewers will still operate; the same cockroaches will feast on your rubbish. The methods will remain - they are a necessary evil to keep your new, modern Ireland functioning. It will always be that way. Now, I have come for that Fenian Whore over there," he said, pointing towards Susan, "and I am not leaving without her. Do you all understand?"

Mary stood up.

"You're a murderer and defiler of women... "

"Oh, you've done your research," he interrupted, as he faced her again.

"The only way you're leaving here is in cuffs," she continued, feeling more confident. Freeny noticed. He stared intensely at her with dark, narrow eyes, leaning across her desk, attempting to intimidate her.

He suddenly straightened up, recognition dawning.

"I recognise you now, even with your clothes on. You're that Cumann Na mBan bitch from Arklow, who murdered a British Captain. A homosexual English officer rescued you from my interrogation that night, spoiling all my fun. Such a pity. I was so looking forward to having a few goes on you that evening. One consolation, I suppose, is that he didn't either, being queer and all. I wonder if he enjoyed his trip to Egypt."

Mary was surprised that he remembered her, or the events of that evening.

"Did the London prison guards finish what I started?

Mary was overwhelmed by memories of her imprisonment. They were always there, in the background, the driving force for her actions. Her face betrayed her thoughts.

"Oh I see," Freeny said, with a sinister smile, "It looks like they did."

Mary was about to lose her temper when the phone on John's desk started to ring. He walked over and answered it. When finished, he slammed down the receiver.

"That was Head Office. We cannot detain or arrest Freeny or Dillon or whatever the hell his name is," the Commandant said, as he walked back and stood behind Mary.

"Thank you Captain 'Coward'," Freeny said, sarcastically. "As I said before, 'I am the system'. I am the law and I answer to no-one. I could murder you all, and the only person I'd have to answer to would be ME."

Mary, supressing her anger, calmly spoke up.

"Would you murder us, like you murdered Lady Bowman?"

"Yes, I would," Freeny said coldly, feeling safe in the admission.

"That stupid bitch is the reason I ended up in this God-forsaken, shit-hole of a country. That fool got caught up in a raid. I did, for a minute, wonder if she was a Suffragette, and it turned out I was right. Talk about being in the wrong place at the wrong time," he said laughing.

"I remember her begging me to stop, in French, whilst I was having a go on her, from behind. Boy was she good. I'm sure, after your own encounters with those prison guards, you fully understand," he said, gyrating his hips.

"But, the bitch started swearing revenge, in English. She knew some very powerful figures who could cause me trouble, so I gave her a good beating with old faithful here, before strangling her," he said, displaying the cosh on the inside of his overcoat.

Once again, he horrified the entire room with his audacious honesty. His boasts clearly gave him a sense of power. He truly believed that he was unstoppable.

"Is that the same one you used on the Carlisle Sisters, before you threw them to their deaths?" Mary said, desperately trying to administer some form of justice to the monster that stood before her.

"Yes, as a matter of fact, it is. I would have used it on you that night as well. Listen to me, Bitch! Do you actually think I give a fuck about them? Or that French trollop, or any other whore that has ever crossed my path? I'm not just above the law, I am the law, and none of you will ever tell me what to do!"

"Would you murder all of us like you murdered Lillie Hicks, and Marsha Littlejohn, your own mother, Anthony?" An elegantly dressed English woman asked, as she entered the room from the kitchen.

Freeny turned, immediately recognising Tracy Hicks, despite the passage of time. He did not answer her, but slowly turned back and stared at Mary with the coldest look she had ever seen. His eyes narrowed to slits of pure rage, as he noticed a photo of his original CID handler, in the open file on Mary's desk. He picked it up, looked at it, and threw it back on the desk, his voice a forced whisper through clenched teeth.

"My you have been doing your research, Bitch!"

He pulled a small pistol from his overcoat, pointed it towards Mary and fired. Thankfully, John anticipated his actions, jumping in front of Mary and pushing her to the floor. The bullet hit him in his side. He staggered backwards and collapsed. Mary scuttled sideways, screaming with fright. She froze as Freeny aimed at her again, but distracted by Moran, he turned and fired at him instead, hitting him in the shoulder.

Suddenly, another loud explosion filled the room. Freeny turned towards the sound, and saw Silvia, pointing the Webley service revolver Mary had acquired from Norman Boland. He tried to aim at her, but she fired again. This time, the bullet slapped loudly into his chest. Freeny fell to his knees, dropping his pistol, staring in utter shock and disbelief at Silvia, before falling over, with a loud thump.

Susan Geraghty, who had remained seated throughout the whole episode, rose and went over to the dying Freeny, closely followed by Tracy Hicks.

Susan rolled Freeny onto his side, as Tracy approached.

"I did get out of the circle of hell and become a journalist, no thanks to you. I'll take this, as it belonged to my Mother," she said, removing the cosh from his pocket.

Freeny gargled, as the life drained from him.

Susan Geraghty stared into his eyes.

"What' is it like to die at the hands of a woman?"

He gargled again.

"Here, choke on this," she said, ramming a Cumann Na mBan pin in his mouth.

"That belonged to Anne Carlisle."

He spat out the badge, and finally managed to splutter out one word.

"Bitch."

"That's Fenian bitch, to you," she said, wiping the badge clean on his upper arm.

Freeny gargled a little, and then stopped breathing.

A Garda Officer checked for a pulse. On finding none, he announced his demise. The other Garda attended to the injured, whilst Silvia telephoned for an ambulance. Fortunately, neither of the men was seriously injured.

That evening, the women met in a restaurant. Susan raised her glass in salute.

"Tracy, you finally got justice. The world is a better place without him."

"Here, here," they all said, as they raised their glasses.

"Silvia! Congratulations on your outstanding marksmanship," Susan laughed

"It was nothing," Silvia replied modestly." All that training in the Boggeragh Mountains finally paid off."

"Boggeragh Mountains? You have such funny place names," Tracy said, before taking a sip of her drink.

"Try saying 'Dun Laoghaire'," Mary said, as the waiters brought over the food.

Two months later, Commandant Mills had just settled back into work, when the Minister of Justice, Kevin O'Higgins, and Garda Commissioner, Eoin O Duffy arrived, unannounced.

"Don't get up," the Minster said, as he watched John struggle to stand.

"Minister, Commissioner, what an unexpected surprise," John said.

"We're here about the Dillon business," O'Duffy interjected. "In future, if you have to investigate anyone associated with Oriel House, you will have to come directly to me, or the Minister's Office. Is that clear?"

"Yes, Commissioner, but .... "

The Minister interrupted John

238

"Commandant Mills, I will cut to the chase. There are skeletons in these cupboards. Details of which, the public is better off not knowing, for the safety of the State. We're not asking, but telling you, this does not go public. Do you understand?"

"Yes, loud and clear," the Commandant said.

"So, can you please explain to the Garda Commissioner, why you were carrying out unauthorised Police work?" The Minister continued.

This prompted Silvia to interject.

"We're not carrying out Police work, Minister. We're applying the recent orders from your office to involve the police in suspected fraudulent claims, as a warning to others. Your office ordered that anyone supporting subversive organisations or who fought on the Anti-Treaty side, during the Civil War will not, nor ever will be, entitled to a State Pension. Mr Dillon's name came up during an investigation, and we simply requested his assistance. Surprisingly, he accepted and arrived at this office post haste. Mary was working at her desk with the suspect claimant, who immediately recognised Mr Dillon as someone else, and challenged him. This led to an altercation, in which Mr Dillon tried to shoot everyone in the office. After he shot Commandant Mills, and the Garda Superintendent, he pointed his gun at me, leaving me with no choice but to defend myself, resulting in the untimely demise of Mr Dillon."

"That sounds very rehearsed," the Garda Commissioner said. "Who was this suspect?"

"A Miss Susan Geraghty," Silvia replied.

"Geraghty, that trouble-maker!" the Commissioner replied, rolling his eyes.

O'Higgins, standing at John's desk, turned to Silvia with anger and contempt.

"You're a woman. A bloody woman doing a man's job. You should be at home, minding children or waiting for your husband to return. What the hell were you doing with a gun? And how, in God's name, do you know how to use one?"

Infuriated, Mary stood up and before Silvia could reply, shouted at O'Higgins.

"Was it Man's work, in 1916, when you lot didn't mind women risking their lives to help ye? And was it Man's work, when those same women risked their lives, carrying arms and messages throughout the War, many of them killed or locked up in English jails? Not just great women, like Nora Connelly or the Gore-Booths, but the innocent woman, raped and murdered in retaliation for the skeletons you so formidably defend. Innocent woman like Eileen Quinn in Galway, a pregnant mother of three, gunned down by the Tans. Will you forget her? Will you forget them all? Are you going to change the constitution, written by better men than yourselves, omitting the part about women, are you, Minister...? Well...? Are you?"

The Minister turned to Mary and looked her up and down. She presented a formidable force, that he had no wish to challenge, but he still felt the same contempt for her that he felt for Silvia.

"Listen to me, young woman. The only thing those deluded fools left this nation, were a load of ridiculous ideas, that it will take years to remove from the minds of people, like you, who have got way above their station. The only place for a woman, is in her home, and what's wrong with that, pray tell?" He asked, shrugging at Eoin O Duffy, who nodded in agreement. "What more could a woman want, when she has her husband and the State to look after her?"

"I'll be sure to remind you of that when we need their help again," John replied.

"Just remember, this new State is built on skeletons, Commandant," O'Higgins said, turning to face John. "Some are exposed and some are hidden in cupboards. So I'm warning you all,

240

if something like this ever happens again, it will be your skeletons you'll need to worry about. Do I make myself clear?"

"Are you threating us, Minister O'Higgins? John said, forcing himself to stand.

"Yes, I am, Commandant," O'Higgins said, leaving with the Commissioner.

John did not have the energy to argue further.

"Let's hope that's the end of that," John said, easing himself back into his chair.

"Yes, and let's make no 'bones' about it," Mary replied laughing.

"What are you like, Mary Bradford?" Silvia asked, with a grin, closing the door.

John laughed.

"Put the kettle on while you're up, and don't get too comfortable in that kitchen, being a woman and all."

He had to duck for cover as Mary and Silvia retaliated with balls of   wastepaper

De Valera

For the next six years, Mary and the rest of the department, worked tirelessly on individual claims and collecting information on the Anglo-Irish and Civil War. Commandant Mills found a few individuals that he would have dearly loved to investigate, but knew there was little point as their crimes would be classed as extra–judicial or State-sanctioned killings. He felt this would be the case with O'Connor, and the landmine incident in Kerry. He was aware that O'Connor now worked as a town foreman, in a small Galway town, and often wondered if his family and friends were aware of his nefarious activities during the Civil War?

Late, one evening, he pondered over bringing the Webley pistol with him on official business, in a town close to where O'Connor worked. He stared at the large fearsome-looking revolver for a few moments.

"If you, Mary Bradford, can wait patiently for the right moment to present itself, then so can I." He closed the drawer, and walked towards the door. Before switching out the light, he paused and looked back at his desk, the memory of the atrocity still fresh. He glanced at both Silvia's and Mary's desks, thinking of them laughing.

"Another time, O'Connor, another time," he said to himself, as he left the room.

For many years, both he and Mary put aside their personal burdens, and focussed on finding a way around the law sanctioned by Cumana Na Gael, which prevented members of the Anti-Treaty forces claiming a pension, or compensation for death or serious injury during the Civil War.

Mary had not given up her quest for justice on those responsible for her incarceration; she simply had postponed it, waiting for the right time to strike. She had given up with John Boland though, knowing he was in Canada, and unlikely to return to Ireland.

Mary had reconciled with Boland's parents, and they moved forward with something akin to friendship. From them, Mary discovered that John was married and settled in Nova Scotia, and had no intention of returning to Ireland. She did, at one time, toy with the idea of going to Canada to confront him, but abandoned that idea, after an incident that occurred on the 12th anniversary of Myles' death.

Every year, on the anniversary of Myles' death, Mary and Mrs Boland tied a bunch of Arklow Rock primroses to railings, near the spot where he died. Mary could see the flowers whenever she left her house. This Saturday morning, she stepped out into glorious sunshine and glanced over at the flowers, just in time to see some boys rip them from the railings, and scatter them across the pavement. She lost her temper, stormed across the road, catching two 8-year olds by the arms, as the rest ran off.

"Why'd you do that, ya pair of curs." she screamed at the startled boys.

The group that ran off, stopped at a safe distance. The eldest shouted at Mary.

"Tommy-lover! Tommy-lover, Mary Bradford's a Tommy-lover".

Mary was horrified; and asked the two she held.

"Is that what you think? Who told you to do this?"

Suddenly the gang of boys scattered. Mary looked up to see the cause, and was greeted by the sight of Commandant Pat Kavanagh, walking towards her, holding the eldest boy by the scruff of the neck.

"Good Morning, Miss Bradford. I believe this one has something to say to you," Pat said, almost lifting the boy of the ground with one hand.

"Sorry, Misses Bradford," the boy stuttered.

One of the boys that Mary held started to sob, pointing at the older one…

"He made us do it Mr Kavanagh."

"Now boys, you're all going to pick up those flowers and put them back on the railings. And then, you're going to take turns minding them for the rest of the week. If I find they've been tampered with, I'll personally call around to your houses."

The boys quickly picked up the flowers and tied them back onto the railings. When they had finished, two of them saw a chance, and ran for their lives, leaving the youngest behind. He started to bawl, loudly.

Mary felt sorry for him. His Mother had obviously cut his hair, which was almost bald in patches. The toes of his shoes had gaping holes, his socks peeking out. He was wearing short pants, exposing cut knees and dirty legs. His jumper was a 'hand-me-down' and almost in rags, and his tears carved tracks down his dirty, freckly face.

Mary opened her purse and took out a sixpence. She looked carefully at the greyhound on the coin, suddenly remembering what Freeny had said about only the stamps and coins changing, and everything else remaining the same, especially the hatred and bitterness. She looked back at the child, and realised it was her own bitterness that had made her want to inflict pain and hurt on this poor wretch. And it was her bitterness that made her want to go to Canada to confront John Boland. She was horrified by this sudden realisation.

"What is your name, child?" She asked.

"Michael," the child blubbered, inhaling deeply between sobs.

"Well, Michael, thank you for picking up the flowers and promising to mind them. Here's a little something for you." She was about to pass him the sixpence, but she paused, and changed it for a florin.

On seeing the large fish on the coin, the boy's face lit up. It was clear that he had never seen, much less owned, so much money in his short life. Suddenly, his face fell.

"I can't keep it, Misses Bradford. Me Ma'll think I stole it," he said, handing back the coin.

"It's fine young Byrne. Tell your Ma that it's payment for something you did for me. Now, away wi' ye," Pat said, as he waved him off.

"Thanks you's," he shouted, running off, before they changed their minds.

"A penny would've been enough, Miss Bradford," Pat said smiling.

"That little boy's made me realise how destructive my bitterness is, Mr Kavanagh. I wanted to hurt him. I was going to take my anger out on him, a child, not even born when my life was turned upside down, 12 twelve years ago."

"You have my sympathy, especially on the week it is. Are you going to town?"

"Yes, I've some messages to do."

"Good, so do I. Will you join me for a cup of tea in the Brook Café? I wanted to talk to you about something"

"Yes, I'd like that," Mary said, "but it's my treat to thank you for your help."

They walked into the town, comfortably chatting like old friends.

As they entered the Café, a small woman showed them to a window seat, and took their order. She turned to an old gramophone, sat on a large dresser.

"Nothing like a little bit of music, Mr Kavanagh?"

"You still have that old thing, Mrs Tracey? I remember the day you bought it from the Kynoch's liquidators at that auction in the old Dining Hall."

"I remember it, Mrs Tracey," Mary said excitedly, as she recalled the machine entertaining the hungry masses, whilst they queued for their lunch. "It used to sit on a table in the Dining Hall, with a selection of records. I never realised this was the one from the factory. I'm so glad it went to a good home."

"Yes, the same one, Miss Bradford," Mrs Tracey said, fumbling with the records.

"Would you like to hear Duke Ellington's 'Black and Tan Fantasy', Mr Kavanagh?" She asked Pat, mischievously.

"You always had a great sense of humour, Mrs Tracy," Pat replied laughing, as the woman disappeared through a back door.

When the door shut Mary turned to Pat and said.

"You wished to discuss something with me Pat."

"Firstly, Mary, I want to say how sorry I am about those boys. I liked Myles and considered him a friend, despite him being an English Officer. We were successfully working together to keep the peace, until his untimely death. Our Area Commander, Thomas Donnelly, ordered his killing. He had a personal grudge against Myles. I don't know what it was, and after his death, I didn't pursue it."

"Mr Kavanagh, thank you for helping me earlier. I don't quite know what I'd have done to that poor child," Mary sighed. "Who is Thomas Donnelly - that's the second time his name has come up? Why would he want Myles murdered?"

"Donnelly was our Area Commander. He delivered orders direct from Collins, and kept us supplied with ammunition and guns. Like I said, I never found out what his problem was with Myles, and stopped investigating after Myles was killed."

"Even if Myles had found out why this Donnelly character wanted him dead, he wouldn't have done anything about it. His resignation had been accepted, and he and I were going to Norfolk, following our engagement," Mary said, removing her gloves.

246

"Myles told me. I was happy for you both. We'd planned to meet up when it was over, but sadly that never happened."

Commandant Kavanagh leaned back to allow Mrs Tracy to place the heavy tray on the table,

"Did you get engaged, Mary? He asked, as Mrs Tracy rewound the Gramophone.

"Yes, we did," Mary said, displaying the ring she wore. "Now, what was the second thing?" She asked confidently, as she poured the tea for both of them.

"Well," he chuckled, "speaking to families you've helped with pensions and compensation, I'm aware you have some political clout in Dublin, so I want to talk about last month's general election. As you know, Mr De Valera's Fianna Fail party won, but shares power with Labour. I'm a member of Fianna Fail, and we've come to understand that most of the women in this town cannot be influenced on whom to vote for by their husbands or families. Believe me, that's led to some very public arguments in the run up to the election," Pat Kavanagh said, with a wry smile. "I believe this stems from their independence gained from working in Kynoch's, which I fully support. But I don't want to see them deliberately waste their vote, just to get back at the family. We want more women involved locally, so they can see for themselves that Mr De Valera is the way forward, and maybe they'll influence their own families, in turn."

"Mr Kavanagh, with all due respect, I didn't volunteer to be involved in the politics of this State. I was dragged into it, because I fell in love with a man. I have watched how, for 10 years, the Cummann na nGaedheal government has chipped away at Women's Rights in this country - keeping the Marriage Bar, refusing women on juries, restricting them from certain jobs. I could go on, but I don't think we have the time," Mary said, with a sad smile. "I've had many memorable meetings with members from all parties, because they had dealings with my office. I'll tell

247

you now, that every one of them showed the same contempt when they realised they had to deal with me,... a woman, and some of them were members of Mr De Valera's Party too. So how can you say this will change now Fianna Fail has been elected?" Mary sipped her tea.

"I agree with you. It'll take time. That's why we want to ensure that Fianna Fail gets two terms. It's not official, but Mr De Valera may call a snap election next year. If he does, we want to be ready, and, with the support of women across the country, we may well win a full house. With women like you, and Marie Curran on-board, I think it can be achieved. Would you be willing to help us?"

"For women, that'd be like being given a choice of which fetters to wear, If De Valera wants our support, he'd better start making radical changes now, from the start. And if these changes benefit women and the nation, then, yes, I'll consider your offer."

"Well said, young Mary," Mrs Tracey agreed.

"You're welcome, Mrs Tracey," Mary said, as she prepared to leave. "I must be getting on. Thank you both for the tea - it was lovely,"

Mary placed a coin on the table and stood to leave.

"You don't have to do that, Mary," Pat said.

"I insist, Mr Kavanagh. I will carefully consider what you've asked, and thank you again for your support this morning - I appreciated it, ".

"My God, she is feisty, Mrs Tracey," Pat said, as he watched Mary pause to put on her gloves, before opening the door.

"That she is. Would you like another cup, Pat?"

"Yes please, and put on that Black and Tan song you mentioned earlier."

Pat stretched out his legs and placed his hands behind his head. He looked at the sixpence on the table and smiled to himself.

"Mary Bradford, indeed you are something else!"

Mary felt obliged to keep her promise to Pat Kavanagh, but desired a better understanding of the policies of all political parties, so she started attending Public meetings held by each party around Dublin. The first was a Cumann na nGaedheal meeting. As she entered, there was a small scuffle outside, quickly supressed by a group of men. Mary took little notice, and went inside. She found the meeting rather fiery, with speakers focussed on comparing their opposition to Communists, rather than discussing their own policies.

The second was a Labour Meeting, which she found dull and dreary.

The third was a Fianna Fail Meeting. The room was packed, and she was glad that she had come early to secure a seat near the front. She was sat next to a journalist, Malachy Foley, with whom she made polite conversation. The hall filled quickly. An elderly man introduced the local TD to loud applause. As soon as he started to speak, fights broke out amongst the crowd. It escalated quickly, becoming a riot, with bottles and chairs thrown across the room. The journalist, fearing for Mary's safety, escorted her backstage. She met the TD who apologised to her.

"We should've guessed the Army Comrade's Association would turn up. That's twice in two months they've broken up our meetings," he said, as he opened the door to an alleyway. He stepped outside, quickly checking all was well.

"You should be safe from here. Thanks for turning up. Don't let those thugs put you off coming again next week. Good night! Safe home."

He stepped back shutting the door behind him.

Mary shared a taxi with the journalist. When they were settled, she asked him to explain who the ACA were. The journalist quoted from a newspaper article he had recently written in a broad, Dublin accent.

"Well now, Miss Bradford, as you know, the IRA split during the Civil War into Pro and Anti-Treaty forces. These two formidable armies were renamed the 'Regulars' and 'Irregulars', which, in turn, became the Free State Army and the IRA. The Free State Army, after a long and bloody struggle, finally won the day, when the IRA Chief of Staff, Mr Liam Lynch, was killed in action. God rest his soul. His successor, Frank Aiken, called a ceasefire. However, to prevent the IRA becoming powerful again, Cosgrave, the leader of the Cumana Na Gael party, and Kevin O'Higgins, arrested all known leaders of the IRA, and introduced the Public Safety Act, banning the IRA, or other paramilitary parties, from legally assembling and holding public meetings."

"Mr De Valera lifted that ban back in March and released a number of leading IRA figures. They immediately re-formed, and started taking revenge on Ex-Free State Soldiers and the Cumana Na Gael Party, for atrocities committed during the Civil War. Ned Cronin, a Commandant from the National Army, now the official name for the Irish Free State Army, founded the Army Comrades Association, the ACA, a society for former members of the original Free State Army. It has become a powerful force, and is now in direct opposition to the IRA. The IRA has taken upon itself to protect all Fianna Fail meetings, and break up all Cumana Na Gael ones, so the ACA have decided the opposite. They protect the Cumana Na Gael Meetings, and break up the Fianna Fail ones, which, as we witnessed, has led to violent clashes between old enemies."

"It sounds like the Civil War could erupt again," Mary said, horrified at the thought.

"That's very true, Miss Bradford, but for now, Mr De Valera will do nothing, as he needs the support of the 'Old IRA' if he's to call a snap election next year. Now, here's your stop," Malachy said, as the taxi slowed down.

"What's the 'Old IRA', Malachy? Mary asked, as she prepared to exit.

"That's the name given to members of the Original IRA before the split that led to the Civil War. A lot of those people are dormant, and don't publicly display loyalty to either side, so their vote can vary between parties. That is why Dev lifted the ban and released prisoners. He's hoping to gain their support. Personally, I don't believe that he foresaw the actual IRA gaining momentum again, as a result."

"Could Dev not talk to Sinn Fein, before this erupts into something terrible?" Mary asked, leaning through the open window of the car.

"I suppose he could, but it'd make no difference – the IRA and Sinn Fein fell out years ago, and don't talk anymore. By the way, I'm covering a Sinn Fein meeting next week. Would you like to come?" Malachy asked with obvious excitement.

"Yes, I'd like that. What time would suit you?"

"I'll collect you from here at 7 o'clock, next Thursday," Malachy said.

"I'll be here."

"I look forward to it Miss Bradford," Malachy said, as the taxi pulled away.

"Not another bloody war, Myles", she said as she walked up her garden path.

The next day, Mary told John about her adventure the night before, and asked his about the Old IRA. He leaned back in his chair, as he began to reminisce.

"The Old IRA is the Irish Republican Army Organisation, or the IRAO, formed by Liam Tobin, an Irish Army Officer, who, like many of us, resented the atrocities committed during the Civil War. He set up the organisation to clarify the difference between the Regular and Irregulars forces. I was one of the first to join, but after the Tralee incident…." He paused and took a deep breath.

251

"After the Tralee incident, and the execution of Childers, O'Connor and Mellows, I realised that Cosgrave and O'Higgins were behaving like dictators, creating questionable laws and giving themselves the authority to eliminate any opposition to their party. That's when I took this job, and resigned from the Army, in February 1923."

"But we live in a democracy John. William Cosgrave would never support that."

"Take the Freeny incident, five years ago. O' Higgins threatened to oust our skeletons in this very room."

"That's true. He was a horrible man. Are you still in the IRAO? Mary asked.

"We still meet from time to time. It's more of an old comrades club now."

"Do you mean the Army Comrades Association?"

"No I don't!" John said firmly. "They are, in my opinion, a Fascist organisation. I was recently asked to consider joining them, but was told they wanted a Blue Shirt uniform similar to the Brown Shirts in Germany and the Black shirts in Italy. That really raised my concerns about them."

"Can Mr De Valera not stop them?"

"Yes, but I don't believe he'll do anything until after he calls a snap election."

"That seems to be everyone's opinion," Mary said, placing her cup on the table.

"Talking of Dev," John said, "This morning, I got a letter inviting senior Pensions staff to a meeting with Ministers in Harcourt Street."

"Why does Mr De Valera wish to address us personally?" Silvia asked entering the room.

"It sounds exciting," Mary said, pouring tea for Silvia.

On the day of the meeting, Mary, Silvia and John entered the building, and were directed to a large room, filled with chairs. The meeting started at 10 o'clock. James Geoghegan, Minister of Justice and Equality, was first to speak. He thanked everyone for their tireless efforts in supporting veteran's, victims, and businesses that had fallen on hard times due to the Anglo-Irish War.

He was followed by a number of Junior Ministers. Finally, the new Taoiseach, Mr Eamon De Valera spoke of his plans for the future. He intended to legalise all political parties, release all political prisoners, and, most importantly, he was going to lift the ban, enforced by Cumann Na Gael, which prevented members who supported the Anti-Treaty side during the Civil War, from claiming a military pension. He would extent the lifting of the ban to all banned organisations, like Cumann Na mBan, Hibernian Rifles, Na Fianna Eireann. He even suggested that members of the disbanded British Regiment, the Connaught Rangers, could claim.

A powerful silence saturated the room. The audience stared in total disbelief, thinking of the workload this would create. Mary could not restrain herself, and started to applaud, thinking of the struggling families she had been unable to assist, because of the previous legislation. The entire room joined in.

"Of course, this won't happen overnight. Minister Geoghegan has suggested it could take two years for your departments to prepare for this. That's why it's imperative that the Fianna Fail Party get re-elected to ensure that these changes are implemented properly and not abandoned by petty squabbling. I can tell from your applause, that you would like to see this plan bear fruit for the struggling families of Ireland, especially those whose loved ones made the ultimate sacrifice for their country."

This comment was met with more applause. This time, Mary did not join in. She sat back, remembering her meeting with Commandant Kavanagh in Arklow.

"Pat Kavanagh, you might just be right about this man," she said to herself, as she looked at the enthusiastic faces of the other women in the room.

When the meeting was over, they loitered, discussing strategies for coping with the extra work this proposal would generate. When Mary was ready to leave, she found John in conversation with Minister Geoghegan.

"Minister, this is Mary Bradford, the lady I just mentioned, who assisted in exposing Judge Lavin."

"Miss Bradford, a pleasure," the Minister said, offering his hand.

"The pleasure's mine, Minister," Mary said, taking it. "May I ask why you exposed Lavin?" She continued.

"I authorised his arrest and sentenced him. The new State inherited a lot of the old Civil Servants, who had previously worked for the British, corrupting the system. Minister Cosgrove and I were determined to remove this corruption, at all costs. I was a member of both the Irish and English Bar Association, and could not stand for this corruption. We were successful at first, but it slowly ground to a halt, because of the nepotism in the last Government. That's why I now fully support Mr De Valera, because I believe he'll carry on with this work and, more importantly, neutralise the animosity between all parties, which played a big part in this corruption."

"I think its great news that banned parties can now claim a military Pension, even if it means more work for us, and less for members of your profession."

"I don't follow? My profession, Miss Bradford?" the Minister said, puzzled.

"I'm sorry, I mean the Bar, Minister. We hire Barristers to countersue cases brought against the State by some claimants. I believe some of these Barristers are deliberately dragging out cases, to extract as much money from the State as possible."

"That's a very serious accusation, Miss Bradford. Those Barristers could sue you for defamation, and I'd support them, unless you can prove your claim?"

"What if I could present hard evidence, similar to the Lavin case?"

"That would be different, as that would interfere with the Bar, and that couldn't be allowed," the Minister replied concerned.

"Would you class this corruption similar to that in other cases you've tried to expose?" Mary asked.

"Yes, Miss Bradford. If true, this is exactly the type of corruption that we try to eradicate. You give me the impression you might know something? A word of warning, though! If you have any evidence, make sure it's concrete. You're accusing Barristers, people considered part of the very fabric of the State. Undermining them could bring the entire judicial system crashing down. That would be prevented, no matter the cost. So, be careful with what you're considering," he said, acknowledging an aide.

"Here's my card. Please contact me when you're ready to present your case, and I assure you, I'll deal with it personally, and in the strictest confidence, without nepotism and regardless of affiliation."

"Thank you, Minister. I look forward to meeting you again. Good day."

"And I you, Miss Bradford," the Minister said, as the aid helped him on with his coat.

On the way back to the office, John asked Mary to expand on her theory.

"John, do you remember that law firm, Dalton and Smith we investigated for corruption a few years ago.

"Yes, we agreed to postpone that enquiry when O'Higgins and O'Duffy threatened to have our skeletons locked in cupboards, if memory serves?"

"Well, the one named Smith is the Lawyer that represented me during my case."

"What? Why in God's name would you allow us to employ him?" John asked, stopping abruptly on the footpath. "It was after all you that suggested we employ them in the first place!"

I'll explain back in the office," Mary said, building suspense. "Now, let's get cake," she said, ducking into a grocery shop.

John Smith

John Smith was an Englishman, born into a prosperous East Sussex family. His Father was a Liberal MP, and a member of the Cabinet. When Smith was 18, he began a degree at City Law School, London, in preparation for a career as a Barrister.

Smith was delighted with a move to London and made friends from similar social circles. In his third year, whilst dining out with friends in a famous Mayfair club, they encountered a group of men from the infamous Oxford University Bullingdon Club, who trashed the restaurant, audaciously paying for the damage. Smith and his friends, fascinated by their actions, decided to set up their own club.

One evening, on a drunken rampage in London, they met a tramp, sitting on a wall next to the Egyptian Obelisk at Victoria Embankment. They gathered around the man, taunting him. The tramp issued a barrage of verbal abuse in return, and lashed out at the closest one, who, punched the tramp, knocking him off the wall and into the river. They panicked and ran as horrified witnesses raised the alarm. The tramp's body was recovered. He was a popular Crimean War veteran, originally from Ireland, and had earned the Victoria Cross for valour. A campaign was launched to apprehend the assailants. After a week, the assailant, unable to bear his guilt, confessed, but remained loyal to his friends, taking full responsibility.

Smith's Father, fearing this event could devastate his son's career, and affect his own, decided to send his son overseas, to complete his degree. Whilst discussing possible options with colleagues from the Cabinet, an Irish Barrister, named Edward Carson, suggested Trinity College, Dublin.

John Smith reluctantly agreed to accept his Father's arrangements, and, in September 1905, 21-year old Smith, stood in front of the large, varnished gates of Trinity College, Dublin, with the prospect of completing his training as a Barrister. It did not take him long to fit in with the Unionist population and, on finishing his degree, he was promised a pupillage in a Dublin-based Law Office associated with Mr Carson.

The Law firm, Dalton and Dalton, was owned by 60-year old, Mr Steven Dalton, and his son, also Steven and ten years' senior to Smith. Dalton Senior was a staunch Unionist, and prominent member of the Irish Unionist Alliance. He tolerated his Catholic neighbours, but did not hide his abhorrence to the Home Rule movement, and the associated Fenian organisations, including the Suffragettes. He took pride in representing the Government against these 'ungrateful vermin', as he described them.

During his final year, John Smith regularly assisted in the office, developing a great respect for this man. Over the past two years, Smith had listened to Dalton Senior's opinions on Catholics, and Ireland's sub-servient role in the British Empire, making him believe he could share with Dalton Senior, the details of the London incident. So, a week before he was due to start his pupillage, he confessed.

"So, he was a Kilkenny Papist with a VC who'd fallen on hard times," Dalton Senior said, from behind his uncluttered desk.

"Yes, Mr Dalton. That's what the Standard said, but the medal wasn't found."

"The Standard? Well, it must be true. I despise these Papists getting our highest awards, and losing them. Truth be known, he probably sold it for drink. They should have their own rewards – they'll never be worthy to wear the Kings medals."

"Well, I just wanted to be honest, Mr Dalton," Smith said, feeling encouraged.

"I appreciate your honesty. Your youthful high-jinx will remain firmly in the past, and will have no bearing on your future here," he said, leaning forward in his chair as he passed Smith, a copy of the terms of the pupillage.

"Your family comes highly recommended by Mr Carson, and your honesty proves his good opinion to be correct. I've always been aware of the London incident, and was assured you'd disclose the details to me before accepting my offer…. The pupillage begins on Monday," he boldly announced. "Welcome aboard! Please do not have me regret my decision," Dalton Senior offered his hand across the desk.

"Thank you, Mr Dalton," Smith said, excitedly. "You won't regret it, I promise."

He left the office with a noticeable spring in his step.

Smith kept his promise. He followed his mentor, Mr Dalton, both into Law, and Politics, joining the Irish Unionist Party. He was given his own cases and started making court appearances. In 1914, a year after the Dublin City Lock Out, he was summoned to the office, where he found Dalton Senior, seated at his desk, with another man in the Visitor's chair.

"Thank you for coming, John. This is Detective Freeny of Dublin Castle,"

Smith shook hands and sat down, listening intently to what they both had to say.

Freeny explained that the prisons of Dublin, and the surrounding counties, were full of insurgents from the riots. Most had been processed, given short sentences, or released, with fines. However, some Ring Leaders were insisting on their cases being heard in Crown Court, hoping for publicity.

"We're planning to hold these cases, at the same time, across the country. This'll strain the supply of Fenian lawyers, forcing them to use state-supplied lawyers instead."

"This is where we need your help, John," Dalton Senior interrupted. "I'd like you to represent one particular person that Mr Freeny has in mind, and to do it in such a way that he'll lose his case. It'll be put down to lack of experience on your part. Do you understand what I'm saying, John?" Dalton Senior asked, flashing a brief smile.

Smith was horrified, protesting loudly at the insanity of the idea.

"John, we're not asking you to break the law, just procrastinate a little with evidence. After all, these Fenian's' are demanding Home Rule, and if successful, it'll destroy our way of life. Its's a 'one off', I promise. The Court's in Galway. Here are the details. I've already set you up as an independent legal aid, supplied by Government. You'll be a complete unknown to the Fenian movement, so should have nothing to worry about. Please don't let us down," Dalton Senior said, passing over the file.

Smith successfully carried out his request. He thought that was the end of it until he was asked to do it again, six years later. This time, it was a murder case in Arklow. Again, he got the result that Dalton and Freeny desired.

Dalton Senior retired in1922, leaving the firm to his son and Smith. The name was changed to 'Dalton and Smith', and they kept busy representing clients with claims against the British Government and the newly formed Irish Free State, for injury and loss of revenue during the Anglo Irish War.

In 1925, they successfully won a bid to represent the Free State in cases arising from its refusal to pay certain claims and pensions. The two men quickly found ways to drag out cases, making a considerable amount of money from the fledgling State. Their preferred method was to delay the presentation of evidence, which, if shown, would quickly conclude the case. The Plaintiffs would be forced to call another hearing, and Dalton and Smith would drip feed the evidence, often resulting in a postponement. They could do this up to three times per case, before finally presenting the damming evidence, allowing the case to be awarded to the State, and making a considerable amount of extra money for their effort.

They successfully applied these methods to every third or fourth case, in order to avoid raising suspicion, but little did they know that Mary was watching them closely, waiting to strike.

The opportunity finally came in January 1933, when Eamon De Valera called a snap election, resulting in a landslide victory. Mary was in full support, believing De Valera would bring significant change to the country, particularly for Women's Rights.

Even though the Pension Office had accumulated enough damming evidence against this Law Firm in 1927, she and John believed they would be forced to drop the case, as the two lawyers were reporting directly to the Head of the Garda, Eoin O'Duffy, and the Minister of Justice, Kevin O'Higgins regarding separate IRA convictions. After the threat by O'Higgins earlier that year, they decided to put off the investigation, but, following O'Higgins's assassination by the IRA in July 1927, the plan was postponed indefinitely, allowing Dalton and Smith to continue unchecked.

After winning the election in January 1933, one of the first things De Valera did was to dismiss Eoin O'Duffy as head of the Garda, on suspicion of encouraging a military coup against his new Government, prompting Mary to finally act on the evidence she had collected. She picked up the phone and called James Geoghegan, the new Minister of Justice.

Over the following months, they sorted through seven years of accumulated evidence with the help of James Geoghegan, who had now resigned as Minister of Justice, and was working independently for the State. Finally, in August 1933, when he was satisfied with their work, they agreed to act on a Saturday morning in September, when the two accused were guaranteed to be in their office, planning for the week ahead. So, on a drab, grey morning, in the second week of September, Mary arrived outside the office of Dalton and Smith, on Capel Street with Mr

Geoghegan, Eamon Broy the new Garda Commissioner, John Mills, and six Garda officers.

A startled secretary allowed them to enter the main office, unannounced. The group was clearly amused to find Smith and Dalton, their backs to the door, unfurling a large Army Comrades Association banner. Both men were wearing the distinct blue uniforms of the ACA, even though neither had ever been in any Army.

"Good Morning, James," a clearly surprised Dalton said, on turning to see who was responsible for the sudden intrusion. He walked across the room to shake hands, having known James Geoghegan, on a professional basis, since the founding of the State. They had an amicable relationship through their long association with the Cumana Na Gael party.

"Good Morning, Steven. As you can see, this is not a social visit," Geoghegan said, refusing the offered hand.

On seeing this hostile reception, Smith loosely rolled the banner and leaned it against the wall. He joined Dalton, standing behind the main desk.

"What can we do for you? "He asked, feigning confidence.

"May we?" Broy asked, pointing to some chairs.

"Of course," Smith replied.

Commandant Mills, Commissioner Broy, and James Geoghegan sat in front of the large desk, whilst Dalton and Smith occupied chairs, on the other side.

"Is this to do with the movement and Commander Duffy?" Dalton asked. "I'm sure you're aware that we've followed the law, and the ACA and National Guard no longer exist," he said, referring to the recent incident in August, when De Valera was forced to ban the National Guard from holding a memorial parade for Kevin O'Higgins, for fear it might force a coup. "These are the uniforms of the Young Ireland Association, part of the new, and legitimate, Fine Gael Party," he said, pointing to the very distinct

262

badge on his left breast, that clearly displayed a large red X, previously used by the National Guard, the words, 'Fine Gael', embroidered above it.

"This has nothing to do with petty in-house squabbles in your Party, or the nefarious ways it bypasses the law with the assistance of Ex- Garda Chief O'Duffy. Broy replied, sharply. "It is about serious allegations of fraud, brought to my attention by the Department of Pensions, which Mr Geoghegan has been investigating."

Smith and Dalton nervously looked at one another. Mary silently placed six files in front of Geoghegan. She looked at Smith. It was the first time she had seen him since her Court Case. Smith briefly glanced at her, as he might any attractive woman.

James Geoghegan explained.

"These files are cases by Ex-IRA men against the state, between 1926 and 1930. In each case, the claimants are demanding a military pension for services to the state, during the Civil War. But, as you know, the Cumana Na Gael Government passed a bill prohibiting that right to anyone who supported the Anti-Treaty forces during the Civil War. This ban was lifted last year, by Fianna Fail, creating a deluge of requests."

"What's that got to do with us?" Smith challenged.

"Everything, Mr Smith!" Broy barked, slapping the desk and startling both men. "Those files contain the original requests from six people, all of whom have re-applied for a State Pension. In each case, there is unquestionable proof that these men were Irregulars, and originally deemed ineligible for a military pension. The proof was handed into this office, and signed for, by you Mr Dalton, two weeks prior to the first hearing of each case. The cases should've been closed immediately, but you failed to present that evidence, and each case dragged on for three more hearings. The Plaintiff lost, and you collected more taxpayers' money, for the procrastination."

Geoghegan interrupted Broy to lay out the extent of the investigation.

"These are only six from up to 100 cases that Commandant Mills' department have accumulated over the last seven years. Gentlemen, the evidence is clear in all cases. This is a blatant act of fraud, committed by this Law Office."

Mary's presence bothered Smith. There was a sliver of recognition, but he could not place her.

"Have we met before, Miss?"

"Of course you have, John," Dalton said, also looking at Mary. "This is Mary Bradford, from the Department of Pensions. She would have delivered these pension cases to this office."

Smith stood and approached Mary, alerting the two Garda. He took a step back, and looked over at Dalton.

"No Steven, I know her from somewhere else."

He stared directly at Mary, trying to intimidate her with his height. She refused to feel threatened by his towering height, or his court room dramatics. Earlier, she had noticed, a framed portrait of a younger Smith, dressed in gown and wig.

"The last time we met, you looked like that," Mary said, confidently leaning around his large frame, and pointing towards the picture.

Smith glanced at the picture and the penny dropped.

"I remember you! Mary Bradford from Arklow, the Fenian murderess Freeny exposed," he shouted "Gentlemen, "this farce is clearly an act of deliberate entrapment by a past Plaintiff seeking revenge on Crown Counsel," he said, pacing the room, using well-rehearsed Court Room theatrics, in front of the bemused group. "Back in 1920, I helped find this woman guilty of luring a British Officer to his death. The crime was worthy of the death sentence, but, I successfully reduced it to 25 years hard labour at his Majesty's pleasure. She was obviously released early and secured employment in a State Office, a position she has clearly abused, by plotting this debacle, as revenge."

He spun around and pointed directly at Mary. "She swore in front of the entire court room that she would get her revenge, and this is her feeble attempt."

"Is this true, Miss Bradford?" James Geoghegan calmly asked.

"No Mister Geoghegan, it's not all true. Firstly, I was engaged to the English Officer when he was murdered by the IRA. Secondly, all I did was hand over case files and supporting evidence, to this Law Office, as instructed by Commandant Mills. I did not suggest they drag out cases in order to extract more revenue from the State. I think you'll find that they managed that all by themselves."

"Which part of Mr Smith's statement is actually true?" James Geoghegan asked.

"When he admitted that he was responsible for my incarceration in an English jail. That was true, but he failed to mention that he was my defence, not the prosecution, clearly proving that he's been corrupt for a long time," Mary replied confidently.

Fear engulfed Smith. He realised that his memory of the case was faulty, and his bold, unprepared statement, had just increased the seriousness of his predicament.

Dalton gave Geoghegan a submissive glance. Their friendship elicited a look of understanding, and they silently agreed that Smith would take the blame. Dalton, feeling more confident from this visual exchange, stood up.

"It looks like we won't be going to the rally this afternoon, John."

Smith shouted, as two Garda approached him.

"This isn't over. We have influential friends and when Fine Gael gets re-elected, you'll pay for this. Do you hear me?"

"John, please don't make matters worse," Dalton said, preparing to leave.

By now, the men had stood up. Broy collected the scattered files from the desk.

Smith pushed away the hands of the two Garda.

"There is no need for that," Broy said. "We're all Gentlemen here."

"This isn't over, you Fenian bitch," Smith said, through gritted teeth.

"Fenian Bitch! You got that bit right," Mary replied, taking the files from Superintendent Broy, and leaving the room, followed by a   grinning   Commandant   Mills.

Fighting Religious Ideology

For the remainder of that year, and all of the following one, Mary felt positively about the Fianna Fail Party, advocating for them. But early in 1935, she was disappointed to learn that the Party was not going to change its policy regarding the Marriage Bar, forcing a woman to give up her job when she married. All of her working life, Mary had found this unfair, ever since she first came across it whilst working at Kynoch's. She had thought De Valera would have removed this draconian law, a hangover from the British regime and adopted by the Cumana Na Gael party.

On a hot Monday morning in June, John handed Mary a letter he had just received. She read it, screwed it up into a ball and threw it onto the floor, angrily storming out of her office.

"This is justice, is it? Nothing changes!" She shouted back at the office.

"Let her go, Silvia," John said, sympathetically, as Silvia rose to follow her.

"What's wrong? Did you share our news?" Worry was etched on Sylvia's face.

"No, of course not. We agreed you would. Here, read this," he said, handing her the now recovered letter.

To all concerned in the Department of Pensions Public Office.

Re: Dalton and Smith Solicitors.

The case brought against Dalton and Smith, Solicitors, by the Irish State, for alleged fraud has been mediated, without the need for court proceedings. The Company will be dissolved, with all costs awarded. Mr John Smith is barred from ever working as a Solicitor in the Free State of Ireland. All charges against Mr Dalton have been dissolved, and he will continue to practice as a Lawyer, and to represent the State and private clients, in Irish Courts of Law.

The Department of Justice thanks those involved in bringing this matter to the attention of an Garda Síochána.

Yours sincerely

P. J. Rutledge

Minister of Justice.

Silvia ignored John's request. She found Mary weeping on a favourite bench, in St Stephen's Green, just below the steps of the controversial bronze statue of George II.

"There's no justice, Silvia. Perhaps the gunmen are right," Mary sobbed.

"Don't think like that. We wanted Smith, and we got him." Silvia comforted her.

"I was hoping he'd go to Jail," Mary sighed resignedly. Changing the subject, she noticed something different about Sylvia today. "You're glowing, Silvia? Do you have news?"

Silvia took Mary's hands.

"You know John and I have been walking out for a few years now."

"A few? Try four," Mary said, excitement mounting.

"Well, John proposed at the weekend. We're to be married this September!"

"That's wonderful news. I'm so happy for you both," Mary said, putting aside her frustration to share their happiness. Mary sat back and studied Silvia.

"That glow, Silvia? Are you....? Mary asked, pointing to Silvia's tummy.

"Yes, Mary! Three months."

"OH! That's even better news! I'm so happy for you," Mary was truly delighted. Suddenly, Mary pulled away.

"Oh Silvia, I've just realised that when you get married, you'll lose your job!"

"I know, Mary, but the baby will need its mother."

"True, but it should be a choice, not the law. Besides, I'll miss you terribly."

"We won't be strangers," Silvia replied reassuringly.

"I hope not, "Mary said, mournfully.

"Come on, let's celebrate over lunch. I'm sure my fiancée won't mind." They linked arms, and walked towards Grafton Street.

Silvia and John Mills were married on September the 5th 1935, in Silvia's home town of Dunloe, County Cork. Mary was a bridesmaid, and had invited the Journalist, Malachy Foley, to accompany her. They were frequently in each other's company, attending the theatre or political rallies together, in and around Dublin.

They had a wonderful time, and Malachy managed to refrain from sharing his communist beliefs with any of the Politicians and clergy present.

At the end of the night, after the bride and groom had left, Mary sat in the bar, resting her head on Malachy's shoulder. They were with other guests, also staying overnight, taking it in turns to sing. For a finale, Malachy sang a beautiful rendition of Kevin Barry. The remaining bar staff also paused to listen.

Malachy escorted Mary to her room on the first floor. They stopped and chatted briefly outside her half open door.

"Thank you for such a wonderful day, Mary," he said, holding her hands.

"Thank you for joining me, and controlling yourself, with the politicians!"

"I'm sure I'll get another opportunity!" He said, straightening the pendent Mary wore. "That's quite beautiful!"

"It's my Mother's," Mary said." I'm surprised you've only noticed it now."

"How could I have noticed it, when it was in competition with your beauty," he said, steeping back to look at her.

"Are you flirting with me, Mr Foley?" Mary asked, pretending to be stern.

"No, no, just saying what I think," he replied, meekly.

Mary felt a rekindled flame of desire. She leaned forward, lightly kissing his lips.

A surprised Malachy was about to speak, but Mary placed a finger on his lips.

"Shush," she said, leading him into her room, and closing the door behind them.

Silvia gave birth to a baby boy on Sunday the 8th of December, 1935. The following Sunday, the child was christened in a Dublin Church by her cousin, who was a Jesuit priest. At the reception, Mary commented on Silvia's absence.

"Where's Silvia?" She asked on seeing John.

"I believe she's in that room," he said, pointing to a side room, where food was being served.

Mary and Malachy entered the room and found guests helping themselves to food from a long table.

"Has anyone seen Silvia?" She asked loudly.

Everyone ignored her. She finally found Sylvia at the back of the room, sitting alone, dressed entirely in black, and wearing a veil.

Mary was concerned for her friend.

"Has someone died, Sylvia?"

This attracted the attention of everyone in the room. Silvia smiled and said.

"No Mary, I just haven't been 'Churched' yet."

"What?" A large woman exclaimed. "I hope you haven't made the sandwiches?"

"You shouldn't be here. You're unclean," another woman added.

"You'll bring bad luck on us all, "a younger woman joined in.

270

"I mean it, Silvia. Did you prepare the food?" The older woman asked again.

"No, Auntie Margaret, the hotel prepared it," Silvia said, standing up to leave. "I just came to collect my mother and baby. I don't mean to cause any trouble. Mary, please tell John I'll see him at home," she said, to a silent, but shocked Mary.

The small, intimidating group of woman were all relations of Silvia, and now gathered around her in a very hostile manner.

"You shouldn't be in public," her elderly Aunt announced, taking the lead.

"You should be ashamed of yourself," a cousin said, supporting her Aunt.

"Why would you do this? I thought you a good person," another exclaimed.

"I'm not going to argue! Mary, please pass on my message to John. Good bye."

At that, Silvia left using the back door of the room.

"And so you shouldn't argue," the elderly aunt said, in a croaky voice, as she and the other women returned to the table, muttering to each other.

"It's you who should be ashamed!" Mary announced to the women.

"How dare you question us!" the elderly aunt shouted at Mary. "You might be young, but I bet your shame would outweigh all of ours," the elderly Aunt said, facing Mary and Malachy, nibbling a piece of cake and hoping to provoke a reaction.

"What the hell is churching?" Malachy asked, completely oblivious.

"Another man-made rule forcing women to be subservient, and turn families on each other. As you can see, it works perfectly."

Silvia's aunt banged her plate on the table in disgust.

"Why you little Hussey, I'll have you know ....."

"Oh shut up, you old witch. Keep it for your cauldron. Come on, Malachy. I want to find John," Mary said, exiting the room, leaving Silvia's Aunt speechless.

Mary found John in the company of the Minister of Industry and Commerce, Sean Lemass. They were in deep discussion. Mary tried to be patient, but, on receiving glaring looks from Silvia's Aunt, she decided to interrupt.

"Please excuse me, Minister, but I just need to pass on a message. John, your wife has been forced to go home because she hasn't been churched."

"I warned her to keep out of sight when she collected her Mother and the baby."

"Well, are you going to do something about it?"

"There's nothing he can do," Silvia's cousin, the Jesuit priest, interrupted. "It's part of Church tradition for women who've just given birth."

"Oh spare me the male hypocrisy, Father. Does John here, need to be churched? I'm sure Sylvia's pregnancy wasn't immaculate."

Minister Lemass chuckled loudly. Everyone looked at him. Embarrassed, he brushed down his jacket, and was about to walk away, when Mary caught him.

"Excuse me Minister. May I have a moment of your time, please?"

Seeing an opportunity to defuse the tension, he replied positively.

"Certainly what can I do for you?"

"My father is George Bradford of Arklow, and whilst I fully agree with the Government's policy regarding land annuities, the resulting Trade War has had a devastating effect on his business, so I was hoping for some advice or assistance."

"Mr George Bradford. That name's familiar. Did you say Arklow?"

"Yes Minister. You know him. He sheltered you and Ernie O Malley, during the Civil War, when you were on the run in County Wicklow."

"Ah yes, I remember. Our dear friend, Marie Curran, organised it. We stayed for three days. You must be Anna."

"No, I'm Mary. Anna is my sister. I was held at his Majesty's pleasure in an English jail, at the time."

"Yes I remember. Your Mother told us. Well, Mary, that gentleman in the orange chequered suit, is in charge of the Industrial Credit Cooperation, set up to help people like your father. His name is Alan Stevens."

"Hello Sean," Malachy interrupted, holding out his hand. He could not contain his excitement any longer, having fought alongside Sean Lemass in the GPO. He had not seen him since the Civil War ended.

"My God, Malachy Foley! What a pleasure," the Minister said, placing his cup on a nearby table, and embracing Malachy with an unconventional hug.

"Are you still dabbling with Communism? " He asked, attracting the attention of the Jesuit priest.

"Well, you know me, Sean," Malachy said. "All men and women are equal."

Mary could tell this discussion would become heated and did not want to be involved. She went over to speak to Alan Stevens, who was guarding a plate of cooked chicken legs.

"Excuse me, Mr Stevens. Minister Lemass said you might be able to help me."

A corpulent, bald man, slightly smaller than Mary, turned to see who had spoken. He wore small, round spectacles that were buried into his plump face.

"What can I do for you?" He asked condescendingly.

Mary felt nauseous at the sight of him, but pressed on, for her Father's sake.

273

"Minister Lemass said you're responsible for issuing loans through the Industrial Credit Cooperation?"

"That's correct, "Stevens said, licking his fingers before taking more chicken.

"I'm asking for my Father. He runs a Coach-Making Business in Arklow...."

"Stop right there, "Stevens said, slobbering bits of chicken over his face. "You're a woman. Is there something wrong with your Father that he can't ask for himself?"

Stevens pointed an accusatory chicken leg towards Mary.

"I beg your pardon!" Mary loudly exclaimed, in disbelieve.

This got everyone's attention, especially Silvia's Aunt, still seething from the earlier incident. She made a miraculous recovery, and walked across the room, intending to share her opinion of Mary with Stevens.

Commandant Mills looked over as the situation unfolded. He rolled his eyes.

"What did you just say?" Mary demanded.

"What is it with Arklow women?" Stevens asked, wiping his mouth with his sleeve. "My office just had to deal with a legacy left by another Arklow woman named Kate Tyrrell, who had the audacity to become a Lady Mariner, of all things. As for Marie Curran, now there's another upstart that has our office plagued. She actually wants women to join the Garda! It'll be the Army next, or the Priesthood, for God's sake. Why don't you woman from that God forsaken town just stay home, where you belong, and leave men's work to the men."

He continued to wag the half eating chicken leg in Marys face as he spoke.

Silvia's Aunt inhaled deeply. She was just about to interject with her opinion, when Mary slapped the wagging chicken leg out of Stevens hand so hard that it was sent flying, hitting Silvia's elderly Aunt on her mouth.

She moaned, in shock, placed the back of her wrist on her forehead and dramatically collapsed, checking behind, to ensure she fell into the arms of her niece.

"HOW DARE YOU, YOU HORRIBLE LITTLE MAN!" Mary exclaimed.

"Without the likes of Marie Curran, and the sacrifice of other women, you wouldn't be standing here stuffing your face with chicken. You'd still be hiding under your bed, shouting for your Mammy," Mary said, through gritted teeth.

Her remark caused sniggers from the other guests, as they enjoyed the show.

Stevens could not reply. He just stood silently in utter shock.

Mary stepped to one side of the fussing nieces, who were fanning their Aunt's face with napkins. Their action seemed to revive her, but with many a loud moan.

"This is entirely your fault. We'll have to return with her to Cork now, and all because of you," her niece said, kneeling over her recovering Aunt.

"Oh, just lend her your broomstick, and she can fly there by herself."

The Aunt swooned again.

Mary left the function room, without another word.

"I think I'd better follow. Please excuse me," Malachy said to Sean Lemass.

"If I were you Malachy, I would, "the Minster replied, trying to supress a grin.

"If ever a man deserved a slap, its Stevens," the Minister said to Commandant Mills, who was still standing beside him.

"And if ever someone needed to be put in their place, its Silvia's Aunt," He replied.

"I'm sorry that you had to witness that, Sean. Mary is known to speak her mind."

"That doesn't worry me. Miss Bradford's right, without help from women like her, we'd still be under British rule. Tell her to contact me direct and I'll help her Father. Broomstick! Now that was funny. I can really picture it," he said laughing.

Minister Sean Lemass was true to his word. He personally visited Mary's parents, the following January of 1936, but even with financial assistance, there was no hope for the company. The majority of its work came from repairing local Schooners and, due to the Economic War, most were laid up, slowly rotting away in the river. The following February, George Bradford closed his business, and retired, gracefully.

Mary missed Silvia terribly. She struggled to work alongside her replacement, a young man named Daniel Condren. He was ten years her junior and lacked experience, but after Silvia intervened, Mary reluctantly accepted the change. She started to help, rather than hinder, this young man, and soon realised that he was very pleasant, with a wicked sense of humour. She came to enjoy helping him improve.

"Miss Bradford, I apologise for bothering you, but I seem to have a double request here. I've checked it over twice, and it's definitely the same man."

Mary viewed both files. The information was almost identical, except for a photo attached to one of the applications.

"This is quite common. Just check the dates. Back in the '20s, when the department first opened, we received requests from almost everyone in the county. It took years to filter the fraudulent claims from the legitimate ones. But, during that process we also had to separate out the claims from banned applicants, due to their affiliations in the Civil War. After that ban was lifted four years ago by Mr De Valera, we received a lot of repeat applications, people assuming their original ones had been lost. The most recent one has a photo attached."

Mary picked up the photo. She thought she knew the applicant, so turned her attention to the older file. The application came from Thomas Donnelly, the man who ordered Myles' execution. The colour drained from her face.

"Are you alright, Miss Bradford?" Daniel asked, attracting John's attention.

"What's the matter, Mary? " He asked, rushing to her side. Both men helped Mary into the small kitchen. They sat her down, and Daniel made tea.

When she had sufficiently recovered, Mary held out the photo to John.

"I've tried to put my past behind me, especially since meeting Malachy. He's actually convinced me to move on. To forget about punishing Boland and Donnelly, and not to let bitterness eat me up. Most days, I manage to do that, but, the tiniest trigger can send me spiralling. Look at this photo. This is Thomas Donnelly, the man responsible for murdering my Fiancée. Do you remember him? We collected damming information on him a few years back, after Pat Kavanagh told me he was involved with Myles' murder. The evidence proved useless in Ireland, so we agreed to put it to one side. But, I need to see this man face justice!"

John took the photo and studied it.

"Mary, I'll do what I can, but bringing Thomas Donnelly to justice is going to be difficult. I recognise him. Thomas Donnelly is now a sitting TD."

Mary took the photo. "Remember your motto, John, 'those that wait, are well rewarded'. Let's reopen his case and see what develops."

"Agreed," John said, as he stood to answer the phone. "Please excuse me."

"What's all this about, Miss Bradford," Daniel asked.

"Well now, where do I start?" Mary replied, pleased with John's reply and knowing that Thomas Donnelly was in their sights. "If

I'm going to tell you the story of my life, perhaps we should start with you calling me Mary," she suggested with a wink, much to Daniel's delight.

For the next few months, Mary worked hard during the week, and enjoyed her weekends with Malachy. She was very fond of him, but stopped short of allowing the relationship to develop into something more serious. She could not bear the thought of losing someone else she cared about, and struggled with irrational feelings of betrayal to Myles' memory. The second time she brought him home to Arklow, her mother and sister convinced her that Myles would approve and would want her to find happiness. However, her father privately voiced his concerns over Malachy's obsession with Communism, believing that, in the current climate, supporting Communism would lead to further trouble for the couple.

Mary respected her Father, and his support of her independence, but she knew his concerns were legitimate. Malachy's Communist leanings never really bothered her. In fact, she often attended meetings with him, still keen to understand all aspects of Ireland's politics. She attended a Republican Congress Meeting, at which, Nora Connelly spoke. Malachy arranged a private audience with Miss Connelly to cover the event for a number of local papers. Mary found Nora Connelly pleasant and honest, and fully supportive of Women's Rights in the New Ireland. However, after the meeting, Mary was alarmed to witness the passion with which Malachy shared his views with other members.

Some weeks' later, her concerns grew during an emergency meeting held by the Congress, in late July, 1936. She obliged Malachy by attending, but was left alone for much of the evening, as Malachy and the Party leaders continued their discussions, late into the night.

The following day, Malachy appeared at Mary's favourite bench, below the George II statue in St Stephen's Green. He apologised for his behaviour the night before. Mary accepted, with a smile, and listened as he explained that the Republican Congress had agreed to send aid to support the Spanish Republicans in the Spanish Civil War. This, he told her, was to countermand the actions of Eoin O'Duffy, who was gaining support from the public and Church leaders, for his suggestion to send an Irish Brigade, made up of members from his Blue Shirt organisation. These men would assist Franco, the leader of the Spanish Fascist Party, in supressing the communist left. Mary was horrified. She stood up abruptly, her lunch falling off her lap.

"Malachy Foley," She reprimanded, ignoring her spilt lunch, "I don't want you fighting and dying in someone else's war for your ridiculous beliefs."

Stunned, Malachy also stood.

"But Mary, O'Duffy is sending......."

"I don't care about Eoin O'Duffy and his bloody Blueshirts. I only care about you!" She said. Tears falling down her face, she was finally forced to accept her feelings for him, the sudden realisation threatening to overwhelm her.

Malachy sat her down. He felt terrible for the pain he had caused her. Not knowing what to do, he picked up her sandwich and tried to clean it off.

"Leave it for the birds," Mary said, slowly recovering. "I know you're passionate in your beliefs, Malachy, but please don't go. I don't think I could survive loosing someone again. I don't want you dying in some foreign and dusty country for a cause only you believe in."

Malachy allowed the passion of his beliefs to cloud his emotions. He was angry that she had belittled them. He stood, threw the sandwich back on the ground, and paced, back and forth, in front of her.

"I'm not the only one in Ireland who feels like this. We won't lie down and be subservient fools, like those that wasted good

279

money erecting monuments to their masters, like the one you choose to sit beneath."

They both looked up at the bronze statue of King George II, sitting on a horse, high on a granite plinth, completely dominating the centre of St Stephen's Green.

"Bronze, Mary! Imagine the difference that money could've made to the poor of Dublin at that time? If I had my way, I'd scrap it, and use the money to feed the poor. But that won't happen, because the two Parties we're forced to choose between, only care about themselves, not the Country, or its people. I don't want the likes of O'Duffy and his cronies taking over this land. If they get into power, they'll unleash a wave of far-right and religious terror across this country, against anyone who objects to their quasi-fascist ideas. They'll put Cromwell to shame. So, if I have to die in a 'foreign and dusty country' to stop that happening, then, so be it."

"But Mr De Valera will stop him, Malachy," Mary said, through her tears.

"Everyone knows the Long Fellow and his crony, Bishop McQuaid, support Franco. They'll both support O'Duffy in sending a Brigade, and Dev will hope that O'Duffy won't return, to rid himself of another problem. But Mary," Malachy said sitting back down and taking her hands in his, "This is what I believe in. Just as you need to get justice for your fiancée, this is something I have to do."

"But you could get killed, and I know I couldn't bear it, Malachy."

Malachy did not reply. He placed a comforting arm around her. Mary snuggled into him, stroking his other hand, feeling at a complete loss. Her emotions were running riot. Malachy was determined that nothing would stop him, even his feelings for her. Mary knew that, so, for the rest of her break, they remained wrapped in each other's arms, staring silently as the birds squabbled over the discarded sandwich.

Between September and December of 1936, Eoin O'Duffy, with funds raised by the Church, started to send small groups of the National Guard out to Spain to assist General Franco. That December, the members of the Irish International Brigade, incensed by O'Duffy's support for the Spanish Fascists, sent out their members to support the Republicans. They left in groups from Dublin, Belfast and Rosslare, planning to meet in Madrigueras, in Spain, for training.

That gloomy December morning, Mary was on the quay at Dun Laoghaire with Malachy. She begged him not to go, or, at least, wait until the New Year. A tall, attractive man noticed the couple. He approached them with a smile.

"Don't worry, Miss Bradford. I'll make sure he returns home safely."

"Who are you?" Mary asked, angry at the interruption.

"This is Frank Ryan, our Commander, Mary. I've told him all about you,"

"He has indeed, told me what an independent and strong minded woman you are," Ryan replied.

Mary recalled meeting him briefly, after Nora Connelly's speech in Union Hall.

"Well, Mr Ryan. I may seem strong-minded, but it's not working here. Please promise me that you'll be true to you word, and keep him safe. I don't know what I would do should anything happen to him."

Mary turned back, wrapped her arms around a clearly embarrassed Malachy and kissed him gently.

"I'll do my best, Miss Bradford," He turned. "Connelly Column, Fall In!"

At that, Malachy obediently joined the others as they marched up the gangway. Mary soon spotted him amongst the waving crowds on the upper decks. She could feel his excitement, as he blew her kisses. The horn blasted loudly, as the ship departed.

Mary waited on the quay, until the boat disappeared over the horizon. As she turned to leave, an old woman approached, dressed in black and covered with a shawl.

"Don't worry, love. God will protect them, for they are going to do God's work."

Mary was taken by surprise.

"But they're Communists. They don't believe in God."

"What?" The woman exclaimed. "Are you telling me that...that... those men were not Mr O'Duffy's men?"

"No!" Mary exclaimed, with a laugh.

"But Father Murray told us to come down and see them off."

"Well, either Father Murray is a Communist, or he was genuinely wrong."

"Well, God's curse on them all. Anti-Christian lot! May they never return!"

Mary was shocked. She was about to issue a rebuke, but thought better of it.

"You clearly don't know much about Communists? It's well-known that if you ask God to wish bad luck on someone that doesn't believe in Him, it will have no effect whatsoever. However, once created, that bad luck has to find somewhere to go, so it whirls around, looking for the person who created it, and when it finds them, it stays with them, Forever! The only way to stop it is to light a candle for the person the bad luck was wished upon. There were over sixty men on that boat, so that's a lot of candles you'll have to light," she said triumphantly pointing towards dark clouds in the sky. "It looks like your bad wishes are already on their way, so here's a few pennies to get you started."

Mary handed the woman some coins, and calmly walked away, leaving the bewildered and panic-stricken old woman, looking up at the foreboding sky, with a handful of pennies.

Mary spent that Christmas at home. She had not heard from Malachy, and avoided reading about the Spanish War in the newspapers. On New Year's Eve, her parents invited some friends to the house for a small celebration. Anna, now married for 9 years, arrived with her husband, Maurice, and their two children, an eight year old girl named Mary, and a six year old boy named Maurice, after his father. Mary absolutely worshipped them. She spent most of the early part of the evening entertaining them in the front room, whilst the adults sat in the parlour. Her nephew had brought some lead soldiers and a toy gun with him, wrapped in old newspaper. He had removed the toys and was playing with them on the floor, beneath the Christmas tree. Mary sat at the table, helping her niece to cut out paper clothes and dolls, from a booklet.

"Auntie Mary, can I borrow your army hat? Her nephew asked suddenly, looking towards her with a face of pure innocence, as he lay stretched out across the floor.

Mary felt awkward. She adored Maurice, and did not want to disappoint him, but felt a strong reluctance to grant his request.

"Maurice, you know Auntie Mary said we mustn't touch that hat, without her permission," his sister said.

"I know! That's why I'm asking for permission," Maurice said, bemused.

Mary's reluctance dissolved when she saw the innocent look on his face as he lay beneath the Christmas tree, surrounded by his lead soldiers.

"Thank you for asking, Maurice. I will fetch it for you."

She returned, and put the hat on his head, his smile glowing brighter that the fire.

"Thank you, Auntie Mary," he said excitedly, and returned to play with his toys.

Mary felt happy as she watched Maurice try to control the large cap on his head. She stood silently, reflecting on the memory of sitting beside Myles, in the Army hospital, doing the same thing.

"Come back and help please, Auntie Mary," her niece said, bringing Mary back to the present.

As she turned towards the table, Mary noticed that the page of discarded newspaper was lying in front of the fire. She picked it up and straightened it out.

"I'll put it on the table, Maurice. We don't want a spark setting fire to it."

Maurice nodded in agreement, the hat sliding over his face. They all laughed.

Mary was attracted to the headlines of the old newspaper. She picked it up, in order to read it properly.

Republican XV International Brigade suffers heavy losses in Battle of Lopera.

Many of the Irish and English Republican Guard amongst the dead.

Below was a brief description of the three-day long battle, followed by a list of Irish causalities. She did not want to read the list, but could not help herself. At first, she tried to glance over the names, but then, she carefully studied each one, hoping that she had misread the spelling of one, in particular.

"Whatever's the matter?" Her niece asked, looking up from her paper dolls.

Mary, unable to control herself, stood up, and ran to her room, without answering, leaving behind two very confused-looking children.

"Thank you, Anna. Now go on down, and I'll follow in a minute. Just let me freshen up," Mary said to her sister, the third person that had come up to comfort her.

"I'll leave the door open," Anna said, with a sympathetic smile, as she left.

As Mary sat up on her bed, her nephew appeared in the doorway.

"I'm sorry I upset you, Auntie Mary. I've put your army hat back on the rack."

"Oh, come here, Maurice. It had nothing to do with the hat," Mary said compassionately, and held out her arms to invite him over.

Maurice rushed over and sat on the bed beside her, holding his toy gun.

"That's a lovely gun Maurice. You know I have a real one. I keep it at work. I'll show you someday"

"Really, I'd love that. Was it yours during the War?"

"No, no," Mary said, as she gently stroked his hair.

"Did it belong to the man who owned the army hat?" Maurice asked. "Mammy said he was very handsome, but died before you could get married, and the hat is all you have left of him," he continued, in one breath.

"Oh I have much more than a silly old hat....I have you for starters," Mary said, pulling Maurice across the bed and playfully tickling his sides.

"Stop, Auntie Mary, stop," he shouted, as he struggled to free himself.

Mary stopped playing. She got up, and brushed herself down. Taking a deep breath, and his hand, she prepared to face the rest of the family.

"Come on, Maurice. Let's go downstairs. We don't want to miss midnight!"

They descended the stairs. Before entering the room, Mary removed Myles' hat from the hall stand, and placed it back on his head. Maurice looked up at Mary, and gave her a heart-melting smile, giving her the extra strength that she needed to enter the room, and join in with the celebrations.

Mary went back to work on Monday the 3rd of January 1937, completely against the wishes of her family and friends. She needed to get away from the constant offers of sympathy and support in order to come to terms with her grief, in her own way. At work, she would be sheltered from the incessant reminders of how she had lost two potential husbands, through the violence of war. Inside, she could not feel any emotion. Nothing seemed to matter. Nothing was important – eating, sleeping or engaging in polite and sympathetic conversation, seemed pointless. Her mind, saturated with a painful numbness that supressed everything, felt like a flower that had fallen into a stream, and was being carried along by the current, no idea of where it was going.

Her father drove her to Dublin, hoping she would change her mind and stay a little longer with her family. Mary stared into the blackness of the landscape, sprinkled with yellow lights from the random and scattered dwellings, whose occupants were preparing for the day ahead. She thought about how life goes on, regardless of the destruction inflicted by others. Her mind was still filled with painful numbness that refused to go away. She could think of nothing else, but Malachy's farewell, the promise from Frank Ryan, and the bitterness of the old woman on the pier. From the beginning, she had deliberately supressed her feelings for Malachy. She never wanted to go through the experience of losing someone she loved, but now it had happened, again. It was this incomprehensible feeling that made her feel numb, and unable to express any facial or physical emotion. She just wanted to be alone, away from everyone and everything, so that she could cry and immerse herself in self-pity.

Her Father glanced at her, feeling her silent pain. He patted a comforting palm on her joined hands which rested on her lap.

"Mary, my love. You don't have to do this. Work is not that important, and your colleagues will understand. Let me turn around and take you home, my dear."

Mary turned her head and looked at her Father. For the first time, she realised how much he had aged. His profile, silhouetted against the colours of the dawn, which stretched across the eastern sky, highlighted the angry scar on his forehead, left by the British soldier's rifle butt. She could feel his love and sincerity for her, but this was neutralised by her inner numbness.

"Thank you, Dad, but I feel I must keep busy. I don't think I could stay at home, getting regular cups of tea and sympathy from Mam."

"I understand, my dear. Plus, Mr Fitzgerald is putting lights in all the rooms this week. I doubt it will be peaceful!"

"The light of a new day will dawn, no matter how long the night," Mary said, leaning her head on his shoulder. He briefly tapped her hands again, continuing their journey in companionable silence, the rising sun evaporating the surrounding darkness.

Mary brushed herself down, took a deep breath, opened the door and entered her office. She was surprised to find John Mills standing in the centre of the room, then horrified when he offered his condolences.

"How on earth did you know?" She asked, angrily taking off her coat and gloves.

"I'm sorry, Mary, but I told him…," a voice replied, from the small kitchen.

Mary looked over, even more surprised to see Sean Lemass standing there, holding a cup of tea. She remembered their first meeting, and his friendship with Malachy. That was the final straw. Her emotions could no longer be suppressed. She embraced him, their mutual pain, evident.

This was the tonic that she needed. Sean sat her down in the small kitchen. John joined them and they reminisced about Malachy and his short life. Sean explained that their socialist beliefs stemmed from joining Na Fianna Eireann, and fighting alongside James Connelly in the GPO. For Malachy, those beliefs developed into a firm commitment towards Communist ideals. He went on to share what he had been able to glean about Malachy's death, from the Republican Congress Party.

"Malachy died beside two English poets, John Cornford and Ralph Winston Fox."

"Fox! That was the surname of my Fiancée!" Mary interrupted him. "Is this generation, born at the turn of this century, condemned to death by War, no matter our circumstances?" Mary mused bitterly.

"It sometimes feels that way, Mary, but Malachy died fighting for what he believed in. Rightly or wrongly, John and I willingly went to war, risking our lives for what we believed in, and even though we survived, we have both suffered personal losses," Sean said, reflecting on the deaths of his two brothers. His younger brother died when Sean was cleaning a pistol that accidently discharged, just before the 1916 Rising. His other brother was kidnapped and murdered by Free State troops, during the Civil War. Sean placed his cup on the table, took out some tobacco and began to fill his pipe. "If you don't mind me asking, Mary, how did your fiancée die?"

"He was murdered, Sean," Mary replied, sharing the unvarnished truth.

Sean looked to John for clarity as he sucked the stem of his pipe. John looked at Mary, pleased to see the familiar spark in her eyes.

"He was murdered, Sean, in cold blood, not as an act of war, but as an act of vengeance, and Mary and I are close to apprehending the assailant," John said, smiling over at Mary.

"Indeed, I've heard this office has exposed some very devious characters, over the years," Sean said, inhaling deeply on his pipe.

Daniel appeared in the doorway, completely caught off-guard when he saw the kitchen full of people.

"Happy New Year, everyone," he spluttered, seeing the Minister of Finance sitting amongst his colleagues. "I hope I'm not interrupting anything?"

"No, you're not. Come in, Daniel and a Happy New Year to you, too," Mary said, standing up and giving him a brief hug.

"Well, I better be getting on my way," Sean said, also standing up. "If there's anything I can do for you, Mary, please don't hesitate to ask."

"You've done more than you imagine, Sean," Mary said, kissing his cheek.

John helped the Minister with his coat, and escorted him from the office.

"Well, Daniel, did you meet any nice girls over Christmas?" Mary asked, focusing on a more positive note as she sat down at her desk.

"Don't embarrass him, Mary," John said, noticing Daniel's shy reaction.

"Ah, he can tell me later," Mary said, looking at Daniel with a cheeky smile. John was delighted. It was clear that the earlier spark was now, firmly ablaze.

Sinn Fein and the IRA

Mary tried to get on with her life. She chose to stop attending most of the political meetings regularly held around the city, and settled into a routine. In February, she received an invitation from the Communist Party, to attend a Memorial for their fallen comrades in Spain. Although this invitation re-opened the wound of Malachy's death, she decided to attend, hoping it would help her with her grief.

The meeting was held in the Quaker Hall, in Dun Laoghaire, at 7 o'clock, on a Thursday night. Mary arrived early, with Silva, against her husband's wishes. They were given VIP seats, near the front of the dimly-lit hall, and realised the guests seated beside them, were also family and friends of the fallen.

The meeting started on time, with short speeches from junior members, before the main speaker, Mr Sean Murray, the General Secretary of the Irish Communist Party, spoke. In his rousing speech, he described the individual heroic deeds of the fallen during the Rising, the Anglo-Irish War, the Irish Civil War, and the Spanish War. He went on to discuss the future plans for the party. He received a standing ovation, followed by a verse of the national anthem, indicating the end of the Memorial.

It had started to rain, and the crowd took longer to disperse. Mary and Silvia shuffled towards the door. They were about to leave the hall, when Silvia noticed Nora Connelly standing in the doorway with Sean Lemass. They approached, and were welcomed by Sean, who officially introduced Nora Connelly.

"Won't people object to your presence at a Communist meeting, Sean?" Silvia asked, after the introductions.

"I'd attend the funeral of a King of England, if he were a friend, regardless of what the public or papers think," was Sean's heartfelt reply.

"Here, here," Nora Connelly interjected, "and let it be said, Mrs Mills, that most of us here, like your husband, John, are Socialists and not Communists.

"Do you know each other?" Mary asked curiously.

"Oh yes, Miss Bradford. John Mills, your friend Malachy Foley, may he rest in peace, and Sean here, all joined Fianna Eire together, and supported my Father's Citizen Army during the Lockout and the Easter Rising. You were all so young at the time," she said, as she lovingly grabbed Sean's arm. "I cooked you all breakfast at Liberty Hall that morning. Do you remember?"

"That you did, Nora," Sean reminisced.

"Are you thinking of joining the Fianna Fail Party, Miss Connelly? We could do with women like you supporting Women's Rights in Ireland," Mary asked.

"If I were to get a penny every time I'm asked that, Miss Bradford, I'd be a very rich woman. No, I'm a Republican and a member of Cumana Na mBan. I have no intention of giving up my beliefs, even if others have." She looked at Sean pointedly.

"Here's our lift," Sean said, changing the subject. "Just in time, as well. The rain is getting heavier," he continued, avoiding a reply to Nora's statement.

"Could you ladies do with a lift home?"

"No thank you, Sean. My husband is collecting us," Silvia said, as she shut the car door for Nora Connelly.

John arrived. Mary sat silently in the back on the way to her Dublin home. She looked out of the window, watching people trying to avoid the puddles, as they picked their way across the wet pavements that glistened beneath the tall street lamps. John pulled up at the recently installed traffic lights that hazily shone through the windscreen, as the wipers noisily swished back and forth.

"My, this country is developing," he said with a smile. "Traffic lights in Dublin! We'll soon be like London."

"It's not developing, in my opinion. It's going backwards. Tell me, did any of you process Nora Connelly's pension application?" Mary asked, leaning forward into the gap between the front seats.

"I think she refused to sign up for it, Mary," John said.

"I processed Grace Gifford's," Silvia said. "She married in Kilmainham Jail, the night before her fiancée; Joseph Plunkett was executed, in 1916."

"My Mother told me about her. Sadly, her family didn't recognise the marriage, leaving her near destitute," Mary said angrily. "But what about the others? Hanna Sheehy Skeffington, or Kathleen Clarke? Their husbands were executed in '16? Have they also refused State aid?

"I didn't notice, Mary," John replied.

"That's the problem. These women are the founding Mothers of this so-called 'Progressive State'. They risked everything fighting for a 'New Ireland', believing they would be treated equally, but they've been abandoned, as Government and Church no longer supports the ideal of equality, which sparked the revolution in the first place."

"Times and attitudes change, Mary, just like these lights," John said, grinding the car into gear, as the lights changed to green.

"Change for the worst, if you ask me," Mary said, sitting back with a sigh.

"Is that Malachy Foley speaking?" John asked, with a chuckle.

"What? Am I not allowed my own opinion, now?"

Silvia reached through the gap in the front seats and placed her hand on Mary's knee.

"I know it's hard, Mary. I felt for you, especially when Sean Murray mentioned Malachy, during his speech."

"Thank you, Silvia," Mary replied, placing her hand on Silvia's. "But this isn't about Malachy. I was thinking of the powerful influence these women still possess. If they just joined a political party, they could do so much more. They wouldn't have to change their beliefs, but would be better placed to advance them."

Silvia turned forward.

"I agree! Other TDs would be forced to act on, rather than slander their beliefs."

"I always said you two would make great Politicians!" John said, pulling up outside Mary's flat.

Mary apologised for her mood, thanking them both, and made her way up the drive. John waited until her door closed, before driving away.

"I knew you shouldn't have gone to that meeting, Silvia. I only hope Mary feels better in the morning."

"Ah, she's just a ball of frustration at the moment. She'll be alright after a good night's sleep. Now take me home, Mr Mills, I'm very tired," Silvia said, cuddling into her husband's side.

For the next few weeks, Mary searched the military records of the most prominent women of Ireland. Most had taken part in the 1916 Rising, the Anglo-Irish and Civil Wars. She was shocked to find that almost all had refused to claim compensation from the State.

She was inspired by this revelation, to attend a public Cumana Na mBan Meeting at Liberty Hall. She met Nora Connelly again, who introduced her to Maude Gonne and Hanna Sheehy-Skeffington, the invited guest speakers.

She wholly supported the issues discussed relating to the equal rights of female workers in Ireland, and the more general demands from the Irish Transport and General Workers Union, the ITGWU, but was disappointed that they did not mention or discuss the social rights of women, especially the freedom to work if married, and the rights of mothers to bring up children born out of wedlock, or keep their children if abandoned or experiencing hard times. When the opportunity arose, Mary raised these questions. Whilst the speaker agreed, she also adopted a 'first things, first' attitude regarding union demands for women. Mary suggested that if some of the powerful women present joined the main parties, they could use their membership and influence as stepping stones to achieving their goals not just for the rights of working women, but for all women in Ireland. Her suggestion was dismissed, and led to heated debate and a reminder, as if needed, of the violence meted out on the woman of Ireland, by members of these Parties. There were personal accounts of beatings and rapes by British, Free State, and IRA soldiers during the Anglo-Irish and Civil Wars, and some openly named their aggressors, many of whom now sat on Town and County Councils, throughout Ireland, representing these Parties.

Mary asked these women if any of them had made claims against the State for compensation for the violence committed against them. Shockingly, as little as one in ten had. The rest declared they wanted nothing from the traitorous bastards now sitting in power, reminding everyone that the power those men now wielded would not have been achieved without the help of the women who risked everything.

When Mary explained to one very angry woman, that she could still make a legitimate claim against the violent rape she had suffered under the hands of Irish Free State troops, the woman replied with a question.

"Have you made a claim for your incarceration, and the defiling attacks you suffered in those English Jails?"

Mary answered honestly, that she had not, realising, that she felt the same - if she was forced to take it, she would donate it to the poor. She sat down, silently reflecting. The meeting ended with the National Anthem.

As she left, alone in the shuffling crowd, she received a sympathetic look from a well-dressed woman. The woman passed her a note, and, without a word, disappeared into the crowd. Mary stuck the note into her pocket and walked the short journey home.

When hanging up her coat, she out took the note, and read the simple message.

'Please call this number, Margaret Buckley'.

A telephone number had been added to the bottom of the note.

Mary paused, trying to remember where she had heard the name before, but tiredness overruled curiosity. She put the note back into her pocket, and retired to bed.

The following morning, Mary was sitting at her desk, lost in thought.

"A penny for them…?" John said, noticing her pensive gaze.

"I was miles away. I went to a Cumana Na mBan Meeting, last night. Well, maybe more of an Irish Women's Workers Union Meeting. Anyway, as a result, I have decided to put in a claim for compensation and a pension."

"Well," said John "you're fully entitled, but why, after all these years?"

"Some of the women at the meeting made me realise I was being hypocritical – I was asking them to claim when I'd not done so myself."

"Fill out an application, Mary, and I'll personally process and approve it."

Mary got up from her desk. Approaching John, she laid a form on his desk.

"Already done!"

She turned, and went back to her own desk.

"By the way John, who's Margaret Buckley?"

John was surprised that Mary was unaware of Margaret Buckley.

"Now, there's a formidable woman. She was one of the founding members of Cumana Na mBan. I first met her during a riot in the Dublin City Lockout; the DMP had attacked a Union demonstration that was marching for better living conditions. God, I was only 16 years old at the time!"

"What was a 16 year old Cork boy doing in a Dublin riot?" Mary was curious.

"My Mother's sister died in childbirth. They lived in a Dublin tenement, so we came to help her family. We were horrified at the conditions they were forced to live in. There were over twelve families in one house in Henrietta Street. Twelve families, Mary – that's over 100 people. I stayed to help my cousins, and they convinced me to join the Na Fianna Éireann." John paused, recalling memories from that time. "I met Margaret again, in Cork, during the Tan War," he said, perking up, "but the last time we spoke was during the Civil War, when I tried to convince her to give up a hunger strike - she was in Mountjoy at the time. We haven't met since. She recently became the Head of the Sinn Fein Party. Why do you ask?"

"Well, I briefly met her last night, and she passed me her number."

"I'd say she's recruiting. Sinn Fein's numbers have dropped since the Party split."

"What split?"

"They split back in 1926, when they couldn't agree on whether to take seats in the Dail. That's when Sean Lemass and Dev founded the Fianna Fail Party, taking most of the Sinn Fein funding and supporters with them. They had another disagreement in '34, when some members agreed to accept the State pension. Remember the deluge?"

"How could I forget! What happened after that?"

"Well, most of the prominent members left and the Party lost all support from the IRA. That's why they haven't contested any elections for years. The Party is broken, and probably won't last much longer."

"Arthur Griffith must be turning in his grave."

"Indeed, he must," John replied.

"I just might give Miss Buckley a call," Mary said, turning her back to her work.

"What're you like, Mary Bradford?" John muttered, pondering her application.

Mary contacted Margaret Buckley, and on the following Thursday they had lunch together in Bewley's Café. John was correct. Margaret was recruiting, and was interested in Mary, after hearing her personal experiences at the Union Meeting. As lunch ended, they shook hands, and Mary accepted an invitation to attend a Sinn Fein Meeting, the following week.

She was apprehensive, but this evaporated, as there were so few people present. Margaret Buckley was delighted to see her. Following some quick introductions, the meeting started and Mary took a seat. The main topic for discussion was how to rebuild the relationship between Sinn Fein and the IRA, which had been lost following the split in 1926. This was followed by a discussion on what to do about Sinn Fein funds, frozen by the State, and finished on whether to run candidates in the coming elections, which De Valera would have to call sometime before the year ended. Margaret and Mary shared their journey home. They discussed personal issues, greatly surprised at how similar their lives had been. They parted on the corner of Merrion Square, and Mary agreed to attend another meeting, the following week.

Mary attended a further five meetings, becoming a familiar face. She shared her passion for Women's Rights, and twice tried to convince the Party they should accept the Oath of Allegiance as a stepping stone, and take their seats in the Dail. She quickly learnt this was like trying to convince a cat to sleep amongst dogs.

Occasionally, famous figures were invited to talk. One such guest, a lady named Margaret Skinner, whose story both fascinated and disappointed Mary, when she learnt that such an interesting woman had given up politics to become a school teacher. Walking home with Margaret Buckley, Mary spoke excitedly about Margaret Skinner.

"I can't believe she was wounded three times in the Rising and escaped from an English hospital, and that she moved about dressed as a man, during the Tan War, and now she just wants to be a school teacher."

"Don't underestimate her, Mary. She's not 'just' a school teacher. She's still working for Women's Rights across the country, and is an active member of the Irish National Teachers' Organisation, the INTO."

"She got to prove herself in both wars. I was locked up in an English Jail."

"Don't punish yourself, Mary. A lot of good women were locked up, myself included, and we survived to carry on the fight for Women's Suffrage."

"But I think that cause is going nowhere. Dev is drawing up a new constitution, after the abdication last year. I know from a friend that Dev is allowing Archbishop McQuaid to influence its construction. My friend told me that women will not be allowed to divorce, work when married, or sit on juries, and all the Church laws that restrain us as women, are to be included. Mothers will still have their children taken away, if their husbands die. They will still have to be 'Churched', after giving birth, and, God forgive her fate, should she become pregnant out of wedlock."

"Well then, we will object to it, Mary," Margaret said, stopping at the corner.

"We always object, but where's the fighting spirit that got us here in the first place?"

Margaret looked at Mary. She could see a familiar anger, lurking behind her sparkling blue eyes. She was inspired to ask Mary to become more involved.

"Mary, I've arranged a meeting with some IRA leaders next Wednesday. We want to try to repair the relationship between them and Sinn Fein. I'd like you to come with me. I could use the moral support, and need someone to take notes."

Mary was surprised but wanted to be a part of this historic meeting.

"That would be interesting, but I am not an official member of Sinn Fein,"

"That doesn't matter. Besides, you never officially left Cumana na mBan."

"I never officially joined either," Mary thought to herself, before replying.

"I'd love to come - it's the only party in Ireland that I haven't attended a meeting with yet!"

"I'll pick you up at 7 o'clock," Margaret said, leaning forward to kiss Mary on the cheek, before departing.

Mary turned, and walked slowly towards her flat. Her shoes echoed across the silent streets. A gentle breeze rustled some litter, as she pondered the events of the evening. The garden gate squeaked loudly, as she closed it. She paused, for a moment, in the darkness of the front garden, glancing up at the barely visible path and inhaling the strong scent of the plants and bushes, pleasantly reminding her of home.

"What am I getting myself into now," she whispered as she negotiated the garden path in the dark.

Mary stopped, recognising the familiar scent of evening primrose. She could just make out the yellow, blossoming plant, in the weak light. She pictured Myles, twirling primroses between his fingers at the Hanging Stone, and the pressed flowers in his journal.

"Oh Myles, my love, even after all of these years, I still miss you, and you have such an uncanny way of reminding me!" She picked the flowers and inhaled their perfume.

The following Wednesday, Margaret collected Mary in a car. Two members of Sinn Fein were also present, as they drove to their Head Office, in Suffolk Street.

Inside, rows of chairs in the main meeting room had been replaced by a large table with six place settings, directly opposite one another. Mary assisted in stacking the surplus chairs and stocking the place settings with pencils, paper and water. At 8 o'clock, four IRA men arrived. Margaret welcomed them and made introductions. Mary recognised two of them immediately, Sean MacBride and Kevin Barry.

"Did you live in France, Mr MacBride? She asked curiously, as the four men finally agreed with the seating arrangements, and sat down.

"I was born there, Miss Bradford. It often confuses people, and, yes, I can still speak French, before you ask."

Mary smiled at him.

"That was going to be my next question."

"Shall we start or wait for the others? They may not make it, given present circumstances," Margret interrupted, sitting next to Mary.

"Let's begin. If Thomas was coming, he'd have made it by now," Sean MacBride said, looking at his watch.

The meeting opened on a discussion on IRA funding, and how Sinn Fein could assist, if, the IRA were to lend its support to the party, followed by intense discussion on Sinn Fein funds currently frozen by the State. Margaret outlined the legal action Sinn Fein was taking, when she was interrupted by the sudden arrival of two more people.

"Ah, Thomas! Glad you could make it," Sean MacBride said to the late arrivals.

"I had to be sure I wasn't followed," Thomas replied, removing his jacket and rolling up his shirt sleeves, as if for a long debate.

Following brief introductions, both men took their places at the table.

Mary was experiencing a rush of terror. She recognised him, but could not remember the circumstances.

Thomas was invited to speak. He suggested a bombing campaign in England, and blowing up all British monuments, throughout Ireland. Sean MacBride agreed, but they got a reluctant reply from Kevin Barry. Margaret interrupted, gently reminding everyone of the true purpose of the meeting, to amicably reconcile the rift between the IRA and Sinn Fein, not a discussion of IRA campaign tactics.

"I beg your pardon!" Thomas replied sarcastically.

Mary could not take her eyes off the crudely-stitched, angry, X-shaped scar on Thomas' left forearm. Suddenly, she was reminded of the evidence Percy had sent her, back in 1932. She looked at his face again, recognising him from the photograph in the file. This was the infamous, 'Thomas Donnelly', the man that had plagued Myles.

Her mind exploded in a tsunami of unpleasant memories. She remembered crawling across the road to reach Myles, and resting his limp head on her lap. Her parents, lying injured, in the hall of their house. Bridie Mackenzie finding her brother's body hanging in the larder. The Court case and the horrific beatings and sexual assaults she endured. As these thoughts raged, she could hear the buzz of conversation and a slew of unconnected words – Constitution; Land Annuities; Bombing Statues.

"Oh, why don't you blow up all the post boxes too, whilst you're at it!" Mary raised her voice, unable to control her anger any longer.

Everyone in the room stopped speaking and stared at her,

"This, burn everything British, but their coal attitude will get us nowhere. Why not direct your energy at something constructive, like repairing this divide and getting back into Government. Dev doesn't hate you, well, not yet at least, but if you carry on like this, he'll not only ban your organisations, but lock you all up, and I wouldn't blame him," Mary finished, staring daggers at Donnelly, who was rendered speechless by her outburst.

An uncomfortable silence ensued, only broken by Kevin Barry.

"I have to agree with you, Miss Bradford," he said.

"This is what always happens!" Sean MacBride interrupted. "Seeds of discontent are planted. We disagree, and the fractures deepen. The IRA has formidable numbers, Miss Buckley, and we're very capable of taking over the State, if necessary. We were ready in '32, if Cosgrave failed to hand over power to Fianna Fail, and we're ready now! So, if Miss Bradford's opinion is that of Sinn Fein, it's very obvious we still have nothing in common, so, I, for one, will not be supporting your Party."

"I assure you that Miss Bradford's opinion is her own, and not that of Sinn Fein, or its member's," Margret said nervously.

Thomas Donnelly leaned forward, looking directly at Margaret.

"Well, you'll just have to prove that, Miss Buckley. You can start by clearing out your pro-British, Cumana Na Gael Blue Shirt Supporters, clearly still present in your ranks," he said, nodding towards Mary. "Secondly, I suggest you replace yourself with a man more capable of doing the job as leader," Donnelly said, standing up.

Margaret was livid, but before she could reply, Sean MacBride interjected.

"I have to agree with Thomas, Margaret. You've a lot of work to do before I would consider sitting at a meeting again. Thank you for the invitation this evening. I'm sure we will be in touch."

At that, the rest of the IRA leadership stood, noisily slid their chairs back under the table, and prepared to leave. Kevin Barry approached Mary.

"It has been a pleasure, Miss Bradford. You remind me of Sean's Aunt, the late Countess Markievicz. Don't let anyone, or anything, break it – it's our spirit that defines us. Good night," he said, kissing her hand, before leaving with the others.

When the room finally emptied, Margaret turned to Mary with a loud sigh.

"I don't know whether to be angry or sympathetic, but I do know that you've just jeopardised six months of hard work and negotiation."

"I'm sorry, Margaret. I don't know what came over me," Mary said, feeling guilty that she was lying to a friend.

"Go on out to the car, Mary. I'll lock up here. I shan't be long."

An uncomfortable silence filled the car on the journey home. Mary wanted to share why she felt the way she did, but refrained from doing so in the presence of others, fearing they might use the information to try and organise another meeting. As she emerged from the car, Margaret called after her, obviously prompted by the others.

"Mary, I'm sorry, but please don't attend next week's meeting. You'll not be welcome."

Mary was about to reply, but the car sped away, leaving her stranded on the footpath. She was hurt, knowing she had lost Margaret's friendship. As she walked up her garden path, she smelt the perfume of the evening primrose, and made a promise to herself.

"Myles, I think we have Donnelly right where we want him," she whispered, sadness replaced by the prospect of delivering justice.

The next day, John handed Mary her daily post. He also passed her a small envelope filled with used stamps, which she was collecting for her niece who brought them to the local convent for the nuns to sell for charity.

Mary looked at the variety and colour of the used stamps, remembering Freeny's words about the stamps and coins changing, but everything else remaining the same. She told John about the previous evening.

"Telling you to be careful would fall on deaf ears," John said, "but please remember, the IRA would not hesitation to kill you, regardless of your sex."

"I was invited to that meeting, John, and attended simply to find out the IRA's view on Women's Rights in Ireland. The last thing I expected was my Fiancée's murderer, a sitting TD, whose only interest seemed to be in blowing up statues," Mary said, the frustration of the previous evening seeping back into her veins.

"I understand your anger, but I think we should follow the original plan to catch Donnelly, and pass our evidence to Detective Broy, once the final pieces are in place."

"We might have it," Mary said, holding an envelope newly arrived from Percy.

In the following weeks, De Valera's Government released a draft copy of the new Constitution. It proposed measures for the Free State to become a Republic. If agreed by all sitting members of the Dail, the draft Constitution would be put to the people as a plebiscite, to be held at the same time as the 1937 general election. Mary read through the draft, disgusted that none of the clauses regarding Women's Rights had been changed, especially the religious suppression of their independence.

Mary wanted to shout from the roof tops, to try and make people understand the stranglehold the Church would hold under this new Constitution, with even more power to suppress the Women of Ireland. She was particularly disgusted to read that young women, who fell pregnant out of wedlock, could be legally removed from their families, locked up and forced to give up their babies for adoption. If Irish families fell on hard times, the State could break up the family, and give the children to a religious order. She wanted to discuss this with Margaret Buckley or Margaret Skinner, but feared a hostile reception. Instead, she arranged to meet Silvia in St Stephen's Green for lunch.

Mary hoped that Silvia could arrange a private audience with Kathleen Clarke and Nora Connelly to understand what these women proposed to do about the loss of Women's Rights under this proposed Constitution.

Mary entered St Stephen's Green from the Boer War Arch, and headed to her favourite seat in the centre of the green, directly below the King George monument, which always reminded her of Malachy. As she approached, she saw a large crowd standing beside make-shift barriers, blocking the path. She made her way to the front, only to be confronted by a sight of total destruction. The bronze statue had been blown to pieces during the night, leaving an empty pedestal.

There were a number of Corporation workers nearby, tidying up the mess.

"What happened?" Mary asked the nearest, a large, round man in dungarees.

"The bloody IRA, that's what happened, Luv. Luckily no one was killed," the man replied, stopping his sweeping to lean, lazily, on his brush.

"That's why they did it at night," his colleague said, brushing the debris nearby.

"What bleeding good will this do any of us?" The big man asked.

"It's so we don't have to look at that ould English King, and be reminded of what he did to this country. I tell you, auld one eyed Nelson better mind himself," the other man said, as he stopped sweeping, and joined his colleague in a lazy lean.

"They'll never get him - he's far too big," the first man said.

"Don't be too sure," the other replied, with a grin.

"What are you going to do with the pieces?" Mary asked, interrupting them.

The first man picked up a piece of bronze and studied it.

"We was told to bring the bits back to the depot. It's only fit for scrap now." He handed the piece to Mary, across the barrier.

"Well then, you should sell it as scrap and spend the money on the poor of the city," Mary said, handing the piece back to him.

"I doubt that'll happen," the man said, throwing the piece to the ground, in front of his brush.

Mary pondered what Malachy would have thought of the incident, and smiled

"There you are, Mary," Silvia said, lightly kissing her cheek. "What's happened?" She asked, seeing the destruction.

"We'll go to Bewley's for lunch. I'll tell you on the way. Good day, gentlemen."

Both men doffed their caps, and went back to their sweeping. The two women linked arms and walked to Grafton Street, where they spent over an hour discussing recent events. Silvia agreed to help Mary arrange a meeting with Nora Connelly.

A month later, on the 14th of June 1937, the Fianna Fail Government dissolved the Eighth Dail, and a General Election was called. Reading the official announcement in the paper, John Mills looked up from his desk.

"Mary, I've some disappointing news – I've just been waiting for the right time to tell you."

Curious, Mary braced herself.

"What is it?"

"Well, you remember a few weeks back, we passed all the information we had on Thomas Donnelly to Eamon Broy, of the Garda?"

"Yes," Mary said, a sinking feeling forming in her stomach.

"Well, yesterday, I got his reply. He's not interested in what Donnelly's done in the past, and won't pursue him for any killings – he thinks they'll be classed as 'Extra Judicial' in any Court of Law."

"What? So he's just going to let Donnelly get away with murder, is he?"

"If Donnelly is found guilty of committing murder during the Tan War, then we're all at risk."

"I'm not talking about the Tan War. It's the new evidence Percy uncovered on the murder he committed in Ireland, way before the Tan War. Surely the proof Percy sent from England, is enough to get a conviction for that one at least?"

"Again, Broy's not interested. He told me he'd passed it on to our old friend, Garda Superintendent John Moran, and left him to decide if it's worth pursuing. He told us to consider that Donnelly is a respected member of the Fianna Fail Party, a sitting TD, running for election. Broy reckons it'd be more trouble that its worth."

"What about the English murder?" Mary asked. "Surely the evidence that Percy uncovered would be enough to convict him of that, at least."

"As I said, anything that happened in England is considered an English matter, and this Irish Government won't extradite an Irish TD."

"What can we do?" Mary asked, close to tears. "He's still a ruthless murderer!"

"Give your evidence to the Fine Gael Party. I'm sure Cosgrave would love to print dirt on a member of the Fianna Fail elite, especially in the run up to an election," Daniel said, looking up from his desk.

Mary and John looked at Daniel. They had forgotten he was there. They looked at each other, completely overwhelmed by the simplicity of such a powerful suggestion.

"The Irish papers wouldn't touch it, especially as Dev owns one," John said.

"What about the English Papers? They love a scandal involving Irish politics. Your friend from London could run the story," Daniel said, expanding his idea.

"You mean Tracey Hicks."

"Yes, that's the one."

John and Mary smiled at each other, silently agreeing to involve Daniel in their future plans.

Thomas Donnelly

Thomas Donnelly was born in County Louth, in 1890. His was a large family. His Father was a Soldier in the British Army, and rarely home. His mother survived on the army pay that arrived monthly. When Thomas was 14, he realised his mother was having an affair with a local RIC Officer. It bothered him, and led to several arguments. One morning, following another confrontation, this time with the RIC Officer, who had stayed overnight, he packed his few belongings, and left for Dublin.

For the first few weeks he slept rough near the docks, and picked up some labouring work, discharging ships. On one ship, two labourers convinced him to go into the ship's accommodation, and steal any valuables he could find. This proved more profitable than the work, the gain far outweighing the risk.

After a year, he got greedy, and was caught stealing from his workmates. He managed to escape into the City, before they could apply the usual rough justice. In the City, he fell in with pickpockets and thieves, and within two years, was well-established amongst Dublin's underworld, working alone, he made a good living stealing from drunks and mugging unaccompanied, elderly Gentlemen.

Early one morning, on his way home from a night of petty crime, he spotted a well-dressed, elderly gentleman, leaving his house on Merrion Square. The man stopped on the pavement to flag down a passing horse and coach taxi, but the driver indicated that he already had a passenger. The Gentleman took a gold watch from his waistcoat, looked at it, and decided to walk. Donnelly followed. When the man turned down an empty side street, next to a park he pounced.

"Give me your watch, now!" He bellowed, at the startled Gentleman.

"I will not, you scoundrel," the man said, waving his silver-topped cane defensively, as he turned to face his assailant.

Donnelly laughed, and grabbed the cane, striking the man hard, on the side of the head. The elderly man fell, and struck his head on the granite plinth, that supported the railings around the park. His top hat rolled away, exposing a large gash on his forehead, oozing blood.

Donnelly heard a scream. He turned to see a man and woman exit the park. They stared at him, horrified. He threw the cane aside, grabbed the watch and chain, and ran. He had to think fast. He knew it would not be long before the DMP would be searching for him. He decided to avoid his accommodation, and head straight to Kingstown, and catch the morning mail boat to England. He could go to London, and sit it out. He would ask a friend to send on his 'stash', hidden in his flat.

There being 'no honour amongst thieves', he never did receive his package, forcing him to work on the railroads in and around London. But honest work was not for him, and he quickly settled back into his old lifestyle, stealing and mugging, once again. He was recognised as an independent amongst the London underworld, his skill soon netting him a small fortune. Shortly after his nineteenth birthday, he saw a well-dressed Gentleman, leaving a brothel in the East End. This usually meant lucrative pickings, but it was mid-afternoon, which confused him. He decided to follow the man. Once on a back street, Donnelly pounced. The Gentleman suspected he was being followed had deliberately led Donnelly down this alleyway. The man turned to face his adversary, pulling a sword from his cane, and slashing Donnelly across his lower, left arm. Donnelly staggered back, in shock.

"I was only going to ask if you were lost," Donnelly pleaded, exposing the slash across his arm to his assailant, hoping to garner some sympathy.

"Fuck off Paddy! Do yer fink I came down in the last shower, you Irish bastard," the man replied, in a distinct cockney accent, which did not support the clothes he wore.

Donnelly was about to say something, when the man lashed out again, catching him across the first wound. This second cut created a large, bloody X-shape on his left forearm. Donnelly cried out in agony, and held his injured arm with his other hand, in an attempt to stem the blood.

"What the hell's wrong with you, you stupid bastard," Donnelly shouted.

"'Fought you were gettin' easy pickin's, did ya, Paddy?" The man said, as he tucked the sword under his arm. He whistled loudly, using his fingers. Donnelly recognised it as a gang distress call, and realised that this man was not visiting the Brothel, he was the owner. Donnelly was in big trouble, so, without thinking, he grabbed the sword from beneath the man's arm.

"Why, you poxy little bastard," the man said, recovering the scabbard, which lay nearby. He tried to strike Donnelley with it, but as he raised his arm above his head, Donnelly struck, plunging the sword deep into the man's chest, killing him instantly.

He could hear the clatter of hobnailed boots, getting louder, as they approached.

"Arfur? Arfur, where are ya, mate?"

He looked to the top of the alley, as two men appeared.

"Arfur, wot's 'appened," one called out, seeing his boss lying on the ground, and Donnelly standing over him, holding the sword.

"Why, you little bastard," the other shouted, and ran towards Donnelly.

Donnelly threw the sword at him and ran for his life.

Both men followed, in hot pursuit, only losing sight of him when Donnelly jumped a railway line, quickly crossing it, just as a train pulled into the platform. He mingled with the departing passengers, leaving the station by the main exit.

The stairs from the platform, led to a large, arched arcade, with shops on either side. As he approached the main exit, panic raced through him. He saw both pursuers at the front of the station, forcefully checking the forearms of young men as they passed. He glanced around the station arcade and saw an Army Recruiting Office, next to a Barbershop. He entered, as casually as he could, and was greeted by a large, jolly Sergeant Major, sitting behind a desk.

"Well hello, young man. Are you here to join up?"

"Yes!" Donnelly exhaled loudly, as he tried to catch his breath and disguise the throbbing pain in his forearm.

"That's the spirit," the Sergeant Major said, delighted that he would not have to spend time convincing this potential recruit of the benefits of Army life. "You know this is the First Battalion, Royal Norfolk, not the London Irish Regiment?"

"Yes, my Father was in the Norfolk's for years," Donnelly lied nervously; as he saw the two thugs search the shops on the opposite side of the arcade.

"Corporal, will you do the honours," the Sergeant said to another man, who had just entered from the back, carrying a cup of tea. Donnelly joined the Corporal at a small desk in the corner of the room, just as the two thugs entered the office.

"Well hello, young men. Are you here to join the Royal Norfolk's as well," the Sergeant bellowed, surprised at the sudden interest in his regiment.

"Not on your life, Mate," one of the men replied. He briefly glanced around the room, concluding that everyone present was office staff.

"He ain't here."

"Let's try the platform," the other replied, as they both left.

Donnelly was sent to Norfolk for basic training, which he completed successfully. He intended to desert, and return to London, when things had settled down, but he got word that a reward had been posted on him, and he knew he could never return. Fearing for his safety, Donnelly decided to stay in the Army, for now.

After six months, he found that regimented army life suited him. He settled in well. It gave him a sense of purpose, and an opportunity to return to Ireland, without suspicion. He still stole from other regiments, but never his own, not out of loyalty, but to avoid raising suspicion. When War broke out in 1914, he was sent to France from Belfast, where the regiment had been stationed. For the first two years, he actually proved himself a good solider at both Mons and Ypres. But his career was marred by accusations of torture and murder. The accusation was made by an Officer, who had witnessed the aftermath of his handiwork - two German soldiers hung with barbed wire in an abandoned stable, brutally beaten. The charges were dropped from lack of evidence and reluctant senior officers.

He instilled fear in his comrades, who witnessed the darker and more sinister side to Donnelly. He felt untouchable. He continued to torture and murder captured German POW's, getting a grim pleasure from the task.

Two comrades were disgusted after witnessing another of his brutal murders. He had gouged out the eyes of a young German conscript, and slowly twisted the corkscrew end of a metal barbed wire picket into the chest of another, laughing maniacally. They struggled with their conscience for a week, before reporting his actions. On approaching their CO, they were surprised to learn that Donnelly had already been a suspect in the murder of a disreputable English Gentleman, from the East End of London, several years earlier, and was being escorted back to England, to face trial in a London Court.

Mary had not heard of Donnelly before 1924, when Bridie Mackenzie first mentioned his name as the man responsible for her brother's death. Mary had overlooked him at the time, from the shock of discovering Father Mackenzie's warped feelings for her. She believed that Donnelly had simply supplied the document to strengthen Mackenzie's allegiance to him, requiring both his support and a safe place to hide, during the Anglo-Irish War.

She did, at the time, briefly investigate his activities during the Anglo-Irish War, which proved rather dull from an active service perspective.

His first application for a State pension was denied, as he had supported Anti-Treaty forces during the Civil War. However, his initial application did contain indisputable proof that he was an Area Commander and not personally involved in any major action against Crown forces. He had successfully supplied money, arms and safe houses to the Flying Columns of Wicklow, Wexford, and Carlow, throughout the conflict. Mary had added him to her list of tormentors, but did not class him as a key figure, so he remained dormant until his name came up again, twice within months of each other, almost eight years later, in 1932.

The first time was when Pat Kavanagh, the Arklow IRA Commander, told her that it was Donnelly who had ordered the killing of Myles, and that his hatred of Myles, stemmed from a personal grudge, the origins of which, were unknown.

She still had his IRA record and his original application for a pension, but the information was limited, so she decided to investigate how he came to possess the damming document given to Father Mackenzie. She knew it might have been stolen from the Cumana Na mBan Office in Wexford, run by three sisters, named Carlisle. She arranged a meeting with the younger Carlisle sister, who still lived there. Siobhan Carlisle agreed to meet her in the Franciscan Church, in the heart of the town.

Mary entered the Church by a side sanctuary. It was unusually bright and looked modern. Huge pillars dominated the main aisle, and a beautiful stained glass window cast an array of colours across the altar.

Mary saw a young woman, around her age, sitting on a pew. As she approached, the sound of her shoes echoed throughout the interior. The woman turned.

"You must be Mary Bradford?" She said, as Mary stopped next to the pew.

"Yes, I am. Thank you for taking the time to meet me," Mary replied, offering her hand, attracting the attention of a nearby priest.

Siobhan invited her to sit down as Mary explained the purpose of her visit. Siobhan, clearly emotional, explained the history of the office founded by her two older sisters with the help of the local IRA Commander, to raise money for the struggling families of imprisoned Volunteers. They also printed propaganda leaflets and held meetings. At one of these meetings, they met Thomas Donnelly. At first, he seemed pleasant and attracted the attention of Niamh, the middle sister, who found him charming. As the months went by, his interest in her became more menacing and he tried to force himself on her, alarming all three sisters. He would turn up at their house at all hours of the day and night, completely unannounced. The eldest sister, Anne, asked the local Commander to warn Donnelly to back off, and stop harassing Niamh and her family. Donnelly ignored the warning.

One evening it came to a head. He turned up unexpectedly and found Niamh alone, in the office. This time he did not mess around. He tried to force himself on her. Niamh was terrified and lashed out, slashing his cheek with her nails. He stepped back in pain. On seeing the blood, he struck her hard, across her head, knocking her to the floor. He pounced on her, like a lion, pinning her down, by kneeling across her chest.

"Look at what you've done, you stupid bitch," he said, tearing open her blouse. "You have no one to blame but yourself. You've been teasing me for months. This is your fault! Do you understand, bitch?"

As Niamh's blouse gave way, he heard another noise behind him. He turned to identify the cause, but, before he could, he was struck on the side of his head, with a typewriter. Whilst he had been wrestling with Niamh, he had failed to notice that her older sister, Anne, had returned. Anne, horrified by what she saw, silently crept up on Donnelly, removed the typewriter from the desk, and struck him on the head with it. Donnelly slumped to the floor, with a loud, hollow thump, but remained conscious.

Anne quickly recovered a loaded .38 revolver that she kept hidden in her desk, and pointed it at Donnelly, as he tried to sit up. Niamh stood up and covered herself with the remains of the ripped blouse. She walked over to Donnelly, and slapped him hard, across his face.

"Shoot him, Anne," she shouted at her terrified sister, trying to cover herself.

Donnelly struggled to his feet, still dazed. He staggered towards the door.

"Shoot him, Anne!" Niamh pleaded, as he struggled to open the door.

Anne could not find the resolve to shoot him, and watched him stagger outside.

"You will regret this. Both of you!" He said, before disappearing into the night.

"My sisters agreed to report the incident to the local Commander, but he had been summoned to Dublin that night, probably on Donnelly's orders. Three days later, my sisters were arrested, and murdered by the British." Siobhan hesitated, trying to hold back the tears that threatened to overwhelm her. She took a deep breath and continued.

"Everyone blamed Father Mackenzie for stealing the document, but he was a good friend to the family. I think Donnelly stole it and used it to extract revenge on my sisters."

The tears won. Siobhan started to cry at the memory, attracting the attention of the Priest. She waved him back. Mary passed Siobhan a handkerchief.

"Some months later, I found Donnelly alone in the office. I confronted him. He was clearly startled by what I knew. He punched me, in the face, almost knocking me out, and told me that if I didn't want to end up like my sisters, I should keep my mouth shut. I was terrified." Siobhan paused, thinking about the incident. "He threw me to one side and left. I stopped attending meetings after that, and left the Organisation. Now, he's a Government TD, which is why I wanted to meet you here," she said, now looking at the Priest, who let Mary know he was watching them.

"He's a friend. I told him about the meeting," Siobhan said, as the Priest looked away, pretending to fuss over a candle.

Mary placed her hand on Siobhan's, and squeezed it.

"Thank you Siobhan. That document was presented at my trial, and, as a result, I spent years in an English Jail. I want to collect the facts and seek justice, now for you and your sisters', as well as myself."

"I hope you can put our demons to rest," Siobhan said with renewed hope. "Promise me you'll get him! Please!" Siobhan pleaded, holding Mary's arm.

"I promise," Mary replied, as she acknowledged the Priest with a nod.

Mary gave Siobhan a hug and walked towards the door. Before she left, she glanced back at Siobhan, and saw the Priest sitting beside her, offering comfort, his arm around her shoulders.

"I really hope I can keep my promise," she said to herself, opening the heavy, wooden door, and flooding the Church with a dazzling, bright light. She walked over to a waiting car. John sat in the driving seat.

"How'd it go?" he asked.

"I'll tell you on the way back, but let's get some lunch first."

317

"Sounds good to me," John said, as he pulled away from the Church, under the watchful eyes of Siobhan and the Priest, now standing in the doorway.

The second time Donnelly's name came to Mary's attention in 1932 was in an old newspaper that Mary was using to light the fire. The article, printed during election season, gave a personal history of each of the Fianna Fail Candidates. Mary unscrewed the ball of paper, and sat at the living room table, reading carefully.

Donnelly was running for a seat in County Louth. In the article, he boasted about what he, and the party, would do, once elected. The brief history that followed described how he had deserted the British Army, the Norfolk Regiment, in Liverpool, back in December 1916, to continue the fight for Ireland's freedom, following the Easter Rising. Then followed a detailed description of how he organised the Flying Columns in Wexford, Carlow, and Wicklow, throughout the Anglo-Irish War, keeping them supplied with weapons and ammunition.

Something bothered Mary about the article. It was the mention of the Norfolk Regiment and the connection to Liverpool. She opened a drawer in the mahogany dresser that dominated her front room, and removed Myles' diary. She scrolled through the pages, stopping at December 1916, bookmarked with the stub of a mail boat passenger ticket. She could not believe what she read. Closing the diary, she turned to the framed photograph of Myles, kept on top of the dresser.

"No wonder he wanted you dead, Myles!" She said to his image. "But, I think we may finally have the evidence we need to bring him down."

She telephoned Percy in London, and told him about the diary entry. Percy, having supplied much of the damning evidence against Donnelly, was relieved that the evidence was coming together. Mary presented her file to John the following Monday.

On reviewing the evidence, John reached out and stroked Mary's arm.

"Mary, I can relate to your pain and frustration, but, this evidence would only be effective if Britain still governed this Country. It only incriminates Donnelly under British law. There's nothing we can do except pass it. You're also talking about extraditing a sitting TD, with serious political ramifications for the entire country."

Mary understood, reluctantly agreeing to wait until further evidence surfaced that might incriminate him, in the Irish Courts, not doubting, for one minute, that it would. She decided to take Malachy's advice, putting her quest for justice behind her, to focus on the fight for Women's Rights in Ireland. This was, of course, until she met Donnelly at the Sinn Fein meeting. She disliked him intensely, even before knowing who he was. The pain of Myles' loss, never far from the surface, punched her, full in the face, with a desire for justice that she found difficult to control.

She had really thought that Broy would be interested in the indisputable evidence that Percy had uncovered on the Dublin murder, committed in 1906. Her own disappointment and that of a clearly grief-stricken, Siobhan Carlisle, on that autumnal day in the Wexford Church, spurred her on.

"Let's do this, John," Mary said, referring to Daniel's suggestion, and feeling a renewed confidence course through her entire body.

They contacted Tracy Hicks, in London, and gave her the information they had on Donnelly, including the damming new evidence, recently received from Percy.

The following Monday morning, 21st of June 1937, an article about the Fianna Fail Candidate for County Louth, one 'Thomas Donnelly', appeared in two British Newspapers, both very popular in Ireland. The headline of the article read:

'Murderers and Gunmen still dominate Irish Elections'

The article suggested that all Irish politicians still lived under the shadow of gunmen. None of the leaders were innocent. Cosgrave, Dalton, De Valera and Lemass were all guilty, surrounding themselves with fellow gunmen. At least democracy would give the good people of Ireland the opportunity to pick their gunman of choice, making the Wild West look like a pre-school training exercise.

Let's take one candidate, a Mr Thomas Donnelly who, by his own admission, deserted the Royal Norfolk Regiment, in December 1916, to continue the fight for Irish freedom. Could this be the same Thomas Donnelly escorted back from France in December 1916, for questioning about the murder of Arthur Scott, a reputable London businessman, and financial supporter of the British Explorers' Club, who was fatally struck down during a failed robbery in London, six years earlier?

Could this be the same Thomas Donnelly that was finally located, following painstaking investigations by Mr Scott's associates, who gave chase to the suspect, on the afternoon of the murder? They mention a large, X-shaped cut to his left forearm, similar to one mentioned in Donnelly's military records, as an identifying scar.

Donnelly was escorted back to England in December 1916, for questioning. Whilst on a train in Liverpool, he murdered his guard, took his identity, and escaped. Captain Myles Fox, on checking the mail carriage where Donnelly was detained, found a seriously injured Guard, Private James Johnson, who sadly succumbed to his wounds the following day, leaving a wife and eight children. All attempts to apprehend Donnelly failed, and he was believed to have absconded to Ireland.

The 'Thomas Donnelly', standing in County Louth, could easily eliminate himself from all suspicion, by publicly revealing his left forearm.

Regardless of whether this is the same man or not, it should not reflect badly on the foundation of the new Fianna Fail Party that he represents, as all members have a somewhat unsavoury past, but this should not bother the people of Ireland, as most seem to enjoy living in the shadow of gunmen.

The article contained two photos. One of the suspect Donnelly, taken from his British Military Pay Book, and the other, a more recent photo of the new Fianna Fail Candidate for Louth, wearing civilian clothes.

The next morning, Eamon Broy arrived at the office, unannounced. He was with Superintendent John Moran, and a very tall elderly man, with mutton-chop sideburns.

"You two have stirred up a hornet's nest," Broy said to John and Mary. " This is Harry Fields, a retired DMP Sergeant, and Superintendent Moran whom I know you have met before " They shook hands.

"Superintendent Moran followed up the information you sent on Donnelly and the killing of Professor Brian Fields, back in 1906. He believed there was enough evidence for a case and was making good progress until that bloody article appeared in the English papers yesterday. It has scuppered our plans, so now; we'll have to act quickly."

"What? If you were following up on Donnelly, why, in God's name, didn't you tell us?" Mary asked, fearful that they might have jeopardised the case.

"You didn't give us a chance, Miss Bradford! It's no mystery, where the information came from, and I have it on good authority, that you should expect a visit from Mr Donnelly tomorrow morning, possibly accompanied by Dev, as well."

"Well, they're all welcome. I'll have the kettle on," Mary said, sarcastically.

"Give it a rest, Mary," Broy said, before issuing his instructions. "Say nothing. Let Donnelly speak first, and fire off his accusations. I

321

want him to confirm he was at that Sinn Fein meeting, just before a number of statues were blown up around the country. Hopefully, he'll recognise you and bring up the meeting himself."

Mary's face turned pale.

"How the hell do you know about that meeting, Mr Broy?"

"If I didn't, I wouldn't be doing my Job, now would I, Miss Bradford?"

Mary sat back down in to her chair, in shock, as she thought about what Freeny had said all those years ago, regarding the legal underworld of modern societies, 'only the coins and stamps will change', echoed in her head, as Superintendent Moran explained his plans for the following morning.

Mary was at her desk when the door opened and in marched Eamon de Valera, followed by Donnelly and two other party members. They ignored Mary and Daniel, marching passed them, and stopping in front of John's desk. John remained seated.

"Won't you stand for your former CO?" de Valera asked, almost whispering.

"I was in the GPO, not the Mill. My CO is dead, executed, even though he was Scottish, refusing to hide behind his nationality to avoid the firing squad."

De Valera ignored the barb, remaining composed.

"Ah, a Citizen's Army man."

"Correct. Now, what can I do for you? As you can see, we're very busy."

De Valera did not flinch. Donnelly slammed his fist on John's desk in a burst of anger.

"We know the leak came from this office, because the photo in the papers was the one I sent you lot two years ago, with my application. THERE WERE NO COPIES."

"There's no need to shout, Mr Donnelly," Mary exclaimed. Everyone turned. John rolled his eyes, suspecting something was coming, not previously discussed.

"And who might you be?" De Valera asked.

"Answer the question!" Donnelly said loudly, walking towards Mary. "You people have no idea how serious this is," he continued.

He stopped in front of the desk and stared at her intensely, for a moment.

"Do I know you?"

"Should you?" Mary replied.

He paused again.

"Yes! You're that Cumana Na Gael Blueshirt Bitch that was at the Sinn Fein meeting a few months ago."

"You're correct, and I see you blew up your statues, regardless of what I suggested that evening. Are the post boxes next?"

"None of your fucking business! It's you behind that article in the Brit papers isn't it?" Donnelly said, reaching across the desk to try and grab Mary.

Mary pulled back, knocking over her chair as De Valera unexpectedly shouted.

"Thomas! Stop!"

"Chief, this little whore is the one behind the article. She infiltrated an IRA meeting a few months….. He paused, and studied Mary a little closer, completely unaware of the damming statement that he had just made,

"I know you from somewhere else…..you look familiar?" He said, as he continued to study her, as if flicking through pages of faces in his mind.

"Yes!" He suddenly exclaimed. "I recognise you now. You're that Priest, Mackenzie's harlot! The one that had him demented. Do you know his last words were, 'I'm soooo sorry, Mary. Please forgive me,' Donnelly said, mockingly. "Mary Bradford. You were screwing that Brit Officer in Arklow. Come to think of it, his last words were, 'I love you, Mary', when I shot him. Were you banging the whole town, you fucking traitorous whore?"

323

"Thomas, calm down. There's no need for this," one of the party members said.

Mary wanted to take her revolver from the desk, and shoot him on the spot, but she managed to remain calm and composed.

"John Boland shot Captain Fox. I saw it. Are you stealing his glory too?"

"John Boland was an imbecilic. He froze. He couldn't pull the trigger. I knew he wouldn't, which is why I had to do it instead."

Mary was horrified.

"But I saw…." Mary could not finish the sentence.

"You only saw what you wanted to see. It's just as well that I got rid of him, and that Scottish traitor, otherwise they would ……"

"So, you were there when Father Mackenzie died, Mr Donnelly," Mary interrupted, for the benefit of those hiding in the kitchen. Donnelly stopped, realising that he had just confessed to Father Mackenzie's death.

"Casualties of war, bitch," he replied

"So, you admit to killing him," Mary continued.

"What're you going to do? Arrest me? I'm beyond the law! We own this country!"

"We've all heard that before!" Mary said, composing herself, safe in the knowledge that help was nearby, if needed. "I'm bored hearing that statement…."

She was interrupted by de Valera.

"Thomas, that's enough. Don't say any more. We'll come back another time."

At that, Donnelly took out his pocket watch and looked at it.

"We've only been here five minutes. We have all day, Chief, and I'm not leaving until I get some answers. This bitch is behind that newspaper publication, because I killed her lover Priest and Brit boyfriend, during the War."

"Enough, Thomas," de Valera said, as three policemen entered. He recognised one as Harry Fields, a DMP man from the '90s, tall as him, and still fighting fit.

"Hello Harry. Haven't you retired yet?" de Valera asked calmly.

"A Policeman never retires, Chief," Fields said.

Casually, he asked Donnelly to show him the Fob watch. Donnelly sat sideways on Mary's desk, pushing her things to one side. He did not think twice, unbuttoned the watch from his waistcoat, and handed it over.

"You have a good eye for quality, Fields."

Too late, he realised his mistake. He had the watch for so long, it was part of him. He had it on every raid and arms drop during the Anglo-Irish War. He had it on him during the first Battle of the Somme, He used to pawn and redeem it, reminding himself of how he acquired it, and the inscription on the inside plate.

"Give it back," Donnelly said nervously, watching Fields try to open the back.

"Push the small button," Mary said. To Donnelly's horror, it flicked open.

"Commandant, please read out this inscription," Fields asked.

John walked over, took the watch, and read the inscription, in a loud, clear voice.

'Presented by the Students and Staff of Trinity College, Dublin, to Professor Brian Fields, for his outstanding research in the field of medicine, 1890.'

"He was my uncle, Mr, Donnelly, and I've been looking for you for over 30 years. I'm arresting you for the murder of Professor Brian Fields."

"What're you talking about? Where's the proof?" Donnelly shouted. "I found that watch."

Mary stood up, took a file from her desk, and handed it to de Valera, who refused to take it. She handed it to one of his deputies, standing nearby.

"Read this," she said.

The deputy opened the file. He found a receipt from the English Mail Boat Company that ran between Dun Laoghaire and Holyhead, dated March 6th 1906, the same day that Professor Fields was murdered. It was a loan of two pounds, against the value of a 22cwt gold Fob watch. It was signed and dated by Thomas Donnelly.

A footnote, describing the watch, quoted the inscription on the inside plate. Another receipt in the file showed that the watch was redeemed three months later, also signed by Thomas Donnelly. The file contained several copies of Donnelly's signature from his British Army days, signing for wages, and, a more recent document, from his County Louth TD's office. The signatures were all exact matches.

The final document was a Dublin Metropolitan Police report on the murder of Professor Brian Fields, on March 6th 1906, whilst on his way to a lecture at Trinity College. The suspect was one Thomas Donnelly, aged 16, a member of a notorious pickpocket gang, working the streets of Dublin. The report indicated that he was believed to have absconded to London. The case remained open.

"You, and your party members, love to surround yourselves with murderers and thieves, just as the papers described, Mr De Valera," Mary said.

This unnerved De Valera.

"How did you get a copy of Thomas Donnelly's membership?"

"She stole it Chief," Donnelly shouted, panicked, not allowing Mary to answer.

"You cannot arrest me! We own this country" He stated, looking at Harry Fields

"This is my country, Miss Bradford, and I have made huge personal sacrifices to get where we are today. I will not let a woman's scorn destroy that work. Do you understand?" De Valera said directly to Mary.

"Then why do you allow Mr Donnelly to remain in the IRA, blowing up statues and planning bombing campaigns in England?"

Donnelly completely lost his temper. He pulled out a short revolver from his coat, and pointed it directly at Mary. One of the Garda quickly stepped in between them, holding his hands up, hoping to calm the situation.

"Thomas! Put that gun down! De Valera ordered, surprising everyone.

Donnelly turned towards De Valera.

"I'll kill them both, Chief. I swear."

Mary seized this opportunity to open her desk drawer, and pull out the Webley. The unsuspecting Garda jumped back with fright, to avoid getting caught in a gun fight.

Mary pointed the heavy Webley at Donnelly, using both hands.

"You've no idea how good it would be to shoot you with this particular gun."

Donnelly stared at the gun, recognising it immediately. He snapped it out of Mary's hand, in an impressive move, startling Mary.

"That's my Webley, the one I took from the Guard on the train in Liverpool. That coward Boland ran away with it," Donnelly said, studying the gun. "How the Hell did you end up with it?" Donnelly said, clearly puzzled.

It suddenly dawned on Mary that the Webley was Myles' missing gun. The one he had lost, after lending it to the Guard on the train. The one his family bought him when he was commissioned. The one he never replaced. She had it all that time. She was overwhelmed with grief, as more unpleasant memories flooded back.

De Valera issued an order in a voice that compelled Donnelly to comply.

327

"Thomas, put the gun down. It's over. Do not make it worse. We can still do something for you right now, but if you squeeze that trigger, it will be all over for good. Now put the guns down. That's an order."

At that, Broy and two of his detectives exited the Kitchen. All were armed.

"Broy's Harriers! Have you no farmers to shoot?" Donnelly said, sarcastically referring to the nickname given to the detectives following the shooting of a farmer in 1934, protesting against restrictions implemented by the Fianna Fail Government.

He looked at the pistols, all pointing directly at him. He thought about shooting Mary, at least, but knew it would have an unhealthy outcome for him, so he placed both guns on Mary's desk. The two Garda grabbed the guns and restrained him. As the handcuffs locked, Broy issued the charge.

"Thomas Donnelly, I'm arresting you for membership of the IRA, destruction of public property, and plotting a bombing campaign in England."

Donnelly stared at Mary, coldly.

"This is not over, Bitch".

"That's 'Fenian Bitch', to you," Mary replied, watching them leave.

As the Party members left, De Valera turned to Mary.

"What's your name girl?"

"Mary Bradford," she said proudly, almost standing to attention.

"Were you part of Michael's team?"

"If you mean Michael Collins, the answer is no."

"Pity! He could've done with someone like you. Miss Bradford. You've just done the Party, and I, a great service, and for that, I'm very grateful. Although some will not believe me, I was genuinely unaware of Mr Donnelly's affiliations, which would have had serious consequences for the election, had they been discovered by

328

the opposition. Thank you for your help. We shall meet again," he said, and left.

"Jesus, Mary! You get worse! You should be a private detective," John said. "I suppose this will lead to another visit from management," he continued, with a shrug.

Daniel, who had remained silent throughout, stood up.

"Shall I put on the kettle? I brought a lovely cake in with me today."

Mary and John turned to each other, and burst out laughing.

"What did I say?" Daniel asked, looking genuinely surprised.

"Oh, just make the tea," Mary said, in the gaps between hysterical laughter.

The elections were held on the 1st of June 1937. The Fianna Fail Party won most seats, but had no outright majority, so, on the 21st of July; Fianna Fail led the 9th Dáil. De Valera's New Constitution of Ireland, also held as a plebiscite on Election Day, was accepted by the people, and to become effective on 29th December 1937.

One morning, in September, John Mills placed a newspaper on Mary's desk. He had highlighted the headline. The article declared that Thomas Donnelly was to face trial for the murder of Professor Brian Fields in 1906. The charge against him for the murder of Father Mackenzie was dropped, classified 'extra judicial'. If found guilty, he could serve at least 10 years, then be extradited to England, to face charges for another two murders.

"She who waits, is well rewarded," John said, as Mary finished reading.

"Thank you, John. That should keep him busy," Mary said, folding the paper.

Two weeks later, Mary pushed open the heavy door to the side sanctuary of the Franciscan Church in Wexford. It was exactly the same as it had been, on her last visit, almost five years earlier. Siobhan Carlisle was sitting near the back with a well-dressed man.

She waved at Mary, and went over to greet her. The man quietly followed.

"We got your letter. I don't know how to thank you, Mary," Siobhan said.

"You don't have to thank me," Mary said, as they greeted each other with a kiss.

"You haven't changed a bit, Mary Bradford," Siobhan said, stepping back and taking a good look at Mary.

"I can say the same for you, Siobhan Carlisle."

"It's Siobhan Bell, now," she replied, holding out a ring for Mary to inspect.

"Oh that's wonderful news. Who's the lucky man?

"Here he is," Siobhan said, steeping to one side to allow the man to join them.

"This is Father...... I mean, Mr John Bell."

Mary recognised him as the Priest that had watched over her, all those years ago.

"How do you do, Miss Bradford. I'd not taken my vows when last we met."

"That's most certainly none of my business, Mr Bell, but you've no idea how happy I am for you both. It reminds me of an incident from my own past, involving a Priest."

"A happy one, I hope."

"Well, let's just say it's better to leave some things buried in the past."

They were standing in front of a shrine. Mary, feeling some remorse as she thought about the fate of Father Mackenzie, inserted a coin, picked up a fresh candle and lit it, in memory of him.

Mr Bell saw the expression of grief on her face, as she struggled to fit the lit candle into a wax-filled claw like slot. He reached out and helped her.

"I'm sorry, Miss Bradford. You came here to help Siobhan bury her ghosts, and it looks as if you may have unearthed some of your own?"

"It's not what you think. It's been a long and weary journey for me, but seeing you both so happy, makes me realise that some good has come from it."

"Let's go for tea and maybe some cake" Siobhan invited, lightening the mood.

"That sounds wonderful," Mary followed the happy couple, remembering meeting Myles for the first time, also in a Church.

Mr Bell opened the door and the two women stepped out into bright sunlight.

"By the way, Miss Bradford, What prison was Donnelly sent to on remand?"

"Portlaoise, I believe. Why?"

"Oh, no reason. It's just good to know where your wife's nemesis is!"

"He's there until the hearing. Now, where is that cake shop you promised?" Mary asked, as she linked arms with Siobhan, and walked towards town.

That November, as the Portlaoise Prison Priest was doing his rounds, he found Thomas Donnelly sitting alone, in the open exercise yard. It was cold, and the sun had not yet penetrated the dismal grey sky.

"Mr Donnelly, I've noticed that you've not been attending Mass," the Priest said.

Donnelly frowned. "Are you serious?" He replied incredulously.

"My job is to help sinners repent, give them absolution and guide them back onto the path of the righteous. Allow me to start, by giving you this small prayer book. The solution to all your troubles may be buried deep within its words."

"I don't want your damned prayers," Donnelly threw it on the ground with utter contempt.

"I advise you to pick that up and have a good read, because you "Will" find the answers to your problems amongst its pages," the Priest reiterated before leaving.

Donnelly looked at the Priest, as he walked away. Curiously, he picked up the book and started flicking through the pages. Several words had been circled, in red pen. He read a few, realising there was a concealed message, hidden amongst the pages.

He hid the book, and casually walked back to his cell.

The Christmas morning mass in Portlaoise Prison was full. Donnelly had been dutifully attending Mass for the past six weeks, as instructed by the secret message hidden in the prayer book. At communion, the Priest surreptitious nodded to Donnelly, who slipped into the side Sacristy. Here he found a prison guard's uniform, lying on a chair. When Mass ended, Donnelly, now wearing the uniform, escorted the Priest, unchallenged, to his car. He acknowledged, with a wave, the presence of two guards, attending the large main gates. They watched him carry out a thorough inspection of the car, before signalling that all was clear. Donnelly walked back towards the prison, but, as the Guards turned their backs to open the gates, he dived into the back of the car. As the car drove past the gates, the Priest waved to the Guards through an open window.

"Merry Christmas," he said as he drove away.

Donnelly climbed into the passenger seat and slapped the Priest on the back.

"Well done, Father. Now for America and away from this God-forsaken country."

"We're not out of the woods yet."

"Quinlan won't fail. He's got it all worked out. He never came to my attention during the Tan War, but he has now!" Donnelly said, getting comfortable.

332

"He's been running the Wexford IRA since the arrest of the key figures, back in the '20s. Some of them were killed by the English, you know."

"Oh, that old chestnut. A country needs Martyrs, Father, and Wexford, without a doubt, has had its fair share. Now, talking of Wexford, what time will we get to the safe house? I'm starving!"

"Sorry for the inconvenience. We'll plan your escape for after lunch next time."

Both men laughed as the car sped through the empty country roads, heading south towards the County of Wexford. They finally reached their destination, late that afternoon. The remains of a burnt out cottage, nestled at the end of a long, overgrown laneway, with grass growing down its centre.

"You took your time, Father. I was hoping to get here hours ago," Donnelly said, as the Priest parked the car on a patch of exposed cobbles, in the overgrown courtyard. He pulled up the hand brake, but kept the engine running, for the heat.

"We had to be careful to avoid the main roads. The route was Quinlan's idea."

"Who's that?" Donnelly asked, suddenly alert, as he saw a woman, wearing a headscarf and wool coat, clambering out of the ruins.

"That's our contact."

She was carrying a small parcel, and got into the back of the car.

"Here are some fresh clothes. Get out of that uniform, Mr Donnelly. Quinlan won't be long," she said, passing over the package.

Donnelly stepped out of the car, and changed into the civilian clothes in the fading light of the evening. When finished, he paused for a moment to examine his surroundings. The old farmyard was completely overgrown, and most of the outbuildings had collapsed. In the remains of the front garden, a large sycamore tree spread bare branches across the roofless building. He noticed that the

333

surrounding land was boggy, and devoid of animals. A white frost still lay on the grassy edges of the hedgerows. It was a bleak and lonely place. Donnelly shivered, remembering the weeks he spent on the run. Hunger added to the memories of living off the land, days becoming weeks. He shuddered at the thought, climbing back into the welcoming heat of the car.

"When can I get something to eat? I'm really starving, "he asked the woman.

"It shouldn't be long now. Quinlan's due at 4 o'clock. Just another five minutes or so," she replied, deliberately avoiding his stare.

Suddenly, the sound of an approaching car shattered the silence. The car parked directly behind their own, and four people exited. Donnelly got out to meet them.

"You're late and I'm starving," he said, ungratefully.

"What, and there I was expecting a 'thank you, Mr Quinlan, for breaking me out of Jail'," the driver said, as he carefully approached Donnelly.

"Come on Quinlan. Stop fucking around. I really am starving. Just get me to the safe house, and a good Christmas dinner."

"Well, back in the day, this one was popular; until the Brits burnt it down after some traitorous bastard gave them documents that led to its discovery."

Donnelly looked at the uninviting ruins and suddenly recognised it as the Carlisle home. Panic raced through him. The occupants of the other car turned their pistols towards him. As the woman approached Donnelly, his world collapsed, recognising Siobhan Carlisle, even after all these years,

"Go on ahead in there, like the good man ya are," Quinlan said, directing Donnelly towards the doorway of the ruined cottage, with his pistol.

Donnelly followed the instructions without objection. Inside the roofless building he saw two wooden chairs in front of the open fireplace, a recent fire still smouldering. It was obvious that Siobhan Carlisle had been waiting for some time.

"Sit," Siobhan ordered, as she took one of the chairs.

Donnelly sat opposite her, and inhaled deeply. The cool evening air could not disguise the uneasy silence that filled the ruins. He still felt some confidence that he would be on a boat to America soon, but when Quinlan tied his hands behind his back, that confidence quickly evaporated.

Once he was secure, Siobhan spoke.

"Do you know, Tom Donnelly, that everything bad that has happened in Wicklow, Wexford and Carlow over the past twenty years, is down to you. If you'd not been born, this country would have been much better off. So many innocent people would still be alive. Not just my Sisters, but that Professor in Dublin, the London Gangster, the innocent Soldier on the train, his CO in Arklow. Then to add insult to injury you provided evidence at the trial of his Fiancée, arrested for a murder that you committed. You chose to extract revenge on my Sisters, by fooling Father Mackenzie into presenting a stolen document at her trial. You knew that document would lead the British straight to us. It did, and not only did those bastards murder my Sisters, they also arrested the entire Column, executing two Volunteers in this very room, …… and then they burned down our house, for good measure….."

Donnelly noticed Siobhan's eyes glassing over as she recalled the event. She wiped a tear from the corner of her eye.

"And you didn't stop there did you? NO!" Siobhan raised her voice. "You murdered poor Father Mackenzie to keep him quiet, which firmly condemned Mary Bradford to a life in prison."

"Mary, Fucking, Bradford! I was wondering when that Blueshirt bitch's name would be mentioned. Is she behind all of this?" Donnelly asked angrily.

"Shut up, and do not speak until I tell you to," Siobhan ordered, angrily.

335

"Because of his feelings for Bradford, Mackenzie, the treacherous bastard, sent a letter to the Brits, confessing everything. We'd have all been arrested…"

Quinlan pistol-whipped Donnelly, from behind. "The lady told you to shut up!"

"I wanted to involve Miss Bradford, but we feared she would be empathetic to you, regardless of your misanthropic attitude."

"Misanthropic! That's a big English word for a little Irish girl, Miss Carlisle?" Donnelly said arrogantly.

Siobhan stood and clenched her hand around Donnelly's chin.

"My name was Siobhan Carlisle, but the little girl you threatened, grew up. Now, you're on the receiving end of threats, not me, you murderous bastard."

Quinlan, concerned for Siobhan, stepped between her and Donnelly. Siobhan took a step back. Quinlan leaned his face into Donnelly's.

"What is it with you and engaged couples? I don't think anyone told you, but Anne Carlisle was my fiancée. We were to be married that December."

"I suppose Christmas dinner is off then," Donnelly said, with a sarcastic laugh, recognising the familiar, cold look of a killer, in Quinlan's steel, blue eyes.

"Step back, Jack," Siobhan said, behind Quinlan.

Quinlan turned to face Siobhan, surprised to see her pointing a .38 RIC service revolver at Donnelly, who recognised it as the gun her sister had threatened to use on him, the night of his attack.

"Siobhan, you don't have to do this," Quinlan appealed to her, stepping back.

"Listen to Quinlan, you Bitch!" Donnelly shouted, clearly anxious.

Without hesitating, Siobhan, overwhelmed with anger and grief, pulled the trigger. The loud bang caused a flock of pigeons, resting in the eaves, to take flight across the open roof. Their fluttering

336

wings created a loud, hollow sound that echoed through the derelict ruins, soon fading to an eerie silence.

Donnelly groaned, lifting his head to look at Siobhan, still pointing the pistol at him.

"That was for Anne," she said, "and this is for Niamh." She squeezed the trigger again and again, firing three more shots, before the gun clicked on an empty chamber.

Jack Quinlan reached out and took the pistol from her as she collapsed.

"You know what to do," he said to the others, nodding towards Donnelly's limp body, as he carried Siobhan out of the ruins.

Outside, her husband was burning the Priest's clothes and the prison uniform worn by Donnelly. Quinlan placed Siobhan back on the ground.

"It's done," she said, standing beside her husband.

"I heard," he said, placing his arm around her. They stood next to the fire, staring silently into the flames, the little heat, barely penetrating the chilly air.

"Come on," Quinlan said, "Let's get home for Christmas dinner. I'm starving."

Another War

The new constitution of Ireland was passed on Wednesday 29th December 1937. Mary was disappointed that it had been accepted by the nation, believing it was only supported to eliminate lingering hostilities between political parties.

In January 1938, she planned to attend an ITGWU meeting, held by Kathleen Clarke, who wished to discuss principals in the new Constitution, which, were completely divergent from the agreed position of women in Irish society, declared in the Proclamation. This was to be followed by an open discussion on the rise of Fascism in Germany.

The day before the meeting, Mary received word that her father had collapsed, and was in St Vincent's Hospital. Commandant John Mills drove her over immediately. They found her father on St Peter's Ward, with her Mother and Sister. He looked weak and frail, lying on the bed, holding his wife's hand. Anna greeted them both, in tears.

"I'll be outside, Mary, if you need me," John said, swallowing his emotions.

Mary stood beside her Mother. They looked at George, who smiled up at them from the bed said.

"Oh look, its Black Beauty, the Irish Rebel."

Mary forced a smile.

"Hush now Dad, and rest."

Angela gave Mary an approving look for the advice. She buttoned up the top of George's red striped pyjamas. He coughed a little as she did, and drifted off to sleep. A doctor entered and invited the family to his office. The news was not good. George passed away three days later.

The reception, following the large Funeral, was held in the Railroad Hotel. Sean Lemass attended and personally stayed in

Angela's company throughout, for which her family were very grateful. Time finally forced him to depart, leaving Angela with Mr and Mrs Boland and the Priest. Mary joined them. They talked of George's successful achievements, before departing. Anna approached, offering Mary and her mother a lift home.

Mary found herself alone in the kitchen, with her exhausted mother.

"Why don't you go upstairs and lie down for a bit, Mam? I'll prepare supper."

"I think I will, Mary," Angela said leaving wearily.

Mary was left alone in an eerie silence, broken only by the rhythmic ticking of the large wall clock. She looked up at it, filled with poignant memories of her Father, standing on a kitchen chair, dutifully winding it every Sunday morning, checking its accuracy against his Fob watch.

Her Mother would now be completely alone in the house. She would be in Dublin, and Anna, three months pregnant with her third child, would not be able to help as much as she would like.

Mary went back to work the following Monday. Silvia came into the office to offer her condolences

"St Peter's Wards, Mary? That was where my Grandfather died. My Grandmother believed it was named after St Peter, because, after staying there, the next person you were likely to meet, would be St Peter, himself," Daniel said, before biting in to a large piece of a cake Silvia had brought with her.

Despite the sombre mood, they all laughed.

When Silvia left, Mary looked at her surroundings, and the thought of her Mother, alone with the kitchen clock, washed over her.

"John, do you remember we discussed an opening for a Pension Clerk at the Arklow Post Office?"

"Yes, it's still available, have you someone in mind?"

"Yes I do…….. Me."

John stopped what he was doing immediately.

"Are you serious, Mary?" He asked, as he stood up, and approached her desk.

"I've never been more serious, John. Mam is alone and frail. She needs my help. I've put my ghosts to rest, with the exception of Boland, and Donnelly is well hidden somewhere in America, but honestly, they don't bother me anymore. I know why there were six bullets in Boland's gun. He didn't shoot Myles, Donnelly did. It feels like the right time to move on. Don't get me wrong, I've enjoyed every minute of it, even the sad times…. But I'm tired, John… I need to move on. I want to go home."

Tears trickled down Mary's face. John hugged her. Daniel approached to offer his sympathy but paused. Mary steeped back, and offered him her outstretched arms, which he willing accepted.

"I really am going to miss you Mary Bradford."

Mary started her new job on Monday 7th March, 1938. She settled in quickly, and was delighted to be home with the opportunity to look after her mother. She also enjoyed spending time with her nieces and nephew. Sometimes she would take them to the beach, or, on rainy days, play games in the house. One time she caught Maurice playing soldiers in the hall. He was lying on a pile of coats, wearing Myles hat. Behind him, his sister, Mary, sat nursing a line of injured dolls, covered in makeshift bandages. Maurice held the large Webley pistol, now deactivated, using it to defend his post from hordes of imaginary enemies.

"Bang! Bang!" he shouted excitedly, as he struggled to hold the heavy revolver.

Mary sat on the stairs, enjoying every second of it.

She saw Silvia and John regularly. They occasionally visited for a weekend, keeping her up to date with Dublin life, which she missed.

During that first year in Arklow, two things happened to remind Mary of her previous life. Firstly, in July, the Fianna Fail Party was forced to call a snap election over the on-going Civil Service dispute. They surprised everyone, winning the first overall majority in the short history of the State. The 10th Dail was in session. She received a personal message from De Valera thanking her for her support during the recent election campaign. The other incident occurred in the Arklow Post Office. Whilst helping at the counter, a man with a French accent asked a question. Mary was delighted to find Sean MacBride, the retired Head of the IRA, standing before her.

"Mr MacBride. What a pleasant surprise. Are you passing through or staying?"

"What a pleasure, Miss Bradford," he said, happy to see her. "I went to school in Gorey, and am visiting friends. May I ask what you're doing here?"

"This is my home town, and I work here now."

"And I thought you were a Dublin girl, with a funny Northern Irish accent."

"My accent's funny! Now that's ironic."

"I suppose it is a little," Sean replied with a chuckle.

Mary served Sean, inviting him to drop in, whenever passing. Sean never failed, and on several occasions, they had tea together, in a local café. At one such meeting, Sean explained that he had retired from the IRA, having been called to the Bar in 1937. He then surprised her, by apologising for his behaviour at their first meeting, which brought up the question of Thomas Donnelly. In reply, Sean admitted that he had no idea where Donnelly was, and believed he had absconded to America.

Throughout the rest of 1938 and early '39, the threat of war loomed closer. Mary kept a close eye on events as they unfolded across Europe. De Valera was adamant that Ireland would remain neutral, should war break out. Finally, in September 1939, War was declared, and De Valera announced Ireland's neutrality to the world.

Almost immediately, causality reports began to arrive at the Post Office. With so many Arkow men in the Irish and foreign navies telegrams, arrived daily.

Although Mary's job was to issue pension payments, she volunteered to support counter-staff when she could. It was here that the harsh realities of war struck home – Wives, Mothers and Children would queue up to enquire about missing loved ones.

The Postmaster, on witnessing a number of people break down, in public, from the contents of hastily opened letters and telegrams, decided to personally deliver all military correspondence direct to the recipient's home. Sometimes the news was positive, where loved ones had survived.

By 1940 , Mary was attending the Dublin Office for a few days, every month. Commandant Mills had volunteered for the 26th Battalion, 2nd Line Volunteer Force, a Battalion consisting almost entirely of Old IRA members, who had stepped into the role of Volunteer Reserves, after most members of the regular reserve were called up for full-time duties. During one of these Dublin visits, in late June 1940, Mary entered the office and was surprised to find Commandant Mills dressed in full uniform.

"Good Moring, Mary," he said, aware of her surprise.

"Good morning John you look smart."

"I've been waiting for you. There's a car outside. We've been invited to a meeting on Harcourt Street, for 9 o'clock. I'll explain on the way."

"On the way, John? I've only just arrived. Can I at least get a cup of tea?"

"Sorry, no time."

On the way, John explained that the Minister of Defence and the Minister of Post and Telegraphs wished to speak to Civil Service staff about censorship. Mary and John were guided into a room on the ground floor of the Harcourt Street building. Mary was delighted to see the Arklow Postmaster, Mr Roberts, already sitting at a table, large enough to accommodate up to twenty people. They joined him. At 9 o'clock, the Minister of Defence, Oscar Traynor, and the Minister of Post and Telegraphs, John Little, entered the room and sat at the head of the table. Oscar Traynor spoke first.

"Good Morning and thank you all for making the journey, especially with the severe restrictions we must endure. As you may have read in the papers, the IRA has increased attacks on British and Irish targets over a two year period. Their bombing campaign in England in 1939, known as the Sabotage Plan, or S-Plan for short, prompted the Irish Government to pass the Offences against the State Act, resulting in a few minor arrests. We now have it on good authority that IRA Leaders have offered to assist the Nazis by continuing their S-Plan. Further investigation, has also uncovered another plan, 'Operation Green', which proposes that the Nazis invade Ireland from the South, with the full support of the IRA. If this happens, Churchill has warned that Britain will intervene, dragging the entire country into this violent war."

Minister Traynor paused to let the seriousness of his words sink in.

"To counter these plans, we are asking trusted members of Post Office staff to monitor overseas post, and censor details that might be vital to German intelligence, which would jeopardise this delicate balance of neutrality we are maintaining."

He finished speaking and poured himself a glass of water. As he drank, he glanced around the room at the stony faces. A Post Mistress from Mayo, Betty O'Connor, broke the silence.

"I won't do it! You can't ask me to spy on old Comrades and friends for the dammed CID, just to appease the bloody Brits. Let me tell you what the CID did to the Mayo Branch of the IRA, during the Civil War when they captured two ...."

"Stop Betty!" John Little interjected. "It's not about past animosities or seeking revenge or assisting the 'bloody Brits'. This is about maintaining the delicate balance of neutrality. The German long-range bombers are very capable of visiting our shores. Perhaps the recent bombings were not accidental, but a way to demonstrate their capabilities? Look at the recent fall of France, and what happened to the British Task Force in Dunkirk. Reports demonstrate that the Nazis are rounding up the public, and shipping them away to concentration camps, or publicly executing them because of their religious or political beliefs. We're in trouble here, Betty! Very serious trouble and it's only going to get worse. We go back a long way and I respect your grievances over the Civil War, but, right now, as a Country, not as individual departments, we need your help. So please, let's not cut off our noses to spite our face."

A deafening silence followed. It was finally broken when Betty, who had been looking down, at the table, throughout, lifted her head and spoke.

"I apologise, John. The Minister mentioned the CID! That name arouses bitter memories for me. I actually have a nephew, a Sailor in the British Merchant Navy. He's missing since Dunkirk, and we're still waiting for news. What do you need us to do?"

"I'm sorry to hear about your nephew, Betty. Let's hope he turns up safe and well. Minister Traynor will explain the censorship program, and what it entails," John Little said, solemnly.

Oscar Traynor explained that it was not possible to monitor ever letter posted overseas. However, simple things such as post cards, and letters to families should be read. Any statements regarding troop movements, the defence of towns, or anything that could be of value to a German invasion, should be erased, with a black marker or, if too explicit, the letter should be sent to the Ministry of Defence.

When the meeting ended, the attendees formed small groups to discuss the proceedings. Mary and John approached the Minister of Defence.

"How have you been, John?" The Minister asked.

"Fine thank you, Oscar," John replied. "And you?"

"Good, given the present circumstances. I'm glad to see you're not wearing your old Green uniform," the Minister said.

"I can, if you want," John replied coldly.

It was obvious to Mary that there was animosity between these men.

"May I present Miss Mary Bradford?" John said, introducing Mary to alleviate the tension. The Minister was clearly captivated by Mary's appearance.

"Why, Miss Bradford, you're more beautiful than I imagined. I've heard a lot about you, within the party."

"All positive, I hope," Mary replied smiling, shaking his hand.

"Of course, of course," he replied. Releasing Mary's hand, he glanced at John.

"I hope Mary doesn't suffer the same fate as the last beautiful lady in our company, John."

John ignored the barbed comment and raised the issue of censorship. After a brief chat on how to detect suspicious letters, Mary asked Oscar Traynor for help with compensation claims, against British Merchant Navy Companies. She explained how they would stop the wages of someone reported lost or missing, and refused to pass on information on what may have happened to them.

"Ah Mary, my Colleagues have spoken of your abruptness!" Oscar Traynor said, smiling. "I agree with you on the plight of these men and we are further concerned by recent attacks on some of our own Merchant ships. The Germans make vague excuses, but are now offering compensation for their actions, both at sea and on land. We've never been under such a threat, which brings me to the question of censorship......"

"With all due respect, Minister, this is not about censorship. I'm asking the Department to help with compensation for the families

345

of missing Irish sailors who worked for British Merchant Navy Companies."

John rolled his eyes, noticing the Minister's look of shock at being interrupted.

"These families seek help from the Department of Pensions, because we've helped distressed families with compensation claims, in the past. They have no one else to turn to, Minister. I've made enquiries on several British Merchant Navy Companies, and have discovered that if a sailor is killed in action, survives in an open boat or is captured, his payments cease immediately, because the shipping company, considers him to be unavailable to work."

"I'm aware of this extra crisis, Mary," the Minister said, sincerely. "I can say, confidentially, that we are presently in discussion with the British Government regarding this issue. I will inform you of the outcome, personally."

"Thank you. I'll remind you, Minister, if necessary, "Mary replied emphatically.

"I'm sure you will, Miss Bradford. I'm sure you will. It's been a pleasure to finally meet you. Ministers De Valera, and Lemass, both speak very highly of you."

"Please pass on my regards to both of them, Minister," Mary said, with a smile.

"I most certainly will. Now, please excuse me. I've another meeting in an hour."

The Minister shook hands with Mary, nodded to John, who politely returned the gesture, with a smile. The Minister left the room.

"Christ Mary! Do you ever give it a rest?" John said, taking papers from the table.

"Me, give it a rest? What was that between the two of you, and don't tell me nothing! Talk about an elephant in the room! And what did he mean about the last woman in your company?"

"I, unintentionally, killed her during the battle of Dublin," John said remorsefully, as he turned from the table with his papers, to look directly at Mary.

"She turned out to be... well, his best friend. But as you know, Mary, some things are better left in the past," John said, sadness etching his face. He turned away, awkwardly putting papers in a small case, distracting himself from the painful memory.

"You really are a mystery, John Mills...." Mary said, fully understanding that he did not want to discuss it further. "Sometimes, I see the same sadness in you that I saw in Myles," she said sympathetically.

"What was that about Sailors?" John said, changing the subject.

Mary invited the Arklow Postmaster to join them.

"We are only trying to help those in need, John, as Mr Roberts can confirm."

"Let's treat him to lunch," John said, starting towards the door.

The three of them left together, Mr Roberts noticeably smirking to himself, as he fell in behind John and Mary, on the busy Dublin street. He had been quietly observing Mary and Minister Traynor and had witnessed, for himself, the full strength of Mary Bradford's personality and her determination to get things done, confirming the rumours of the high esteem in which she was held, by Irish politicians.

"What are you like Mary Bradford," he said to himself, noticing that she had stopped walking and was waiting for him to catch up.

"Hurry up, Mr Roberts. We don't want to lose you now, do we?" She said, and linked his arm. They walked to Bewley's Café, on Grafton Street.

In October 1940, Eamon De Valera paid a brief visit to Arklow to inspect the East Wicklow branch of the Old IRA, whose members had proudly volunteered to join the 26th Battalion for Ex-IRA members. After the Parade, Minister De Valera held a public meeting in the Railway Hotel, renamed Hoyne's, after its new

347

proprietor. The visit was designed to boost morale and ensure the continued loyalty of the 26ᵗʰ Battalion and the public, on the wane since the State executions of two IRA men, that September. The men were hung in Mountjoy Jail for killing two Garda, during a police raid on an IRA safe house, in Dublin. The role of the Fianna Fail Government in these executions, unnerved De Valera, as he was acutely aware of the risk of losing support from the public and the Old IRA, who were now legally armed, having joined the 26ᵗʰ Battalion.

De Valera need not have worried, as everyone was well aware of the threat posed by the Nazis, and the consequences, should they invade. The nation unconsciously supported the difficult decisions of Government, as demonstrated by the large crowds that turned out to support him. It was particularly evident in how the Old IRA still protected Dev, gathering around him, on his short walk to the Hotel from the Parade ground, as if still defending him from possible arrest, by the National Army.

The public meeting was held in the hotel lounge. Rows of chairs had been set out in front of two tables, pushed together beneath the large street windows. De Valera sat in the centre of this table, between Pat Kavanagh, now the Commandant of the East Wicklow Brigade, and Lieutenant General, Daniel McKenna, the Chief of Staff of the National Army. Beside these men, were junior ministers and their aides.

De Valera read a prepared speech on the security of the country, and laid out the reasons why the Fianna Fail Party had distanced itself from all IRA subversive action, action that was giving both the Nazis and the British, the excuse to invade. He went on to say that this had been official policy since the founding of the party in 1926, and openly demonstrated in 1932, when the party was officially elected, and announced a withdrawal from all past allegiances with subversive organisations and its members.

"That's not true!" A voice shouted from the back of the room.

Everyone turned to see who would dare to interrupt the Taoiseach of Ireland.

"With whom am I speaking?" De Valera asked, remaining composed.

"Mary Bradford," Mary said loudly, in a clear and angry tone, as she stood up.

"Ahh. Miss Bradford. I thought it might be you," Dev replied. "Is there somewhere we can talk privately?" He asked the proprietor, Mr Hoyne.

"Yes, in here," Mr Hoyne replied, opening a door to a separate lounge area, normally reserved for residents.

"Shall we, Miss Bradford," Dev said, inviting Mary to join him.

As Mary walked past the rows of chairs, people started to applaud. Having heard rumours of how she had sought revenge on Judges, Priests, CID Officers, Barrister's, and Ex- Castle Agents during her time in Dublin, The local Postmaster had described Mary's recent meeting with the Minister of Defence, a story that changed more and more with every telling. Now the townsfolk saw for themselves how Mary dealt with Government Ministers. The Taoiseach of Ireland seemed to know her, personally, and had invited her for a private audience, confirming the rumours were true.

"Pat, could you please…?" De Valera said to Pat Kavanagh, indicating he would like a guard placed on the door. This was more for show than security purposes. Two armed men from the 26th Battalion stood on either side of the door, as De Valera closed it behind him.

The room was full of small tables and chairs. Mary recognised it as the dining area that Myles and Percy had frequented during their lunch breaks. It looked like the new proprietor had separated it from the main lounge, by installing a brick wall.

"Please have a seat, Mary," De Valera said, pulling out a chair.

Mary sat without speaking, as De Valera joined her.

"Now Mary, something is obviously bothering you, so please tell me?"

"In your statement, you said that you did not support the IRA since the founding of the Party in 1926. Yet, as we both know, one of your sitting TDs not only remained a member of the IRA, he was instrumental in planning and carrying out attacks on the State, right under your nose. Then, you allowed him to escape from Jail, without pursuit. That makes you a hypocrite, in my book."

De Valera remained calm, his voice a whisper.

"Mary, I spoke the truth when I told you that I was unaware of Mr Donnelly's chicanery, and I can promise you, that neither I, nor any member of my Party, had a role in his escape. I can also assure you that Mr Broy is leaving no stone unturned in trying to find out what became of him, which, I will admit, is something of a mystery."

"Myself, and a good friend of mine in Wexford, are both living in constant fear, waiting for him to turn up. I work at the Post Office in Arklow. For all I know, he could turn up there, demanding a stamp, just like Sean MacBride! What do I do if Donnelly turns up? Invite him in for tea to discuss old times?"

"Sean MacBride, the proverbial thorn in my side," De Valera sighed loudly.

"Well, at least he's honest, and I believe him....."

"Mary, you speak with such passion! You and Michael Collins would have got on well. But I'm sure you wouldn't have shown him the same disrespect you show me."

"Well, I would if he were still alive and proved a liar too?" Mary said coldly.

"Mary please…, I have no desire to discuss Michael's memory - he will always be remembered at my expense," De Valera said, supressing his anger at Mary's non-verbal accusation. "Now, please understand we're in difficult times. If I exposed the seriousness of the threat we all face, the country would be in complete turmoil.

The British Government would love the excuse to invade, and take over, not just the harbour Ports they so desperately want, but the entire country. And, I know for a fact, Mr Churchill would not politely leave when the mess was finally over. So, I have to make some very difficult decisions. Hanging old Comrades who fought beside me in the Easter Rising, is not something I did lightly. What choice did I have? Please tell me what you'd have done in my situation?"

"I can't speculate on that, Mr De Valera. Unless I was in that position, I can't tell you what I'd do. I agree, these are difficult times, but my reason for this unexpected meeting is not State security, but because Thomas Donnelly is still at large. You don't seem bothered by it, yet you hunted down and hung other comrades."

"Mary, I promise I'll find out what became of Donnelly. In return, can I be assured of your loyalty, at least to the end of this Emergency? I can see from the rapturous applause that you received for challenging my authority, that support for the Government could change very quickly which would be catastrophic. And I'm sure Mr Cosgrave would love nothing better, than to roll over for Mr Churchill."

A loud knock on the door interrupted them.

"Enter," De Valera said, poignantly.

"Chief, we must be going," an Aide said, using the English word for Taoiseach.

"Thank you, Jack. Leave the door, we're almost done," De Valera said.

"Mary, it's been a pleasure, as always. I look forward to our next meeting, perhaps under better circumstances."

"Yes indeed, and thank you for taking the time to speak with me."

"Are we in agreement then?" He asked, walking Mary towards the door

351

"Yes, and should you fail on your part, I will remind you."

"I'm sure you will, Miss Bradford, I'm sure you will," De Valera said, as he held the door for Mary, so she could enter the busy room, ahead of him.

The Chief of Staff had continued with the prepared speech in the absence of the Taoiseach. When he finished, he took the opportunity to vent at those that had deserted the National Army, in favour of the British Armed Forces, calling them 'nothing but traitors', and 'no better than subversives, hell bent on wrecking the delicate peace' and promised they would be punished, on their return.

"Can we offer you a lift?" An Aide asked Mary, as everyone started to drift to the exit.

"Is it raining? She asked Pat Kavanagh, who was standing next to the Aide.

"No, not at the moment, Mary, "Pat replied.

"Well then, thank you for your kind offer, but I shall walk. Good day Gentlemen."

The Aide shrugged his shoulders and returned to collect papers from the table.

Pat looked at Mary, as she shuffled along with the crowd. Their respect for her had increased tenfold as they stepped back to allow her ahead of them.

"What are you like, Mary Bradford?" Pat said to himself, as he watched his old comrade's fuss over her.

The following year, the number of telegrams increased, as the tentacles of war touched so many. There was rationing, restrictions on travel, and a general lack of supplies. During her weekly walks with her niece and nephew through the ruins of the Kynoch's Factory, Mary noticed an increase in its destruction, as the local people, desperate for building materials, had started to remove the wood, bricks, pipes, steel girders, and anything else that could be useful. They even started to remove the sand surrounding the explosive houses. One winter's day, she went to the beach alone, to view the aftermath of a storm. When she arrived, she was surprised to see a large crowd of locals, who had arrived by donkey and cart, bicycles, old prams and any other means of transport. Despite the strong, bitter wind blowing in from the sea these people were cutting down large sections of the wooden piles, exposed by the storm, for fire wood. Mary watched this sad performance by desperate people until the cold, easterly wind finally drove her home to the warmth of her front room.

Despite everything, there were still moments of happiness. One day, when Mary was assisting on the counter, a large, elderly woman exclaimed, in a Cockney accent.

"Well as I live and breathe, if it's not young Mary Bradford that sits before me."

Mary looked up, bewildered, not recognising her.

"It's me! Bridie Murphy, your old Supervisor from Kynoch's."

Mary could barely control her excitement at seeing her old friend.

"You went to England when the factory closed. What have you been doing?" Mary asked as she lifted the hatch to give Bridie a hug.

"Oh, I worked for Nobles Explosives for years, and then moved to Plaistow, London," Bridie said, with a gasp, as Mary hugged the life out of her.

Are you here on holidays?"

"No, I've come back to live here, until this bloody war is over. I can't handle those bloody Nazi bombers every night. They come with a loud drone and then drop their bloody bombs, forcing us all to sleep in a bloody Anderson shelter at the bottom of the garden. You just don't know if your house will be standing the next morning."

"Oh, well, apart from the rationing, you should be safe here."

"I hope so. We should meet up and chat about the good old days."

"I'd love to, "Mary said. "I'd better get back to work, now. What can I get you?

"Oh, just to post some letters home."

Mary smiled to herself as she watched her leave. Bridie had looked out for her during her time in Kynoch's. She thought of the changing rooms, and all that she had learnt of life there. Thinking of the changing rooms, bought Myles to mind....

"Can I have a stamp please," a voice asked, depositing a penny coin on the counter, and bringing Mary back to the present.

"Certainly Sir," Mary said, grabbing the larger blue folder.

She picked up the English penny and looked at Britannia, thinking of the Norfolk Regiment cap badge on Myles' hat, as it lay on the floor of the abandoned changing room.

"Can I get a stamp today, please," the man asked loudly, breaking the spell.

"Sorry! Bridie's just awoken some incredible memories for me."

"I'm glad for you. Now, may I have a stamp!" Mary completed the transaction.

On Monday the 2nd of June 1941 the war firmly arrived on her doorstep. That night, the German Luftwaffe dropped bombs on Arklow. The drone of the bombers woke the entire town, just one of many bombing raids that took place on the East coast of Ireland. Luckily, on this occasion, no one was injured.

The next day the town was buzzing with a large Army presence. Mary was serving at the counter, when Bridie Murphy approached.

"Hi Bridie. How're you settling in?"

"Settling in! Are you serious? You obviously didn't hear those bloody Dornier's last night, and their bloody bombs. Have those Nazis got it in for me? I'm away to bloody Scotland, Mary, to live with my eldest daughter. They won't get me up there."

Mary started to laugh.

"I think it would take more than a few Nazi bombs to stop you, Bridie Murphy."

"Maybe, but I just want sleep! I'm leaving in the morning, so until next time…."

Mary came around the counter and gave Bridie a hug, and watched her leave.

As she turned to go back to work, a woman's voice rang out.

"Hello Mary".

Mary looked around, and recognised Siobhan Bell from Wexford.

"Siobhan, what a lovely surprise!" Mary exclaimed.

"Hello Mary. Can you stop for lunch?" Siobhan had a serious look on her face.

"Certainly. Is everything alright? Has Donnelly turned up?" Mary asked, concerned by Siobhan's unemotional reaction to their reunion.

They went to a restaurant, just up from the Post Office, and ordered tea and sandwiches. When the order arrived Siobhan began to speak.

"Mary, I need to tell you that Donnelly will never bother either of us, again. A friend in the Free State Army told me you and Commandant Mills are still looking for him, and won't rest until you find him, so I want to assure you that it's over."

Mary remembered it was rumoured that the Wexford IRA had assisted in Donnelly's escape, waiting until Christmas Day, to break him out. Donnelly had not been heard of since, and it was widely thought he had absconded to America.

"Were you involved in his escape? Why would you help him go to America, after all that he did to you and your family?" Mary asked angrily.

"He didn't go to America, Mary. In fact, he's still in Wexford."

This horrified Mary. The thought of him living nearby was unbearable.

"He's dead, Mary," Siobhan said coldly, when it became clear from the fearful look on Mary's face, that she had misunderstood.

"The IRA told me not to tell anyone, especially you, for fear of a deeper investigation into his escape. But after I heard how distressed you were, I realised how cruel that was, especially after the help you've given so many near destitute families."

"How do you know he's dead?"

"I was there," Siobhan's eyes welled up with tears. "My Sister's fiancée planned his escape, with the help of my husband. We hoped for justice. Hoped he'd admit what he'd done. But things went wrong.... I did it! I killed him, Mary," Siobhan whispered.

"Oh Siobhan, you poor dear. What happened? Mary asked horrified. She reached out and took both Siobhan's hands in her own.

"I didn't mean to do it. It was just ....well I had brought my Sister's gun along, for personal safety, just in case things got out of hand. As I watched him sitting there, in the remains of our parlour, arrogantly demanding to be fed, I remembered him behaving the very same way when he used to hide out at our house, demanding food from our poor Mother, and whiskey from our harmless Father. The thought of him assaulting my Sisters, and causing their deaths...., I just couldn't help myself. I was overcome by a blinding rage and well..... I just shot him....over and over. My God Mary! He has turned me into a monster, like him."

"Oh Siobhan," Mary said, squeezing both of Siobhan's hands. "Don't blame yourself. You could never be like him. It was an impulsive reaction. I wanted to shoot him myself, that day in my office, when he boasted about killing Myles, and I think I would have, had he not unarmed me. Men like him bring out the worst in all of us. But, rest assured, you'll not be judged for this, in fact, I think you'll be commended."

"Thank you, Mary. Thank you. That's what my husband says."

"Well, he's right! How is he?" Mary asked, deliberately changing the subject.

"He's at home, minding our children."

"I never knew! Congratulations! How old are they?"

"The oldest is two, and the baby, six months. We named them after my sisters."

A man entered through the café door.

"Sorry to rush you, Siobhan, but we really must start heading back."

"Five minutes," Siobhan replied, holding up her hand.

They stood, and hugged for a while. Mary, knowing Siobhan had put herself at great risk by telling her of Donnelly's fate, thanked her.

"I've lived in fear for years, worrying he'd return to carry out his promise. You helped me put that fear to rest, Mary, so I'm returning the favour. You don't need to live in fear of him, either," Siobhan said, as she put on her gloves and walked towards the door. After seeing her out, Mary returned to the table. She sat silently, in shock.

As she composed herself, she said, under her breath.

"Well Myles Fox, justice really does come to those who wait."

Mary settled back into her chair, and asked for the bill, feeling completely relieved, knowing that she could stop harassing Broy and De Valera for answers about Donnelly, and knowing that he would never suddenly turn up, unannounced.

The War made its presence felt again in Arklow. The following year the bodies of two RAF pilots were recovered from the sea in February 1942. Pat Kavanagh and a local policeman brought their personal effects to the Post Office, to confirm their identity to the British Embassy. Mary saw the items on a table. There were private letters, a wallet, RAF identity cards, a large pistol, and some photos. Everything was wet. She looked at one of the photos. It was a young girl of about eight years, wearing a floral, summer dress. It reminded her of her niece, and the harsh reality of War and the effects on the innocent, especially children. She left abruptly, tears in her eyes.

Later that year, a sea mine was spotted floating off the South Pier. For safety, the police evacuated the nearby Pottery Factory, only to see all the employees' climb the pier to get a good look. During the night, it washed up on the rocks of the North Beach, and exploded, shattering a number of windows on a nearby street.

At the end of the year, Mary was surprised to read in a paper, that the Government had banned all British companies from advertising in Irish newspapers. She could not understand it. Most of the work that the poorer families undertook to bridge the poverty gap were seasonal, and there was almost £4 million pounds a year coming through the Post Office, in remittance for Irish Employees working in England.

Mary had little concern about the ban, as the letters she had opened under her censorship duties, proved that word of mouth was a much better form of advertising. However, she did mention the issue during the election campaign, in May 1943, but, most of the TDs that she spoke with were more concerned with the restrictions of the Emergency Act, now in place since 1939. De Valera had hoped to extend the term of Government from five to six years, due to the Emergency, but got little support from the opposition. The election was held in June 1943. The Fianna Fail Party won again, but new opposition parties meant they did not have a parliamentary majority when the 11th Dail sat on the 1st July.

In June 1944, Mary purchased a large, wooden Pilot radio set and Mr Fitzgerald, the electrician, wired it up in her front room. Mary poured the tea, whilst he demonstrated how it worked. As he tuned the dial, they were surprised to hear Germany's Irish service, 'Irland Redaktion'. They briefly listened, laughing at the constant propaganda, but shocked at the seriousness of other statements, like the German promise to 'respect Irish neutrality' when they eventually took over Britain. Mr Fitzgerald used a pencil to mark the most common stations on the glass display. He realised it was almost 12 o'clock, so he tuned the radio into the BBC World Service, and they both settled down to listen to the news.

Good Afternoon and welcome to the BBC World Service. Here is the news. Today, Tuesday the 6th of June 1944, the Allied forces successfully landed on a number of beaches in France and have firmly established secure beach heads, and started the push inland, towards Germany. Causality's are high, but not as high as expected.

Mr Fitzgerald looked towards Mary. He was surprised to see her wiping tears from her eyes, with a hanky. He stood up and turned off the radio.

"Whatever's the matter, Miss Bradford? This is good news."

"I know, I know. I'm just thinking of the telegrams that we'll receive in the Post Office, with so many Irishmen in the Allied Forces.

"Well, think of the telegrams that have good news, when the POW Camps are liberated. They may well locate some of the missing sailors from the town."

"That's very true. Please switch it back on, so we can hear what's happening."

The radio came back to life, and the old friends settled down to listen to the broadcast, companionably sipping tea.

The month before, De Valera called a snap election. It was a tactical decision, as a result of the very obvious fractures appearing in several of the opposition parties. This time, he won a Parliamentary Majority, and on the 9th of June 1944, the 12th Dail sat, just 3 days after the D-Day landings.

The War raged on for another year. Mary and Mr Fitzgerald were both right about the telegrams. The Axis Forces increased their submarine activity, in a last-ditch attempt to starve the British, sinking a number of Irish Merchant Ships, in the process. This increased the number of enquires for missing loved ones, but, at the same time, several missing Arklow men, sailors and soldiers, were located in liberated German Prisoner of War Camps across Europe. The War finally ended in May 1945, but both the Town, and the whole Country, did not feel they had anything to celebrate, especially after Churchill's derogatory remarks about Ireland retaining its neutrality throughout the entire conflict. De Valera waited a few days, before replying. In his statement, he outlined Churchill's bullying tactics towards the Irish, and defended his offer of condolences on the 2nd of May 1945, to the German Embassy, on the death of their leader, a statement that not only enraged England, but the entire Allied Force.

Later that summer, Mary got some wonderful news - a letter from Percy, informing her that he would be in Ireland shortly. He had official business in Dublin, and had set aside some time to spend a weekend with her, in Arklow.

He parked his car outside her house. As soon as he got out, he was greeted by Mary, who had been eagerly waiting, on the footpath. She hugged him until Percy, desperate for breath, glanced up at a figure that had appeared on the top of the steps. It was Mary's mother, Angela, with her adoring smile, still very beautiful, for her age.

"Mrs Bradford," Percy said, breaking away from Mary's embrace. He gently kissed Angela on the cheek. "You look radiant, Mrs Bradford."

"You were always so charming, Captain."

"Oh, call me Percy."

"And I'm Angela. Now come in," she said, leading him into the parlour, where tea was waiting.

Soon they were deep in conversation about old times. Mary asked after Andrew.

"I couldn't tell you in a letter because of the censorship, but Andrew volunteered for the National Civil Service in 1939. He went to Singapore, and was there when it fell. I tried everything to find him, even with all my contacts, I couldn't.... I just couldn't..."

Percy tried to disguise his emotions, picking up the spoon that lay on his saucer, and stirring his tea with it, before placing it back down. He looked towards Mary and her mother, who sat opposite him at the kitchen table. Mary got up and sat beside him, taking both his hands in hers.

"Oh Percy. We know exactly what it's like to lose someone you love."

"Mary, I tried everything back in '39 to locate him. I really did.... but with all that was going on at home with Germany, nothing was ever done, and anyway, who would ever have thought that Singapore would fall."

Percy took out a box of cigarettes. He was about to light one.

"May I?" He asked

"Of course," Angela replied, passing over an ashtray.

"Did you find out what happened?" Mary asked, once he had lit the cigarette.

"It was only last July when I heard from the Red Cross. He died in a camp, on some island, off Singapore. I hate to think of his suffering," Percy said, inhaling deeply from the cigarette.

Mary was truly sorry as she thought of the bright and carefree Andrew, who had unselfishly given so much of his time, when she was released from prison.

Angela stood up and firmly clasped Percy's shoulder.

"My husband, Mary's Father, always said, 'let's not dwell on the past, but embrace the future', and I am sure that's what Andrew would have wanted."

"You were always so kind, Mrs..Angela," Percy said with a sad smile on his face.

"Come into the front room, Percy. There's much we have to discuss." Mary said.

"Mary can show you Mr Fitzgerald's Radio. You might be lucky and catch a show," Angela said.

"Good idea! Come on Percy," Mary said excitedly, as she led him through.

As Percy entered the front room, Mary saw Myles' hat on the hall stand. She quickly took it down, and followed him in. Percy was greeted by the photo of Myles in uniform, standing on the large dresser, next to the fireplace.

"Ah, there's the man himself. Dear old Myles. I do miss our chats, Old Boy," he said, picking up the framed picture, and staring at it.

"Look Percy, here's Myles' hat. Do you remember me writing to you about the day we found it, hanging on the hall stand, beneath my coat?"

Percy turned and looked at the hat. He carefully took it from Mary.

"My word, Mary, it's like having part of him here."

"That's not all I have," Mary said, excitedly, "but first, let's warm up the radio."

The radio gave a loud, concussed hum, as it fired into life.

Percy sat at the table, staring silently at the badge on the hat.

"Oh my, the Norfolk regiment. This brings back memories."

Mary opened a drawer in the dresser. She removed the Webley revolver, Annabelle's letter, Myles gloves, and finally, his journal. She placed everything in front of Percy, just as the pips rang out for the 5 o'clock news.

Percy ran his fingers across the items.

"Oh Mary, our dear friend Myles is so alive in this room, right now."

That evening, after supper, Mary linked arms with Percy and took him for a walk around the town. Percy pointed out notable changes that Mary had forgotten about, such as the electric lights that had replaced the gas lamps, and the new Council Estates that had been built around the town.

"My word Mary, the town used to be full of Fishermen's cottages, made of mud and thatch. Now look at it – solid, stone structures, fit for a King."

"It was part of Mr De Valera's Rural Development Plan in the '30s. Most towns across the country benefitted."

"I love the names, Mary," Percy said.

"They're named after famous leaders, killed in the Anglo-Irish and Civil Wars - Griffith Street, Rory O'Connor Place, Connelly Street, and Liam Mellows Avenue."

"Some of these estates were built in the '30s, you say? But that was during the Great Depression and the Economic War?"

"That's right. Both had a devastating effect on business. Farming and sailing also suffered. That's why there're so many abandoned schooners in the river."

"I thought it was due to the end of the days of sail, engines being more efficient?"

"No, Over half the Arklow fleet was laid up, and never used again."

"How did the Economic War start? I read about it in the papers, but never took much notice, to be honest."

"Where do I start, Percy? 800 years ago, perhaps? You see, as part of the Treaty in 1921, there was an agreement to pay land Annuities to England, which drained the country of substantial revenue, every year,

"Land Annuities?"

"Loans, given by the Land Commission to tenant farmers in the last century. They used them to purchase the land they farmed. When Ireland became a Free State, the new Government, under Mr Cosgrove, continued to collect the loans, and pay them back to appease the British. But De Valera's Government of 1932, refused to pay them back, believing they were part of the public debt that the Free State was not required to pay back. His government continued to collect them, but refused to send the funds to England. He passed the Land Act in 1933, which allowed the money to be spent on local government projects, like the housing estates that you see all around us, and the building of the Pottery factory, on the South Quay."

"I can't see the British liking that!" Percy said fascinated.

"Well, good old England, in all its sagacity, slapped high taxes on Irish imports, and Ireland returned the favour, doing the same on English imports."

"A stalemate! How did it end?"

"Five years later, the Government struck a deal with England. The English Government agreed to accept a one-off payment for the land annuities, and to hand over the remaining occupied ports to the Irish Navy."

"The ports! I remember them as a very sore point. Churchill was very disappointed that he wasn't allowed to use them during the war," Percy mused as they ambled along the streets of the lower end of town.

"The whole country feared Churchill would take them back by force," Mary replied

"Believe me, their fears were justified!"

Percy stopped in his tracks.

"My word, the Brook House, where the IRA planned to shoot me!"

"Shall we?

"Assuming they don't want to finish the job!" Mary said, giggling.

"I think we can risk it," Percy said, holding open the door.

It was a Friday evening and the pub was busy. A number of heads turned to stare at them through a thick, white haze of cigarette smoke. The barman, pulling a pint, looked at Mary, and indicated, with a flick of his head, that the snug was empty. As they made their way through the bar, a number of people who knew Mary, doffed their hats and greeted her, mostly curious, to know who the well-dressed gentleman was, with her.

In the back they found a single, small table, next to some empty kegs. As they settled in, the barman appeared at a hatch in the wall.

"Well folks? What's your poison?" he asked, with a grin.

"A Guinness for me and the Lady will have a mineral, please."

"Coming up," he replied. When he returned, Percy opened his wallet, to pay.

"It's already paid for," the barman said grinning, leaving without an explanation.

Percy looked to Mary for an answer as a figure appeared in the doorway of the snug, holding a pint of Guinness.

"There's your answer, Percy," Mary said, pointing to Pat Kavanagh, whose large frame almost filled the doorway.

"Thank you," Percy said, and introduced himself.

"Oh, I know well, who you are, Captain Harper. I'm Pat Kavanagh, your old adversary. May I join you?"

"As long as you don't want to shoot me, Mr Kavanagh."

They laughed as Pat sat down. For the rest of the evening they reminisced on the good times and reflected on the death of comrades, especially Myles.

"For an English Officer, I liked him! We came to an amicable agreement, and, with no disrespect to you Captain Harper, I hoped to be having this conversation with him, rather that yourself tonight."

"None taken, Mr Kavanagh. I was aware of your agreement. Myles shared everything. He trusted me with his life, you know."

This created an awkward silence, which Pat broke by raising his glass.

"To Captain Myles Fox, a good Officer, Gentleman, and friend."

"Here, here," said Percy.

"To Myles," Mary said, and raised her glass.

As they spoke, Mary was amused by the faces that appeared in the doorway, to see what was going on. When Pat left for the toilet, two drunks entered, and made a nuisance of themselves, but left abruptly, on Pat's return. Eventually, Mary realised it was her presence attracting this unwanted attention. Being a respectable single woman, in a pub, late at night, in the company of two men, was seriously frowned upon. After a number of unruly comments, directed at her through the door, causing Pat and the barman to come to her defence, Mary decided to retire for the night, before she lost her temper and challenged the individuals. She deliberate over-exaggerated a yawn.

"It's time to go home, gentlemen."

Percy stood up and shook hands with Pat.

"It's been a pleasure, Mr Kavanagh. Thank you for your hospitality."

"You're very welcome. I look forward to the next time," Pat said, as he held open a backdoor in the snug that led to a laneway.

Mary linked arms with Percy as they strolled home in the coolness of the evening, briefly pausing on the bridge, to admire the sunset that stretched out across the distant Wicklow Mountains.

"I'd forgotten how beautiful this town is. Thank you for the warm welcome."

"Oh Percy, you're always welcome here," Mary replied, snuggling into his side.

For the first time in years, Mary felt warm and comfortable, the memory of Myles more alive than ever, as they made the short journey   home.

Sean MacBride

During the War, Mary developed a reputation for successfully helping distressed families with compensation claims from the British Merchant Navy. This was made less arduous for her in May 1941, when the British Parliament passed the Emergency Work Order for the Merchant Navy. Sailors would now be paid if their ship was sunk, unlike before when they were considered, 'unavailable for work', and pay, immediately severed.

As the War ended, Mary found herself personally inundated with requests to assist in compensation claims for lost soldiers and sailors and help locate official graves. Mary found the Commonwealth War Graves Commission useful, helping many families find the final resting place of their loved ones, her success enhancing her reputation. In 1947, she was asked to help a completely different group of distressed families those of Irish Soldiers, who had deserted the National Army to fight for the Allies.

On their return, they were victimised by a new law, 'the Barring Order', known as the 'Starvation Order', it saw thousands of men barred from State employment and refused a pension. This discrimination, unpoliced at local level, bled across to include all returning Allied Soldiers, including those that had not deserted the National Army, regardless of the proof they presented.

Mary met these desperate men to better understand their circumstances and help them present their case. They would describe the horrors they had witnessed at the hands of both the Nazi and Japanese armies. When she heard these horrific accounts, Mary demanded a meeting with the Minister of Defence, in a bid to help them. She was refused and told they were all traitors, regardless of whether they had deserted or not. She asked Sean Lemass for help, who proved sympathetic to the cause.

Early one Tuesday morning, in October 1947, Mary stood beneath the statue of Queen Victoria, in the grounds of Leinster House, waiting for Sean to collect her and bring her into the building, to meet Oscar Traynor, the Minister of Defence. As she waited, she studied the condition of the statue, still sitting proud against the brilliant blue of the autumnal sky. It looked dilapidated from neglect. She was wondering how this statue had survived the IRA campaign, when a voice interrupted her thoughts.

"Good Morning, Miss Bradford," Oscar Traynor said, offering his hand.

"Good Morning, Mr Traynor. Sean was going to bring me in to see you." She shook his hand.

"He may be a little late. There's a collision at the top of the road. The Garda are re-directing traffic. I had to walk," the Minister informed her.

"I see you admiring 'auld Vic'? We're thinking of having her removed, but maybe not until after the elections next year." Oscar Traynor mused as he surreptitiously admired Mary.

"I wonder why the British left so many statues behind. Perhaps they left this one just to upset us!"

"Maybe they did." Oscar replied.

"And that's not all they left to upset us," Mary said, turning to him. "There are the graves of thousands of famine victims that died on that woman's watch, most unmarked."

"Very true! My own family suffered terribly, and now we know she had full knowledge" the Minister replied looking up at the statue.

"And it's happening again, Minister."

"I don't understand, Miss Bradford," he replied, confused by her statement.

"Irish families are starving, once again, Minister Traynor, but this time, it's the Irish causing it, and it's happening on your watch."

"What're you talking about?" He was horrified at the comparison to Queen Victoria.

"I'm talking about soldiers that joined the Allied Forces. They've returned home, and are going hungry, because of the 'Starvation Order', issued by your Department," Mary informed him angrily.

"Well, they should have thought of that before deserting the National Army," he replied abruptly, a feeble attempt to defend his Department's decision.

"Do you mean the same National Army that hunted you down and murdered your colleagues? The same Army, whose formation you so vehemently opposed? Is this the same Army you are now defending Mr Traynor?"

"That's in the past. We risked our lives for what we believed in, but we've moved on from that now," the Minister replied, angry at having to explain himself.

"So it's 'forgive and forget' those that would have murdered you, as they did your friends? Can you not show the same empathy to these returning soldiers? They risked their lives for what they believed in. They fought against an enemy that would have willingly invaded this country, and inflicted punishment on its people, that would have made Cromwell and 'auld Vic here, turn in their graves? It would have happened, and the likes of Thomas Donnelly and Eoin O Duffy would have supported it, to extract their personal revenge on the lot of you," Mary exhorted angrily, thinking of what those soldiers had witnessed, and how their families had been punished.

"Miss Bradford! May I remind you that these men deserted the Army when their country needed them most? They deserve to be punished."

"What about their wives and children, and the wives and children of the men that didn't desert? They are also being punished by your Barring Order."

"They should've joined the National Army, not run off to join the Bloody Brits."

"That's 70,000 men, Mr Traynor, and not all joined the British Army! What, in God's name, would the National Army have done with that many?

"Miss Bradford! I will not stand here and listen…" The Minister was cut short.

"Good Morning! Sorry to be late, but there was an accident on Kildare Street."

"Good morning, Sean," Mary said, his presence calming her.

"Good morning, Sean," Oscar said, nodding his head in acknowledgement.

"Would you like to come to my office to discuss the issues with the Barring Order?" Sean asked Mary, pointing towards Leinster House.

"We can talk it over," Minister Traynor said, hoping to relieve the tension.

"Are you going to change your mind, Mr Traynor?"

"It takes time, Miss Bradford," Oscar Traynor said, relaxing with Sean present.

"Well then, I don't see any point in eating biscuits and drinking tea, at the taxpayer's expense, whilst Irish families starve," she responded, as blunt as ever.

"What on earth's been said?" Sean asked, clenching his pipe between his teeth.

"Mr Traynor has made his position perfectly clear and has no intentions of lifting the Barring Order against returning Irish soldiers. It fascinates me how you can pass laws overnight, but it takes years to remove them."

"I'm sorry you feel that way, Mary," Sean said, clearly disappointed.

"Sean, thank you for the invite, but, I've better things to do that listen to this lack of empathy for those that risked their lives to

370

prevent this country being overrun by Fascists! Good day, Gentlemen," Mary said, as she turned to walk away.

"Please! Just wait a moment, Mary. Let's discuss this in my office," Sean said, reaching out and lightly touching Mary's arm, hoping to change her mind.

Mary turned and faced them both.

"Remember Gentlemen, Elections are looming! The people are unhappy with your party and new Republican parties are forming. So, not only are you risking the votes of women, following countless failed promises on Women's Rights, but now, 70,000 hungry men and their voting wives, are angry as a direct result of your Party's orders."

"There are 5,000 names on the list. 70,000 is a gross exaggeration," Oscar Traynor said angrily.

"What list? Have you made up a list of these men?"

"Well yes, we had to keep a record of them," Sean replied sheepishly.

"Your facts are wrong. There are 5,000 so called 'deserters', but another 70,000 men who did not desert, but are still considered traitors. That number's not exaggerated! You've been in power for over 16 years, and feel invincible! But you're not." She paused, thoughtfully adding, "Have you ever read Orwell's 'Animal Farm'? If not, you should, before the next election. Thank you both. Hopefully, next time we meet, will be under better circumstances."

Mary turned, and left the two men staring after her, as she confidently walked away, both men, in awe and admiration of her.

"What did you do, Oscar? Mary's a good woman and we need her support."

"What difference does one woman's vote make?" Oscar said, preparing to leave.

"Don't underestimate Mary Bradford, Oscar. She represents more than one vote. Anyone that I know who has ever crossed her has definitely come off the worse for it," Sean said, remembering the christening.

"The book she mentioned? Do you have a copy?" Oscar asked sheepishly.

"I believe I do. I'll drop it to your office," Sean said, pausing to light his pipe.

As he sucked on the stem, he turned and caught sight of Mary in the distance.

"What are you like, Mary Bradford," he said, exhaling a long plume of smoke.

The following November, Mary had business in the Dublin Office, which would take a few days. She organised it around the first 'Ard Fheis', annual conference, of a new political Party, called 'Clann Na Poblachta', the 'Family of the Republic', founded a year earlier by Sean MacBride, and gaining serious political ground against Fianna Fail. The electorate felt alienated by Fianna Fail, believing the party had betrayed its founding principles, especially after the executions of Republicans during the War.

During a passing visit, Sean MacBride had invited Mary to the Party's first Ard Fheis, held in the Balalaika Ballroom in Dublin. Mary invited Susan Geraghty as her guest. They met in the foyer and were escorted to their seats, pleasantly surprised to be seated with Margaret Buckley and Nora Connelly. They exchanged hugs, any lingering animosity between Mary and Margaret, long forgotten.

Mary was pleased with the presentation and enthusiastically joined in with the applause. After the meeting, an aide invited the women to a private meeting with Sean MacBride. They found him standing amongst a small group of men, all of whom turned to see who had just entered. The man nearest Sean MacBride spoke, in fluent Gaelic.

Cén fáth a bhfuil tú fós ag siamsaíocht ar an Léine Gorm sin, a Mháire

372

("Why are you still entertaining that Blue Shirt, Margaret?")

Mary smiled at Margaret and replied, her Gaelic perfect.

"Is chuig an Uasal MacBride is cóir duit an cheist sin a dhíriú, a dhuine uasail, mar táim anseo trína chuireadh pearsanta."

("It's to Mr MacBride that you should direct that question, Sir, for I am here by his personal invitation.")

A look of horror crossed his face, as Sean MacBride replied, also in Gaelic.

"Sea, thug mé cuireadh don Iníon Bradford, más í an té a dtugann tú 'Léine Gorm' uirthi?"

("Yes, I invited Miss Bradford, if she is the one you're calling a 'Blue Shirt'?")

The man was speechless. He muttered an excuse, and left the room.

"Welcome ladies! Please take a seat," an excited Sean said, holding out his arms.

The four women joined him and other party members, and were soon in deep discussion on gathering support from the various Women's organisations, in return for lifting the Marriage Bar. Mary also mentioned the Barring Order, and Susan discussed women joining the Garda and the Army. Sean felt the need to temper expectations.

"Ladies, the issues you've mentioned, are close to my heart. I'm well aware of the sacrifice of Irish women in forming this State, and, how other parties, once elected, have dropped their support. If elected, we will address these issues, but I have to be honest with you, in order for this party to quickly gain the support needed to challenge Dev and his cronies, we will focus on the declaration of a full, Irish Republic for the 26 counties, and work on removing the border to finally unite the entire country."

The women understood, and accepted the need for this 'Steeping Stone' approach to gain support from Fianna Fail supporters, agreeing that policies should take priority. Once established, they could address the matters of Women's Rights.

Eamon De Valera called a snap election in February 1948, intending to catch Clann Na Poblachta off guard. Before calling the election, he increased the number of seats in the Dail from 138 to 147, hoping it would split the vote for MacBride's Party in some counties. The electorate saw this for the gerrymandering it was, and the government lost support. The revised boundaries ensured that Fianna Fail gained the highest number of seats, but Dev failed to achieve the Parliamentary Majority required to form a single-party Government. He also failed to foresee the growing dislike of both himself, and Fianna Fail, enabling the other parties to successfully create the first, Inter-Party Collation, under the leadership of Fine Gael. On the 18th of February 1948, the first Inter-Party Government of the Free State, sat, forming the 13th Dail.

Everyone thought this amalgamation of parties would fall at the first hurdle, but they actually seemed to work well together. Within a few months, they agreed to pass the, 'Republic of Ireland Act', allowing them to leave the Commonwealth. The statue of Queen Victoria was removed from the grounds of Leinster House. The coalition wanted to remove all vestiges of British rule from the seat of the new Republic, before officially declaring it to the world. On the 18th of April 1949, after a year in power, John A Costello, the Taoiseach and leader of the Fine Gael Party, officially announced that the 26 counties was now a fully, independent Republic. Sean MacBride refused to attend the inauguration ceremony, angry that Costello had stolen his original election idea.

The Doctor

Sadly, Mary's mother passed away in May 1949, following a short illness. Mary and her sister were devastated. Sean Lemass attended the funeral, supporting Mary throughout. At the reception, he passed on condolences from Eamon De Valera, Oscar Traynor and other party members.

"Oscar believes he should have listened to you, that day beneath 'auld Vic."

"About what?" Mary asked, exhausted, and secretly desiring to be home.

"You told us the people disliked the party," Sean said, pouring milk into his tea.

"That wasn't intuition, but fact," Mary said in her usual blunt manner.

"Sometimes, we don't see the woods for the trees," Sean replied, sipping his tea. "Did you know that Oscar read 'Animal Farm'? He was horrified that we might be seen in that light," Sean said, pondering over a plate of sandwiches. "He suggested other TDs should read the book!"

"Please thank them for their condolences, Sean."

"So what do you think of our full-blown Republic?" Sean changed the subject.

"Michael Collins was right all along," Mary replied, sitting up straight. "He said the Treaty only a stepping stone to a Republic. If you'd listened to him that day at the Four Courts, imagine what might've happened? No split in the Sinn Fein Party? No Civil War? Collins, Mellows, O'Connor, Lynch, and many others, would still be alive, and everyone would have got a pension! God only knows what else might've happened. Maybe there wouldn't even be a border?"

"Hindsight is a wonderful thing," Sean sighed. "That's for sure," Mary said with sadness.

"The British split our country to suit their needs. They did the same in India, and now Palestine! Divide and conquer, Sean! Divide and conquer!" Mary sat back in her chair, completely drained.

"Thank you for the reminder, Mary. I believe this Republic will be a stepping stone to total unity," Sean said, defending Ireland's Republic declaration.

"Do you really think the English will allow this country to unite? For centuries they've divided our culture, religion and nationality!"

"But the new Republic will unite all Parties and Religions helping us to achieve a shared goal," Sean said, frustrated by Mary's negativity.

"Our new Republic, Sean! Tell me, what has really changed but a few lines in an administrative paragraph. That's all! As that thug, Freeny once said, only the coins and stamps will change. Everything else will remain the same. Women will still not be allowed to work when married. Surviving children will still be sent to the Church, should one parent die, and pregnant girls will be sent to the laundries! Nothing really changes, Sean. Nothing," Mary sighed. "We're all victims of our innocence. You, your poor brothers, God rest them both. My mother bayonetted by an English soldier, the poor Yorkshire lad who died saving my life. My beloved Myles and Malachy. The list just goes on and on, Sean. All of us, dragged into a war of attrition by our innocence. Does that make sense? And nothing changes, not in the old Free State or in this new Republic!"

Sean gave Mary's hand a reassuring squeeze.

"It makes perfect sense, my dear. That's why this country needs women like you, strong honest women who never give up, no matter the obstacles. You're a strong woman, Mary, and you will get through this."

"Thank you, Sean I'm sorry to be so negative."

"Don't apologise Mary I fully understand."

Sean's Driver approached, quietly indicating the time.

Sean let go of Mary's hands, and stood up.

"I'm so sorry to rush away. You know where I am if you need anything!"

Mary stood up to accompany him to his car, but was forced to sit down again by a sudden and painful stitch in her side. She expelled a loud moan, startling Sean, and Anna, who was sitting nearby. After a while, the pain passed. Mary insisted that she did not want a fuss, blaming it on stress and indigestion.

Sean gently kissed her on the cheek, and left.

Over the following year, the pain returned at intervals, but Mary chose to ignore it, until one bright, summer's day, in early June 1950, when she was walking through the ruins of the Kynoch factory, now converted to a caravan park. She was wearing a floral dress and enjoying the sunshine, when the pain made its presence known with a vengeance. She had to sit on a nearby chair, outside of a caravan.

As she rested a large dog appeared and rested its head on her lap. He looked up at her, with big, black, sympathetic eyes. She smiled and stroked his head.

"What's your name, Mr Dog?"

"Rommel," a posh English voice replied.

Mary looked up to see the owner, standing at an easel, holding a painters palette.

"I apologise. I just needed to sit down for a moment, "Mary said, embarrassed.

"Take your time. You're most welcome," he replied.

He was in his early 50s, with short, grey hair and a manicured moustache, and wore only khaki shorts. his entire body bronzed by the sun. Mary thought him handsome, as she glanced at the painting on the easel. It was the old water tower.

"He won't bother you. He's waiting for some local's boys. He goes swimming with them every afternoon."

"Aren't you worried he won't come back?" Mary asked, fighting the pain in her side.

"He knows where his bread is buttered."

"What did you say his name was?"

"Rommel."

"Rommel? After the German General?"

"Yes. I actually met him when I was captured at Tobruk. Dammed nice man! Great command of the English language. Oh where are my manners I do apologise "Major Basil Maynard", MD, retired," the man said, approaching Mary with an outstretched hand.

"Mary Bradford. Pleased to meet you, and Rommel," she said, shaking his hand.

"That's a beautiful painting," Mary said, admiring his work, the pain subsiding.

"It helps pass the time. I love painting these abstract constructions. They're the remains of an explosive factory, called Kynoch's, so my wife told me."

"She's correct," Mary said.

"Was," he corrected. "She passed away, two years back. She originally came from Arklow. I met her when she was training as a nurse in London, back in the '20s. That's why I love to spend the summers here, meeting up with family and friends. Keeps her memory alive," the Doctor said, pausing briefly. "Damn, I miss her," he said, snapping back and touching up the painting with a brush. "She loved to walk through the ruins, and tell me what the different parts were used for. She worked in it as a teenager you know. She went to England after it closed."

"I may have known her? I also worked here."

"Heavens alive! Her name was Mary Kearon," he said excitedly, "Yes! I did know her. She went to England and married a Doctor."

"Well, I'm that Doctor, "he replied, delighted his wife was still remembered.

Suddenly Rommel pricked up his ears. A group of boys appeared at the top of the path. He looked up at Mary, as if to say goodbye, and ran off to join them.

"Here they come. That's him gone for the afternoon. Would you like a cup of tea, Miss Bradford?"

"Yes. That would be nice," Mary said, taking advantage of the chance to rest.

He disappeared into the caravan, reappearing with a tray of tea and scones. Mary could see he was excited to be in company, as he fussed over her, buttering a scone.

"Made them myself! You have to add the cream before the jam, or you lose the taste. I come from Devon, and people get very upset if you do it the wrong way round!"

Mary laughed.

"Can you imagine going to war over how you butter your scone?"

"Well, in 'Gulliver's Travels', the Yahoos fought over which end of an egg you should open," the Doctor said, with a chuckle, cutting open another scone.

"That truly does prove the futility of wars!" Mary said laughing.

She was enjoying his company and his stories, until one statement about Africa.

"I was captured, in Africa in '41. That's when I met Rommel! I was sent to a POW Camp, and not liberated until '45, missing out on all the action."

This sparked Mary's anger, as the families of the missing and dead she had helped came to mind.

"What is it with you men and your love of war? Missed all the action, be dammed! War destroys, Dr Maynard. Ask the wives and children of the two Air Men, buried her. Ask the families of the dead that litter the fields of Europe. Ask them if they're happy their loved ones didn't miss out. Ask the families of the soldiers and sailors that died in both wars. Some have had to wait years to find out what happened to their loved ones. Some still don't know. Do you think they're happy their loved ones didn't miss out? I haven't been to War, Dr Maynard, but, by Christ, I've experienced its devastation! Your caravan is pitched on the ruins of one of the largest munitions factory ever built in the British Isles. I worked in it, manufacturing explosives that killed and maimed thousands. We got weekly updates on how our work added to the War effort, killing the Hun in their thousands. If we questioned this slaughter we were branded unpatriotic pacifists. War takes fathers from children and husbands from wives, and the copper discs attached to silk ribbons offered as compensation, doesn't fill hungry bellies or replace broken hearts. Missed out on all the action! God give me patience."

As Mary stood up to leave her suddenly, she let out a large moan, and collapsed across the table, knocking the contents to the ground. The completely bewildered Doctor rushed to her aid.

Dr Maynard drove Mary home in his orange Volkswagen. He contacted a local doctor, and stayed with her until her sister arrived. As he left, he apologised to Mary for his remarks, and promised to check in on her the following day. This he did, with a bunch of flowers and some homemade scones. Their friendship blossomed, both delighted to have a friend to go to the cinema with, or take long walks.

Through his contacts, Dr Maynard arranged for Mary to be examined in a Dublin Hospital. At first, she refused, despite endless pleas from Anna. She was finally convinced by John and Sylvia Mills, during a weekend visit.

One Thursday afternoon, in late August, Dr Maynard arrived at Mary's house in his orange Volkswagen, with Rommel. He had made plans to spend the weekend in Dublin, with some friends, and Mary was to look after the dog. Rommel rushed straight past her, raced upstairs, and jumped into a box she kept for him, at the foot of her bed.

"Sorry about that, Mary. He seems to know his way about!" the Doctor laughed.

"Oh, don't worry Basil. It's not his first time to sleep over now, is it?"

"No, I suppose not! I'll be back at 6, Sunday evening," Basil said, walking back to his Volkswagen. "Oh, I almost forgot. This came today." He turned and handed her a letter. "It's from my friend in St Vincent's Hospital. Your results, I think, have a read, you know where I am if needed."

Mary chose to ignore the letter.

"Yes, I'll do that. Now, get going or you'll be late."

She waited for his car to disappear from sight, before going back into the house. She placed the letter on the hall stand and called out to Rommel.

"Come on boy, its supper time," she said, walking towards the kitchen.

Later that night, Mary was sitting at the base of the sand dunes, on the North Beach. A full moon shone low on the horizon, casting shadows on the abstract ruins that littered the beach. A gentle breeze blew from the land, carrying the perfumed scent of the cool night air. Rommel buried his head in her lap.

"You see those ruins?" Mary said to Rommel, pointing to the silhouette of a roofless structure, half-buried in the sand. "That was the Ladies Changing Room. I could tell you stories, but you're too young! That was before the sea washed it away, because the wooden piles were removed for firewood, during the War. Everything's to do with War, even us. We met because of War, even your name is from the War. But it doesn't matter now does it."

Rommel lifted his head and looked at Mary. His eyes, pools of darkness set in a sympathetic face, seemed to know something was wrong. Mary stroked his head. She took the Doctors letter from her pocket, held it aloft, and let it go. It briefly flickered in the moonlight, as the wind caught it, carrying it a short distance, before dropping it on the surface of the calm sea.

"Nothing matters anymore," she said, as the letter sank into the murky waters.

That Sunday evening, at 6 o'clock, Mr Fitzgerald was surprised to see a man knocking loudly at Mary's door, whilst a dog barked furiously from inside,

"It's Miss Bradford. She's lying at the foot of the stairs. I think she's fallen?"

"Is that your car?" Mr Fitzgerald said, pointing to the Volkswagen.

"Yes! The key's in the ignition."

"Stay here. Her sister has a spare key."

"Please hurry," Basil whispered, as the car disappear over the bridge.

Mary regained consciousness in St Vincent's Hospital, surrounded by Anna, her family and Basil Maynard. She remembered going upstairs to bed, then nothing more. The doctor informed the family that it was pancreatic cancer, likely to have developed over time, from working with chemicals, as with many ex-employees of Kynoch's.

This had all been explained in a letter.

"Yes, she kept very quiet about it," Basil said to the consultant.

"Well, as I said, it's only a matter of time. We can make her as comfortable as possible, but, sadly, she will not be going home."

Basil choked up as he tried to supress his emotions.

Anna hugged her family, and started to cry.

"I'll be in my office if you need anything," the consultant said, leaving the room.

They took turns to spend time with Mary. Some days she would be well, and others, very poorly. One day, Basil and Maurice arrived with a large bag, which they struggled to carry. Anna, who was sitting with Mary, quizzed them on the contents.

"Whatever have you got there?"

"Oh, a surprise for Mary," Basil said secretively.

Maurice slowly unzipped the bag, allowing an excited Rommel to poke his head out. On seeing Mary, he escaped, and jumped onto her bed, excitedly licking her face. Mary was delighted to see him and kissed him back. Maurice, who was keeping watch, warned them as a nurse approached, and Rommel was quickly concealed, but barked when the nurse entered the room. Maurice tried to convince her that he had made the noise by faking a cough, but she would have none of it. She glared at the men.

"I'll give you two minutes to leave, and take your cough with you."

Another morning, Maurice arrived, lifting Mary's spirits.

"Did you bring it?" She asked excitedly.

"Yes, it's here," Maurice said, pulling Myles' cap and journal from a bag.

"Thank you," she said, hugging the cap and kissing Maurice on the forehead.

"Maurice, I want you to have this hat and all of Myles' belongings."

"But, Auntie Mary, I can't!"

"There's no point arguing. I know it meant a lot to you, so I want you to have all of Myles things. It will help keep his...., our memory alive. I want your sister to have my engagement ring. Your Mother will want to bury me with it, so I'm giving it to you to pass on after..., it's all over. It's here in this envelope with a note. Oh one last thing. Please place the primroses on the railings every year, and make sure they come from the Rock. Promise me Maurice?"

"I promise, Auntie Mary," Maurice replied, wiping back tears.

Mary, realising she upset Maurice, changed the subject.

"Any news from home anyone dead or dying?"

""Dying" Auntie Mary? Can't you put that another way?" Maurice scolded her.

"Sorry! Well, is there any news?"

"Actually yes. Norman Boland died last night," Maurice informed her.

Mary was sad as she thought of Norman. She had made peace with him and his wife years earlier. She often helped him up the steps of the Church, and Mrs Boland still put flowers on the railings with Mary, each year.

Maurice stayed until the nurse gave Mary something to help her to sleep.

Four days later, a nurse approached Mary and said.

"Sorry, Mary, but we have a patient that's in for an emergency operation. We'll have to put him in with you for a few days, until he's well enough to travel."

"I'll enjoy the company," Mary replied.

An attendant wheeled an unconscious man into the ward, parking him next to Mary. He did not wake until the following morning. Mary glanced over at the new arrival. She could see that he was weak, but did not look too frail.

"Good, morning," she said, as he opened his eyes. "You're in good hands."

"Oh, I know. I'm very grateful," he replied, in a soft American accent. "Dr Anthony saved my life. I had a clot, but he successfully removed it."

"The nurse said you're from America?"

"No, not America. I live in Nova Scotia, Canada, but I'm originally from Arklow. I'm home to bury my Father, but fell ill at the funeral."

Mary reeled with shock. Her desire for justice still burned. She looked at him, as he slowly pulled himself into a sitting position. He looked pale. Her heart was racing.

"Is your name John Boland?"

"Yes," he replied, looking over curiously. "Do I know you?"

Mary thought she had overcome her need to punish John Boland, especially when she discovered that it was Thomas Donnelly that had killed Myles. But, the thought that he had forgotten about his part in the drama that changed her life forever, was too much to bear. His presence eroded years of acceptance.

"You should know me. John Boland! You murdered my Fiancée in front of me. You rifled his pockets and stole my engagement ring. You left me to face a trial, and be found guilty of his death! You could have saved me from three tortuous years in an English jail. You surely do know me, John Boland."

Mary was exhausted. Her breathing became shallow, and she passed out before seeing Boland's reaction. Boland, fearing the worst,   pulled   the   emergency   cord.

John Boland

The doctor sedated Mary and it was several hours before she regained consciousness. John Boland watched her resting face. He clearly recognised her now, and still thought her a beautiful woman. Mary opened her eyes.

"Is that you Basil? Is Rommel with you?" She asked weakly.

"No Mary. It's me, John Boland. Please rest. I'd like you to listen to what I have to say. I hope it will bring you some solace, and maybe some peace for me."

"I don't have strength to argue, John Boland, so have your say," she whispered.

John Boland finally spoke his truth.

"I was under enormous pressure from a man named Thomas Donnelly, a friend of Father Mackenzie and my Father. He made the local lads run errands and spy for him. We'd deliver arms and ammunition, and, in return, he'd give us cigarettes and promised jobs when the War was over."

"Back in '19, a week before Christmas, he drove me to the RIC Barracks. We waited, outside for ages, watching soldiers and Police come and go. After about an hour, Two Captains came out. Donnelly told me to find out all I could about the tall one with the moustache. It was Myles,

I think that was before you'd met him?" John looked to Mary for clarity, but she refused to engage. He continued

"The responsibility felt great, and I did what I was asked with great efficiency, but I always suspected Donnelly that had known this man before?"

"The less you know, the better," he said, "but I can't move freely whilst he's wandering around."

"I was still following the Captain when you started walking out with him, and this made me jealous. That's why I started that fight on the street. It wasn't to do with the War, just my jealousy." Tears welled up in John Boland's eyes.

"Donnelly was mad because I picked that fight. I found out later that he'd planned to shoot both Captains that day, and I'd messed things up." John Boland gave a hollow laugh.

"I saw you kiss, out at the Hanging Stone, and was overcome with anger, I loved you, Mary, and had, since our Kynoch days, but I was young and naïve, and couldn't express myself. When the factory closed and the War started, I behaved badly, not just to you, but to everyone. When I found out the Runner named Payton wanted me to lead you into a trap so he could assault you. I deliberately treated you badly, hoping to drive you away. Sadly it worked, and although I tried to explain later, you wouldn't have anything to do with me."

Boland paused, and reflected on the mess he had made of everything. He looked at Mary, as she lay in her sick bed deserving an explanation – he continued.

"Mary, I cannot express the emptiness I felt when I saw you and him together, I told Donnelly. He convinced me that if we shot both the Captains, I could get you back. Stupidly, I believed him. We hatched a plot. Captain Harper would die when both Captain Fox and Commandant Kavanagh were away in England. I didn't know until years later, when my father told me in a letter, that these assassinations were not sanctioned by Dublin. They were part of Donnelly's personal vendetta. He gave me his pistol. I remember him saying how ironic it would be if they were shot with that particular pistol, but when I asked why, he wouldn't say."

"Some other time," he kept repeating.

"I couldn't do it, Mary. I really couldn't. On the day of the first attack, I gave Steven Kelly a message, which he successfully passed it on you.

"Captain Fox returned the following week, and when I saw how happy you both were at the railway station, and seeing him

387

buy a ring in Powers Jewellery Shop the day after, I felt a great remorse about the planned attack. Donnelly had me escorted to the Wicklow Mountains the day before the attack. He correctly feared I would try to pass a message to you. The following morning we drove to Arklow. Donnelly and I stood outside the hardware shop, across the road. I wore a woman's dress. The car continued across the bridge, turned and came back, as it slowed. I saw my chance – I wouldn't jump, but at the last second, Donnelly pushed me into the car. It knocked the wind out of me. I lay on the ground, bruised and dazed. The next thing I know, Captain Fox is leaning over me, trying to help. I rolled over, and he saw my Pistol. I panicked, thinking he was armed, so I pointed it at him."

John Boland cast a sideways glance at Mary, but she was resolutely staring ahead.

"Mary, I can still see the look of terror in his eyes, as he tried to shuffle away. Suddenly, he stopped, crossed himself, and said, 'I love you Mary'. I knew I wouldn't shoot, but still, a shot rang out, passing through his hand, hitting him in his chest. I turned to see Donnelly put away a Mauser pistol."

"Quick, get his pistol, you cowardly bastard."

"I didn't know what to do, so I opened his holster. To my horror, it was empty."

"Search his pockets," Donnelly screamed. I did, and found a small box. I swear I didn't know it was your ring. Donnelly dragged me away and we escaped across the marshes. I knew the area better, and lost him. I got home, muddied and in shock. My parents were horrified. My mother just cried."

"His poor parents! Poor Mary."

"My Father drove me to Cork and bought me a ticket to New York the next day. Mary, until I got the letter from my father, years later, I never knew that you were implicated. Every day since, I have prayed for you and your English Captain."

"Mary, I hope you can find the strength to forgive me. I'm so very sorry for what happened and for the burden that you've carried for 30 years."

Mary was feeling exceptionally weak. She called John Boland over.

"Please call my family, John," she asked him.

"Yes, anything Mary," he replied.

Later that afternoon, Mary's family, John and Silvia Mills and Basil Maynard entered the ward. She was still very weak, but could speak to them. She introduced John Boland, omitting their personal history. They all left together at 6 o'clock. Out of ear shot, Dr Anthony told them to expect the worst within hours. Maurice and Basil chose to stay close and John Mills offered a room so they could do shifts. Maurice took him up on the offer, leaving Mary and Basil alone. Mary asked Basil to write out two letters for her. She would dictate. The first was for Silvia and John, the other, to her family.

In the letter to her family, she told them she loved them. She spoke of her Will, and explained that Maurice should not be blamed, as he was carrying out her wishes. This almost broke Basil's heart. It was 9 o'clock, when the Nurse came onto the ward, and told Basil to wait in the canteen, as Mary was clearly exhausted,

Before Mary settled down for the night, she wanted to talk to John Boland.

"John, the time we worked together in Kynoch's was amongst the happiest of my life. I loved you. When the factory closed, you went astray. You were horrid, but I still loved you. Now I know why. I'm grateful for the sacrifice you made, but I can never trust you. I will forgive you, as I know a lot more about the people you were involved with, and how easily they could manipulate others. Goodnight, John"

Mary turned out her bedside light, and went to sleep. John copied, but lay awake, staring at the rising moon though the window. The only other source of illumination was a slash of yellow, coming through the ward door, left slightly ajar.

At 2 o'clock, John Boland woke, sweating and unable to breathe. He felt a terrible tightening in his chest. The moon was high, flooding the room with silvery light that failed to penetrate the dark corners. John looked over at Mary's bed, and was surprised to see her sitting on it, fully dressed, staring back at him. He could not move.

"Mary," he cried out. "Mary please, pull the cord. Something's wrong." Mary did not move. His breathing worsened and pain filled his legs and arms. "Mary, please! For God sake, pull the cord." She still did not move. His panic turned to terror. "Mary, please don't do this. We've made our peace. "

Out of the shadows, a tall figure emerged. John could just make out the features of a young man.

"Thank God! Maurice. Please get help."

Mary stood up. He could see her smiling, in the pale moonlight. Maurice took her hand and guided it towards the nurse call. They pulled it together. Mary opened her bedside locker and took out a military hat, handing it to Maurice who placed it smartly on his head. John thought Mary looked much younger, and the man was not Maurice, but Myles Fox. John heard a commotion outside, and just before two nurses burst onto the ward, Mary and Myles faded into the darkest corner.

An hour later, John Boland was stable. He asked the doctor to thank Mary for alerting the Nurses.

"John, Mary couldn't call the Nurse. She passed away, at least two hours before your relapse. It must have been you?"

John was speechless looking over at the empty bed.

"But Doctor, I saw her. I saw her with Myles. I watched them pull the cord."

"Perhaps you were dreaming? Now, get some rest."

The next morning, Maurice came to collect Mary's belongings. John told him what had happened during the night. When finished, Maurice opened the locker and showed him the hat. John Boland wept openly.

Mary was buried, with full State. A huge crowd turned out to pay their respects. Percy and John Boland attended. Pat Kavanagh was surprised at the number of Irish dignitaries and TDs present. There were representatives from Fianna Fail, Fine Gael, Sinn Fein, the Garda, and even the Communist Party. Among those present, were Sean MacBride, Sean Lemass, Eamon Broy, Margaret Buckley, and Nora Connelly.

"Whatever did Mary Bradford get up to in Dublin? Pat asked Sean Lemass, when he caught him alone at the reception.

"Just about everything, Pat," Sean replied, while lighting his pipe.

Silvia and John Mills approached Percy who was alone in the hallway outside the reception room. Sylvia held an envelope, containing information about Mary's state pension, which would have to be cancelled.

"Excuse me, Captain Harper. Do you have any idea where this address is?" Silvia asked, presenting the letter to Percy.

"Why? It's the churchyard where Myles is buried."

It dawned on Silvia that Mary had been sending her pension to Norfolk for years for the upkeep of the Church and graveyard.

"What an honourable thing to do," Percy said.

"My God, Mary Bradford! You can still spring surprises on us," John Mills said, taking the letter from Percy and reading the address for himself.

He reflected on the contents of Mary's letter given to him by Doctor Maynard, where she had requested his promise to carry on with her work for woman's rights and the destitute across the country regardless of their creed or loyalty's.

"Mary Bradford, what are you …." He paused and changed his statement.

"Mary Bradford, what were you like? "

Silvia, smiled a sad smile at his statement, and snuggled in to his side as they entered the room together, where a most interesting reception was certainly guaranteed.

THE END

Printed in Great Britain
by Amazon

79294015R00231